WILLIAM H.

W⊕RLDWIDE®

TORONTO · NEW YORK · LONDON · PARIS
AMSTERDAM · STOCKHOLM · HAMBURG
ATHENS · MILAN · TOKYO · SYDNEY

"A thriller in the pure~~st~~ ~~diff~~ ~~ker~~

"The book builds to a~~n~~ better spy thrillers. It~~s~~
—Asbury Park Press

"...moves briskly...should make Old Hand espionage fans nostalgic..."
—Kirkus Reviews

"So well paced...the reader is literally glued to the page... You won't put this one down until the very end..."
—The West Coast Review of Books

"...a suspenseful, fast-paced novel..."
—University of Illinois Alumni News

"...a rainy-day adventure with each chapter ending with a cliff-hanging encounter."
—Orlando Sentinel

"...a thrilling tale of espionage..."
—Newport News Daily Press

"...several cuts above the norm..."
—Baltimore Morning Sun

"...a dandy new espionage and adventure thriller."
—Seattle Post-Intelligencer

In 1962 two missile crises brought the world to the brink of nuclear war. In October Kennedy and Khrushchev went eyeball-to-eyeball over Soviet missile bases in Cuba, until, as Dean Rusk said, "the other fellow blinked." But four months earlier a smaller yet far more deadly crisis was played out thousands of miles away. It never made the six o'clock news or the front page of the *New York Times*. Hints of that story are only now beginning to be believed through the memoirs of the intelligence agents involved.

1

EGYPT: JULY, 1962

MAHMOUD YUSSUF HATED the desert, especially at night.

He hated its eerie silence, the snakes and scorpions lurking among the rocks, and the dim shapes that moved through the shadows. But there were other things he hated even more. He hated being poor. He hated the sight of guns in other men's hands. And he hated the mere thought of pain. Yet for enough money, Yussuf could force himself to tolerate almost anything.

Landau's money. Yussuf cursed it now. He was lying on a dark sand dune: cold, alone, and paralyzed with fear, staring over a high, barbed-wire fence into an old army base, waiting for that damned fool to come back, while the imagined terrors of the desert night slowly wrapped themselves around his fat body like the coils of a giant snake. Yussuf wanted to scream. He wanted to jump up and run away, but he couldn't. He was trapped between his own fear and Landau's money. So he burrowed his fat, sweating carcass deeper into the sand, praying to a long-ignored Allah that he'd survive this night.

They made a strange pair: the squat, greasy Arab with the gold tooth, and the gaunt Israeli with the dull, haunted eyes. They had only one thing in common: Landau's money. That was Yussuf's dilemma. If he ran away now, he'd never see it. So he stayed.

It had been an hour since Landau had left. He'd handed Yussuf a pistol, then calmly cut a hole in the fence and disappeared into the dark base. Yussuf peered into the darkness. He tightened his grip on the pistol until his knuckles turned white, convinced he had seen something moving in the shadows. The guards would be back soon. Had they seen him? Had they found the hole in the fence and come looking for him? If they had, the old pistol was useless. The guards carried submachine guns. They would kill him if they caught him here: slowly, painfully, and without the slightest mercy.

He cursed the place. He cursed Landau, wishing he'd never met the man. Then he cursed himself. How could he work for this Jew? Not that the breed mattered to Yussuf. In his day, he'd spied for the Russians, the Americans, even the British. So why not the Israelis? After all, business was business.

But this time it was different. Landau was insane. He had taken a risky job and turned it into a suicide mission. He was determined to cut his way into that compound and take more of his stinking photographs, even if he got them both killed doing it. Suicide. But there was the money to think of.

Yes, Landau would pay well for this night's work, if they lived to tell about it. So Yussuf forced himself to think about the money. Concentrate on the money, he told himself over and over. He thought of all the lovely things he'd spend it on: a crisp, new, white-linen suit, the down payment on a used Fiat sedan, and a juicy whore, this very night. He closed his eyes and ran his tongue across his parched lips, feeling himself getting hard at the thought. He'd find that one with the reed-thin waist and small, hard breasts who laughed at him when he had no money. He'd settle that score properly, and she wouldn't be laughing when he was finished. He'd ride her until she was bow-legged, then slap her raw.

Yussuf opened his eyes and groaned. The pleasant thoughts of money vanished. The whore and the stiffness in his pants faded with them. He found himself lying on his belly in a cold, shallow trench he'd gouged into a low sand ridge, barely thirty feet from the hole Landau had cut in the fence. Yussuf had gotten down on all fours like a dog, scooping the sand aside with his bare hands, terrified of being seen. An hour ago, the hole in the wire had looked so small, hardly big enough for a child to crawl through. Now, as Yussuf stared down at it, minute after agonizing minute, the hole gaped and yawned at him as if it were the mouth of hell itself.

Landau had told him to bend the wire back into place and cover the hole with dry brush. That was a reasonable thing to ask. Reasonable. And to Yussuf's eternal credit, he had managed to kick a few dry branches near the hole before scurrying away into the darkness as fast as his short, panic-driven legs would carry him.

"Forgive me," he now prayed. But Allah didn't grant miracles to fools like Yussuf. No, he reserved special punishments for them, ones that precisely matched the sin. Allah had condemned Yussuf to lie on this sand dune and stare down at the hole he'd failed to cover, sweating and terrified, knowing it would be his own sloth that would get him killed. The guards would see the fresh cuts in the wire. They would hunt him down and they'd kill him. Yussuf knew that, but he could not summon even half the courage it would take to crawl back and make it right. He was doomed to watch and wait and die for it.

"Landau, where are you?" he moaned and pounded the sand with his fist.

Slowly, he raised his head and took another desperate look into the compound. What could be so damned important down there? He saw two groups of buildings inside the compound. Most were old army barracks, like the ones bunched together off to Yussuf's left. But Landau had ignored them. He was only interested in the bigger buildings sitting by themselves farther back to the right. They looked like airplane hangars and were lit like the Nile Hilton during holiday.

Why didn't Landau care about the barracks? Yussuf wondered. They were old and decrepit, but someone was using them. And what about all those tanks—dozens and dozens of tanks—enough to outfit a whole armored regiment. Someone had tried to hide them in the groves of trees at the far side of the compound, but nothing stayed hidden from Yussuf's prying eyes for long, at least nothing of value.

Why were they here? Why was any of this here?

That was the real mystery. The British had abandoned this place years ago. There weren't supposed to be guards or lights out here. Everyone knew the closest Egyptian armored regiment was in the Delta, or across the canal in the Sinai, where they could protect the country from the Jews. Cowards! They weren't supposed to be hiding here, less than fifteen miles from Cairo.

Well—Yussuf tapped his gold tooth for luck—Landau could look wherever he wanted. If the Israeli didn't care about the troops and tanks, someone else would. Yes. Yussuf never had a shortage of customers.

But he had a bad feeling about this place. This was no ordinary army base. What army base was crisscrossed with strings of tall light poles? Between their cones of harsh, white light ran the thinnest ribbons of black shadow, too narrow for any sane man to trust with his life. Yussuf never would, even if the hounds of hell were snapping at his heels. Landau was insane.

And there were the guards, real ones, not the stinking militia. Yussuf hadn't seen crack troops like these since the British had left. Methodically and relentlessly, they swept through the compound and around its perimeter. They certainly weren't Egyptian. Those troops asleep in the barracks might be, but not the guards. They were too professional.

Landau talked a good game, but what would happen if they caught him? What if they'd already caught him? Yussuf broke into a cold sweat. What if Landau was down there right now spilling out his guts to them, telling them about his "partner" waiting on the other side of the fence? Yussuf was crazy to trust his life to a madman like that. The money had looked so sweet back in Cairo. Now, he knew he'd sold himself too cheap by half.

A sound! This time, it wasn't his imagination, either. He pressed his face deeper into the sand and prayed. Footsteps! Slow and steady, coming closer, walking along inside the fence. Guards! He saw them now, two of them, backlit by the lights down in the compound. And voices! He heard voices and hushed laughter. He strained to hear but couldn't understand the words. The language sounded foreign. Russian? No, he understood a smattering of Russian. That wasn't it. More guttural. German? Yes, a few words here and there, now a few more. German! Yussuf frowned. What were Germans doing here in this cursed desert, with all these troops and tanks? It was a mystery all right. But if Landau wanted to know, then it must be valuable, and Yussuf knew what to do with things of value. They were like gold nuggets, to be snatched up and pocketed.

Germans! Yussuf guessed what that might be worth. Yes. He licked his lips and thought of that smart-mouthed whore again. He'd keep her all night. And the next day too. She'd be too sore to work for a month after he finished with her.

Then the guards stopped walking. Yussuf stopped breathing. They weren't forty feet from where he lay and not ten feet from the hole in the fence. Surely they had seen him. Surely they could see the hole in the fence. After all, it was right at their very feet! With the slightest turn of their heads, the slightest glance, they'd see it and he'd be dead. He'd hear the shouts and the angry chatter of gun shots, just before their bullets punched him full of holes. When the sun rose in the morning, he'd be little more than a bloody lump of carrion left for the vultures.

But what if they didn't kill him? His stomach jumped. What if they took him alive? Torture? He closed his eyes, thinking of the terrible pain they'd inflict on his body. He could never let that happen. They'd never take Mahmoud Yussuf alive.

He gripped the pistol tighter, pulling the hammer back with a muffled *click*. Better to die right here, he vowed, than to be taken alive. His hand quivered. He raised the barrel to the side of his head and the touch of cold steel made him whimper. Gritting his teeth, he slowly took up the slack on the trigger, trying not to think of the white-hot pain to follow.

Then, just as he was about to squeeze, he heard a soft laugh. The guards were laughing. Yussuf forced one eye open for a final look. To his utter amazement, the guards were walking away. They were moving away from the fence. His finger froze on the trigger. He couldn't believe it. As quickly as they'd come, their footsteps faded away into the stillness of the desert night. They were gone.

Yussuf's entire body shook. The pistol dropped from his limp hand as if it weighed a ton. He felt drained: numb, giddy, and astonished to still be alive. Then he remembered what he had almost done. His blood ran cold. The bile rose in his throat, making him gag. Had he lost his mind? Allah have mercy. He had almost blown his own brains out and those jackals hadn't seen a thing. He had almost pulled the trigger and blown his own brains out!

He cursed Landau. "That son of a whore! That's what he is. And he's insane!" Yussuf mumbled, his voice rasping painfully. "That crazy Jew wants to get himself killed. He wants to commit suicide. That's bad enough, but now, he's got me doing it!"

Not anymore. The money be damned! Yussuf rose to his hands and knees and began to crawl away across the sand when a new sound made him drop flat once again. Someone was coming! "The guards," he groaned. They had only been taunting him, pretending to leave. Now they'd come back to kill him. Yussuf couldn't bring himself to look. He shut his eyes and listened to the pounding of his heart, certain it would jump into his throat and strangle him.

He prayed to the cold sand, "I'll never do this abominable work again. Never! Let me live? Mecca! I'll take the pilgrimage. I swear, the Prophet's beard."

But the prayer died in his throat as a pebble plopped onto the sand next to him, followed by a faint whisper. Someone was whispering, calling to him from the other side of the fence. "Yussuf!" The whisper had actually called his name. He frowned, lifted his head, and realized it was Landau. Landau had finally come back.

Yussuf couldn't see him. The Israeli wore a dark sweater and slacks and his face was blackened like a commando's, but Yussuf knew he had to be near. The Arab scrambled down the sand dune as if the Israeli was his long-lost brother. Forget the money, and the car, and even the whore, all Yussuf wanted was to grab Landau and run as far away from this place as he could get.

He reached for the hole in the fence. Pull that crazy Jew out, he thought, then run. But Landau stopped him.

"No," he ordered. "I'm not finished yet. I must go back."

Yussuf was stunned. "Back? You . . . you can't! I won't let you. We must go. Now!"

"You go, if you must," Landau whispered calmly, as he fumbled with something in the darkness.

"The guards . . . They'll feed us to the dogs if they catch us here."

"Then go back to the car. I'll meet you there in thirty minutes."

"They'll kill you. Can't you see that? Then they'll kill me! Have you no pity," he begged, his gold tooth flashing in the dim light.

"Then leave. And don't worry." Landau smiled in the darkness. "I'll still pay you."

"Pay? How? How does a dead man pay people?" he demanded, his voice growing shrill with anger.

"Hush! If you don't shut up and do as I say, you'll get nothing. . . . I'm not finished. You want to come back tomorrow night and do it all over again?"

Yussuf groaned.

"I thought not. Here . . ." Landau reached his hand through the fence and pressed something hard into Yussuf's palm.

Yussuf jerked the hand away, as if Landau had dropped a red-hot coal in it.

"Take it," Landau snapped. "Go back to the car if you want, but take this with you."

"You're insane," Yussuf whimpered, looking down at his hand and realizing he held a small, silver can of film. "More photographs? Haven't you taken enough?"

"Don't lose them. And don't get any cute ideas, either! You and the car had better be there in thirty minutes."

"And what if you don't come back? What happens to me?"

"You?" Landau chuckled. "Yussuf, you'll land on your feet like the overfed alley cat you are. If I don't come back, get the film to Evans. He'll know what to do. And he'll pay you, have no fear about that."

"You're mad," the Arab muttered in frustration. "What if they catch you this time? What happens to . . ." His voice trailed off as he found himself talking to the empty night. Landau was gone.

YUSSUF WAS RIGHT and Landau knew it. Sneaking into the compound once was risky enough. Trying it a second time was suicide. But he had to try. He needed proof. He'd searched everywhere, except the big hangar. That was where it must be. It must.

Egypt was sinking into chaos. The revolution had driven out that fat fool Farouk and his British protectors, but the mobs in the street now ruled. The army colonels danced for them like trained bears in the circus. The colonels had little to offer except the torch of nationalism, socialism, and a hatred of all things foreign. Cairo was a tinderbox. With a quarter of the country's population crammed into its slums, all that was needed was a spark. The resulting firestorm would engulf the entire Middle East.

Why should he worry? Hadn't Israel beaten them to a pulp twice already? Yes, but the second war was more painful and more bloody than the one before. They ended in victories, but that didn't matter. All it would take was one defeat. Each time, that abyss grew closer.

Would the Egyptians really attack? And if they did, where? When? How? And what were they doing at this abandoned base in the desert? It was his job to find out. The answers might start a war—or stop one—but he must find out.

Germans. The memories were cold, gray ash now, dead, but not the hate. He still saw the rusting barbed-wire fence of the death camp as if it were yesterday, with cruel-eyed men dressed in black and the wispy plumes of smoke from the ovens rising against a pitiless sky. He had survived. He remembered. And he hated. Death? He had died and gone to hell every night for three years, only to awake and be forced to start the journey anew the next day. So death held no fear for him. It was an old friend. That was why he could push himself back into the compound. Afraid? Insane? Not really. He was blessed with the reckless abandon of a man with absolutely nothing to lose.

He floated through the dim shadows of the old army base, blending into the night, until he reached the edge of the tarmac. Then he stopped and flattened himself against the sand, watching and waiting, barely fifty feet from the side wall of the hangar. It was the biggest building in the compound, nearly three stories of rusting sheet metal. Hard to believe this was where anyone would hide a secret, Landau thought to himself, but the signs all pointed here. He looked at the other buildings, the storage tanks, the stacked crates, the bright lights, and noted the way the guards checked the hangar more closely than the rest. Yes, this was the place and he had to get inside.

There were two big doors at the front end, but they were bathed in broad pools of light. That way would be suicide. The smaller door at the far end didn't look much safer.

Landau saw that his only chance was through one of the windows that ran down one side of the building. They'd stacked a half-dozen oil drums near the wall, casting a long shadow beneath the closest window. The glass was painted black. With no lights on inside, if he could pry it open, he could get in. That is, if he could cross the brightly lit tarmac without being seen.

Landau took a last look around and thought, This is as good a time to die as any. He rose to his feet and sprinted toward the oil drums. The bright glare of the lights made him squint but he ignored them, concentrating on the window. It was suicide. A black figure floating through the dark shadows was one thing. A black figure running across the brightly lit tarmac was something else: a clear target. The thought made him run even faster.

His knife was out before he reached the window. He drove the blade up through the gap between the upper and lower sash, tugging and jerking the handle from side to side, pushing up until the steel tip touched the latch. He pushed harder, expecting the latch to pop open. It was old and rusted. Surely the coats of faded, chipped paint were all that held the wood together, he told himself. But the damned thing fought back. Landau pushed the knife up again, straining, praying its thin blade wouldn't snap. The latch squeaked in protest and the blade bent, almost breaking, before the latch surrendered and sprang open. He gripped the lower sash with both hands and pushed. The old paint gave way with a loud, splintering crack and the sash slid up.

Landau cringed, twisting his head toward the front of the building, expecting to find himself looking down the barrel of a submachine gun, but no one was there. Too late to worry about the guards, he thought. If they'd heard the noise, he was dead already. All he could do was keep moving and get out of sight. He crawled through the narrow opening and pulled his legs inside, closing the window and pressing his body flat against the wall. He held his breath and listened, waiting for the empty silence to be shattered by whistles and shouts, waiting for the darkness to be slashed by the crisscrossing beam of a powerful flashlight, and waiting for the gunshots that would follow. He dared not move, not until he regained his night vision. Besides, Landau was patient. If he waited, and if there was someone else hiding in the dark with him, the other man might make that first, fatal mistake.

Nothing. No lights or shouts or gunshots. The agonizing seconds stretched into minutes and Landau could wait no longer. Time was running out. He raised his flashlight and flicked it on, letting its thin beam probe the floor nearby. He saw stacks of big wooden crates, some storage tanks, and two huge workbenches. They were ten feet wide and a hundred feet long, littered with tools and shiny metal parts. Overhead, he saw a heavy crane, its empty hook dangling over the workbenches.

Slowly and silently, Landau edged toward the center of the hangar, keeping his light on the floor. As he moved closer, he saw the dim outline of a long, shrouded object in the darkness ahead of him. No, there were two of them, sitting side-by-side on the floor. They were at least fifty feet long, covered with tarpaulins, and taking up most of the space in the center of the hangar. Their front ends were tapered and the rear ends jutted toward the ceiling. Beneath the edge of the tarpaulin, he saw several sets of rubber tires. Trailers! Whatever they were, they were set on trailers.

Landau felt an old twinge. He stepped closer and lifted the corner of the tarpaulin. He hoped he was wrong, even if it meant he'd die for nothing, but he wasn't. He wanted to scream. He stared, unable to move, feeling the old hatred rise in his throat. It had all changed now. Just getting away and warning Tel Aviv wasn't enough, not anymore, not with what he'd found here. Besides, if they caught him on the way out, the secret would die with him. The warning would never be sent. No one would ever know until it happened, until it was too late. That thought terrified him more than anything else, certainly more than dying.

Even death was relative. Landau welcomed it, which was why he made the perfect agent. To a corpse, what did it matter who the gravediggers were? But suddenly, in this old dilapidated hangar, that had all changed. His life now meant something. It had a value equal to their secret—more than it had ever been worth before, and more than he had ever wanted. That thought paralyzed him. He couldn't die. He had to stay alive, at least long enough to send a message. But after seventeen years of not caring, he wasn't sure he knew how.

To have any chance of escaping, Landau needed a diversion. A diversion? He smiled. Why not a big one? Why not the biggest! Why not destroy this precious work of theirs before they could finish it? That would set them back a few months and be a sweet bonus, indeed. Even if he did not get away, even if they killed him, it wouldn't matter.

Yes, Landau knew what he had to do.

And quickly! He raked the narrow beam of light across the workbenches, desperately searching for something to use. Then it came to him: fire. Yes! Find something that will burn. He spotted a pile of rags lying on the end of one of the workbenches. On the floor next to it sat a metal locker. He guessed what was inside it. He used the knife to spring the cheap lock, and smiled when he saw the cans inside the locker. He punched holes in the tops of four of them and bent down to smell. Turpentine and paint. Just as he'd hoped.

But where? Where would be the best place to set it? The flashlight beam sliced through the hangar until it came to rest on a large, concrete-block bunker set against the rear wall. Odd, he thought. A concrete bunker, inside a hangar? That made no sense. His brain wanted to ignore it, wanted to stick to the urgent task at hand. But his eyes kept turning back to the bunker and the flashlight followed.

"Forget it! What does a bunker matter? Hurry. Set the fire, you fool, before it's too late," he whispered to no one.

Yet the bunker held his attention like a magnet. Landau soon found himself walking toward it, the can and rags hanging forgotten in his hands. As he got closer, he saw that the bunker had a thick, reinforced-steel door and no windows. On the door was a small red warning sign. The flashlight beam danced across it and he squinted, trying to make out the words and the symbol printed on the sign. He was still too far away to read the letters, but the symbol, with its three interconnected yellow rings, registered deep inside his brain, sending an icy flash down his spine. The words were German, but the symbol was international, in bright yellow, and instantly conveyed the larger and infinitely more terrible secret this place held.

Landau stopped walking; his body stood frozen to the spot as if it wouldn't permit him to go any closer. The bunker suddenly repulsed him, with shock and horror. He hadn't guessed the half of it. How could the Egyptians be this foolish? The Egyptians? Never. They might be paying the bills, but his stomach told him that his old enemies in the black death's-head uniforms were behind it. Landau had never been more certain of anything in his life.

He stepped back, his eyes still riveted on the sign. A diversion? No! He must destroy this place if it was the last thing he ever did. He hurried back toward the wooden crates, stumbling, the weight of their secret more than he could bear. Tripping over his own feet, he fell, dropping the can and spilling the turpentine all over himself and the floor. He rose to his knees, shaking with anger and ignoring the fumes. He rubbed the handful of rags in the puddle, sopping up as much of the turpentine as he could. He emptied what was left in the can onto the rags, and fumbled in his pocket, groping for a book of matches.

Forget the storeroom, he told himself. Forget the hangar. And forget escaping. None of that mattered now. All he cared about was destroying this monstrous evil before it was too late. He tore a paper match loose and scratched it across the back of the matchbook, but didn't even get a spark. The emery paper was wet, soaked with turpentine and sweat. He tried again and watched in agony as the second match head crumbled beneath his fingertip.

He tore at another as the blackness of the hangar exploded with a blinding, white light. Someone had thrown a switch and the main bank of overhead lights burned bright. Landau covered his eyes with his hand, shrinking back, but it was too late. He couldn't see them, but they had seen him. And in that instant, Landau knew his gravediggers had arrived.

The match! Light the match! he told himself. It would be his last, defiant gesture to a cruel world. He struck it across the back of the matchbook as the first fusillade of gunshots ripped through the silent hangar.

The man was standing inside the front door, less than fifty feet away. Landau was little more than a black shadow in the dim clutter of the hangar, but the guard reacted instantly. He fired, and the heavy slugs ripped into Landau's chest, punching him backward across the concrete floor until his limp body came to rest against the steel leg of a workbench.

Odd, Landau thought as he smiled through the haze. He knew he'd been shot, but he felt nothing: no pain, no anger, merely a dull sadness. His eyes were open, staring at the ceiling. He turned his head and saw a match lying near his hand. A match? Yes! He remembered. It was still burning, its pale orange flame resting inches from the pile of turpentine-soaked rags.

So close, close enough for him to hope.

He heard the pounding of boots on the concrete and voices shouting in German. "Major Grüber! I got him!"

There was no reply, only a long silence, and then a pair of brightly polished jackboots appeared next to him. He heard a soft, satisfied grunt, then a boot rose in the air and stomped down on the match. The tiny flame was snuffed out, and with it went Landau's last hope.

A painful groan escaped his lips. He looked up. There, towering over him, was a giant, blond with bright blue eyes and the same kind of sadistic half-grin Landau had seen in a thousand nightmares.

"*Ja, ja,*" the man finally said, staring down at him as if he were a trophy elk he'd just bagged. Then the man's face, his bright blue eyes, and even that hateful smile grew hazy. The colors and shapes faded to a dull gray, then a deep, eternal black.

2

THOMSON LEANED BACK in the chair and continued to draw circles on the greasy tabletop with the tip of his finger. He glanced around the dark, nearly empty bar and sighed. It was a dump, but it was a good place to hide away. The only face he recognized was the bartender's, and that was just the way he wanted it.

He belted down the last of the gin and tonic and raised the glass above his head, dangling it back and forth until Jeremy couldn't ignore him any longer. Jeremy frowned, but he finally poured him another drink. They both knew he wasn't drunk, not yet anyway; but that wouldn't last long.

The first night after he got back, Thomson had tried the Hilton and almost thrown up. The crisp white tablecloths, soft jazz, and air conditioning were nice, but he couldn't take a whole room full of those smart-assed Harvard kids, with their tortoise-shell glasses, button-down collars, and cute, condescending smiles.

"Packed you off to Cairo?" That was how it always began. "We wondered. Rotten luck, that deal in Damascus. Made all the papers here. Don't worry. The Agency can't blame it on you. Could have happened to anyone."

Maybe things looked different when you were twenty-five. He wondered. The age of immortality. How old was he? Forty-two, going on seventy? Whatever. His face just didn't fit in their class picture anymore. Not his face. It had more lines and scars than an old oak tree. Why not? He'd earned every one of them the hard way, like hash marks on a sergeant's sleeve. What did they call it? Character? Well, he had all the character he could stand.

Damascus. He had gotten two of his own men and a local killed. That was bad enough. But he had also committed the cardinal sin: he wasn't one of them. If he'd gotten blown to pieces with the rest, everything would have been fine. They would have planted him in Arlington and mumbled a few nice words, whether they meant them or not. Better a dead hero they could lie about than a live embarrassment.

The plan had been so simple. "You see"—he could still hear his own words as he tried to explain—"there was this Syrian air force colonel with a sweet tooth for redheads and Switzerland. He offered us a bag of Red Army tech manuals for an even bigger bag of cash."

But the colonel's bag had blown up and taken what was left of Thomson's career right along with it. Lights, camera, action! The next thing he knew, the Syrian secret police were all over him. They rousted him good, grilling him for a week. After the bruised ribs, the cuts, and the half-dozen beatings they gave him just for fun, the only thing that made it worth the price was imagining that last look on the dumb-ass colonel's face when he opened the bag.

Washington had finally pried him loose. Not because they wanted to, but because they had to. They had patted him on the head and given him two aspirins before they dumped him here in Cairo like last week's garbage.

He had tried to fit back in. He even wore the same company uniform they did—a tan Brooks Brothers suit and a rep tie—but he wore them badly, the shirt collar open and the tie pulled down. The suit hung limply on his awkward frame, so stained and wrinkled it looked like he'd slept in it, which he vaguely remembered he might have done, and couldn't have cared less.

Not that it mattered anymore. The Harvards had taken over. It was their day and they swarmed through the Agency like an army of carpenter ants. They were on their way up, all bright-eyed and eager, while Thomson was on the express elevator back down. No, he was well past down. He'd hit bottom, crashed through the floor, and was still going.

They weren't to blame. They were the children of the "new Camelot," the "super spooks," and they knew every spy trick the Agency could teach them from a book. Old OSS vets like Thomson were quaint, dented antiques, to be kept around for display only. "See the fine craftsmanship, children? But for Heaven's sake, don't touch."

Shit! He swore he wouldn't start feeling sorry for himself. Anger and frustration? He had a right to those, but not to self-pity.

Finally, he looked up and saw Jeremy threading his way between the tables with the drink. A sly grin crossed Thomson's lips. He dug into his pants pocket and came out with a fistful of quarters, dumping them in the center of the table.

Jeremy set the drink down as Thomson looked up at him with his broadest, friendliest smile. "Want to try another one?" he asked.

"Not again, Mr. Thomson," Jeremy groaned. "Look—"

"Double or nothing? I thought you'd want to earn some of it back?"

"Like hell you did! You've drunk free three nights running, and I'm not making any money as it is."

"Triple then," Thomson offered, as he arranged the coins in a triangle. "It's easy. Ten quarters: four in the

bottom row, three in the next, then two, and one at the top."
He raised his eyes and knew he had the Englishman
hooked. "The tip of the triangle is pointing toward you.
Right? You get to move three of the coins, no more. But
when you're done the triangle has to be pointing at me."

Jeremy stared at the coins, then at Thomson, and his face
took on an expression of grim determination. "All right,
mate, but I'll work on it back at the bar. Triple or nothing!
And if I win, I get to keep your bloody quarters, too!"

"Good man!" Thomson laughed and raised the fresh
drink in mock salute. "Here's to Jeremy Throckmorton
and his gin. They're the only decent things you Brits left
behind in this sand trap."

"You ain't won yet!" the bartender growled as he
scooped up the coins and walked away.

Thomson leaned back and took another sip. Then he
frowned. Games. Even winning had become depressing.
It was too damned easy, and a pathetic substitute for the real
thing. In his time, he'd been good. No, he'd been the best.
Now he was sitting on the bench and there wasn't a damned
thing he could do about it.

That was when he saw the Arab.

Thomson glanced up and saw the fat bastard staring at
him from the front door and that got him mad. An Arab in
a Western bar? They'd never allow it at the Hilton. It was
reserved for men of a much whiter persuasion. And you'd
never see it in Damascus, not with all the religious taboos
against alcohol. But in a dump like this? In Cairo? Why not?
They never took anything very seriously in Cairo.

So why the hell was this one staring at him? Thomson
wondered, half-drunk and ready to get mad at something.
The Arab looked seedy—short, dark, and fat, with a sleepy
mustache that drooped below the corners of his mouth.
From the looks of him, he hadn't seen a razor or clean

clothes in a week. His old, gaudy sports car was all him: two sizes too small and popping its buttons.

Don't judge the bastard too quickly though, Thomson warned himself. He might look like a sweaty lump of lard, but his eyes were alert. He had that quick, hard look of a carpet merchant in the Souk. His eyes darted nervously from table to table, checking them out one at a time. Satisfied of something, the Arab looked back at him and made his move. Unless he turned off or headed for the kitchen, he was coming straight for him.

Thomson did nothing. He ignored the Arab as if he weren't even there.

When the Arab reached the table, he pulled out a chair and quickly sat down, uninvited, carefully keeping his back toward the front door. He leaned across and smiled, showing a silly gold tooth, then whispered tentatively, "You are Thomson?"

The American didn't reply. He maintained his hard expression and watched the Arab sweat. The man's face dripped with it, and his shirt was stained and wet. The night was hot and humid, but not that bad. Either Fats had been running, or something had scared the hell out of him.

The Arab threw a quick, nervous glance back toward the door and leaned even closer, licking his lips, trying to twist them into a more pleasant smile. "I...I am Mahmoud Yussuf," he announced, as if that was supposed to mean something. When it became apparent it didn't, the phony smile wilted and his face grew visibly worried. "Mr. Thomson, we..." He paused, struggling to keep his voice under control. "We...must talk!"

Thomson's expression remained blank. He picked up his glass and took a long drink, keeping his eyes riveted on the Arab's, boring straight through the man.

Yussuf shifted uncomfortably. "I know who you are, Mr. Thomson. You are CIA, so we *must* talk.... It is important and my time is short. I have the photographs," he blurted out triumphantly. Still no response. "The photographs, for Evans! The ones Landau took?... Well, I have them now."

"So what?" Thomson shrugged indifferently.

"Mr. Thomson, please!" Yussuf sounded desperate. "Do not pretend. These must go to Evans. And soon."

"Then give them to Evans."

"No, no! You don't understand." Yussuf blinked. Whatever he had expected, this wasn't it. "I ... I cannot find him. Landau did not tell me how to make contact. But your picture was in the newspapers. You are CIA, like Evans. He is waiting for these photographs, this very minute. They are worth much, I assure you. So you must help me. Tell Evans that Yussuf has Landau's pictures. Tell him that. He will know what to do."

Thomson gave the Arab a long, amused look, then slowly sat his glass down on the table and said, "Get the hell out of here before I toss you out." His voice sounded flat and bored, but his eyes were hard and angry. "I don't know any Evans and I sure as hell don't know you, so take your photographs and shove them!"

Yussuf's mouth dropped open in shock. "Mr. Thomson," he stuttered, "please, no jokes! You don't understand. This is important." He glanced nervously at the door once more. "All right, all right," he relented. "I know, you have rules. You do not know me. I am not one of your agents, am **I?**" He giggled as he dragged the sleeve of his jacket across his brow. "You need proof, is that it?" he asked as he thrust his hand inside his jacket.

When Yussuf's hand moved, Thomson lunged across the table and grabbed the man's throat with one hand and his wrist with the other. He wrenched the Arab's hand out of his jacket, but there was no gun, only a thick envelope dangling from his short, fat fingers.

"If you ever do that again," Thomson said, as he shoved Yussuf back into the chair, "I'll jam your pinkies so far down your throat you'll touch your toes."

The American's loud voice made Yussuf cringe. The handful of people in the bar were all looking at them, and the Arab didn't like it. "It's the photographs," Yussuf whispered, shrinking down in his chair and trying to become invisible. "Here!" He ripped the envelope open, pulling the bottom photograph from the stack and dropping it onto the table. "A sample. For free even! For you to take to Evans. Please!"

"Go peddle it to some tourist," Thomson snapped back, surprised and angry that the man still persisted with this idiotic story. "I'm not that stupid anymore. You got that? Once, maybe. But not anymore. Go tell them that."

The Arab didn't seem to be listening. His head was turned back toward the door and he sat frozen in the chair. Thomson's eyes followed the Arab's, until he saw two more men standing inside the doorway, looking slowly around the bar, just like Yussuf had done.

Before Thomson could ask, Yussuf slipped out of his chair and bent over the table, his face only inches from the American's, his mouth twisted into an angry snarl.

"Take the photograph to Evans," he hissed. "Tell him Landau took this at Heliopolis. And if he wants the rest, my price is ten thousand dollars! One hour, that's all I'll give you. Be at the rear of your apartment building, in the alley, him or you, in one hour! Not one minute longer! If no one shows, then I sell them to the Russians. They are not as stupid as you!"

Yussuf slipped through the beaded curtains that hung across the door to the kitchen and was gone.

Thomson turned his head and looked toward the two men at the front door. Even in this dim light he saw they were Arabs, and they were after Yussuf. One of them took a quick step to follow him, but the other one grabbed his arm. It was too late. He glared at Thomson as they backed out the door and ran away.

Thomson stared at the empty doorway. The months of lonely anger and frustration had built up inside him, bringing him to the flash point. He slammed his fist on the table. The glass jumped, spilling the watery gin. Thomson slumped forward and closed his eyes, shaking his head, disgusted with everything. Hadn't they had enough fun with him in Damascus?

But "they" weren't to blame. He was. He'd screwed it up, every way you could screw it up. And now he was a marked man. It was open season on Thomson, so why blame them? He had fallen for a doozy of a setup once. Why not twice? It was the safe play. They knew he was desperate, and desperate men do desperate things. Maybe he'd grab at anything that could resurrect his sorry ass.

Well, he *was* desperate, but they'd never know the half of it. Even if he fell for the bait and ran straight to the embassy, no one would listen to him. They wouldn't listen to a damned thing he had to say. Not anymore. He'd been cleaned and hung out to dry, finished, a tired old joke no one wanted to hear anymore. Damascus? That was just an excuse. Thomson was obsolete, a brown shoe in a glossy, patent-leather world. So the Agency had dropped him here, hoping he'd dry up and blow away on the hot desert wind.

He was so lost in his own maze that he didn't see Jeremy standing next to him until the bartender sat a fresh drink down on the table. The Brit was no dummy. When a customer had the leave-me-alones, that's exactly what he did.

Thomson forced a smile. "Sorry about the spill."

Jeremy already had his towel out. "Look, if that wog was bothering you, you should have given me the high sign. I'd have chucked him straight out."

"No, no problem, really," he muttered.

"Used to be, they'd never set foot in a white man's bar. Knew better. That's what you get with them running the country and all. Place is going to hell in a handbasket. And it won't take too damned long, either!"

"What then, Jeremy? You, me, and the wogs?"

"Not me, Mr. Thomson," he snorted. "Not me. Maybe just you."

"Maybe . . ." Thomson reflected sadly. Then he smiled. "Figured out the coins yet?"

"Ah . . . another minute. I nearly got—"

"Tell you what." Thomson waved it off. "Forget that one. And you keep the coins. I got a better one for you. Bring me three gin and tonics and three empty glasses."

Jeremy looked around the room, then back at Thomson suspiciously. "Oh, all right. What the hell. One more." He laughed and went back to the bar.

Thomson picked up the fresh drink and downed half of it in one gulp. The bite of raw gin was strong, but not strong enough to cut the sour taste in his mouth. He looked down and saw the photograph, still lying on the table where Yussuf had dropped it. He fought with himself, but finally gave in to the temptation and picked it up. He squinted, tipping the glossy side of the photo toward the dim light, but couldn't make it out. Either the room was too dark or his eyes were getting as bad as the rest of him. He fished in his shirt pocket, pulled out a box of matches, and lit one.

The bright yellow flame hurt his eyes, but as he held the match closer to the photo, he saw a gaunt face staring back at him. It was a black-and-white shot of a man, from the chest up. No, more like a photograph of a framed portrait hanging on some wall. The original was mounted in a cheap, thin frame. The guy looked middle-aged, pale, and half bald, with his hair slicked back for the camera. He was wearing wire-rimmed glasses and had that bland, humorless expression you'd expect on a high-school math teacher from Omaha. He stared straight into the lens, taking the whole thing ever so seriously.

A math teacher? Maybe. Judging from his face, he could have been a watch repairman or even a mortician. He could have been, but he wasn't. Not this guy. From the neck down, he was wearing an SS uniform.

The flame touched Thomson's finger. He cursed and dropped the match on the floor, then quickly lit another one. The uniform attracted his attention. There had been a time when he could name every ribbon and medal they wore, but this proper little Kraut looked naked. He might be SS, but not the fighting type. No, he was nothing more than a bureaucrat. All he had were the party service ribbons you'd find on some desk clerk. What did they call them? Golden peacocks? Yeah, Thomson thought, he might be a party hack, a technician, or maybe one of Himmler's exterminators, but he wasn't a soldier.

Thomson took a last look at the face, then lowered the match to the bottom corner of the photograph. The yellow flame warped and curled the paper until it caught fire. The flame quickly ate the man's jacket, gobbled up his ribbons, and charred his face, before Thomson dropped it in the ashtray. The bright yellow flame did the rest, leaving behind only a stiff, black ash.

Thomson stared at it. He'd been down before, but he'd never sunk this low. What an insult. The Egyptians probably had a squad of security police waiting outside the bar right now, expecting him to walk into their little trap with the photograph of that old, pathetic Nazi and $10,000 in his pocket. How lame can you get? Yussuf? Surely they could dig up a better Judas-goat than him? And Evans? That was the dumbest part of all. Why not pick someone he knew? How stupid did they think he was?

Unfortunately, he knew the answer. But Jeremy was back before he could dwell on it and get even more depressed.

"Now look, Mr. Thomson, if this is the one where you belt the drinks down and say they're on the house, I'm not playing," he announced firmly.

Thomson smiled and began arranging the six glasses in a line, with the three full ones on the left and the three empty ones on the right. "Listen. You can only move one glass, then the six glasses have to be alternating: full, empty, full, empty, full, empty. Got it?"

Jeremy frowned. "Another of your damned tricks?"

Thomson smiled. "No tricks. Just a little creative problem solving." He sat back and laughed quietly to himself. "Evans? What a crock!"

3

THOMSON DRANK THOSE THREE and that many more again, as best he could remember. When Jeremy flipped the last chair upside-down on his table and stood with his arms folded across his chest, Thomson knew it was time to go.

"Closing time, right?" he asked, as he rose slowly to his feet and dropped some loose bills on the table.

"You won, mate, not me," Jeremy confessed.

Thomson shook his head. "Next time. I drank too much to stiff you tonight." Then he headed toward the door, feeling the gin and carefully brushing the edge of each table with the tips of his fingers like a blind man navigating by braille.

"How 'bout I call you a cab? It can get rough out there."

"No, I'll manage. Besides"—he laughed as he waved good-bye—"tonight, I'm the best protected man in Cairo."

Outside, the night air closed around him like a warm, damp blanket. He'd never known anything like it. By day, the wind blew hot and dry off the desert, hissing and filling the air with a shimmering veil of dust. But at night, the wind died. The air grew soft and damp, reeking with the smell of a million charcoal cooking pots, the exhaust from too many Italian sedans, and the stench rising from the river. They'd even desecrated the Nile. That magnificent highway of the pharaohs was little more than a brown, open sewer. What was the line in the tourist brochure—"Ah, the

Cairo nights, full of mystery and sin''? Bullshit, Thomson thought. The night was like a big vat of rancid sweet-and-sour sauce.

Okay, where the hell are they? he wondered.

By now, the opposition knew he wasn't buying. The appointed time for him to meet Yussuf had long passed, but they wouldn't stop watching him. So where were they? In an unmarked car? In that dark, second-floor window across the street? Were they a couple of late-night shoppers loitering nearby in cheap suits? Thomson couldn't have cared less, but he was drunk enough and mad enough to insist they do it right. They could stomp the rest of him into a bloody pulp, but he had his professional pride.

So at each corner he'd stop to listen and look. What was that sound? A car door closing? Footsteps? Did he see a shadow in that doorway? He knew they were here somewhere. He could feel the old adrenaline pumping again—the anger brought it out. But deep inside, he heard a tiny voice praying they really were there, because it would mean he was still in the game. In the game? Who was he kidding? He was finished the minute they yanked him out of Damascus. Even the stupid Egyptians ought to know that.

Thomson kept walking, blocking out the memories and keeping mental notes on each car he passed, certain he'd see it again, waiting up ahead. He noted the coats, hats, and shoes on everyone he passed. Amateurs never remembered the shoes. He smiled, looking into store windows, searching for careless reflections. He crossed the street and crossed back again, throwing them every trick he knew, determined to blow their cover. Finally, he gave them his patented dipsy-do. He turned a blind corner, counted to ten, and came storming back around, head down and shoulders set, knowing some poor clown would be racing to catch up and hoping he'd knock him flat.

But no one was there.

Thomson stopped in his tracks, his confident expression fading away as he realized no one was following him. He leaned against the building, feeling older and more tired than he'd ever felt.

Set him up? The more he thought about it, the more it made him laugh. The incompetents screwing with the King of the Incompetents? That was incest.

All they had to do was ask Kilbride.

"Mr. Ambassador," they'd gloat, "we have arrested your man Thomson, and—"

"Good, keep him!" *Click!*

Well, this time he was clean. All he wanted was to be left alone. No, that wasn't what he wanted. He wanted back in the game, but not like this. He wanted back in the real game, not the bush leagues, but he might as well wish he was on Mars. Not too damned likely.

True, he'd lost a step or two, but not many. Starting with those suicide jumps into Germany in '44, he'd given them eighteen years. None of that mattered. After the Bay of Pigs, they had filled the gutters with heads like his. That was Allen Dulles's last stand, and Custer had gotten better odds. The smart guys saw it coming. They read the signs and grabbed for a teak desk in Virginia. Thomson was the dumb schmuck. He stayed in the field and got burned. When it happened, all they did was smile.

Before he realized it, Thomson found himself standing in front of his apartment building. He looked around one last time, squinting into the dim shadows, but they were empty. He could swear he felt their eyes on him. Or did he just want it that bad, like an old junkie with a twitch? Well, he needed his fix too, and all the gin in Cairo couldn't make him forget it.

He pushed through the glass door of the apartment building, more depressed than ever. Looking up, he spotted a sign on the elevator door. "Out of Order," it read, making his day complete. It figured! Nothing in this damned town ever worked right, or often. With all the Russians around, you'd think they might send somebody who could fix an elevator. The Egyptians? They couldn't fix a camel in heat.

He trudged toward the stairs, knowing it was five flights up. That put him above the worst of the city stench, but he had to pay the price of climbing the stairs at least once a week. Tonight, with the way his head felt, it wasn't worth it.

Why couldn't they play their little games with one of Kilbride's pets like Collins? Harvard '59 needed a little street training. He was such a perfect ass. But one of these days, the bright glow of Camelot would fade away along with the Hula-Hoop and bouffant hairdos, and they'd eat Collins for breakfast.

Why not get out? Why fight it? Thomson must have asked himself that question a hundred times a day. Get out and do what? Be a "security consultant" in some banana republic? Run a few guns? Maybe go back to the States. Then what? Guard the door of the First National Bank of Omaha? No, Thomson would stay on their merry-go-round. He'd keep riding until it threw him off, because it had the only brass ring in town. One more try, that was all he'd asked. He'd stretch his fingers and grab for the ring, even if he fell flat on his ass again.

Thomson reached the third-floor landing and slowed down. He was wheezing, and dripping with sweat. Hard to believe this was the same body that had finished jump school at Benning, then special ops training, and then run across half of Bavaria one step ahead of the Gestapo. When was that? Eighteen years ago? Look at him now: jumping at shadows and huffing up the back stairs. Thomson, my good man, it had been a lousy trip, but you got here all by yourself.

He finally reached the fifth floor and doubted he'd ever breathe again. Keys? They were somewhere. He rattled the coat and found the right pocket, then lurched toward his apartment door, bone-tired. Fiddling with the key ring, he found the most likely looking candidate and shoved it into the lock, giving the key a quick twist. He turned the knob but the door didn't open. The key fit, but the door didn't open. How could it still be locked? he wondered. Odd. Maybe it was one of those damned double locks. Thomson turned the key again and kept turning until the key wouldn't turn anymore. He tried the lock again, but the door still wouldn't open.

Thomson was in no mood for this. Even the mechanical world was lashing back at him. And the door was still locked. Locked? He stepped back and frowned. If the door was still locked, then it had been unlocked when he got here. That was the only explanation.

Unlocked? It sure as hell hadn't been unlocked when he left.

Thomson stared at the door, the sweat on his back turning cold. He sobered up fast, realizing how incredibly stupid he'd been.

No wonder the bastards hadn't followed him home. They didn't need to. They were already here, waiting inside. Or were they? Maybe they had just left him a present. Thomson's mind raced ahead. What had they planted? Drugs? Papers? Maybe more of those damned photographs? Since he hadn't taken the bait in the bar, they'd decided to take him out the easy way. If he stepped through that door, a whole squad of security men would pop out of the wood-work.

He backed away, knowing the smart move was to run as fast as he could. But his feet stopped moving. They wouldn't go, and he wasn't sure he wanted them to. Maybe it was the gin, or that fat Arab with the gold tooth, or the look in the eyes of those two gorillas in the doorway, or Cairo, or Damascus, or the whole damned thing rolled into a big ball of dung; whatever it was had become an insane challenge to him. They had gotten him mad. It was their game—their field, their rules, and their ball, and Thom-son wanted to ram it down their throats and make them choke on it. He wanted to beat them bad. Besides, what did he have to lose? What more could the Agency do to him? Send him to Cairo?

Instinctively, he slipped a hand inside his jacket. Then he remembered. No gun. Another of Kilbride's stupid rules. "No incidents!" The ambassador had spouted that one from the top floor of his mountain. "No trouble, no guns, no nothing." And he had been looking straight at Thomson when he said it. Unfortunately, the big Mick wasn't standing here, wondering what was on the other side of the door. He was probably in some reception line, sip-ping martinis with the Russian Ambassador, comparing notes on the best shopping buys in Rome.

No gun. So be it. Thomson bent down and slipped his shoe off, slowly cocking his arm like he was Sandy Koufax, thinking fast ball as he edged back toward the door. Some weapon, he thought, an old penny loafer with a worn heel. It wasn't much, but he could always throw it and run like hell. And if they were quicker? It would be a swell way to go: stretched out on the worn hall carpet of a third-rate Cairo apartment building with a bullet in his back, one bare foot, and a wry smile.

"Incidents!" he spat as he slowly turned the key. He twisted the knob and kicked the door open, pressing himself against the wall, waiting to hear gunshots, angry shouts, something.

But he heard nothing. He waited at least a full minute, until his curiosity got the better of him and he groped his hand around the corner, feeling for the light switch inside. He flipped on the living room light and listened to nothing but dead silence. He felt his nose twitch and sniffed the air, smelling the faint aroma of Turkish tobacco wafting slowly out of his apartment.

That was when he heard the voice.

4

"MR. THOMSON, IF YOU are quite finished with the theatrics, come inside and stop making an ass of yourself." The voice was Egyptian: mild, cultured, and arrogant, and Thomson knew he'd never heard it before.

He edged forward and peered around the door frame, shoe held high and arm cocked, just in case. But the scene in his living room hardly looked threatening. Against the far wall, sitting in the only decent chair Thomson owned, was a dark, thin Arab in an immaculate white-linen suit. He was perched on the front edge of the chair, with one leg thrust awkwardly in front of him, leaning hard on the ebony cane propped between his knees. The man inhaled deeply on his cigarette and slowly exhaled, looking up at Thomson with an expression of utter contempt.

He hadn't come alone. Flanking him in opposite corners of the room were two huge goons, even bigger than the ones in the bar. They were the little man's muscle, and Thomson had their undivided attention.

"Comfortable?" Thomson finally asked, trying to sound calm.

The man in the white suit glanced around the shabby living room. "Not particularly. You have kept me waiting for nearly an hour. If you had not returned soon, I would have sent Sergeant Sayyid to track you down. He would have enjoyed that. You would not."

"You knew where I was."

"I did?" the man asked, sounding surprised.

"Knock it off," Thomson said, irritation creeping into his voice. "We both know I'm not playing. And you aren't half good enough to make me."

"Playing?" The Arab frowned. "Neither am I. I've come here for answers."

"Got a search warrant?" Thomson held out his hand. "Or did you forget about diplomatic immunity?"

The Arab's eyes flared. "Mr. Thomson, do not make me angrier than I already am. Diplomatic immunity?" The words were calm and precise, but Thomson felt the burning anger behind them. "Diplomatic immunity? I do not concern myself with the shams you Westerners use to protect your spies—"

"State Security can't touch me. Call the Foreign Office," he interrupted.

"I am not with State Security, or the cursed Foreign Office. I am Captain Hassan Saleh of the Metropolitan Police, Chief of Homicide. If that means nothing to you, perhaps a few nights in our drunk tank will cure your 'diplomatic immunity,' and your clever mouth."

From the look in his eyes, Saleh meant it. Thomson shut up, no longer certain what was going on.

Saleh waited too. When the American did not reply, he looked disappointed. "Good. Maybe you are smarter than you look, Mr. Thomson. Now you will tell me where you have been this evening."

"In a bar." Thomson heaved a disgusted sigh. "All night. And we both know it. Your own men saw me there and I have witnesses. Go ask."

Saleh frowned again, looking puzzled. He turned away and rubbed his front leg, deep in thought. Finally, he motioned to one of the goons. The man walked over and bent down as Saleh whispered something in his ear. The goon glanced at Thomson and nodded, then quickly left the room.

"I shall do just that, Mr. Thomson." Saleh eyed him suspiciously. "And while I'm waiting, you will tell me everything you know about Mahmoud Yussuf."

"Who? Never heard of him." Thomson shrugged, hoping Saleh was only fishing.

"Permit me to refresh your memory. Yussuf was scum, one of those pathetic things you people drop behind you like excrement. Calling him a spy would be ludicrous. He was a leech. He would have been a pimp, if he weren't so crude. Even the whores would have nothing to do with him. So he stooped even lower. He dealt in information. He sold anything to anyone, regardless of what it was or the damage it might do, provided the price was right. Scum!" Saleh spat as he rubbed his leg even harder, his face lined with pain. "Scum. But without you Americans and Russians or the damned British before you, men like Yussuf would not have been scum."

"The name means nothing—"

"A lie," Saleh interrupted quietly, reaching inside his jacket to hand Thomson a small photograph. "Examine the face. This time, tell me the truth. It is your last chance."

Thomson knew it wasn't, but he pretended to study the photograph anyway, knowing Saleh's eyes were looking for the slightest reaction. It was a police mug shot, front view and side, and the face was Yussuf's. But why? What was Saleh up to? Still, if he was going to this much trouble, Thomson knew he'd better tread softly. Saleh was no fool. Thomson frowned and pretended he wasn't sure.

"Take a long look," Saleh said. "As you can see, Yussuf was no stranger to us."

Why did he keep using the past tense? Thomson wondered. When that came from a homicide cop, it was time to duck. "This guy? I don't know. It could be," he offered blandly. Saleh could prove they had met, but not a whole lot more. If he kept his story straight, they'd have to work like hell to catch him in a lie.

"It could be what?" Saleh pressed.

"Look," Thomson conceded sheepishly, "a guy came up to me in the bar tonight. It was dark and I'd had a few to drink. We only talked for a minute or two. Maybe it was him. Maybe it wasn't. He wasn't handing out business cards, you know."

"What did he want?"

Another question? Thomson wondered. Why not skip straight to the threats? Saleh already knew the answers. It didn't make sense.

"He tried to sell me something, like you said." Thomson shrugged. "Some photographs. But I wasn't buying. I told him to get lost. Bip. Bam. That's all there is."

"He was one of your agents then?"

"Him? Get serious."

"Then why did he go to you?"

"Maybe I've got a friendly face?" Thomson snapped. "Look, Captain, half of Cairo knows who I am. It was in all the papers. And they all want to sell me something."

"I don't care about half of Cairo, just Yussuf and the photographs you said he sold you."

"Not sold. Tried! I'm not in the market anymore."

"Photographs of what?"

"I don't know. I didn't see them!" Thomson had lost his patience. "He said they were 'interesting,' that's all. How the hell should I know? Maybe they were pictures of his thirteen-year-old niece waiting in the alley? The bar was dark, maybe he thought I was Egyptian."

Saleh's face turned crimson. He glanced sharply to his right and snapped his fingers. One of the goons came across the carpet like an avalanche, big and quick. Before Thomson could ward off the blow, the goon gave him a monstrous backhanded slap across the face that seemed to erupt from the floor and lift his head to the ceiling. Thomson rocked back on his heels, then slowly straightened up, feeling the heat pulse through his cheek. He wiped his fingers across his lower lip. Blood. How did that old Polish proverb go? "Don't get mad, get even." The goon didn't have much to worry about, not unless he found a spare tank lying around. But that little bastard Saleh better stay out of dark alleys.

"That was just to get your attention," Saleh said, his eyes every bit as hard as Thomson's. "If you want to be cute again, Sergeant Sayyid will gladly oblige. I hope you do, because you and your humor are equally repulsive to me."

Saleh was seething. "Who do you think you are? We Egyptians ruled the greatest empire in the world while your ancestors squatted in mud huts and scratched each other's fleas. You stand there stinking of gin and have the audacity to insult us? I don't understand it. How could a great power like yours send us a piece of dung like you?"

He stared at Thomson, hoping for a response, but Thomson wasn't that stupid. He glared back, keeping his mouth shut, stone-cold sober now.

"I thought so," Saleh said with a faint, sarcastic smile. "Now you will tell me the details of your arrangement with Mahmoud Yussuf. All of them!"

"We had no arrangement—"

"How was it to work?" Saleh hammered away. "Were you to meet him, or was he to meet you? How was it to be done?"

"We had no arrangement! I had just finished telling him I wasn't interested, when your two men stepped in the front door. Yussuf took one look at them and tore out the back like a scared rabbit. He left and I stayed, right there, all night, and we both know I can prove it."

Thomson stopped, expecting the grilling to get worse, expecting something, but not the expression on Saleh's face. The policeman shook his head. "Why do you keep saying my men?" he demanded, sounding frustrated. "What men? What did they look like?"

More games? Thomson wondered. "Two goons, not quite as big as these two. Arabs, with short-cropped hair and cheap suits with bulges. Cops? State Security? Take your pick."

Saleh listened intently. "Is that the truth or another of your lies?"

"The truth. Just like the rest."

"We'll see." He turned and snapped his fingers at Sayyid again. Thomson flinched, but the burly sergeant only smiled and handed him a large manila envelope.

"Perhaps this will impress you, Mr. Thomson." Saleh had a strange smile on his lips. "Open it."

Thomson opened the flap and pulled out another photograph. It was much bigger than the mug shot, grainy and black-and-white. He held it toward the light and squinted, trying to figure out what he was looking at.

"No, take a good look! If I were a CIA agent in Cairo and the police found that lying on my doorstep, I would suddenly become very cooperative."

As the pieces suddenly fell into place, Thomson's stomach leaped for his throat. He closed his eyes, but the gruesome image wouldn't go away.

"Oh, no, Mr. Thomson"—Saleh's voice dripped with sarcasm—"take another look. A good, long one this time. Remember? I said I was from homicide!"

Thomson opened his eyes. He saw a body lying on a slab of concrete, looking like a lumpy sack of potatoes with arms and legs poking out at odd, obscene angles.

"Does the picture disturb you? Well, it is nothing. You should have been there to witness it firsthand, Mr. Thomson, in full color, as I did! If you had, you would understand why I do not find you amusing tonight."

Thomson's stomach lowered itself into place and he took a closer look. The body was lying in a huge pool of blood, more blood than he ever dreamed a body could hold. But Thomson hadn't noticed the worst part: the body had no head. Instead, it was sitting a few feet away on a concrete step. Some sadist with a terminal case of the funnies had placed the man's head so that its vacant eyes could stare down at its own body. The mouth hung open, the jaw gone slack. The face was swollen and grotesque, but Thomson saw the gold tooth and knew who it was.

"Your agent Yussuf, correct?" Saleh said.

"No. He wasn't my agent—"

"And are you ready for the big surprise?" Saleh bore in. "That photograph was taken behind this building, in the alley, less than two hours ago. Imagine that! And imagine my surprise when I discovered who lives here."

Thomson felt drained, barely able to stand and listen, but Saleh was just warming up.

"How interesting. Someone separated poor Yussuf from his head, right after he had a secret meeting with a CIA agent. How interesting." Saleh was toying with him. "Can you imagine how powerful an arm and how sharp a blade it takes to do something like that, to sever a man's head from his shoulders, to slice through all that muscle and bone and simply lop it off as if it were a ripe melon on a vine, with just one stroke? No, I doubt you could imagine that, Mr. Thomson. An Arab might. You see, this is not some routine back-alley murder. Call it an execution, a punishment, a gesture, a statement, or a message, if you like. But someone had a perverse desire to make a very, very violent point of it all. I want to know what that point was. So why don't you tell me?''

Thomson was stunned. The booze, the hot, foul night air, and now this: each had taken its toll. "You don't seriously think I did this, do you?" he whispered.

"You?" Saleh laughed derisively. "How ridiculous. Look at yourself. There isn't enough gin in Cairo to give you the courage to do a thing like that. No, you did not wield the sword. But I think you know who did, and I think you know why."

Thomson swallowed hard and tried to regain his self-control. "I had nothing to do with this. Yussuf asked me to meet him in the alley later. I didn't go, but it looks like someone did."

"Ah, a bit more of the story slips out."

"He asked me to meet him. I said no and I meant it. I didn't go. I stayed in the bar. Check it out."

"Perhaps you set him up?"

Thomson tipped his head back. It was his turn to laugh.

"You find that amusing?" Saleh grew angry. "Why?"

"Why? Because I thought he was setting me up, that's why! I thought the whole thing was one big setup. And until just now, I figured you were the next part of it. But you aren't, are you? You're just another dumb cop who doesn't know any more about this than I do!"

Saleh's eyes flared and he looked over at Sayyid.

"Don't waste your time," Thomson said, shaking his head. "So Yussuf had some good stuff after all. Too bad.

But if I'd gone for it, you'd have two bodies lying out there on the concrete, wouldn't you? So go talk to the KGB or your own security people. Somebody chased that poor bastard out of the bar. Use your head. It wasn't me. And if it wasn't you, it had to be one of them. You ought to find out why."

Saleh gave him a quick, angry look. But for once, he kept quiet. He was considering Thomson's arguments, and he didn't like the conclusions he kept coming up with. "I know you are lying, Mr. Thomson," Saleh finally replied as he rose to his feet. "So be it. You had your chance." His words were quiet and unemotional, but his eyes raked Thomson like a fistful of nails.

"When I get my proof, all the 'diplomatic immunity' in the world will not save you from me. I am Bedouin, Mr. Thomson. Do you know what that means? My people spend their lives wandering the blistering desert, dressed in heavy, brown robes. Some say it makes us all a bit mad. I prefer to call it determined. Every now and then, an old Bedu will stop in his tracks, look up at the blinding sun, and utter a prophecy, as if he were reading words carved deep into a stone tablet. Well, Mr. Thomson, you just heard a Bedouin prophecy. Remember it."

Saleh limped painfully to the door, ignoring Thomson. When he reached it, he stopped and turned back. "You see, Allah permits each man one blind, irrational passion in life, Mr. Thomson. Mine is my nation, and I will stop at nothing to protect it. For the first time in two thousand years, Egypt is ruled by an Egyptian. We are one, and nothing else matters. Nothing! And certainly not you!"

"I'm not involved in this, Saleh. Check it out. You're seeing spies under the bed."

"Am I, Mr. Thomson? We'll see. You must excuse a bit of paranoia among the poor, backward peoples of the world.

Nine years ago, it only took five of your CIA agents and ten thousand dollars to overthrow the Mussadegh government in Iran. You hate Gamal Nasser even more, but you aren't going to get him. Not while I live. Remember that.''

Their eyes met, and the challenge was understood.

Saleh laughed and turned away. He and his men walked out the door, leaving it open behind them.

Thomson reached out and slammed it shut. He slumped back against the wall, shaking with rage and frustration, and not a little fear.

They had gotten him good this time, and he knew it. But why? Why him? And to think he was the one who had wanted back in the game.

5

HUNG OVER AND CHEWED OUT, Thomson had had a bad night. And when he stepped into the embassy lobby, he knew his morning was going to be even worse. The receptionist didn't even let him get halfway to the elevator.

"Not so fast!" Her chewing gum snapped a warning shot. "His Eminence wants you, Thomson, and I mean right now."

"Can't the condemned man get some coffee?"

"I wouldn't recommend it, honey." She shook her head. "My orders are to have your butt in his office, if I have to get the Marines to drag it there."

"You're a peach, Doris," he deadpanned.

"Yeah, I guess I am. So do us both a favor and go, huh?" Her limp arm pointed toward the elevator.

There was no escape. But why should he need one? He hadn't done anything wrong. And by the time he strode down the long, carpeted hall and opened the door to the ambassador's office, Thomson had worked himself into a good case of outraged indignation.

Who did Kilbride think he was anyway? He hadn't given them eighteen years and two wives to be treated like some flunky. Eighteen years! What had he gotten in return: nine hundred dollars in the bank, an old Dodge in storage, and a couple of Christmas cards from two spoiled brats he wouldn't even recognize. Yeah. The more he thought about it, the more he figured it should be him who gave Kilbride a piece of his mind.

He didn't. Kilbride's secretary sentenced him to a hard-backed armchair in the far corner. She knew the score, just as Doris had. She sat behind her desk and painted her nails, watching him over the top of her glasses, with a faint smirk on her face. She knew Kilbride was going to eat him alive, hangover and all.

When the intercom buzzed, she didn't need to say a word. She just cocked her head toward his office door and smiled with all the warmth and sincerity of a cemetery groundskeeper.

As he stepped into the ambassador's office, Thomson could see that she had pegged it about right. Kilbride was sitting center stage, leaning back in his black-leather chair and surveying his world from behind the brightly polished ramparts of his immense oak desk. Thomson had to admit he cut an impressive figure. With his flowing white mane, blue pin-striped suit, wrinkled brow, and long expressive fingers, Kilbride looked every inch the suave, skilled diplomat. Thomson knew better. This was Standard Pose #5—"The Angry Ambassador," straight out of the manual. Kilbride hadn't actually read it, of course, but he might have scanned the pictures, or colored them.

Standing the precise number of steps to the ambassador's right was the ever-present Collins, probably on the X Kilbride had drawn for him on the carpet. Collins had his arms crossed and was scowling like his boss. They were the Caped Crusader and his Boy Wonder, just as Thomson remembered.

The ambassador didn't waste any time. "What the hell have you got to say for yourself? The foreign minister woke me at the crack of dawn. Guess what was on his mind? You! You and your goddamn CIA, running around town without the brains God gave a moose, leaving bodies lying on your own doorsteps, and being stupid enough to get caught doing it! That's what was on his mind.''

Kilbride leaned forward, red-faced, and used a long, manicured finger like a pointer. "Listen and listen good, boy. I don't like your outfit. I don't like surprises. And most of all, I don't like you. There I was, just starting to make some headway with the boys at the Foreign Ministry, when you go crap in their well. They didn't like that, Thomson. So I don't like it much, either!''

He finally came up for air, his eyes squinting, his voice turning more sarcastic. "Let me put it in itty-bitty words even a screw-up like you can understand. My job's to get along with these people. I talk their language; not Arab''— he made it sound like two words—"just good old back-scratchin' politics, and that's no different here than back home.''

Thomson tried hard to keep a straight face, because the man really was serious. Next to ambitious, Kilbride was nothing if he wasn't serious. That made him doubly dangerous. Thomson focused his eyes on the wall above Kilbride's shoulder, where Kilbride kept his big picture gallery, hoping to keep them out of trouble. Somehow the bastard had managed to pose with every Back Bay politician imaginable, from Old Man Kennedy and Jim Curley, to Mike McCormack and a gaggle of short, fat mayors, congressmen, and judges. They were the ones who were smiling. Why not? He was the tall, shanty-Irish businessman who was writing the checks. Someone had said he'd been "big in concrete." Not big enough or deep enough, Thomson told himself.

"You know what they sent me this morning?" Kilbride waved a familiar black-and-white print in the air. "Jeezuz, Mary, and Joseph! They cut that guy's head off! Makes me want to puke every time I think about it.'' He closed his eyes and tossed the print on the desk between them. ''Have you people gone nuts or something?''

''I had nothing to do with that,'' Thomson answered quietly.

''Don't insult me! They said this guy was peddling pictures to you—''

''And I told them I wasn't buying.''

''And that doesn't wash any better with me than it did with them. Damn it!'' Kilbride slammed his palms on the desk with a loud slap. ''I told Langley I didn't want you, but they pushed. I was new. I didn't want any stink, so I gave in. Now look what I got. Well, I ought to ship your sorry ass back to them right now. But I can't, can I? Be as good as admitting you're guilty, wouldn't it? So I'm stuck with you, Thomson, at least until things cool off. Damn! As if I don't have enough problems.''

He ran his fingers through his white hair and scowled again. ''You listen good, mister. If I'm stuck with you, then you're damn well stuck with me, and this is my embassy.'' He poked himself in the chest with his thumb. ''I'm in charge here, not a bunch of spooks from Langley. From now on, you don't go to the can without asking first. Don't even sneeze or fart loud without a 'teacher may I.' Because if you do, I'll have you out in the desert with a clipboard counting camels so fast your head'll spin. You got me?''

''Yes, sir.'' Thomson held his tongue, but barely.

Kilbride glared across the desk at Thomson. He wanted an argument, but none was forthcoming and that took most of the satisfaction out of it. So he leaned back and decided to dig a little deeper. ''What the hell was going on last night, anyway? What were you doing with that Arab?''

''Nothing. I never saw him before.''

''You expect me to believe that?''

"I don't expect a damn thing!" Thomson had finally cracked. He kept his voice low, but he took a step forward, right up to the desk, and leaned on it with both hands, so he could stare straight down into Kilbride's eyes. "You can believe whatever you want, Mr. Ambassador. I'm telling you I never saw that guy before last night. It wasn't an Agency operation. He wasn't working for me. I didn't kill him and I don't know who did any more than you do. So get off my ass!"

Kilbride looked up into Thomson's angry eyes and blinked. "Well"—he coughed, not accustomed to people who talked back—"you didn't, huh? Then what about those photographs? I suppose you don't know anything about them, either?"

Thomson stared down at Kilbride for another second, then backed off. "I'm not sure. He only showed me one of them, but it meant nothing. It was an old wartime shot of some SS officer. Yussuf said he had a whole envelope full of pictures to sell us. The price was ten thousand dollars if we wanted them. He said they were the ones somebody named Landau took out at Heliopolis."

Kilbride almost came out of his chair, his eyes wide open and scared. "Jeez! You didn't tell that to the cops, did you?"

"Of course not! He said they were for one of our Agency people, for some guy named Evans I never heard of. I figured it was a setup, so I stayed away. But I'll tell you one thing." Thomson looked straight at Kilbride. "If there is an Evans and I get my hands on him, he's going to have some questions to answer."

"No!" Kilbride snapped, shaking his head nervously. "You're finished with this business, Thomson, as of right now."

"That guy almost got me killed last night. Don't you think I have a right to know why?"

"No! You're out! There is no Evans. If there was, don't you think I'd know it?" He cocked his head toward Collins and scowled. "You ever heard of any Evans?"

"No, sir!" the young agent replied, a bit too quickly and innocently.

"There." Kilbride smiled and shrugged, sounding remarkably friendly. "The Arab made up the whole story. It was a setup, like you said. He was trying to con us out of a few bucks, and it didn't work. A crook like that? Figures someone took him into a dark alley, just like they do back home. Might even be the cops. So, I shouldn't have yelled at you. You didn't fall for it last night, did you? I'll give you credit for that much. You smelled a setup and steered clear. That was quick thinking, Thomson. You did the right thing." Kilbride was on a roll now, probably even believing himself. "The only part I don't understand is why the guy hit on you in the first place?"

"He said this Landau never told him how to contact Evans. He remembered me from the newspapers. What else could he do? Knock on the embassy door? But if he was running a con, he was good at it. He didn't look to me like he was pretending, and neither did the guy who cut off his head. No, I think Yussuf had some good stuff, whatever it was. He tried to free-lance it and got burned. The rest is anyone's guess. That's why I'd like to go out to Heliopolis and sniff around."

"No! You're out! I mean it, Thomson. Nothing's going on out there and I don't want you to even mention it again." Kilbride was nearly shouting. He heard himself and quickly lowered his voice, twisting his mouth into a sly, knowing grin.

"Look, Thomson," he snorted, "you've been around. You can see who's behind this, can't you? It's those damned Israelis. That's who. Stop and think—a photo of some old Nazi, a guy named Landau, and now a dead Arab? It's clear as a bell to me. The Jews are in this up to their beanies; them, or the KGB, or both. But they're not after you. They're after me."

Kilbride leaned forward and started to whisper, as if he was letting Thomson in on a family secret. "The Jews would do anything to drive a wedge between me and Nasser. They're scared. They know what I'm doing, and they're out to stop me, any way they can."

Thomson looked down at Kilbride in amazement, trying not to laugh. "Then what's going on out at Heliopolis?" he asked.

"Nothing! It's an old British army post. That's all!"

"We ought to check it out—"

"Fine. I'll send Collins. He can ask a few questions. Will that satisfy you? You do what you're told. Stay away. You never heard of the place. Never. Just keep playing it smart and we'll forget about last night."

"Aren't you worried about this SS officer?"

"God, man. This is 1962, not 1945! Nobody gives a damn about some old Nazi. The Egyptians have been hiring them for years. Maybe a few do smell. Who cares? If Nasser likes them, that's fine with me. I'd rather he use a few Krauts with shady records than the Reds."

Kilbride leaned back in his chair and stared at the ceiling. "Let me read you into the big picture, Thomson. The president didn't send me here to take snapshots of pyramids. No, sir! There's a war out there. There may not be any bombs falling, but it's real and I'm not going to be the one who loses it. Jack wants these Arabs on our side and my job's to get them there, any way I can. He's counting on me,

and I'm not going to let him down. That's going to take
some hard work, a lot of stroking, and a big fistful of dollars, but I'm going to get them.

"Look," he continued, deep in thought, pressing those
long fingers together as if his hands were doing push-ups
against each other. "No sooner did Nasser bump off old
Naguib in '54, than he signed that big arms deal with the
Reds. Khruschev had him right in his pocket. But that old
fox Nikita had bigger ideas. Two years ago the local com-
mies stirred up some trouble, tried to dump Nasser. So he
slapped a bunch of them in jail and the honeymoon's been
over ever since. The Reds won't give him any more toys."

Kilbride looked up at Thomson with that very serious
expression again. "You just watch. I'm going to reel them
in like a big, fat cod. Not just neutral. A full-blown treaty.
A treaty! With trade, naval bases, the whole nine yards.
And I'm not going to wait too damned long to see it happen, either."

"A treaty? With Nasser?" Thomson almost laughed.

Kilbride ignored him. He gave a little condescending
smile and spoke carefully. "With . . . the Egyptian government. You know what these two-bit countries are like.
Colonels come and colonels go. One of them gets on top for
a little while, pretty soon he forgets what his people really
want. Well, we got lots of friends over here. All I have to do
is 'encourage' the right ones. That, and keep the British and
the damned Israelis out of my hair long enough to get it
done."

Kilbride suddenly looked nervous, as if he'd said more
than he should have. He pointed with his finger again. "So,
you see why this little business last night got me all worked
up. This is no time to rock the boat, Thomson. I need you
and the rest of the crew pulling on the oars, stroking in time
to my beat, just like Collins and the rest of my boys. If you

do, we'll get along fine. I'll even put in a good word for you with Langley. If you hear anything, anything at all, you tell Collins. He'll take care of it for me. Got that?''

Thomson knew there was no sense arguing, so he nodded and kept his mouth shut. Kilbride was nuts—and lying through his teeth—but there wasn't much he could do about it.

"Good." The ambassador flashed a broad, contented smile. ''Then that's the end of it. It'll just fade away. State will be happy with me, and Langley will be happy with you. See how easy it's going to be?''

6

MAJOR ERNST GRÜBER leaned against the fender of the black Mercedes sedan, as the full fury of the noonday sun beat down on his head. Tiny beads of sweat popped from every pore of his body, but he ignored it, as well as the searing heat of the open city square around him. Grüber could take the heat. He'd known far worse on the sweltering steppes of Russia. And he'd be damned before he'd show the slightest weakness.

Bored with even a brief wait, Grüber permitted his eyes to wander. He hated the place: the crumbling old stone buildings, sun-bleached and sand-blasted to a dull, muddy brown; the pushcarts and the cacophony of rude noises; and the dark, filthy people who weren't fit to lick his boots. Tall, blue-eyed, and blond, Grüber was the only person in the square who wore clean clothes.

The intense glare of the sun hurt his eyes. He squinted. It must have been over 120° where he stood. There was an inviting patch of shade at the base of a tall building barely a hundred feet away, but Grüber stayed where he was. The shade might offer some relief from the merciless sun, but it was filled with swarming flies and stinking children singing the Egyptian national anthem: eight-year-old beggars screaming, *"Baksheesh, baksheesh!"*—Money, money!—accompanied by the ever-present buzzing of flies.

Grüber had been summoned. The colonel's men had told him to wait by the car, so that was precisely what he would do. *"Zu Befehl!"* To obey. Regardless and absolute. It was the SS motto and his personal code of honor. The colonel knew full well what the square was like at high noon, but he enjoyed his little sadistic tests. Grüber would not fail them.

He lifted his head, hearing the last wailing chant rise from the mosque on the far side of the square. *"Laa ilaaha illa llaah!"* Their voices rose as one. "There is no God but God! . . . Mohammed is the messenger of God! . . . Come to prayer! . . . Come to salvation!"

Grüber looked at the entrance to the mosque. The stairs were covered with long rows of empty shoes, placed there by the faithful. His lips curled into a sarcastic smile. The beggars and thieves of Cairo would steal anything in Egypt, including the Sphinx, but they would never touch a pair of shoes left outside a mosque.

Looking through the wide doorway, he saw dim rows of men bowing, kneeling, and bending forward, touching their foreheads to the carpet. What a strange cross section of humanity: bus drivers and doctors, pimps and carpet merchants, bankers and army colonels. Their bodies moved in perfect unison, here if nowhere else, as their individuality melted into the rhythms and emotion of their prayers. How ludicrous. They had been a mob before entering the mosque and they'd be a mob after they left. But inside, they became a homogenized whole. Or a mongrelized one, Grüber thought, turning his eyes away from the disgusting scene.

Finally, the chanting stopped. The dim shapes rose to their feet and the monotonous drone reverted to the chatter of a raucous mob. Outside, a crowd of the less than faithful surged forward to block the exit—to beg, to sell, to steal, or whatever.

The first worshipers stepped out into the blinding light. They groped for their shoes with one hand and clutched their wallets with the other, resigned to fighting their way through the crowd. At the back of the column, Grüber saw the colonel towering above them. He stepped into the sun and paused, standing stern and ramrod straight in his full parade uniform. While an aide fetched his shoes, the colonel slowly placed his hat on his head and surveyed the mob. As his head turned, the brass emblem on his hat caught the sun's rays and flashed from the doorway like a bright beacon. The colonel's gaze fixed itself on the crowd of beggars standing directly in front of him. They scurried aside as if he'd cleared a path with grapeshot.

The colonel looked neither surprised nor pleased. It was expected, but the crowd's fearful reaction made Grüber smile. The German knew the power hidden behind those hooded eyes. It was rooted in violence and madness. Hitler had had it, and this Arab colonel had it too.

Finally, those eyes looked across the square and came to rest on Grüber. Only then did the colonel take his first steps toward the Mercedes. He marched through the crowd at double time, leaving his three bodyguards running to catch up.

When he reached the car, he gave Grüber a quick, withering stare. "Get in," he ordered, bending low as he stepped inside, and slamming the door shut behind him. Grüber obeyed without uttering a word and slid into the backseat beside him.

The car was as hot as an oven, but the Egyptian didn't seem to mind. Another test? Grüber wondered. But this time there was intense anger written across the colonel's face.

"You failed me," he began slowly, almost quietly. "I paid the price your General Hoess demanded, because he said you were the best. I paid, and I placed you in charge of my security because I can afford no mistakes. None!"

The colonel turned slowly and his eyes locked on Grüber. "You failed me. It was bad enough that you allowed the Jew to penetrate the compound, but you did not even know he was there, did you? He could have destroyed everything. Everything, all my plans. And now this," he hissed, as he tossed a thick envelope into Grüber's lap.

Grüber was seething inside, but he said nothing. His worst fears had been confirmed. He knew what must be in the envelope, but he wasn't a man who offered excuses.

"The Jew had a camera when you caught him. Why wasn't I informed?"

"The camera was empty. I didn't think it mattered."

"You fool! What kind of spy carries an empty camera?"

"We are searching for the film—"

"And you will never find it, Herr Major"—the sarcasm in the colonel's voice was not lost on Grüber—"because it isn't there. He gave it to an accomplice before you caught him. You would have known that, if you had not indulged yourself by killing the Jew before he could be made to talk."

The colonel's voice turned hard and cruel. "You Germans can kill, but you cannot think. So you chased your tails in little circles for the past three days, not learning one more thing than you knew in the beginning, have you?"

Grüber bristled. How much more of this outrage must he suffer? He had shot dozens of men for less, far better men for far less. Yet he was forced to submit to this humiliation. General Hoess had been very specific on that point. He knew Grüber too well. Someday, Grüber knew those orders would change. Until then, he would obey, because he was a survivor. He would listen to every word this Arab spoke, concentrating on each scrap of information he doled out. Someday, those little scraps might save his life.

"Do you think I am idiotic enough to rely on your reports alone, Grüber? No, I have other sources of information. The Jew had an accomplice, a wretch named Yussuf who tried to sell the photographs. We searched the Souk from one end to the other, but we found him. And none too soon. He was trying to sell the film to the CIA! Fortunately, neither Yussuf nor the stupid CIA agent knew the value of what they had."

With that, the colonel pointed to the envelope lying in Grüber's lap. "Open it. Look at them! I want you to see the things this man was able to photograph, despite your 'crack' security guards patrolling the compound."

Grüber pulled the prints out, slowly examining each one.

"He had it all," the Egyptian hissed. "The assembly building, the fuel bunkers, the army tanks, your guards, Fengler and his technicians, even you! Look at yourself, standing there so arrogant and content, chatting with the guards, gazing across the blowing desert sand like Rommel himself. Looking for Montgomery, perhaps?" The colonel's voice dropped to a deadly whisper. "He was selling those to a CIA agent."

"So?" Grüber shouted back. "We caught him! He paid dearly for his treachery and you have his photographs. No damage has been done!" He had called the colonel's bluff.

"Damage? No damage? Count the photographs, Grüber."

The German's heart sank as he quickly fanned the edges of the prints, one by one. "Eleven," he whispered.

"Yes, Herr Major. Eleven! But the roll of film held twelve shots, didn't it? One is missing. That means he gave the twelfth one to this American, Thomson." The colonel paused, letting the ominous words sink in.

It was Grüber who broke the silence. "What do you want me to do then? Kill him, too?"

"No! I don't want him killed! I want the missing photograph. I want to know how much this Thomson knows, and I want to know who he told it to. The police questioned him, but he told them nothing. That is irrelevant. I know them. They will hound him, trying to pin Yussuf's murder on him. But if they hound him enough, the American may trade the photograph for his freedom. I can't permit that. In a few days it won't matter. The police will be obeying my orders, not those of the Great Traitor. Until then, I cannot afford to have them suspicious."

"Suspicious?" Grüber asked sharply. "I understand you cut the man's head off. Don't you think that might make the police a little suspicious?"

The colonel glared. "An infidel like you can never understand our ways, Grüber. Yussuf was a traitor—to his people, to his nation, and to his faith. The punishment is prescribed. That is our way. Nothing else would suffice."

"Perhaps," Grüber argued. "But Landau would never have talked. If you had turned that fat Arab over to me, I'd have had him singing like a bird. I know the type," he added slowly, not bothering to hide his contempt. "He'd have spilled his guts out before I finished with him!"

With that, Grüber turned away and rolled the window down without asking. He took a deep breath. He had had a bellyful of this Egyptian and needed fresh air to clear his head. "After I had made him talk, you could have 'prescribed' whatever you wished. Now tell me what you want me to do." The colonel's eyes were burning into the back of his head, but Grüber no longer cared.

When the Egyptian did speak, his voice was surprisingly subdued. In the last analysis they needed each other, like it or not, and they both knew it. "Find the American.

Find him alone and learn what he knows about Heliopolis. Then see that he disappears, like Landau. I will handle the rest. The police will be told he boarded an airplane, that the CIA shipped him home. They will believe that, because it is what they want to believe—that it is all a CIA plot.'' Then his voice pressed down on the German, smothering him. ''Do you think you can do that much, Grüber? Can you carry out my orders, without fail?''

''Ja!'' Grüber snapped his head around and met the challenge. His arm, wanting to salute, twitched from old reflexes they'd drilled into him over the years, but he stopped it. He'd never salute this Arab. That would be unforgivable. Never. His orders be damned!

''When you finish with him, return to Heliopolis. Stay there. You are to keep a close watch on Fengler and the rest of his technicians—''

''They can be trusted,'' the German interrupted. ''You've been given assurances on that.''

''Trust?... Assurances?... Those are of no value to me. Only success is. And you Germans have failed me once already.'' The colonel spat in disgust. ''You have always failed, just as you failed with your 'final solution.' Because you failed, your problem was visited upon my people. We are the ones who are paying for your failures. They were your Jews, Grüber, not ours. If they needed a homeland, the British should have given them Bavaria. It would have served you right! So do not waste my time with your 'trust' or your 'assurances.' We poor Arabs can no longer afford them.''

He stared at the German with hate and contempt, his dark eyes threatening. ''If you or Fengler or the rest of your ilk fail me on Thursday, nothing will save any of us. Thursday, Grüber! It works perfectly on Thursday, or we die. There is no second chance.''

The German swallowed hard, his throat suddenly as dry as the air outside. Thursday. On that one point, if none other, the two of them agreed.

"Now go!" The colonel gave a casual flip of his hand, as he would dismiss a waiter in a cheap restaurant.

And Grüber went, glad to leave. If he hadn't, he might have strangled the man right then and there, and that would have meant the end of everything.

Grüber hated him. He had met more than his share of fanatics. In fact, he considered himself one. But this Egyptian was over the edge. He was insane.

THE COLONEL WATCHED Grüber hurry away. He leaned back against the seat cushion and closed his eyes.

A faint smile crossed his lips, then quickly vanished. Getting other men to do his bidding was his forte. He knew the precise volume of anger to pump into Grüber, and he'd inflated him to the point of bursting. Good! he thought. The more the German hated, the more determined not to fail he became, and the more he focused his vicious temper on their mutual enemies. With that, he smiled again, thinking of what lay in store for the American.

He hated Americans, but no more than he hated the British, or the Russians, or even the Germans for that matter. They were all godless infidels: foreigners, white barbarians, Christians or Communists, but all with Crusader mentalities. They thought they knew everything that was worth knowing and he hated them for that arrogance.

Of the lot, the Nazis were the most despicable. They were supremely arrogant, racist, and amoral. That was why he had hired them. They were lepers, men without a country, and could sink no lower, so they could be trusted to be exactly what they appeared to be: cruel, totally venal, and self-serving. And that was exactly what he needed.

The Nazis thought that *they* were using him, like the monkey who persuaded the old alligator to ride him across the river on his back. Well, the colonel thought, the far shore is drawing near. Soon, we shall see who ends up as dinner.

They would all get their due, each of them in turn: Israel, the United States, Great Britain, and Russia. Oil! By next winter, the godless infidels would have reams of their own broken promises to burn, and little else. The lights would dim in Washington, London, and Moscow. They would no longer have the oil fields of the Arab Crescent to suck dry. Not after Thursday.

The black flag of Islam would flash across the sky once more, he thought. It had been twelve hundred years since the Army of the Faithful first rode into battle beneath it. Thursday! He would be the man who unfurled it, awakening dreams that had lain cold for all those centuries.

Nasser thought he could outlaw and suppress them, but no one could outlaw a dream or suppress a movement that springs from the heart of the people. It would begin here, in Egypt, as it must. The great Saladin had known that. Once Cairo and Egypt were purified, the rest of the Middle East would follow. He would cauterize the Western cancer growing in their midst. Their most hated enemy would be incinerated in a rain of fire and the people would rally to him.

Thursday! By sunset on Thursday, all Islam would bend its knees beneath the black flag of the Moslem Brotherhood, in Baghdad and Riyadh, Damascus, Tripoli, Amman, and a thousand mosques between.

Yes. The world would tilt on its axis. On Thursday!

7

THOMSON SPENT THE AFTERNOON and most of that evening in Jeremy's bar. All he wanted was enough time to get himself roundly smashed. That was the one remaining pleasure they couldn't deny him.

Had he sunk to self-pity? What if he had? He'd earned it. He'd have liked to dunk Kilbride, the fat Arab without the head, Saleh, Damascus, and the whole damned world into a tall glass of straight gin. Maybe if he soaked them until they were numb, they'd leave him alone.

And gradually, that pleasant thought made things look a shade brighter.

Until Reggie Perper walked in.

Thomson figured it was about nine-thirty. Perper skipped through the door, smiling and whistling as usual, and headed straight for Thomson's table.

"Two, Jeremy." Perper raised his fingers in a broad V. "And bring one for me, too."

"You're not staying that long, Reggie," Thomson warned, knowing simple rudeness wouldn't be enough. Sure enough, the man pulled out a chair and sat down at Thomson's table anyway.

"Be nice for a change." Perper laughed as he glanced around the dark, nearly empty bar. "I don't see anybody else buying you free drinks? After what you went through this morning, I figured you needed one."

"What do you want?" Thomson groaned.

"Nothing. I don't want a damned thing from you. Your name was mentioned prominently on the old jungle drums today. Thought I'd let you know. Italics, bold caps, and exclamation marks. Made quite a stir. They said you got your ass put in traction, so old Reggie stopped by to console the patient."

"Or gloat? Go away, Perper. Don't smile. Don't giggle. And don't give me any of your bullshit. Just go away."

"Thomson, only winos drink alone. And only hermits drink in a cave like this."

Jeremy set a tray of drinks on the table and cast an angry glare at Perper.

"Put them on his bill," Thomson ordered. "All of them! And add a big tip."

Perper laughed and drummed his fingers on the table-top, saying nothing until Jeremy took the hint and went away. Then he began to whistle, taking a long look around the room. "How can you stand this place, Thomson? It's so depressing."

"Not until you came in."

"And with all the hours you spend here, Jeremy ought to make you pay rent. Shit, move your damn desk in! Why go halfway?" He leaned forward, drumming his fingers on the table louder and louder. "Thomson, look at yourself. Haven't you ever heard of that big thing in the sky, the sun? You look like a mole, for chrissakes. And—"

"All right, Perper! I surrender." Thomson grabbed Perper's wrists, pressing his fingers flat on the table. "No drumming, no whistling, no fidgeting, and no more crap. Sit perfectly still and say what you came to say, then get out. Please?"

"Much better, old man. See how fast I can grow on you?" Perper's grin was infectious. "And maybe you're right about this place. These days, it's a damned sight safer than the embassy.''

"Except for code clerks?" Thomson released his grip on Perper's wrists and gave up.

"Except for code clerks," Perper readily conceded, as he jabbed the tip of his finger on the tabletop. "Don't you knock it. Reggie Perper paid his dues. He was in the field, just two classes behind you. Remember? And he ducked every bit as much lead as you did—Norway, Hamburg, even Hungary in '56. So don't get uppity with me." Perper's eyes narrowed. "The only difference between us— and I mean the only damned difference—is that you didn't have the smarts to hang it up a long time ago. What the hell did you expect they'd do? Give you a medal?"

"Beats the desk," he mumbled.

"Keep telling yourself that." Perper leaned back in the chair and smiled contentedly. "Codes is nice and sweet. Perper hassles nobody. Nobody hassles him. He's a day-shift paper pusher who doesn't get his name written up in cablegrams, like some people he knows."

"Kilbride's that pissed?"

"Mild understatement. Messages have been cascading down from the top floor like confetti on a Fifth Avenue parade."

"All right, Reggie. Why? Why are you telling me all this? I thought you were the piano player in the cathouse. Hear no evil, see no evil? Just busy little fingers on the ivory?"

"Did I say anything?" Perper looked up innocently.

"What's going on?"

"Beats me." Perper turned serious. "Kilbride's a real shit. He doesn't trust any of us regulars anymore. We're 'tainted,' beyond hope. He's surrounded himself with his own private mafia, all loyal and eager, tagging around behind him in their three-piece suits."

"Collins?"

"Ah, you've met!" Perper grinned. "Collins sends Kilbride's messages for him, not us. All of them."

"Complain to the union."

"Can't. If we took away his Captain Midnight decoder ring, it would break his heart." Perper shrugged and took a stiff pull on his gin. "I don't know what's going on. But reading the tea leaves, I gather your little conference this morning had something to do with it."

"Okay, Reggie. Why?"

"Why what?"

"Why your sudden interest in what happens to me?"

"Oh, I don't know," Perper frowned. "Call it brotherhood week. You and I never got along much, Thomson, but we're both OSS fraternity brothers. We're like two old dinosaurs, and the breed's nearly extinct. It's that simple. If Kilbride has his way, there's going to be one less of us big, humpty-backed monsters rutting around in the grass. So think about old Perper for a change. What am I going to do when you're gone? Who the hell will I swap war stories with? Huh? Some snot-nosed Harvard kid half my age? No, that would do me in. So I figure us dinosaurs got to stick together, for the sake of the species."

"Reggie"—Thomson smiled and shook his head—"take that crap someplace else. I know you. Tell me why you really came."

"You don't believe me?" Perper's face broke into a thin, conspiratorial grin. "All right, I don't either. Let's say I can't stand Kilbride for my own sublimely delicious reasons . . . and she shall remain nameless."

"Much better, Perper!" Thomson smiled back. "Now I'll start listening. The ambassador caught you with some broad? What else's new?"

"Nothing, but the guy really got righteous about it. Would you believe, he actually packed her off to Istanbul. Now that's a bit much!" Perper tried to act outraged. "You need a better reason? Let's say I'd cheer for anyone who jabbed him in the ass with a pitchfork."

"Knowing you, Reggie, the whole thing has suddenly become perfectly understandable."

"Look, Thomson." Perper leaned forward, his voice turning serious. "I like you. I really do. But there's one big difference between us. We both want to see Kilbride jabbed in the ass, but I only do the cheering. You're the one he's going to catch holding the pitchfork. Watch out. Kilbride's a jerk, but he is the ambassador. That's grounds for most men to steer a wide path around him. He's a size-fifteen SOB with heavy political connections. You ought to see his mail. Even the damned State Department busts a vest to keep him happy. Guys like us? We don't stand a chance. So be careful, Thomson. Kilbride doesn't like you much."

"And I don't like him, either."

"Cute. Real cute! How many times do you need to get kicked in the head before you wake up? He's stupid and he's naïve: a classic bull-headed Mick Irishman. But he's got big plans. If you screw them up, he'll chop you into little pieces."

Thomson conceded the point. He leaned across the table and started probing. "All right, Reggie. You've been around longer than me. What the hell's Kilbride really up to?"

"I'm not sure. All I get is whiffs and whispers."

"Has he gone native?"

"He ain't the first, and he sure as hell won't be the last. He's like a kid with a new toy: a dumb big-city politician who found an embassy in his Christmas stocking and the swelled head that goes with it. Guess I can't blame him for wanting to score. But Kilbride wants it too bad. He's bitten. He sees it as his express train to the Cabinet, maybe a governor's mansion, or even the Senate. Who knows? But what he lacks in brains, he makes up for with ambition. Any jackass who wants it that bad is pure dangerous. Gone native? For chrissakes, Thomson, he wears it like a hair shirt. You heard about the movie?''

Thomson shook his head.

"Three weeks ago. He got a copy of *Lawrence of Arabia* from some crony back home. He showed it eight times down in the basement, and he didn't miss once. Thinks he's God's gift to the Arabs now. The man's more Egyptian than the Sphinx! So watch out. Kilbride intends to make them happy, and he's going to keep them that way, regardless.''

"He's nuts.''

"No, just arrogant and naïve. That's worse, and there's a lot more back at State just like him. They love the Arabs. It's all the rage, you know. So they love him. Eventually he's going to take the big fall. When he does, you don't want to be caught underneath, Thomson.''

Perper leaned forward, his expression serious. "What the hell did you step in yesterday, anyway? I've seen Kilbride mad, but he stormed around like you'd tracked the barnyard all over his white carpet.''

"Damned if I know, Reggie. Look, you work in Codes. Ever heard of an Agency guy named Evans? Maybe a cover? Anything?''

"Here? Evans?'' He frowned. "Nope.''

"Figures.'' Thomson nodded. "What about Heliopolis? Heard any stories about something going on out there?''

Perper shrugged. "Not really. Nothing hot. Word was the Egyptians have a base out there, that's all. Who the hell knows anything for sure around this place? They're always getting ready for a war, or licking their wounds from the last one. Hell, wars and coups are the only thing that keep the wheels greased in these parts. And right now, there are more secrets and conspiracies floating around than even I can keep straight.''

''Like Heliopolis?''

''Like . . . something. I heard one story that they're making something out there. Even that isn't new. Maybe it's an airplane factory? Who knows? Remember, Heliopolis is only fifteen miles from Cairo, straight up the road. It could be a new army garrison. Ever heard of a dictator who didn't like to have a few friendly battalions close to the capital? Nasser's no fool. He remembers how he got the job. So he isn't about to give the next guy the same chance to do it to him. Like I said, who the hell knows?''

Thomson thought about it as they sipped their drinks, then asked, ''What about Germans? Are there any of them working around here now?''

''Germans? Damned right there are!'' Perper snorted. ''Just open the guest register at the Hilton or the Semiramis. They aren't a bunch of traveling bankers from Frankfurt, either. Nasser has brought in some real sweethearts in the last two or three years, guys like SS General Oskar Dierlewanger. Remember him—'the Butcher of Warsaw'? Or Daimling? I think he was head of the Gestapo in Düsseldorf. Leopold Gleim commanded Hitler's bodyguards. Willi Brenner ran the death camp at Mauthausen. And he's got more Panzer generals and colonels than a Wehrmacht rest home. Germans? They're all over the place.''

''Hasn't Kilbride said anything about it? Hasn't he bitched or filed a protest?''

"Kilbride?" Perper scoffed. "He invites the Krauts to our receptions! Why do you think I'm here? The whole thing really stinks."

Thomson shook his head and took another sip before he asked, "Are there any Israelis still working Cairo?"

"I guess. But they've only got a skeleton crew at best. It's tough. When they do sneak a guy in, they don't waste him. They keep him busy on military stuff—like troop movements across the canal bridges—when he isn't being chased all over town by State Security. But everyone is real tight-lipped about the Israelis these days."

"Kilbride?"

"Yeah. We used to play big brother for the Israelis. Not anymore. Kilbride put that in the deep freeze. He hates them. Maybe it's the new Peter O'Toole role he's playing. Let's hope so." Perper tried to sound charitable. "So be careful. If he catches you playing footsie with them, you're dead."

Reggie suddenly looked at his watch and belted down the last of his drink. "That's enough commiseration for one night. The meter's run out and so must I."

Perper stood and turned to leave, then paused and looked back down. "Thomson, I don't know what kind of shit you got yourself into and I don't want to know. But go easy. You aren't over the hill. You're buried beneath it. Quit. Stop fooling around, huh? Climb back into your coffin and take the long sleep before Kilbride pounds a stake through your heart."

Thomson raised his glass in mock salute.

But Perper was truly worried. Thomson wasn't about to listen. "All right," he said. "Just remember. I wasn't here. And I sure as hell didn't say anything to you if I was. Good luck. You'll need it."

Perper turned and bounced away, whistling even louder than when he came in. As he passed the bar, Jeremy called him over. The Englishman had been waiting with a broad smile and six glasses.

"You look like a sporting man, Mr. Perper. Double or nothing. See these glasses here. Well, three of them are full and three of them are—"

Reggie didn't even let him finish. He picked up the middle of the three glasses full of whiskey, poured it into the middle empty one with a quick splash, and set it back down where it came from.

"There!" He chuckled sadistically. "Now I got one for you, Jeremy. How many Brits does it take to screw in a light bulb?"

The Englishman growled and almost leaped over the bar after him. By then, Perper had backed out of his reach. "See ya!" He laughed as he dashed out the door.

Thomson smiled to himself, thinking Perper might not be such a pain in the ass after all.

8

AFTER PERPER LEFT, Thomson sat in the bar for the better part of an hour, so lost in his own thoughts that he never touched his drink. He didn't want it, and for the first time in a long time, he didn't need it. He was sky-high without the gin, twirling little puzzle pieces and an old black-and-white photograph round and round in his head.

Jeremy had another customer, a tall European, blond and well-dressed. The man was sitting alone in a far corner, slowly nursing a drink. When Thomson rose to leave, much earlier than usual, Blondie frowned.

Thomson stepped through the maze of tables, smiling and holding his arms straight out from his sides as if he were a tightrope walker. Jeremy laughed as he watched the American stroll out the door. "Hate to lose the business, Mr. Thomson," he called after him. "But it's good to see you leave this way for a change."

Outside, Thomson threw his shoulders back and took a deep breath. The city even smelled better. He looked around and saw that the street was deserted. Yet Cairo never seemed as vibrant and alive as it did to him now. Even the dim shadows sparkled with a new clarity.

He knew the city hadn't changed. He had. He felt the old juices flowing inside him again. The sap was racing up and down the trunk of that gnarled old oak tree, making him feel young and alive for the first time in months. If that was an illusion, Thomson didn't care. He felt great.

Sure, he knew he was in deep trouble, but someone else was in even deeper. The bastards had made a mistake. No, they had made two of the biggest mistakes of their lives. They had left a few pieces of their puzzle lying on the ground. Only a few, but Thomson was the guy who had found them. That was their first mistake. Their second mistake had been not killing him. Thomson had those pieces clutched tightly in his fist, and he wasn't about to let go. He had no idea where they would fit. But when they did, he'd jam the whole puzzle down their throats.

He felt alive again. He was working. He might not have sanction to, but he had the time. So screw Kilbride. And screw the rest of them, too. He was working again, and there wasn't a damned thing wrong with him that work wouldn't cure.

His angry thoughts were cut short by a friendly, heavily accented voice calling to him from behind. "Herr Thomson, a moment please?"

Thomson looked back over his shoulder, and slowed down a step or two, curious, without giving it much thought. It was Blondie, the guy from the bar, smiling and walking quickly, trying to catch up. Strange, Thomson thought, Blondie had his hands jammed deep inside his coat pockets. Coat? Why the hell would anyone even wear a coat on a hot night like this?

Little things. No one of them would arouse suspicion in an ordinary person. But Thomson wasn't ordinary. His old reflexes took over without being told. They were a bit sluggish, like an old car buried all winter in a snowbank. After a few well-deserved gasps and sputters, the reflexes finally kicked over and started running, rough as a cob, but they were running. They checked the situation out, and didn't like what they saw.

It had something to do with Blondie and a deserted street, and Thomson didn't like either one. So he kept walking, faster, not letting Blondie close the gap. Reflexes, reflexes, he thought, as his head twisted from side to side, his eyes and ears scanning the surrounding turf, taking in every detail and filing it away. He checked the parked cars, the buildings, and the dark doorways, searching for any movement, straining to hear the squeaks and scrapes, separating the safe places from the dangerous ones, and noting the soft spots where he could bail out. In seconds, he had the whole scene recorded.

He was hemmed in on the sidewalk. He had a solid wall of dark, empty buildings on his left, and a long line of cars parked bumper-to-bumper on his right. Up ahead was the safety of the next street corner. Thomson had started to walk even faster when he saw a car door open and two big men get out. One stepped into the middle of the sidewalk and stopped, neatly blocking that escape route, while the other one stepped into the street.

The night was dark and their faces were cast in shadows, but Thomson knew they were the two goons who had chased Yussuf from the bar the night before. He stopped where he was. He couldn't grapple with either one of them, much less both, so he had to use his head. One glance told him they weren't amateurs. They had picked their spots well, too damned well, cutting him off and boxing him in, all the while standing there with the casual nonchalance of professionals. They didn't even have to move. If they stayed where they were, Blondie would drive him into their waiting arms.

"Herr Thomson." Blondie smiled as he slowed down, deciding not to get too close too soon, and not alone. "About that word with you . . . ?"

"Not tonight, Fritz." Thomson smiled as he edged toward two parked cars. "My bowling team's in the finals tonight. You know how mad those guys get when the high roller is late. Maybe next time." Then he jumped over the bumpers and took off running, doubling back and heading toward the bar.

The odds were three to one. He was a sucker to play against the house, but he didn't have much choice. He'd have no choice at all if he let them get any closer. He managed to get past Blondie before he was cut off, and that gave him a fifty-foot head start on the two goons. If he ran like hell, it might be enough.

But they knew all the tricks. One of the goons broke into a dead run as soon as Thomson made his play. At first glance, the goon had looked big and lumpy. But as he got closer, Thomson saw that the lumps were hard, and lightning-quick. The goon's short pounding strides gobbled up the pavement and closed the gap in seconds. Once he had caught up, he didn't try anything fancy. He raised a balled fist and snapped off a short punch that caught Thomson in the middle of his back and felt like a Mack truck.

The goon was an artist, and he had painted a masterpiece of destruction with that one quick stroke. It sent Thomson flying forward, hopelessly out of control and heading straight toward the side of a parked car like a perfectly guided missile. All the goon had to do was slow down and watch the fun.

Thomson saw it coming. He raised his arms to try to protect himself from the worst, but nothing was going to help him now. His head struck the car door and the other parts of his body piled in from behind like a string of runaway freight cars hitting a mountain. That took most of the wind and all of the fight out of him. Stunned, he felt his body slide down the door and collapse in a heap on the pavement.

Before he could catch his breath, the goon leaped on top of him and wrapped his short, powerful arms around his chest. Thomson threw his head back and heard a sickening crunch as he caught the goon flush on the bridge of his nose. The goon grabbed his face and cursed loudly in Arabic, then grabbed for Thomson again, but it was too late. The American had pulled his arms in and curled into a ball. Good thing, too. The goon would have crushed his ribs if he'd gotten a decent grip.

They wrestled and rolled around on the pavement. Between the grunts and groans, Thomson wasn't doing all that badly. He was battered and bloody, his jacket was torn, and one of his shoes had been ripped from his foot, but the goon hadn't gotten him yet. He was even entertaining a glimmer of hope he could break free when he saw the legs of the other two men standing next to him, waiting to grab the first piece that popped out of the pile. So much for getting away, he thought. Maybe he could catch his breath and scream like hell. Maybe someone would hear him. The goon must have read his mind, because his arms clamped around Thomson's chest like a vise. He couldn't even breathe, much less scream.

Thomson let his body go limp. He dropped his mouth over the meaty part of the goon's forearm and chomped down, hard, drawing blood. The goon roared in pain. Furious, he squeezed even harder and slammed Thomson up and down on the concrete as if he were a rag doll.

That did it. Playtime was over. For the coup de grace, Thomson saw a dark blur out of the corner of his eye. He twisted away, but the second goon kicked him in the side of the head. It was only a glancing blow, but enough to cause him to see flashing bright-red stars. Rough hands pulled him to his feet, and his brief, one-sided tag-team match was over.

The second goon held him up, while the first goon cocked his arm back, taking careful aim with a huge fist. From the gleam in his eye, he was going to make the punch a good one. Why not? He had the time and there was nothing Thomson could do to stop him.

Just as the fist was about to smash his face, Thomson was blinded by a harsh, white light. No, two of them, from a set of headlights on high beam, filling the street and pinning Thomson, Blondie, and the two goons in their powerful glare. The car's horn blared as it raced straight toward them.

The fist froze in mid-air. The goon couldn't help being distracted. At the last second, the car skidded sideways to a halt, not fifty feet from where they stood. The goons panicked, instantly forgetting about Thomson. Their hands pulled away and Thomson found himself standing upright, tottering back and forth on rubbery legs. Then he toppled backward and sat down hard on the pavement.

The two goons dug inside their jackets, frantically reaching for their guns. But Blondie wasn't that stupid. He didn't know who was inside the car, and he wasn't waiting to find out. He ducked between the parked cars and ran down the sidewalk, bent low, determined to get away before his carefully laid plans went even further awry.

Thomson wasn't that stupid either. With the two goons distracted, he rolled beneath the parked car, trying to shake the cobwebs out of his head and figure out what was happening. He looked up and saw the two goons silhouetted in the bright headlights. The goon with the bent nose and bloody arm pulled out his revolver and pointed it in the general direction of the car. He hunkered down, trying to shade his eyes and find a target. He fired the first shot, but before the echoing blast had died away, he got his reply.

Bright orange flashes erupted from the passenger window of the car and Thomson heard the hacking cough of a silenced submachine gun. There was only one short, chopping burst, but it was expertly done. The bullets hit the goon in the chest, ripping into bone and muscle, lifting him off his feet, and dropping him hard onto the pavement.

The other goon didn't even try. He dove aside, tumbling across the trunk of a parked car as a second burst flashed from the car window. The bullets skipped off the pavement, chasing him with a shower of white sparks. They missed but did the next best thing. The goon took off running after Blondie, zig-zagging into the darkness without even looking back.

Good riddance, Thomson thought. He was battered, bruised, and glad to still be alive. He reached up with one hand and groped for the door handle, slowly pulling himself to his knees. Dimly, through the fog bank inside his head, he heard a shrill whistle. Police, and not very far away. That was all he needed. He was in no condition for another grilling from Saleh, but he was in no condition to outrun them either.

The sounds of the police whistles were drowned out by the roar of an automobile engine. Thomson looked up to see the mystery car race toward him, then skid to a halt only a few feet away. The rear door flew open and hands grabbed at him, pulling him into the car. Thomson tried to shove them away, until an angry voice from the front seat said, "Don't be a fool, Thomson. Get in!"

He heard the dull chatter of the submachine gun again, and decided it wasn't a good time to argue. He didn't know who these people were, but for the moment, they would have to do. Maybe they weren't on the right side, but they weren't on the wrong one either. He let them pull him into the car. He was treated roughly, but they weren't trying to hurt him, they were just in one understandably big hurry. Thomson slumped onto the floorboards, too numb to move.

The tires squealed and the car sped away, chased by several loud gunshots. The driver took the first corner on two wheels and careened into a sidestreet. He made another quick turn, then several more before finally slowing down.

Thomson looked up through the rear window. The lights of the city streaked past, thinning out, until he could see only black sky and a high, thin crescent moon. Wherever they were going, they were well outside the center of the city.

His head slowly cleared. He lifted himself to his knees, then the rest of the way up, turning around and sitting painfully on the backseat. He ached everywhere, his body in complete rebellion against what he'd put it through. Slowly, his brain inventoried the moving pieces. Some were bruised and dented, but nothing seemed to be missing, broken, or shot full of holes—not yet anyway.

Thomson looked up to see the man in the front passenger seat staring back at him. "You must be more careful, Thomson." He sounded calm and confident. "Late-night walks in Cairo can be bad for your health."

He was dark-skinned, with a bushy mustache and curly black hair, and older than either the driver or the other man in the backseat. They all had the same olive-brown skin, which could have come from anywhere around the shores of the Mediterranean. The man's accent was strange, but the nasty-looking submachine gun he held in the crook of

his arm was an Israeli Uzi, with a long silencer on the end
of the barrel.

"Yeah . . . and thanks," Thomson acknowledged belat-
edly.

The man casually laid the Uzi across the back of the seat,
still pointed in Thomson's general direction. "You've had
a rough day," he said in a friendly voice. "You look tired.
So why not relax and enjoy the ride?"

9

CAPTAIN HASSAN SALEH let his police cruiser roll to a halt. He turned the engine off and sat quietly, staring through the dust-streaked windshield at the all too familiar scene a half block farther down the street. The flashing rhythm of red lights and the crowd of gawking late-night thrill-seekers never failed to turn his stomach. It was all so futile. He saw the occasional pop of a reporter's flashbulb, clusters of uniformed police officers milling about waiting for someone to tell them what to do, and, in the center of it all, a body and a pool of blood.

Saleh had seen it too many times before. Regardless of the who, or the why, or the how, there was a sickening sameness to every murder. Someone slashed someone with a blade or pulled a trigger, instantly transforming another human being into so many pounds of dead, raw meat. Then they called for Saleh. He was the butcher's handmaid.

Slowly and painfully, he opened the car door and swung his legs out. He kept his hand on the steering wheel for support as he flexed his knee, testing it, gradually adding weight until it was ready to support his reed-thin body. But the leg hurt much worse tonight. Not that it would ever hurt much less. He had known that from the beginning. The doctors had threatened him with that over and over again.

Pain. A lifetime of pain thanks to the white-hot explosion of an American artillery shell, from an American howitzer, fired by Israeli hands from Arab soil. The doctors had wanted to cut the leg off, but he had refused. Doctors! What did they know. There were things far worse than a lifetime of pain. Spend his remaining days in a wheelchair? Hobble about with crutches and a stump? No, he would never permit an abomination like that. Better the pain. Or better to have died.

He'd been sitting too long and his leg muscles had cramped. That was why he had parked up the street in the shadows, so he could do his suffering in private. Leaning heavily on the ebony cane, he took the first painful steps. He stopped and shook his leg, punching it with his fist, trying to beat it into submission.

Gradually, the cramp subsided and the knee supported his weight. Bent over at the waist, he limped slowly up the street, until he reached the bright lights at the corner and his private sanctuary disappeared in the flood of illumination. He became Captain Saleh again. Closing his eyes, he pushed down on the top of the cane, forcing his torso upright. Waves of pain rolled and crashed inside his head. He almost passed out, but concentrated on the flashing red lights and blocked the pain from his mind. Finally, it ebbed. He pulled a sweat-soaked handkerchief from his pocket and wiped his brow. How long? How long before the tricks wouldn't be enough?

Saleh gritted his teeth and stepped into the light, commanding his leg to move at a normal pace. There was a rope barricade strung across the street. Saleh pressed it down with his cane. As he lifted his leg over, a uniformed policeman turned his head and bellowed, "You there! Where do you think . . ." But the man's voice faded as he recognized the distinctive white suit and cane. "Captain Saleh," he said apologetically, "I did not..."

Saleh dismissed him with a harsh glance and continued over the rope. Once inside the perimeter, his eyes searched for Sayyid. He finally found him standing in the midst of a group of young detectives, laughing and joking with them. When the sergeant saw Saleh, he quickly separated himself from the others and hurried to join him.

Saleh didn't wait. The captain's eyes methodically began to sweep the murder scene. Slowly, he walked a line down the middle of the street, alone, noting and absorbing each detail. Sayyid fell in step beside him, knowing not to offer any comments or explanations until he was asked.

When he reached the far end, Saleh turned and looked back down the street, pausing, deep in thought. "Nothing has been touched?" he asked quietly.

"Nothing... as you ordered."

"Good. Clear the street." He eyed the milling crowd of dark faces. "It is time the circus closed for the night."

Sayyid hurried away as Saleh began to retrace his path, studying the crime scene more carefully this time, his head turning from side to side, nose slightly raised, eyes narrowing like an old hunting dog's seeking the scent.

They were all there. All the signs were there: the skid marks, coming and going, the glimmer of brass shell casings scattered along the pavement where they'd flipped out the car window, and the body. He stopped and looked down at one of the shells, rolling it from side to side with the tip of his cane. Painfully, he bent over until his trembling fingers grasped the piece of brass. He pushed himself upright and held his hard-won prize up to the light.

Saleh grunted. It was nine-millimeter: big, deadly, and effective. They made them for one purpose and one purpose only: to kill a man, even with a bad hit. What did a nine-millimeter shell prove? None of the Russian or American weapons used nine-millimeter ammunition, but the brass could have come from a British Sten, a French MAT, an old German Schmeisser, or a dozen others, including an Israeli Uzi. Even if he knew the make of the gun, however, Saleh wouldn't know the nationality of the finger on the trigger. The brass shell was something, though. It was a beginning.

His eyes searched the pavement again, examining the deep gouges in the concrete. Some of the bullets had missed their mark. He looked at the body, lying in a heap beneath a gray field blanket, and knew that some hadn't.

Sayyid was back. Saleh felt his presence next to him, watching and waiting. Finally, the sergeant spoke. "One of our officers was patrolling in the neighborhood when the shooting began. He came running, but it was too late. There was gunfire and all he saw was a dark sedan racing out of sight around the corner. Do you wish to question him?"

"No. I doubt he will have anything to add. Would you? If someone was shooting a submachine gun at you?" He smiled, knowing that Sayyid probably would. He might not be much of a detective, but he had been in the infantry and was hard. "Tell him to go back to whatever it was he was doing."

"He found this lying in the street," Sayyid replied quietly as he handed Saleh a badly scuffed shoe.

Saleh's eyes widened as he cradled the shoe in the palm of his hand as if it were a piece of rare porcelain, turning it over and over in the dim light. The label was American, and Saleh immediately knew where he had seen it before. He nodded. "What do they call this? A penny-loafer? Show me. Show me where he found it."

Sayyid pointed toward a parked car. "There, behind a tire."

Saleh stepped closer and ran the tips of his fingers across the dents and scratches on the car door. He noticed a few drops of dried blood. In a way, he was relieved. Thomson had been injured, but they hadn't killed him. If they had, there would have been more blood and a second body. What of the first? he wondered. Whose side was he on? Had he attacked the American or tried to help him? Whichever, it had cost the man his life. Why?

Saleh hobbled toward the body. He used the tip of his cane to flip the blanket back. He stood quietly for a moment, examining the man's wounds. Five bullet holes in his chest, forming a neat line from the bottom of the rib cage to the middle of the left shoulder. A thoroughly professional job, Saleh told himself, neat, effective, and deadly accurate.

The man was Egyptian, or Arab at any rate, thick-set and muscular, with a powerful chest and arms, of average height, clean-shaven, and dark. Nothing terribly remarkable about that. Except for his hair, which was unusual: closely cropped on the sides and the top. Sheared might be a better description, and not by the most fashionable barber.

"His hands. Show me his hands," Saleh said impatiently.

Sayyid frowned as he dropped to his knees and raised the man's right hand to the light.

"Rub your fingers across his palm. What do you feel?"

"Feel?" Sayyid questioned. "Why, it is rough . . . very rough, with calluses."

"And?"

Sayyid strained for the answer that wouldn't come.

"The calluses? What do they tell you? Use your imagination, Sayyid. Think! What does that palm tell you of the man?"

Sayyid shrugged and rubbed the palm again. "The hand is big, rough and scarred. . . . He worked with it, outdoors, and he used it often."

"Good! What of the muscles? How do you think he got them? Sitting behind a desk? And what about the dark, weathered skin on his face? Outdoors is correct. This is no simple street tough like that fellow last night, is he? No, *his* hands were soft, like a pimp's, like someone who spent his mornings in bed, weren't they? Look at this man's suit. Look at the fabric."

Sayyid nodded with a glimmering of comprehension.

"His hair. Notice how short it is cut," Saleh hurried on, his voice fading as his mind raced ahead, losing interest in the lessons. He opened the dead man's jacket with his cane. The waistband of the slacks was gathered in awkward tucks beneath the belt. They were a cheap local brand, ill-fitting but new, as if he'd just purchased them and hadn't had time to see a tailor.

"No papers on him, I assume?"

"Nothing. Not even a matchbook or a pack of cigarettes. His pants pockets didn't even have any lint in them."

Saleh nodded. Completely professional, he thought. Precisely what he expected.

"You have the gun?" he asked, holding out his hand.

Sayyid pulled a plastic bag from his pocket and handed it up. "American. An old Smith and Wesson revolver, a cheap one," he commented. "Four rounds were fired. I'll order the usual tests run, but the gun is quite common."

"Yes. And take the man's fingerprints. But they won't match anything in our files. I'm certain of that," Saleh stated as a curious expression crossed his face. "Send the prints to the army, to the personnel department, with this fellow's photograph. We'll see if they have any record of him."

"The army?" Sayyid frowned. "Why would they be involved in this? With the American?"

Saleh volunteered no answer. Instead, he turned away and stared back down the street, trying to picture what had happened. He could smell it. The scent was so strong, it burned the lining of his nose. He hated it and knew he'd never rid himself of that stench until he hunted them down. And when he reached the end of the trail, he knew he'd find the American.

His eyes narrowed. "At first light I want this entire neighborhood canvassed. Question everyone in these buildings."

The sergeant nodded as he stood up. Then, in an unusually formal and almost hesitant voice, he asked, "Begging the captain's pardon, but should we not refer this matter to State Security? Surely it is now in their—"

"What?" Saleh asked angrily.

"It . . . it involves . . . foreign agents. This man Thomson. We know he is—"

"A material witness in a murder case! Two cases, now. This is murder, not espionage. That makes it my business, not State Security's. Murder, nothing more! Unless you have some evidence I have not seen."

"No! No, sir," Sayyid stuttered. "It is just—"

"Then you have your orders," Saleh snapped, looking deep into Sayyid's eyes. "I have no intention of stopping this investigation, now or ever—not until I have them all by the throat!"

Sayyid shuffled his feet uncomfortably. Finally, he asked, "Do you want the American arrested?"

"No. He is merely a pawn. They would sacrifice him to us willingly if we permitted it. But I want them all. Our arrogant American friend will return. When he does, I want him free to roam and I want him followed."

"Isn't that dangerous?"

"Dangerous? Certainly. But wherever Thomson goes, interesting things happen. That is why I want him free. He is my bird dog. Let him raise the game for us. We'll see what he chases from the bushes. So have him watched, *closely*," he warned. "Thomson is not to leave Egypt until I say he may go."

Saleh dismissed Sayyid with an angry wave of his cane. This made one too many dead Arabs thanks to these accursed foreigners. Saleh had seen good men clubbed to the ground by their batons in 1935, crushed beneath their tanks in the streets of Cairo in 1942, shot by their bullets in the riots of 1952, and bombed by their airplanes in the Delta in 1956. These foreigners had shed a sea of Arab blood, and the time had come for retribution.

But Saleh was a soldier no more. Now he was a policeman and he had learned his new profession well. He was on Thomson's trail and nothing would shake him lose, politicians be damned. He hated them no less than he hated foreigners. They all had blood on their hands, and Thomson would lead him to them. He was the bait. They could swallow Thomson whole for all Saleh cared. He'd see they choked on him!

The only answer was to drop the proof at Nasser's very feet. Nasser was no fool. He would not ignore it. He would act! He would throw the foreigners out: the CIA, the KGB, and the whole lot of them together. Not even the foreign minister would dare intervene. Not when Nasser had the proof.

The foreigners must be taught a lesson. Then they would never dare do these things again. Never! Those days were gone! Saleh would smash them like an avenging angel. He'd have them all expelled: the bankers, the businessmen, the foreign "advisors," the leeches, the spies—all of them.

They would be banned for the next hundred years. Only then would their stench begin to fade.

Egypt belonged to the Egyptians now. The pharaoh was back on his throne.

SAYYID HURRIED AWAY into the night. Captain Saleh had that look in his eyes, and Sayyid was terrified thinking about where it might lead.

Besides, Sayyid had many things to do, and quickly. There were fingerprints to take, photographs to distribute, a door-to-door canvass of the neighborhood to organize, and a phone call to make.

10

WELL OUTSIDE THE CITY, the Mercedes turned down a narrow dirt road and came to a stop behind an old house. Thomson was ushered through the rear door, with the driver leading the way and the man with the Uzi close behind.

The house was dark, but Thomson saw the dim outline of more men standing in the shadows, watching him. Firm hands guided him down a short hall, into a back bedroom, to a hard-backed chair facing a long table. Thomson's eyes had just begun to adjust to the dark when a goosenecked desk lamp was switched on and pointed straight at his face.

"You guys have been watching too many George Raft movies," he commented dryly.

They didn't find it funny. Neither did he. The room was quiet, except for feet shuffling on the dusty floor behind him and a few muffled whispers as men entered and left. Thomson didn't know how many, but counting the guy with the Uzi, there had to be at least six or seven. He was about to ask what they wanted, when a soft, quiet voice spoke to him from the shadows beyond the glaring lamp.

"What happened to Landau?" came the first, simple inquiry.

The man's voice was unlike any interrogator's he'd ever run into. It sounded tired and hollow, like an old man who should have been tending his garden or napping in the late-afternoon sun. And it was imploring, not threatening. It was clearly in charge, but it was asking. The threatening would come later.

"Who?" Thomson tried to act confused.

"Mr. Thomson," the old man sighed. "I have neither the time nor the patience for protracted conversation. Suffice it to say your answer is very important. So please spare us any additional anguish. Tell me what happened to Landau."

Thomson shifted uncomfortably on the chair. "You know," he answered with an amused smile, "lots of people have been asking me questions like that today: strange questions about people and places I've never heard of. So welcome to the crowd. I don't know anything about any Landau. Never met him. Never even heard the name before last night. And don't bother asking me about Evans either, or the Arab without the head, or Blondie, or the two goons who tried to grab me tonight. I don't know what's going on. That's the truth and you can do whatever the hell you want with it."

He folded his arms across his chest and sat back in the chair, expecting an angry reaction, and was surprised when none came. All he heard was another weary sigh from beyond the desk lamp.

This time, it was the guy with the Uzi who broke the silence. He was standing behind Thomson and his voice was sharp and angry. "We did you a favor tonight! If we hadn't, you'd be sitting in front of Grüber right now, and he isn't nearly so polite. He'd pry the answers out of your skull with a tire iron and a blowtorch. He enjoys doing things like that."

"Who's Grüber?" Thomson asked.

"No friend of yours," he snapped.

"German? East or West?"

"Thomson, you amaze me. He's neither. He's SS! Not was or maybe. Is! And he's a killer. He learned it fighting partisans in the Ukraine and the streets of Warsaw during the uprising. We had a name for him. We called him 'the Devil's Bastard.' He was one of Himmler's pets. After the war, your people caught him and let him go. The fools!"

"Sounds like a real sweetheart."

The guy wasn't amused. "He is a killer, Thomson."

"So why's he after me?"

"That's what we'd like to know. Grüber is a 'consultant' now, working for State Security, for Colonel Rashid. And you don't want either of them to get their hands on you."

"Why? You think they'd use bright lights and the boogeyman treatment on me?"

Thomson waited, but the guy didn't reply. It was the voice of the old man behind the desk lamp that reasserted itself again.

"Mr. Thomson, heed Jani's advice. It can save you much pain. Surely you see we are not on opposite sides in this matter. Our interests are...similar. And we need your help. So please tell us what happened to Landau. We had given up all hope, until we heard you met Mahmoud Yussuf in that bar—"

"He met me. I didn't meet him."

"The distinction escapes me. What matters is that you met. You see, Yussuf ran errands for Landau, and Landau worked for me. Yussuf was a stringer, a free-lance local we used when we had no other choice. I am told even your CIA, with all its vast resources, uses such people from time to time. Do they not?" he asked with a soft chuckle. "We never trusted Yussuf, but he filled a need. He was available, and he was totally loyal...to the highest bidder. Landau understood that, so he paid Yussuf well and told him nothing. The situation was not ideal, but we do not live in an ideal world, do we?''

Thomson nodded. He was in uncharted territory here, but he wasn't worried. He found himself liking the old man, and he couldn't disagree with what he was saying.

"Now"—the man's voice faded to a sad whisper—"Landau is missing. We believe he found something, something important, which he desperately wanted to get to us. But something went wrong." He paused, struggling for the right words. "Thomson, you are in the business. You understand how an agent and his control can come to know each other's very thoughts. Well, Landau was a good agent. The best. I knew him like my own sons. And I trained him to take no unnecessary risks unless the prize was worth it. That was how he worked. And that is how I know Landau found something important."

"Who are you? You aren't Germans. Your voices don't sound Arab, and you don't act like the KGB. So who does that leave? Israelis?"

"Let us simply say we are friends." He stopped the guessing game. "Friends who happened to be in the neighborhood when you needed help. Call it...brotherhood week."

"I didn't know Perper traveled in these circles."

"Why should that surprise you? We have many friends, some inside your own government. Friends, Thomson! Not spies or informers. They choose to help us because it is the moral thing to do. They are friends we have earned, Mr. Thomson."

"Then why the bright lights? I thought we were on the same side."

"We used to be." The old man's voice grew sad again. "Now? Who can tell? Let us say the bright lights prevent any temptation. If you cannot see my face, then you will not need to lie about it, will you? Regrettably, we don't always know who our friends are these days."

"Like Kilbride?"

"You know that answer as well as I do." The interrogator conceded the point as he leaned forward, his hands stretching into the bright cone of light. They were old and brittle, white, and wrinkled. And as his soft voice spoke, those hands pleaded, adding a poignant emphasis to each word.

"Mr. Thomson, I have seen your record. You were in Germany. You saw what we are still up against, and you are neither naïve nor a fool. Look around. You have eyes. You can see Egypt drifting in that same dangerous direction. So is your ambassador. We must know where it will take them. Please! Tell me what Yussuf said."

Thomson couldn't stop himself. "He didn't say much of anything. He tried to sell me some photographs, but I wasn't buying. I sent him away."

"You fool!" the guy with the Uzi exclaimed.

The old man's voice behind the lamp cut through the room like an angry razor, silencing the others. There were no more interruptions. Then he apologized. "You must excuse Jani, Mr. Thomson. He and Landau were like brothers. Naturally, this business has us all upset. So please continue. Did you look at the photographs?"

"No," Thomson admitted guiltily as he slumped back in the chair. "I didn't. The whole thing looked like a setup, so I steered clear of it."

"Of course . . . Damascus." The old man clearly understood. "Most lamentable. And I can understand your reluctance to become involved. Unfortunately, those photographs might have been the best lead we have had. That is even more lamentable. Didn't Yussuf say anything to you? Anything at all? A single detail could help."

Thomson hesitated, then said, "We talked for a few minutes. I wasn't very friendly. He had a thick envelope of pictures. He said they were the ones Landau took at Heliopolis. If we wanted them, the price was ten thousand dollars."

He could hear the shuffling of feet behind him, but no one spoke. After almost a minute the voice behind the lamp finally asked, "Why did Yussuf bring them to you? Surely he knew you would be suspicious, and Evans would have quickly paid his price."

"Evans?" Thomson exclaimed. "Yussuf said he couldn't find him. Landau never told him how. So he was stuck."

"Ah!" The fingers reappeared in the cone of light. "Your picture was in the newspaper. Of course. It all fits now."

"If you say so." Thomson looked skeptical, and wished he could read the man's eyes, uncertain whether this was another test.

"You don't agree?" The voice sounded puzzled. "Why?"

"Because it doesn't wash. The whole thing just doesn't wash. Who the hell is Evans, anyway?"

"You do not know? Evans was Landau's contact with your CIA. They worked together for the past two months. He was the conduit. Landau passed his information through Evans to your embassy in Tel Aviv, then on to us."

"Did you ever meet Evans?" Thomson asked. "Do you know who he is, or what he looks like?"

"Of course not," the old man replied, without losing a shade of his certainty. "Landau made the arrangements at this end. He had to. It was all unofficial, but it worked well for several months. No, Thomson, you are wrong. Evans does exist. Or he did, until Landau's reports stopped coming. Why are you so positive he does not?"

"Because Kilbride said he'd never heard of him."

"Kilbride?" he scoffed. "What does that prove? I doubt he was even informed of the arrangement. Perhaps it was handled directly with your Langley headquarters. Perhaps Evans did it on his own. Or perhaps Kilbride lied to you?"

"Oh, Kilbride lied to me all right. But why? That's what I want to know. And the only way to find out is to ask Evans."

"You may have a point."

Yes, Thomson thought. He had a point, but he didn't have a damned thing more. So he started asking some questions of his own. "What about Heliopolis, then? Doesn't everything point to Heliopolis?"

"Perhaps. Perhaps not."

"Your turn to talk." Thomson leaned forward. "What's going on out there? Everyone says it's an old army base. Even Perper heard the rumors. Something about a secret airplane factory?"

"Ah, rumors!" The voice laughed. "The Middle East would be an insufferable bore, were it not for the rumors. But an airplane factory? What sense would that make? Do you really think the Egyptians could make their own jet airplanes? The Egyptians?" It laughed even louder. "What kind of airplane? One that is good enough to fight us? How absurd. And why bother? The Russians will sell them as many as they want at bargain prices. Airplanes? That is simply a smoke screen."

"Then what are they doing?"

"We do not know. Something, but not airplanes." The hands opened, reaching out to him for the answer. "Tell me. Have you heard any stories around your embassy regarding troop movements? That is why we sent Landau here. Last week, for no apparent reason, one of their tank regiments left its base in the Delta. It simply disappeared." He went on, as if he were thinking out loud. "That is most unlike the Egyptians. They are not good at maneuvers, especially secret ones. Someone always gets lost. So they usually hold their war games in the Sinai or the Western Desert. They aren't there. We checked. They aren't anywhere. The tanks did not cross the canal. They simply disappeared. So you can appreciate our concern. One mystery we can handle, but this one is sprouting questions faster than we can answer them."

Those long, expressive fingers stretched toward him again, pleading. "We must have your help, Thomson. We must! There is too much at stake. Can you tell us nothing more?"

Thomson squirmed uncomfortably. "The chair's hard," he whispered, watching those fingers and feeling a dozen eyes pressing in on him. "Well, maybe." He cleared his throat and confessed, "There *are* a couple of other things. Maybe they'll help. First, I'm pretty sure those two goons in the street are the same ones who came into the bar when I was talking to Yussuf. He knew who they were, because he took off like his pants were on fire."

"That explains why Grüber came after you tonight. If his men saw you with Yussuf, he is convinced you know something, or he is not sure. Whichever, your life is in grave danger. And the other thing? What is that?"

Thomson turned his eyes away, embarrassed to tell him. "Yussuf gave me one of the photographs. He said it was a sample."

"You have it?" The man's hands twitched anxiously.

"No...I...I burned it," Thomson admitted, feeling guilty as he watched the hands slump onto the table. "Sorry," he added pathetically. "I...I couldn't keep it."

"Do you remember anything about it?"

"Yes. That was the strange part. It was a photograph of a photograph, a portrait shot. It was in a cheap wooden frame and it showed a man from the chest up... in an SS uniform. Not our friend Grüber, either. This guy was a real worm: balding, middle-aged, wearing thin silver-framed glasses. Not much rank or medals, either.... Not much to go on, is it?"

"No, but it is something. And we appreciate it."

The hands pulled back, seemingly content. The room was silent for a while, then the old man spoke again. "Thomson, you have done us a service. We owe you one in return."

A hand reappeared in the light, holding a slip of paper. He pushed it across the desk. "It is a phone number. For emergencies. You never can tell when you might need some friends on short notice. Someone will be there. And if you learn anything else, please tell Perper."

Thomson felt a hand on his shoulder and he knew the grilling was over. He rose to his feet and let the man with the Uzi nudge him toward the door. When he was halfway there, the old man spoke once more.

"And, Jani, find this man a new shoe." He chuckled. "It would not do for us to send him home with one bare foot."

THE RIDE BACK to the city was a blur. There was so much more Thomson wanted to ask, but he knew Jani wouldn't give him the answers. Soon, the Mercedes was pulling over to the curb only a few blocks from his apartment.

Thomson stepped onto the sidewalk and heard Jani warn, "The police are watching your place. Be careful, Thomson. And remember what the old man told you. Call us if you learn anything. Right now, we're the only friends you have in Cairo. Even your own people won't help you, not now."

Thomson stared down at him for a moment. Their eyes met and Thomson could see Jani was serious. He nodded and took a deep breath, then turned and walked up the empty street, feeling very much alone.

Jani was right. The cops were there, but they weren't hard to spot. There was a small, plain sedan parked across from his apartment. Inside he could see the tops of two heads in the dim shadows.

What had he blundered into? Thomson wondered. Was there any chance this really could be an Agency operation? Kilbride sure as hell was sensitive about it. If it was, why hadn't the pompous bastard just said so? There were a hundred easier ways to call him off than this. Easier, that is, if the operation had Agency sanction. If...

So screw it. And screw Kilbride, too! Thomson was mad, good and mad, and he felt alive, for the first time in a long time. He was going to keep doing what they had trained him to do, whether they wanted him to or not, because it was the only thing he knew how to do. He had something to prove, to himself if no one else. His career? That couldn't sink any lower, but he still had his self-respect. He still had his instincts, too, and they told him he was right about this one.

All he needed was proof and he knew there was only one place to find it.

11

HE WAITED UNTIL midafternoon.

Leaving the city wasn't difficult, not dressed as an eccentric English tourist on a rented motorbike, complete with baggy shorts, a pith helmet, and a picnic basket. Five minutes in the crowded streets and back alleys of the Old Quarter did the rest. He left the police mired hopelessly in the pushcarts and clutter, cursing a donkey and their own bad luck.

Thomson steered northeast, through the city and its suburbs, until he reached the main highway to Heliopolis. "The City of the Sun" had been built in the early decades of the century by the British, for the British. From its high plateau, the colonial emperors rode into the capital each morning and escaped back to their safe, white enclave each night. The emperors were gone, but their aura remained—for those with the cash to afford it. The proud villas and apartments of the British were occupied by the native upper class now—wealthy merchants, powerful government mandarins, and army colonels with their brightly colored ribbons.

Fifteen miles of blistering sun and dry desert air left the skin on Thomson's hands and face as parched and cracked as old leather. As the first houses on the outskirts of the city appeared on the shimmering horizon, he swung the motorbike into the shade cast by a scraggly palm tree and reached into the picnic basket. He grabbed one of the canteens he'd stashed there and splashed half of it down his throat and the other half onto his face. The rush of warm water turned the powdery road dust into a river of slimy mud. It ran down his chest and soaked his shirt, but even that felt luxuriously refreshing.

On the other side of the road he saw a narrow dirt track branching off from the highway and fading away into the low, rocky hills of the desert. The army base was out there somewhere. Thomson forced his aching rear end back onto the bike, kicked the motor in gear, and went exploring.

Before he'd traveled the first bumpy mile, the heat of the desert had dried his shirt. And before he'd gone the second mile, he ran into a military police roadblock.

Two Egyptian soldiers were asleep at the back of their jeep and a third sat on the front bumper, dozing on his rifle. It was hard to tell who was more surprised, Thomson or the MP. The Egyptian jumped into the road and flagged Thomson down with the barrel of his rifle.

"I say," Thomson protested in his best British accent, "let me pass, my good man."

It was hopeless. The MP didn't understand a word of English. He grinned and nodded, but he kept motioning with the rifle for Thomson to turn around.

"Oh damn!" Thomson pouted and stomped his foot on the ground, but he had no choice. He wheeled the bike around and headed back up the road, making a mental note of the markings on the jeep's bumper and smiling. The roadblock was tangible proof that something was going on out here. Someone was worried enough about security to post guards and cordon the area off.

Thomson backtracked to the main highway and pointed the bike toward Heliopolis again. After another mile, he found a second dirt road slicing away into the desert. This time, he'd barely gone a mile before he ran into another roadblock. The result was the same, except one of the MPs spoke English.

"Oh, be a sport, old chap," Thomson pleaded. "I'm a geologist. That's the Semiramis Fault out there," he said, making a bold, sweeping gesture toward the empty desert, winging it as he went. "Oil shale! It's the future, mark my words—"

The MP silenced him with a fierce scowl. "No! Off limits. Off limits. You go back. Go!"

"Now see here!" Thomson put his hands on his hips and blustered. "I have friends in the ministry of—"

"Go! You go!" The guard continued to scowl as he leveled the rifle at Thomson's chest. And from the look in the MP's eyes, Thomson knew he'd love to pull the trigger. So why give him an excuse? He quickly backed away, hopping on the motorbike and throwing it into gear.

Thomson didn't get much from his second encounter, but as he looked back at the MP, he saw him coughing and cursing in the cloud of choking dust Thomson had left behind. He smiled, but he didn't slow down until he was well out of sight and halfway back to the main road. Then he swung the bike off the narrow track and into the soft sand, muscling it a few hundred yards into the desert until he was hidden behind a low, rocky outcrop.

This would do.

Thomson dropped his aching body onto the hot sand next to the bike and tried to relax. His muscles were still tingling from the bumpy ride. He needed rest. He needed sleep, but it would have to wait. He shielded his eyes and turned his head slowly to survey the rugged wilderness around him.

Waves of heat shimmered off the hard-packed, coppery-red sand. The blinding glare made him squint. Who would even want this hellhole? he wondered as he glanced at his watch. It was four P.M. Time for a late lunch and a long nap. Judging from the landscape, he'd need them both before the night was over.

THOMSON WOKE FEELING stiff and cold. There had been nights when these old bones hadn't objected to the hard ground, but he was having trouble remembering that far back.

The shimmering heat of the afternoon was gone. Now, the night air bore an eerie chill. Overhead hung a cold quarter moon. Thomson slapped his arms and rubbed them hard, amazed at how quickly this blinding oven became the black inside of a refrigerator.

His watch showed nearly eleven P.M. His body had been right; it had needed the sleep and this was the biggest chunk he'd stolen in over forty-eight hours. He rose to his feet and stretched, then dug both hands into the bottom of the picnic basket. There was a pint of brandy squirreled away down there, and he grinned when he found it, twisting off the cap and taking a big nip.

"Watch out, world, here I come." He shivered and coughed, trying to convince himself he might actually make it. He changed into dark clothes, threw his small mountaineering pack over his shoulder, and set off, checking his bearings with an old army compass and a Michelin road map. In less than twenty minutes, he noticed a faint white glow above the far horizon. Thomson put the compass away and smiled. So much for the abandoned army base. Something was going on, and it sure as hell wasn't maneuvers. So take it slow and easy. If he ran into the MPs dressed like this he'd never pass for a wandering geologist. He stayed low, following the terrain, winding through meandering rock-strewn valleys, moving quietly, blending into the night like one more dark shadow, until he reached a fence.

It wasn't new, but it was tall and well maintained, patched and painted, with the underbrush hacked away and a double coil of concertina wire strung along its top. Like any obstacle, it couldn't keep a good man out, not if he really wanted to get inside, but it upped the ante by slowing you down and making you decide how bad you really wanted in.

Thomson wanted in, but he was in no hurry.

He pulled a pair of binoculars from his pack and focused them on the compound. In front of him sat dozens of long wooden army barracks. Beyond them, farther inside the compound, stood a big grove of palm trees. Peeking between the trunks and branches, he saw the flicker of lights, as if someone were trying to hide something. That might work during the day, but not at night. He cocked an ear and heard the banging of metal and the deep-throated rumble of a diesel engine. Looking through the thick shroud of trees, he could see the dim shapes of men and machines backlit by powerful lights. It was a motor pool! From a glimpse here and there, Thomson recognized the unmistakable outlines of a half-dozen Russian T-34 tanks. The old iron monsters looked small and outdated now, but in their day they had smashed anything the Germans threw at them, and had carried the Red Army on their backs from Moscow to the gates of Berlin. Now, the Russians pawned them off like worn-out shoes. There were enough dark places in the compound to hide a whole army of tanks, and Thomson knew he'd just found the tank regiment missing from the Delta.

Thomson swung the binoculars and focused them on the gate where the main road entered the compound. It was floodlit, barricaded, and guarded. Beyond the gate, the road branched into three smaller ones. One curved toward Thomson, passing by the barracks. The second went on toward the big buildings at the center of the compound. And the third curved sharply away until it disappeared into a long row of wood-frame bungalows.

The buildings in the compound dated from the war, and had been built by the British. The bungalows probably had housed the NCOs and their families, since British officers always lived in town. It wasn't hard to imagine how the dilapidated cottages had looked back then, with a coat of fresh paint, windowboxes of petunias, and clotheslines bending under loads of bleached laundry. Not anymore. As Jeremy said, it had all gone to hell in a handbasket.

Thomson had more questions than answers, so he crawled away from the fence and back into the shadows, slowly working his way around the outer perimeter of the compound toward the main gate. Every hundred meters there was a sign hanging on the fence, warning any foolhardy trespasser in both Arabic and English that he'd be shot. And there were enough guards to make the threat real. He'd seen at least six heavily armed men patrolling the fence and he hadn't covered more than a fraction of its perimeter.

When he got within thirty feet of the main gate, he stopped and lay still, content to watch and listen. It didn't take long for his patience to be rewarded. A big sedan came speeding up the road, its headlights illuminating the entire entrance with the glare from its high beams.

The two Egyptian sentries slouched at the gate looked up. When they recognized the sedan, they braced to attention. At the same time, the door of the guard shack behind them flew open with a loud crash. A short, burly sergeant strode out, glaring at the guards as he hurried over to the car. There was something odd about him, Thomson thought.

He wore the same Egyptian army uniform as the other two, but even from a distance he looked different. The light was dim, but his skin looked shades paler than theirs. He was older and well built. And he didn't walk, he strutted—casually, but with the smug confidence of a man born to be a soldier. As he laughed and chatted with whomever was inside the car, they seemed to be sharing some old, familiar joke.

Thomson strained to hear their words above the low rumble of the car's engine, but all he caught were snatches. *"Ja, ja . . . diese Scheissidioten!"* The sergeant nodded and looked at the two guards with contempt. *"Ja, ja . . . in Ordnung . . . Naturlich . . . Wann? . . . Gemacht."* The sergeant snapped to attention and Thomson swore he heard the man say, *"Zu Befehl, Herr Sturmbannführer!"*

There was only one military organization in the world that used titles like that, the SS. The sergeant snapped his fingers at the guards and they quickly raised the gate. As the sedan passed through the floodlights, Thomson got a brief glimpse inside and saw the same profile and arrogant smile he'd seen the night before. It was Blondie!

The guards quickly dropped the gate back into place, as the red taillights of the sedan drove away toward the big buildings in the center of the compound. The German sergeant stood with his hands on his hips, snarling at the two Egyptian sentries. He spat in the middle of the road, then stormed back into his shack. The two sentries looked at each other and smiled. Soon, they were lounging against the gate again, no more concerned than before. Good, Thomson thought, as he silently crept away into the shadows. He wouldn't have to worry about the Egyptians. But the heavy duty was pulled by Germans, and they were worth avoiding.

Thomson made a wide arc around the main gate and reached the fence again near the row of old bungalows. This was the darkest part of the compound, and Thomson didn't have to debate his next move. He had already learned a few things, but not nearly enough; he needed to know more. He pulled a pair of wire cutters from his pack and went to work on the fence.

From up close, the small bungalows looked even more dilapidated than they had through binoculars. Decades of sun, sand, and neglect had left them gray and drab, shingles were missing from the roofs, and the rear porches sagged badly. Even their once proud gardens were neglected, reduced to a few scraggly patches of weeds; all, that is, except the bungalow at the far end. It had a garden, small and well kept. Even more surprising, a flowerpot sat on the rear window ledge. And there were curtains! Someone had actually hung curtains in the window.

"Be it ever so humble," he muttered and shook his head. Someone called the place home. And since it was the farthest from the bright lights of the gate, it would do nicely.

Thomson crept across the backyard and onto the back porch, taking a few cautious steps to test the old wood. It looked solid, but he didn't need any loose, creaking boards giving him away. With a small, light stride, he reached for the doorknob and gave it a gentle push, only intending to make a gap so he could jimmy the lock. But the door opened. Thomson's heart jumped into his throat as he realized the damned thing wasn't even locked. Why should it be? With a barbed-wire fence, dozens of armed guards, and ten miles of desert in every direction, who needed locks? They couldn't be safer out here, could they?

He pushed the door open and edged inside the kitchen. He stopped, waiting quietly, listening for some sound of life but hearing none. The room was pitch-black and the house was as quiet as it had been when he entered: no strange sounds, no alarms or growling dogs, nothing, not yet anyway. Satisfied he was alone, he pulled a small flashlight from his pocket and let its thin beam explore the room. It was as neat as a pin. The counters were clean and the evening dishes were stacked in the sink. With the flowerpot and the garden, Thomson was pretty sure there was a woman around the place somewhere, and he'd bet she was German.

He took a few steps and passed through an arched doorway into a tiny dining room. To his right, a staircase rose to the second floor and what he assumed would be bedrooms. He stopped at the foot of the stairs to listen. Somewhere above, he heard the faint creak of bed springs as a body tossed and turned in its sleep. He froze, but all he heard was more silence and soft snoring.

He backed away from the stairs and stepped to his left, entering the living room, or what used to be the living room. Now, it was an office. Two long cluttered tables filled the center of the room and an old, threadbare couch covered with stacks of books and reports sat against the far wall. There were so many, Thomson didn't even know where to start.

He picked a folder from the top of a stack and turned his flashlight beam onto its cover. The paper was old and water stained, so covered with dust that the print was barely legible. Still, the words were German. Thomson tucked the folder under his arm and continued his search, knowing he didn't have the time to try to translate it now.

His thin flashlight beam cut across the far wall, which was covered by a huge gallery. He stepped closer, his eyes darting over the rows of thin frames. Most held old black-and-white photos, but some contained ornate diplomas and certificates. The books and reports could wait, he thought, as the light danced among the photographs, searching for the one he knew was there. "Landau, you sneaky bastard," he muttered with a satisfied smile.

Near the far end of the wall hung the original of the photograph Yussuf had dropped on his table just two nights before. He stared at it, marveling at the sour face of the SS officer—the one with the pale skin and wire-rimmed glasses. His expression was so banal it was hard to believe he could harm anyone. Still, Thomson felt a shiver run down his spine as he realized he was standing where Landau had stood when he'd snapped that picture. Two men had died because of it. Two so far, and Thomson didn't want to make it three.

He turned the flashlight beam away, taking a quick look at the other photographs. They told more about old Sourpuss's life than Thomson wanted to know. He was in each one, always looking timid and unsure of himself, hiding at the side or rear of large groups of men. He was always the odd man out. The others smiled and laughed at the camera. Not him. He appeared nervous, as if he didn't fit in and knew it.

In the ones where he looked youngest, the men were dressed in civilian clothes. But in later shots, they all wore uniforms—Luftwaffe and army for the most part—except for Sourpuss. He wore the black and silver of the SS. No wonder his smiles were strained, Thomson thought.

One particular photo drew Thomson's attention. It had the same old faces, but they were posed on the front steps of a modern brick building, as if they were attending a grand opening. Behind them, a sign was mounted on the wall of the building that read *"Hechingen..."* That's all Thomson could make out; the heads blocked the rest.

He swore to himself and turned his attention to the certificates and diplomas. They were from the Universities of

Tübingen and Berlin, and from the Kaiser Wilhelm Institute: big certificates with gold ribbons and ornate lettering. Thomson moved the flashlight even closer, trying to decipher the tiny Gothic script, when the light fixture above him suddenly flashed on. The room was filled with light, and Thomson found himself staring down the barrel of an old Luger.

12

THOMSON COULDN'T SEE much through the blinding glare of the light except for the black muzzle of the old Luger and the shaking hands that were pointing it at him. They belonged to a woman.

She wore a heavy cotton bathrobe clutched tightly at the throat like a suit of armor. She'd obviously been asleep. Her eyes were as round as teacups and her face was pale and nervous. He would have laughed, if it hadn't been for the gun. Her hair was tied up in dozens of those silly, pink hair curlers and she wore no makeup. Not that she was unattractive. She just looked to be all business. And out in this godforsaken place? Who cared about makeup? Besides, she was no spring chicken. Thomson figured the woman and the Luger were about the same vintage: somewhere on the downhill side of thirty.

She had her back against the wall, as if she were the one caught in the trap, and was holding the gun at arm's length, gripping the butt with both hands and keeping its barrel pointed straight at him. At least she hadn't used it. Not yet, anyway.

"*Hande hoch!*" Her voice trembled as she tried to sound firm, not quite making it.

"*Ja ... Ja ... Bitte!*" He thrust his hands high above his head and dropped the folder on the floor. "Don't shoot ... Uh, *nicht schiessen*. Okay?" he stammered. "I don't speak

German. And point that thing someplace else, before it goes off. Lord, you scared me half to death sneaking in here like that."

"Me?... Sneaking?" Her eyes bulged out as she responded in heavily accented English. "How dare—"

"Thank God you understand! There must be some mistake. You see, I...I have an appointment..."

"A thief? A thief makes appointments?" she demanded.

"Why yes. Uh no! Look, I'm not a thief and I do have an appointment," he said, gesturing toward the photographs on the wall. "With...him, with the doctor."

"Here? At this hour?" She sounded confused. "Impossible. He would have told me."

"Well, then he forgot." Thomson gestured insistently. "It was all arranged by our...'friends.' Go ask him."

"I...I can't. He went to the laboratory."

"That isn't my fault. The plane was late, it was catch-as-catch-can." He smiled, becoming more animated and waving his arms as he took a few cautious steps toward her. "Do you know what it's like getting a cab to drive out here from the airport, at this hour?"

She extended the barrel farther, keeping it pointed at him, but she was clearly confused.

Thomson wasn't about to let her sort it all out. "Look," he babbled, "the guys at the gate said I could come in and wait. The lights were out. How the hell did I know anyone was home. I figured I'd sack out on the couch until he came home. Don't blame me if they didn't let you know. That's what you get from Security. Right? Here." He took another step toward her. "Let me show you the pass they gave me."

Thomson lowered his eyes and dug his free hand inside his jacket pocket, ignoring the look of panic on her face as he closed in. "It's right here." He smiled as his hand flicked out and grabbed the gun barrel, twisting it out of her grip before she realized what he was doing. When she did, she blinked and stared at him, her eyes filling with hate and fear. She dropped into a crouch, her hands out, ready for the last round.

Thomson chuckled and stepped back and shook his head. "There. Isn't that better? You scared the hell out of me with this thing," he scolded her, as he examined the old Luger, careful to keep it pointed in her general direction.

"I should have shot you with it!" she snarled.

"That's a hell of a friendly note! If that's all you have to say, I won't even apologize. Go sit on the couch," he said as if she had hurt his feelings, using the gun like a pointer. "Go on. Go sit down. I've had enough excitement from you for one night."

She went, but she wasn't happy, moving slowly, keeping her back against the wall, trying to stay as far away from him as she could. When she reached the couch, she squeezed between two stacks of books and looked up at him warily.

"I saw your flowers out back," he commented in a friendly voice. "I should have guessed that wasn't the male Aryan touch." He glanced around at the stack of books and reports that filled the tiny living room. "I bet he never gets much farther than here, the bed, and the lab. Right? But who are you?" He frowned. "You're too young to be his wife. What are you then? His secretary? His mistress?"

"I'm his daughter!" she shouted.

"No kidding? From the expression on old Sourpuss, I'd have never guessed he had that much passion in him. A long time ago, eh? Duty to the Führer and all that? But now that you mention it, there is a strong family resemblance. What's your name?"

"Ilsa . . . Ilsa Fengler."

"Ilsa? That's a nice little name."

"What do you want?" She slumped back in the couch, her voice drained.

"Me? Oh, I'm just a tourist. I like out-of-the-way places in the middle of the night."

"You are a thief! Look at your clothes—and that flashlight. How dare you come breaking into people's homes, sneaking around in the dark like this." She was starting to get suspicious. "No, you aren't a thief after all, are you? You're a spy, that's what you are. Another filthy spy!" she shouted, her face turning beet-red. "I knew I should have shot you."

"Think of the mess that would have made." He laughed, and glanced around the small living room.

"Your little jokes won't get you out of here. Neither will that gun. The guards will catch you."

"Oh no they won't." He shook his head knowingly, intent on keeping her off balance. "They didn't stop me from coming in, did they? Haven't you asked yourself why? You're a bright girl. You've been around. Why didn't they stop me?"

She bit her lip and her eyes filled with doubt.

"I wasn't lying." He mocked her. "I was sent. You should have figured that much out by now."

"That is preposterous," she said, trying hard to convince herself. "Major Grüber would have—"

"Grüber? What makes you think he knows?" He cut her off, quickening the pace, hoping she'd say something useful before she caught on.

"But, Stuttgart would never—"

"Oh yes they would, and you know it. Stuttgart trusts no one: not you, not your father, and certainly not Grüber. Do you?" Her eyes answered that one. "He doesn't call the shots anymore, not after the mistakes he's made."

"Of course he's made mistakes. We all have, but...
You're an American!"

"And you're German, and some of us are British, some
are Swiss, and this is Egypt. So what?"

"This is impossible!" She shook her head. "Even if they
did send you, you have no business—"

"My dear girl, do you realize how important this project
is?" he countered, talking to her as if she were a child.
"And things are falling way behind schedule."

"That isn't our fault...not my father's, anyway."

"How do you explain the mistakes then?" He quickly
changed his tone of voice, tearing into her like an angry in-
quisitor. "Delays? Accidents? Spies? Call them what you
like, Ilsa, but Stuttgart wants answers. Maybe some of it
was intentional."

"Intentional?" She almost leaped off the couch at him.
"What are you accusing him of? My father's work is flawless. Höchengler is in charge of the rockets. Papa has nothing to do with them. So go break into his house, if you like.
Just leave us alone."

So that was it. Rockets!

Thomson was stunned. It was all so obvious. The pieces
were all there, if he'd only put them in the right places.

"Höchengler is someone else's concern, not mine," he
blustered, trying to think. "And I don't need to be told how
important your father's work is to the program."

"Then why does he waste time on trash like you!" she
hissed, her voice trembling as her feelings rushed out. "He
has always been loyal. He gave you the best years of his life,
since 1937, and he has done nothing to deserve this. If you
have questions, go to him honestly, in the open. Don't
break into his house in the middle of the night," she said
in disgust.

"You're right." He bowed and tapped his heels together like a polite headwaiter. "That is precisely what I should have done. I'll go to the doctor right now and confront him with the accusations. Get your coat. You're coming with me."

"Gladly!" Her eyes flashed angrily as she jumped to her feet. "I can't wait to hear what he says to you."

"Neither can I." He smiled.

"The car is outside. I'll get my keys." She marched past him to the tiny foyer, grabbing her coat from the closet and storming out the front door.

He followed her across the barren front yard toward a battered old Fiat. She started the engine and gunned it, barely waiting for him to get in before she backed into the road, her face still livid. She ground the gears, but the car lurched forward with a groan and a squeal from the tires. Thomson was delighted; the madder she got, the less likely she'd be to think clearly.

She slowed down at the fork in the road, intending to turn right, toward the big hangars. That was when Thomson jabbed the Luger into her ribs, gently, but with enough force for her to get the message. "Let's go the other way"— he gestured—"to the left. Toward the gate."

She let the car roll to a stop as she turned her head and stared at him, her eyes big and round.

"Do it." He nudged her again with the gun. "Now, and you won't be hurt, Ilsa. If you don't . . . I'll have to shoot my way out of here and somebody's going to get hurt."

"You . . . !" she spluttered, unable to speak, her knuckles turning white as she gripped the steering wheel.

"Probably. So humor me. You've got a big mouth. And if you can't talk us through that gate, then Papa Fengler is going to be minus one precious daughter. I doubt you care, but think of him. He'd tell you to do what I say, wouldn't he?''

"You're insane!'' She glared at him, but she dropped the car into gear and turned toward the gate.

She drove right up to the barrier, skidding to a halt, and took out her wrath on the two Egyptian guards. "Open the gate,'' she shouted through the window. "You know who I am, Faisal. So open it. I'm in a hurry.''

The Arab began to raise the pole, but stopped when the door to the guardhouse swung open. It was the German sergeant. Thomson poked her with the gun again and whispered, "You're doing fine. Just keep up the good work, Sweet Pea.''

"Was ist los?" The sergeant bent down and peered into the front seat, leering at her bathrobe until he saw that someone was sitting beside her. "And who is this?''

"My friend... He's no business of yours, Klaus. Just let us through!''

"I know nothing of any... friend. When did he arrive?''

"At noon, before you came on duty. Just tell Faisal to open the gate, or I'll have another talk with Major Grüber about you.''

Klaus's round, fat mouth twisted into a vicious snarl. His eyes shifted back and forth from her, to Thomson, and back to her again. Finally, he backed his head out of the window. *"Sehr gut,* Fräulein Fengler. You and your... friend may pass. But this incident shall go in my report. You may be certain of that! We'll see who has the last laugh.''

He snapped his fingers and the terrified Egyptian raised the barrier. She didn't wait. She pushed the accelerator to the floor and drove off in a billowing cloud of dust. Thomson looked back and saw Klaus fighting the dust, cursing as the car sped away. His face was filled with an animal fury that Thomson didn't want to see at close range again.

They drove down the road in complete silence until Thomson estimated they were halfway to the main highway. "This is far enough, Ilsa," he said. "You can stop now."

"Here? What next?" she asked. "After burglary and kidnapping, are you going to add rape and murder to your list of crimes?"

"No." He laughed. "I'm too old for that. Just a pleasant walk on a mild summer's evening." He nudged her out of the car with the gun barrel. "You can go back to Papa now, Fräulein Fengler, no worse off than I found you."

She took a few steps and turned back, staring at him, still trying to figure him out. "You know you'll never get away with this. Don't you?"

"Oh yes I will." He smiled. "I already have. And don't fret your little head about the car. I'll park it outside the German Embassy. You can get it in the morning. Fair enough?"

"What am I supposed to tell them?" She glanced at the dim glow from the camp above the horizon.

"Tell them I stuck a gun in your ribs and made you drive me out the gate. They'll find it under the seat. That should be enough. Besides, you can blame the whole thing on Klaus. Tell them you tried to signal him, but he never took his eyes off the front of your bathrobe. Tell them he was hitting the schnapps a bit hard tonight."

For the first time, he saw her smile.

"You know," he said, "your face doesn't crack into little pieces when you do that. No telling what a little more practice would do. So have a pleasant walk home, Fräulein. Maybe we can meet under more pleasant circumstances next time."

"Who are you?" she suddenly asked.

"Why? Does it matter?"

"It does. To me anyway," she replied.

"Then it's Thomson. Okay?" He dropped the car into gear and drove away, leaving her standing by the side of the road with another of those silly smiles on her face. Women, he thought. He needed them like he needed a hole in the head.

13

HIS NIGHT ENDED LATE and his morning came too early. Sandwiched between were a few hours of restless sleep and the same old nightmares.

It was dark. He was running down a long, narrow tunnel, desperate and out of breath, chased by a black limousine. The walls on each side gleamed like wet glass, rising from the ground into the mists above. Every time Thomson looked back, he saw the bright headlights of the car looming closer and closer.

In the dark shadows beyond the walls were hideously distorted faces, laughing and taunting him, cheering as he ran faster and faster, cheering for the car. Kilbride was there. So was Blondie, and Saleh, and that fat Arab. He was holding his head high above the crowd so he could watch the show. The boys from Damascus were there too, playing catch with a smoking bomb and waving at him. That prim bastard Collins was there, and Doris too, snapping her gum. Worst of all, Thomson saw his first two wives, laughing hysterically and slapping each other on the back. The only face that seemed the slightest bit concerned was Ilsa Fengler's. She stood by herself in her bathrobe and hair curlers, crying.

All Thomson could do was keep running, knowing he'd lose in the end, no matter how hard he tried. But he wasn't going to quit. The car would get him, but he'd never give those faces the satisfaction of seeing him quit.

The one nice thing about his dream was that he never felt any pain. Every time the car was about to smack into him, he'd wake up, in a cold, chilling sweat.

But this time, it was a loud knocking that saved him. He threw on a pair of pants and went to the door, only to be greeted by the unfriendly faces of two big security guards from the embassy, and Collins.

"Get dressed, mister," the Boy Wonder ordered, wedging the door open with his foot. Thomson looked down, tempted to slam it shut and break the fool's ankle, but the two meatballs pushed him back. Collins kept his distance, knowing he didn't want to get too close to Thomson.

"Collins, it's the middle of the damned night!" Thomson fumed.

"It's five A.M. Ambassador Kilbride wants you, now. That's all the reason I need, Thomson."

Collins was his usual officious self, and he let the meatballs do the dirty work. They shoved Thomson into a chair and began tossing the contents of his dresser into a suitcase, which didn't take long. Thomson could have moved everything he owned in the backseat of a VW Bug and still have had room for passengers. In five minutes they were out the door, then it was the fast lane to the embassy and a slow elevator ride to the fifth floor.

Kilbride was waiting, sitting in his chair, looking red-faced and well-rehearsed. "Are you nuts, Thomson?" he started off in his loudest, most sarcastic voice. "Is that it? Should I have the shrinks toss you in a rubber room?"

Thomson didn't respond. He stood directly in front of the ambassador's desk, arms folded, staring down at Kilbride, relaxed, confident, and bored.

"Damnation! What's the reason, Thomson? You nuts? Stupid? Or maybe you're out to get me like the rest of them."

Thomson kept quiet, wrecking the script. He stared down at Kilbride, watching him shift uncomfortably in his chair.

"I can't believe it." The ambassador started to back down. "How could you break into an army base and kidnap that woman? Too bad you didn't get shot! That would have solved my problem the easy way. And by the time I'm finished, you'll wish they had. I got another phone call from the foreign minister in the middle of the night. That was bad enough. Then I got one from the German ambassador! Who's next, Thomson? The Russians? The British? The goddamned Norwegians?"

Thomson had had enough, more than enough. He leaned forward, putting the palms of his hands on Kilbride's freshly polished desk and pressing uncomfortably close to the ambassador's face only inches away. "Since you had them all on the line, did you bother to ask them about Fengler and the rest of the Germans they have working out there?" he demanded.

"Fengler? Fengler?" Kilbride's eyes bulged.

"Yes, Fengler! You heard me," Thomson answered back in a tone of voice Kilbride wasn't accustomed to hearing. "Did you ask them about Fengler? Or are you afraid of what they might tell you? Well, let me jam some facts into that thick skull of yours. There's a bunch of Krauts working out in the desert, and they aren't making cuckoo clocks. They're making rockets. Rockets, Kilbride! Those are German rocket scientists, and they've got a small army of goose-stepping SS guards to watch over them. You wouldn't know about that. Would you? You don't want to know anything except your neat little plans. Do you?"

Kilbride's face turned white. He shrunk into the cushions of his chair and turned his eyes away.

That was when it hit him. "You already know, don't you?" Thomson asked in disbelief. "You know, and you haven't done a damned thing to stop it? Have you?"

Kilbride wiped his hand across his lips, looking small and scared, with no place to hide. "Now you've really done it, mister," he blustered, trying to regain control. "I told you to stay clear. And now I'm going to have your head on a platter before I'm done with—"

"Kilbride, it's too late for threats! Don't you understand? Can't you see what they're doing out there?" He shook his head in disgust. "Do you think you can sit up here and just let it happen? What are you going to tell State? Wash your hands and claim you knew nothing about it?"

Kilbride jumped to his feet, his angry expression giving way to a cynical belly laugh. "State? You want to know what I'm going to tell State? You moron! You half-witted, bumbling moron!" Then he laughed even harder. "Is that what you think? That State doesn't know?"

This time it was Thomson's turn to be stunned, as the enormity of Kilbride's words hit him full force.

"You silly son of a bitch," the ambassador crowed. "Why do you think I wanted you and your damned CIA to keep out of it? Why do you think it's so sensitive? Of course we know there's Germans out there—Fengler, Höchengler, and the rest of them. So what! And so what if they did bring a few goose-stepping gorillas to baby-sit them? Does that offend your tender sensibilities, Thomson? Well, tough!"

"What do you think they're making them for?" Thomson asked with equal sarcasm. "You think they're saving them for the Fourth of July?"

"Who cares? They don't mean a damned thing, Thomson. What kind of rockets do you think they're going to get from those Peenemunde retreads, anyway? We got Von Braun and the pick of the litter back in '45, and the Russians got the scraps. So believe me, that bunch of 'Mister Wizards' out at Heliopolis couldn't make good cow shit on a dairy farm. They're third-rate. Worse. All Nasser is going to get for his money is a couple of V-2s with a fresh coat of paint. So who cares?"

"And when they drop one on Tel Aviv?"

"They won't!" Kilbride shook his head. "Nasser's fighter planes carry a bigger payload than a V-2. Besides"—he dismissed the point with a wave of his hand—"he's never going to use the damned things. Wouldn't dare. Told me so himself. The Israelis would paste him good, and he knows it. But what's wrong with him having a few to show off to his pals? He's on a Third World ego trip, and he wants to go first-class. What's the harm? If it makes him happy, then I'm happy."

Thomson shook his head.

"It's like I told you yesterday, Thomson, but you were too hardheaded to listen. Okay, they aren't making airplanes. I lied. Big deal. Nasser wants some new toys and we can't sell him any, not with that Israeli lobby in Congress. But I'll be damned before I let the Russians get their damned hooks in any deeper, either. Remember the Aswan Dam? We turned him down. Moscow didn't. This time it's going to be different. His little deal with the Germans solves everybody's problem, doesn't it?"

"You really think you can keep the genie in the bottle that easily, Kilbride?"

"It's policy, boy! Mine and Washington's, so you damned well better believe it's going to work. Everyone knows about it, and they know when to play dumb, too. I told you before, boy. My job's to get Nasser on our team, and that's exactly what I'm going to do. Besides, if Nasser has a few rockets, he might even teach the Israelis some manners. The more worried they get, the more they'll toe our line. So everybody benefits. Everybody. Except you, that is!"

Kilbride leaned across the desk and his eyes turned hard. "That's why I can't have some washed-up Sneaky Pete coming in here screwing the whole deal up for me. Not now. So I'm going to drop a great big lid on top of you, Thomson."

"Like you did on Landau and Yussuf?" Thomson said. "Is that what you called it, 'dropping a great big lid on them'? You fed them to the Egyptians, didn't you, Kilbride? Landau trusted us. He found out what was going on and he tried to get the word out, so you set him up, didn't you? You cynical bastard!" Thomson shot a quick glance at Collins. "Who played Evans? You, Collins? Yeah, I bet it was you." He nodded, but the young CIA man turned his eyes away. "You'd be the perfect choice: Judas in a three-piece suit."

"Collins did what he was told to do!" Kilbride snapped angrily. "You'd be smart to learn that lesson, Thomson. And don't go laying that dead Arab at my feet. We had nothing to do with him or Landau. They got themselves caught. And what happened afterward is none of my business."

"Bullshit. You were the only ones who did know. Yussuf did get in touch with you, didn't he? He was desperate after I threw him out of the bar. What did he do? Phone the embassy looking for Evans and say the magic word—'pictures'? That's it, isn't it? The pictures. That must have scared the hell out of you. So you fed him to State Security, or to Grüber and his SS playmates. Just a little word to the right people and the problem went away, permanently!''

"That's their business, not ours!''

"Like hell it is. You let them drop it around my neck, didn't you? And if I hadn't had an airtight alibi, you'd have let them hang me for it, wouldn't you?''

"No! And what the hell are you complaining about? They never did anything to you. Did they?''

"Who killed Yussuf? Who's behind this?''

"I don't know and I don't want to know,'' Kilbride said flatly and firmly, but he wasn't a very good liar.

"If your pals know it wasn't me, why the hell are the cops still on my tail?''

"Because they aren't in on it, dummy! This thing is way above the police. You ought to know that. So they're following you? So what?'' He shrugged. "We can't tidy up all the loose ends, you know. Besides, you act like you've never been tailed before. It kept the cops busy and kept them away from what really counts. But you're in no danger, Thomson. If Saleh got really nasty, we'd have chucked your ass on an airplane. Which brings me to my last point.''

Kilbride glanced at his watch and looked up with a satisfied smile. "I hate to end this little confession on a sour note, but that airplane I just mentioned will be all fueled up and waiting for you. Good-bye, Thomson. Wish I could say it was a pleasure, but it wasn't. You're Langley's problem now. Not mine.''

Part of Thomson wanted to fight back, but the rest of him was too fed up to care anymore. What good would it do? The deck had been stacked from the beginning. What was the saying? Never bet against the house? So he'd go along. But as he did, he glanced back and gave Kilbride one long, disgusted look.

The ambassador pointed his finger at Collins. "All I want to hear from you is your happy voice at the other end of a phone telling me his plane's in the air and the big bird is soaring out of sight. Got that, Collins?"

The two meatballs were summoned from the outer office. They hustled him out the door and into the service elevator, none too gently. With one of them on each arm, he was crammed into the rear seat of a waiting car before he even realized it.

As they drove away, Thomson slumped back, more angry and frustrated than he'd ever been in his life. He'd been had. But for once, he wasn't to blame. Damascus was all his, plain and simple, with no excuses. He had blown it and deserved what he had gotten. Not this time, though. This time he hadn't done a damned thing wrong. In fact he'd done the first right things he'd done in years.

As he spun it around and around in his head, he kept hearing little alarm bells going off, ringing louder and louder, telling him something was very, very wrong. He closed his eyes, concentrating on Kilbride's words, but the alarm bells kept drowning them out. He heard the woman's voice too, jumbled up in a mishmash of words and voices and alarm bells. And none of it made any sense.

What had she said? Her father had nothing to do with the rockets? Then what *did* he do? And why had Kilbride called him a rocket scientist, if he wasn't? The wall full of pictures and framed certificates flashed across the inside of Thomson's eyelids as if they were movie screens, but it still didn't make any sense. Peenemunde? Kilbride had said Peenemunde. But the building in that photograph said Hechingen. Rocket scientists? Then why wasn't Von Braun's face in any of the shots? Or any of the other top guns like Willy Ley, or the rest? From the number of picture frames on the wall, it was obvious that Fengler had a monumental ego. Surely he'd want a few shots with Von Braun, wouldn't he?

Questions. Questions up the yin-yang, but not one damned answer. And before any could come, the car was at the passenger terminal of the airport.

Collins and the two meatballs wasted no time. They gave him the two-armed hustle through the main concourse, marching double-time, until they reached the departure gate. Collins wanted to go on, right across the tarmac to the airplane, but an Egyptian customs agent stopped them, standing in their way like a rock. He had his rules, and no one in Egypt was more determined than a minor bureaucrat with a rulebook.

Thomson smiled, turning his head toward the runway. Kilbride was wrong about one thing, he told himself. The plane wasn't ready, it was still refueling.

"The gentleman has no luggage?" the customs agent asked.

"No!" Collins said anxiously. "It's already been checked. Can't you see this is official business? We're in a hurry. So if you'll just step aside and let him get on his plane." Collins raised the chain and flashed his diplomatic passport. The customs man gave him a dirty look, but he inched aside.

The two meatballs pushed Thomson through the gate. He moved mechanically. His mind was buried in old files, thumbing through photos of Von Braun and the other rocket scientists at Peenemunde. Something was wrong. Every time he conjured up images of them, they were standing in the bright sunshine: proud, robust men, posing in front of a launching pad, windblown and smiling, with the sandy beaches of the North Sea spread behind them. That scene with Von Braun must have been mandatory, like a class picture, or a souvenir. They had to pose out there with him, standing in front of one of their shiny new toys.

But there was no picture like that on Fengler's wall. Not one. No rockets. No Von Braun. No proud, smiling faces on a sandy beach. Fengler's group looked like a bunch of nervous gnomes. They stood on the steps of that heavy brick building as if they'd been ordered there, hiding behind each other, afraid and unsure about the whole thing.

No! No matter how hard Thomson jammed the pieces together, they didn't fit Kilbride's picture, and he knew it.

Collins nudged his shoulder. "Come on!" he said, anxious to get him on the plane.

The bastard sure was in a hurry, Thomson thought, as Collins pushed him through the gate. "Sorry, old man," Boy Wonder said with a real note of sympathy. "But you know how it goes. The chief was right. You could have avoided all this trouble if you'd just done what he said."

"Yeah, you're right, Collins," Thomson replied as seriously as he could. "Maybe I'll remember next time."

Thomson stepped onto the tarmac, his hands thrust deep into his coat pockets, hunched over against the hot, gritty wind. But he couldn't get that photograph out of his head. What could they have been doing in Hechingen?

With every step he took, the alarm bells rang louder and louder, like fire bells that wouldn't quit until he had answered their call. They just rang louder and louder, until he stopped walking and stood on the runway, looking up at the airplane.

Thomson slowly turned and looked back at Collins and the two meatballs. None of the pieces fitted. None of them. And Kilbride was too stupid to ever understand. Thomson had the sick feeling he never would either, until it was too late.

So he took his hand out of his jacket, stood erect, and gave Collins a classic one-fingered salute, then turned and began running down the tarmac, running as fast as he could.

14

ILSA FENGLER WAS too weary to continue arguing with him. He was her father, but that was no longer enough. Over the years he had lost her, piece by lonely piece, until there was nothing left for him to grab onto. More sad than angry, she turned away and stared out the kitchen window at the pot of wilted geraniums sitting on the ledge.

"No," she said quietly, slowly shaking her head. "The American, Thomson, didn't harm me, Papa. He wouldn't have done that. I know he wouldn't."

"What would you know of men like that?" he scoffed, trying to make her feel like a child again.

"Papa, I know. That's all. I just know." She looked back over her shoulder and glared at him. "He was far less dangerous than Grüber, or the rest of those animals he brought with him."

She knew he could never deal with the truth. He had insulated himself from it for too many long years. Instead, he turned his eyes away and resumed his incessant pacing across the kitchen floor, pulling his handkerchief from his pocket and wiping it across his brow.

"This heat," he mumbled.

That wasn't the reason he was sweating. They both knew it. And wiping his brow wouldn't help. Neither would ignoring her words, but he kept doing them both anyway. She knew him better than he could ever know her. Or at least she used to. Now? She wasn't sure.

"What did the American want?" he asked quietly, but insistently. "Why did he come here? Why to you, Ilsa? Why did he come here and take you with him, you of all people? Surely you know how that must look."

"Look? To whom? To you?"

"Of course not to me, Ilsa. To..."

"To Grüber then? Well, I answered his questions last night, Papa. I answered them until the sun came up. And I don't care how anything looks to him anymore. Do you? Do you really care?" Her eyes studied his face, and what she saw made her sick. "Is that what this is all about? Did Grüber tell you to keep after me? To keep asking? Or don't you believe me either?"

"Of course I believe you, Ilsa." He fidgeted and tried to smile, but he refused to look at her. "*Gott*, Ilsa. How could you leave the compound with him? He might have killed you. Or worse! I couldn't stand that." His hands were trembling and she saw that his eyes were filled with terror. "Not after what happened to your mother. You are all I—"

"Father, stop it! That won't work anymore." She had lost her temper and shouted at him. He cringed like a small child after a scolding. That should have made her feel worse, but it didn't. Those feelings had been dead too long and she despised him for trying to use them to dominate her. But she knew it was Grüber and General Hoess speaking, not her father. He had died in the air raid with her mother. The shell of a man standing in front of her deserved her pity, but not her love or her hate.

She turned back to the window and leaned heavily against the old porcelain sink. "I am twenty-nine years old, Papa. Stop treating me like a child of twelve."

"Ilsa, you are all I have left," he whispered. "The American is a dangerous spy. Don't you understand? He came here to sabotage my work—to kill me if he got the chance. And he isn't the first. They've sent others, and they'll send more after him. They won't leave us alone. Don't you see how dangerous that makes him?"

"He might be many things, Papa, but he isn't dangerous. He was clever and infuriating, but he would never harm me."

"He is a murderer! The police want him for murder!"

"No, Papa," she answered quietly. "I've never been more certain of anything in my life. It would have been a simple enough thing, if he had wanted to. But he didn't. And if he had wanted to harm you, all he had to do was wait here in the house until you returned. But he didn't do that, did he?"

She remembered how silly she must have seemed to him, and how gullible. "Yes, he was clever and very infuriating, Papa," she said with a bittersweet smile, recalling the excitement of that hour and the anguish that followed. "Thomson did exactly what he said he would, didn't he? He left the car at the embassy and the gun under the front seat." She pointed at the old Luger lying on the dusty kitchen table. "Doesn't that tell you anything?" she asked, waiting until he finally looked at it.

"Of course I was scared when I found him in the house," she went on. "I was terrified. But I wasn't the one who let him in. Where were all your precious guards? Isn't that why Grüber is here? Isn't he supposed to protect us? So who is he to accuse me?"

Fengler didn't reply. He kept staring at the old gun until he mumbled again, "I detest those things." He slowly reached out and picked up the Luger, letting it dangle from his fingers as if it were a dead rat. Then he opened the kitchen cabinet and placed it on the top shelf. "You are right, Ilsa. I shall file a protest with General Hoess about this entire situation when he arrives. After that intruder last week, and now this . . . it is all Grüber's fault!"

Ilsa watched him, trying to remember what he had once been like. But those memories were old and faded now. Maybe it was the times. Maybe it was her. Maybe she was the one who had changed, not him. Maybe she had just grown up and looked at things differently now.

She stared out the window at the geraniums again, pulling the pot closer, moving it into the shade. She filled a small pitcher with water and poured it into the flowerpot, knowing it wouldn't help, not for long. The water disappeared into the parched earth. Like everything else out here, the sand and hot desert wind sucked the life from whatever they touched, leaving nothing but crumbling stone monuments and desiccated mummies.

"I can't take it anymore, Papa." She sighed, gazing into the empty desert. There was nothing but heat, swarms of angry flies, and a gritty coating of sand on everything. She'd had enough, enough for a lifetime. Why couldn't he understand?

But his voice droned on, shrinking to a pathetic whine. He wrung his hands and stepped closer to her. "Ilsa, you must realize how dangerous things are right now, how critical. An incident like this . . . You know how it could look if . . . if you, of all people, were suspected of helping a foreign agent. . . ."

"Papa, I want to go home," she stated quietly, completely ignoring his words as she turned to face him.

If he heard her at all, he didn't react. But she knew he had heard. And she knew he was blocking it out. He did that so frequently now. If he didn't acknowledge it, then it didn't happen. "Did you hear me, Papa?" She grew insistent. "I said I want to go home."

"Home?" he finally answered, sounding confused, as if he didn't understand. "You mean . . . to Germany? But we cannot go there. My . . . my work . . . It isn't finished. . . ."

"I've never complained before. You know that." She must make him stop his rambling if she was ever to make him understand. "I've always followed you, wherever you went—Spain, South Africa, Argentina—even here. But it never changes, does it? It's always the same. We go from one backward military outpost to another, don't we? Why, Papa? Why? What has it gotten you? What has it gotten us? And where will we go next? There will be a next, won't there? And another one after that? Until I too am old and gray. So tell me why, Papa. I have a right to know that much. At least tell me why."

"Ilsa, it is . . . my job. It is research, you know that." He dismissed her words with an impatient wave of his hand.

"Papa, I am not a stupid child. Stop treating me as if I were one. I've never asked what you are doing, or why, but open your eyes. Look at the kind of people you are working for—Hoess, Grüber, and all the rest of them."

"I do not work for them," he bristled.

"Oh, yes you do, Papa. You think you're above all that, but you aren't. You're lying to yourself."

His eyes flashed, but he didn't reply.

"I'm frightened, Papa. It was never like this before. I have eyes. I can see the guards and the tanks, and I've talked to the others. You aren't doing research. That isn't why they brought you here. I've seen the rockets that Höchengler and his people are making. And I know what you are making. What do you think the Egyptians are going to do with it? What do you think they are going to do with your 'research' when you are finished . . . ? So please take me home,'' she pleaded. ''Take me home now, before it's too late.''

''Home? To Germany?'' he scoffed, his voice becoming more agitated as it rose in pitch. ''We are nothing there. Nothing. Do you want me to go back to become . . . some lab assistant, to do all the work, and see others take all the credit, as they did during the war? Never! I was right, and they were the ones who were wrong. No, Ilsa. You ask too much.''

He had that faraway look in his eyes again, and she knew it was useless to keep arguing.

But he had only begun. ''If they had listened to me back in 1943, things would be far different today, wouldn't they?'' He began pacing the kitchen floor again, faster and faster. ''And I would be Germany's leading atomic physicist. Me! Do you think I like this place?'' His hand swept around the room. ''Working year after year in pestholes like this? I hate them more than you can ever imagine, Ilsa. But I will never go back, not until my work is recognized, not until they drop to their knees and beg me to come back.''

''Papa,'' she moaned, looking up at the ceiling and trying to fight back the tears, ''the war is over. It was over long ago. Can't you see that? How can any of it matter now, if it ever did? What did it accomplish? Men like Grüber almost destroyed Germany. But Germany has risen from the ashes, and Germany has forgotten. Isn't it time we forget, too?''

''Forget? Forget?'' He stared at her, his mouth hanging open as if he could not comprehend the word. ''Is that what you think we should do? Forget?''

He grabbed her arm. His hands were trembling and his face was livid. He had never touched her like this before and she had never seen such a look in his eyes. It terrified her.

''What could you possibly know, Ilsa? Your generation could never know what it was like to be a German in the twenties. We were disgraced, shattered, and beyond hope. The Communists were rioting in the streets and a bushel basket of marks couldn't buy you a loaf of bread.''

He paused, slowly releasing his grip on her arm. But he couldn't release the idea, which gave his eyes a strange glow. ''The shame of it, Ilsa! Then the pride. Yes, the pride: in a people, a nation, and in a man. He gave us something to be proud of. He saved Germany. You hear none of that today. No, they never talk of that, only of the destruction they blame on him. But none of it is true. They lied and they deserved what they got!''

He began to pace again, talking loudly, more to himself than to her. ''You are right, Ilsa. None of it matters. Not anymore. The war is over. All that matters now is my work. That is all that ever mattered. But if they had only listened to me—Göring, Himmler, and the rest of those cretins who surrounded him—things would be different today. There were too many small minds crowding in around him by then. They corrupted him and sapped him of his strength.''

He stopped pacing and faced her, standing upright as she hadn't seen him do in years. His voice was loud and firm as he declared, ''So they deserved what they got. All of them! But go home? Never! Not now. This is my last chance, Ilsa. My last chance. It took me fifteen years to get this close, and I will never have this chance again. No. This time I will show them I was right. Thursday at noon. That is when I will show the whole world I was right!''

She stared at him and saw something in his eyes she had never seen before. It made her shrink back in fear.

15

WHY NOT? Thomson laughed as he raced along the rear wall of the passenger terminal, his feet pounding on the hot tarmac. The old legs might not be good for distance, but they could still give 'em hell in the dash.

Collins and the two meatballs fought their way past the customs agent, but Thomson had a good lead on them. He found the exit door to another passenger lounge, yanked it open, and began walking briskly through the main concourse. Time wasn't on his side. Collins and the meatballs were half his age. He couldn't outrun them for long. He couldn't hide either, not here anyway. But he couldn't quit. His only hope was to get away from the airport as fast as he could.

Outside the main entrance, a long line of cabs sat waiting under the harsh midmorning sun. The drivers were doing what bored cab drivers do everywhere, standing in small groups, smoking, arguing sports and politics. Others sat inside their cars, reading the morning paper or taking a nap. Thomson ran to the car at the far end of the line, opened the rear door, and jumped inside.

"Back to Cairo," he told the startled driver. "Now!"

As the other cabbies howled in protest, Thomson threw a twenty-dollar bill into the driver's lap, squelching any objections he might be harboring. The man grinned and tromped on the accelerator. As the cab roared away from the curb, he raised his arm and saluted the others in an obscene gesture. Seconds later they were on the main highway, merging into the heavy traffic.

Thomson looked through the rear window but saw nothing, not yet. He leaned back and closed his eyes, still trying to catch his breath. Collins was an idiot. Damned Harvard amateurs. And then he laughed to himself.

But the little victory was like wetting your dark pants on a cold day. It gave you a brief warm glow, until the chill of reality set in. What the hell was he doing? Where was he going? One man, alone, in a foreign city? It was crazy to run. Then again, it was probably more crazy to let them pack him on an airplane. That would have been the end—not just of his career, but of him and whatever thin thread of self-respect he still held onto. After all, wasn't he the one who had begged to be back in the game? Begged for one more chance? Well, he had gotten it, in spades.

"Hurry up," he told the cabbie. They were halfway to the city, but the morning traffic was getting as thick and slow as cooling fudge. He looked back again and saw a big, powerful American sedan weaving in and out of traffic, trying to catch up. Collins must really be desperate if he was trying to beat the natives at their own game. And remembering Kilbride's words, he knew Collins was desperate.

Before they reached the city, Collins had cut the gap between them in half. With the limo's horsepower, it was only a matter of time before he closed it completely. Thomson leaned forward and tapped the cabbie on the shoulder. "See that car?" He flashed a conspiratorial smile at the sedan. "My girlfriend's brothers. Understand? Three of them, and big," he said, drawing his thumb across his throat. "Take the side streets and lose them. Okay?"

The driver answered with a cackling laugh. At the next narrow sidestreet, he spun the wheel. The small cab heeled over and Thomson braced himself, grabbing the door handle for dear life. The cab sped on into the Old Quarter. It had once been ringed by sixty massive stone gates, but only three still survived. Egyptian cab drivers had probably knocked down the other fifty-seven, Thomson told himself. Inciting one to reckless driving was redundant—and suicidal.

The cab darted through the teeming, narrow streets, rounding corner after corner, using the road or sidewalk interchangeably and sending pedestrians scrambling for the sanctuary of the nearest doorway. Collins might try to keep up, but he had the wrong car and the wrong genes for the job.

Thomson had begun to think they had made it when the cab made a sharp turn and the driver suddenly hit the brakes. The car skidded to a halt, throwing Thomson onto the floor. He quickly pulled himself up to his knees and looked through the front windshield. They'd reached the end of the line. Directly in front of them, only inches from the bumper, sat an old delivery van, completely blocking the street.

The cabbie looked back and shrugged. This would have to do, Thomson thought. He pulled out another twenty and dropped it on the front seat. "Good try," he said with a smile, and jumped out. He squeezed around the side of the delivery van and ran up the street toward the next corner, hoping he could disappear before Collins caught up.

Just as he reached the corner, the snout of the big American sedan swung into view at the other end of the street. Thomson didn't have to see the rest. Collins was driving too fast. Over the sounds of his racing feet and heavy breathing, Thomson heard the screech of brakes, the sharp crunch of metal, and the sound of breaking glass. That would slow them down a stride or two, he told himself, and then broke into a grin.

The next few minutes were critical. Collins was Mr. Safe. He'd play it by the book and order one meatball to stay with the car. That would cut the odds to two-to-one, but now Thomson had a whole city to play in, not just an airport terminal. Time and distance were on his side now. And he could become a very tiny needle in this stinking haystack if he had to.

He set a fast pace, knowing he couldn't hold it for long. After only a few blocks, he was dripping with sweat and was badly winded. The air in the narrow streets of the old city was hot and foul, as if it had lain there unflushed for decades. He ran another block and had to stop. Collapsing in the shade of an old brick wall, he dug a fist into his side, trying to stave off the sharp cramp starting in his gut. A cramp! That was all he needed. He couldn't stop, not yet. He got to his feet and forced his unwilling body on, breaking into a slow, painful jog. Just one more street, he told himself, then another, until he could go no farther.

He stumbled into an alley, desperate for a refuge. Halfway down the alley, he found a low, shadowy archway. It would have to do. He stumbled inside and fell against the far wall, panting and wheezing, trying not to throw up. It felt so good to stop, to escape the heat, to rest. Nice. And it was so dark and cool he almost forgot the stench.

Think! he ordered his brain. The best way to block the pain was to put his mind to work. So think! What were his options? His resources? Liabilities? Opportunities? Catalog and analyze. Go down the punch list, just like the bastards had taught you.

Where could he go? The apartment was out. So was the embassy and what was left of his friends. Those would be tops on their list. But Kilbride wouldn't dare call the cops.

No, he had to handle this strictly in-house. So how fast could he pull in enough men to cover all the bases? Six, maybe eight hours? At least. And by then, it would be dark. If he could keep away from them until sunset, he could move again, and the darkness would give him another twelve-hour lease on life.

Resources? That was a joke. He emptied his pockets onto the dirt. Keys and wallet. But no passport. And no gun, of course. Money? He pawed through the small wad and counted the bills. In Egyptian pounds and U.S. green, maybe he had seventy-five dollars and change. That wouldn't last long, or get him far, not on the run. One day, two at the most. Two days—doing what?

Thomson ran his hand through his hair in desperation as he closed his eyes. It had been stupid to run away and even pretend he could beat them. Damn! They had him trapped like a rat in a corner. The trap was big, with lots of room to run around in circles, but sooner or later they'd drop a net on him.

Thomson knew he'd broken the First Commandment. He'd gone lone wolf. That was a mortal sin, and all the Hail Marys in Christendom wouldn't get him absolution. By tomorrow, they'd have every snitch and free-lance gun in Cairo looking for him, dead or alive. And right now, Kilbride was probably pushing for dead.

He was flexing his knees and considering pushing on when he heard footsteps enter the alley from the left. He pressed his body against the wall and froze, listening to the loud, confident strides. Maybe it was some *fella* out for a stroll. Please pass by, he prayed. But they didn't. The footsteps slowed down and stopped, just beyond Thomson's line of vision. Then he heard a second set of footsteps enter the alley from the right.

The new ones sounded slower and more uneven, awkward and out of sync, accompanied by the crisp *click-click* of a steel-tipped cane. As they came closer, the awkward sound became the distinct, scratchy shuffle of a foot being dragged across the old bricks of the alley.

Thomson was trapped and as good as blind, able to see only a small patch of rough red-brick wall on the other side of the alley. He waited, barely breathing, until he heard a voice. It was the first man, speaking softly in Egyptian. He heard footsteps as the second man approached the archway and his shadow fell across the bright patch of sunlight. Thomson held his breath as a brightly polished shoe came into view, followed by the white cuff of a well-tailored linen suit.

The cane rapped on the side of the stone doorway.

"Mr. Thomson, you may come out now," the man said in an amused voice. "Your friends are blocks away by now, so come out of your hole before I send Sergeant Sayyid in to get you."

It was Saleh. But why?

16

THEY DROVE TO THE CENTRAL police station in silence, sitting side by side in the rear seat of the police cruiser. Saleh offered no explanation and Thomson wouldn't give him the satisfaction of asking for one.

Sayyid parked in a rear lot. Thomson was hustled through a service door and up a dim flight of stairs. Saleh led the way, limping painfully, with the big sergeant playing caboose. Thomson walked along, curious as to why they were sneaking into the building. Why didn't Saleh just book him and send him straight to the lockup?

Saleh's office on the third floor was furnished in old bureaucrat with a cheap rolltop desk, three ancient armchairs, and badly worn linoleum on the floor. They seemed to contrast so sharply with the man, Thomson thought. But maybe he wanted it that way, grim and Spartan, so he'd never feel the temptation to be comfortable here.

The Egyptian pointed to one of the armchairs. Like any good prisoner, Thomson took his seat and kept his mouth shut, watching Saleh slowly lower himself into the swivel chair behind his desk. Saleh motioned toward Sayyid, who was watching intently from the doorway, "You may leave us, Sergeant. This man is not going anywhere, are you, Mr. Thomson?"

Saleh seemed to be enjoying himself. He looked across the desk at Thomson and studied him closely as he lit another of his strong Turkish cigarettes. "I consider myself a good judge of men, Mr. Thomson," he finally said. "But you are a complete mystery to me. Two nights ago, when we found your shoe lying in the street, it appeared you had finally gotten what you deserved. No such luck. You keep popping up, again and again, like a jack-in-the-box. So you must excuse my confusion. Why didn't you get on that airplane? They had us completely fooled. You would have escaped me, if you hadn't run away. So tell me why? Can't you bear the thought of leaving this pleasant country, Mr. Thomson?"

"It would have been a shame, wouldn't it?" He smiled.

"Indeed." Saleh smiled back. "Think of the questions you would have left behind. The poor things would have been orphans, left to wander around Cairo without the slightest hope of an answer. So what am I to do with you? Arrest you for murder? Espionage, perhaps? I suppose there is always breaking and entering, and kidnapping, but they seem so plebeian for a master criminal like you."

"No doubt." Thomson nodded.

Saleh leaned forward, his smile fading. "Tell me why you ran away, Thomson? I can appreciate the CIA's desperation in wanting you out of Egypt, but why did you disobey them?"

"Kilbride wanted me out. The Agency had nothing to do with it."

Saleh shook his head. "A CIA plot, with a CIA man in the middle of it, and the CIA is not involved? You insult me."

"There is no CIA plot. You've got CIA on the brain, Saleh," Thomson answered in a tired voice.

"There is always a CIA plot, Mr. Thomson!" The policeman's hard eyes flashed. "I admit it is an obsession of mine, but your Agency never tires of meddling with little people like us. This time, they were sloppy. I caught you, and I shall hang you around their necks before I am finished. So why didn't you escape when you had the chance?''

"I had my reasons," he answered with a shrug. "And you're wrong. The CIA has nothing to do with this. Neither do I. In fact, I don't know what's going on, and it's obvious you don't either. So let me ask you a question for a change. Do you people really want another war? With the Israelis?''

Saleh frowned, considering the question. "No. Not that we don't hate them, but we've bled enough for other people's causes.'' He tapped his thigh. "It is time we put our energies into building a nation."

"All right," Thomson ventured, "then what's going on out at Heliopolis? At that old army base?''

"Why don't you tell me? You thought it was so important, you broke in and tried to kidnap that woman.''

"It's a secret research center, staffed by Nazi scientists.''

"Mr. Thomson''—Saleh shook his head derisively—"I expected better. Nazi scientists? No one cares about that anymore. During your world war, many of us preferred the other side. Not that we liked Hitler, but anyone who fought the British was a friend of ours.''

"Agreed." Thomson waved the point aside. "But I'm talking about today. Somebody's doing something out there and a lot of people are scared to death about it.''

"Good! They should be. But even if your story is true, what they are doing or not doing out there is none of your damned business!''

"Would a secret airplane factory surprise you?''

Saleh cocked his head and considered the point. "No, that wouldn't surprise me. It wouldn't interest me, either.

Neither would your story about German scientists. If that is the best you can come up with, I have wasted a good deal of my valuable time on you for nothing."

"Well, it isn't an airplane factory," Thomson answered, carefully studying Saleh's face for a reaction. "That's the cover story they're using, and it's not a very good one. Would a secret rocket base surprise you?"

Saleh raised his eyebrows and paused. "Yes. That would surprise me, and pleasantly so I might add."

"Well, maybe I'm crazy, but I don't think that's the whole story either. The minute I began poking around, a lot of people got real nervous. So I think there's more going on out there than that."

"For instance?"

"I don't know. But the best way to keep a big secret is to wrap it inside a bunch of little ones."

"Naturally, you think that's why your friend Yussuf met his early demise?"

"Him, an Israeli agent named Landau, that goon you found lying in the street, and maybe a couple more besides them."

"All of them—killed by a group of gray-haired head-hunting German rocket scientists?"

"No. Your people did the killing."

"This story is wearing thin, Mr. Thomson. If Yussuf and the rest of them were foreign spies, why shouldn't they pay with their lives? What's wrong with that? And why should I care?"

"Because it doesn't make sense. There's got to be more to it, and that's the dangerous part, the part they're willing to kill for to keep secret."

Saleh stared at Thomson, but the American's eyes never wavered.

"Look." Thomson edged closer, trying to explain. "Someone caught Yussuf and shut him up for keeps, right? Assume for the moment it wasn't us."

"Why should I?"

"Humor me. Assume Yussuf really was a spy. If we caught him, or the Israelis, or even the KGB, wouldn't we want to keep him alive? Long enough to make him tell us everything? Think about it. Give me one reason why we'd want him dead. And dead like that? Come on, Captain. It's not our style."

Saleh let him continue.

"Whoever caught him didn't want a damned thing, except his life. It was an execution, an example to others, and by some real fanatics. For my money, that leaves the Germans, or your own State Security."

"State Security? That is preposterous!"

"No it isn't. We would have bought his pictures. So would have the Israelis or the KGB. No pro kills a good snitch. It's bad manners, especially if you might want something from him in the future. Use your head. Who would want to shut him up? And if this whole thing's on the up-and-up, why didn't State Security push you aside a long time ago? We all know who I am. Why did they want to keep it a simple police matter? Answer that one."

He watched Saleh's face as the words sank in. Thomson had him stumped.

"But I got a better one. This isn't wartime. Doesn't the army notify the police about major troop movements?"

"Of course. There are many things to consider. Traffic, missing persons . . ."

"What if somebody moved a crack armored regiment, maybe even two, from the Delta. Wouldn't they tell you, before they moved them to Cairo and hid them in the desert not fifteen miles from here?"

"You're insane—"

"That's what I thought!" Thomson sat back and smiled. "You don't know a damned thing about them, do you? Well, they're here, Captain. I saw them. There's at least a full armored regiment hidden under camouflage nets at that base, and I'll bet there's a second one not far away."

"You are lying." Saleh didn't believe a word of it. "I don't know why. But I have no doubt you are."

"Am I? Why would I make up a story that you could check out with a couple of phone calls? Am I that dumb? So I'm telling you those tanks are out there. T-34s. I saw them, and here are the markings I saw on one of their jeeps." He grabbed a pad of paper and a pencil from the desk and began to sketch. "This may not be perfect, but it's close enough," he said as he spun the pad toward Saleh.

The Egyptian's eyes flashed as he looked down at the paper.

"It does mean something, doesn't it? What unit is it? The Third Armored Regiment, or the Fourth? Whatever; they're supposed to be up in the Delta, aren't they? And you know as well as I that there are only two things you need that much muscle for: to start a war, or to overthrow a government."

"That is preposterous!"

"Prove it! Prove I'm lying. I've bet my life on those tanks, so you prove I'm wrong."

"To satisfy you?"

"No, to satisfy yourself."

Saleh glared at Thomson, then picked up the phone. "Police headquarters in Alexandria. I want Sergeant Khatib, in the inspector's office. Put it through immediately!" Then he sat back and waited, trying to maintain his confident facade, but not as successfully as he would have liked.

Ten interminable minutes later, the phone rang. Saleh yanked it from the cradle and forced a broad smile. "Khatib! You old rascal. Saleh here... *Aywa, aywa.* Yes, yes. Too long, I know... No, I'm calling on business. Perhaps you can save me some time. We had a murder last night. The unfortunate victim was wearing army fatigues and tanker boots, but the thieves got away with his wallet. You know what it's like to ask the army... Yes. But I heard some armored units from the Delta came down here for maneuvers."

Saleh picked up the pad and stared at Thomson's crude sketch. "Really?... What about the Fourth Armored?... Of course you ought to know. That is why I called.... They're not? What about the Third Armored, then?... You are sure about that?... You saw General al-Baquri yourself. This morning," Saleh said, his confidence returning. "No, do not bother. I shall call them myself, Khatib.... Yes, *shokran*, old friend. Thank you. You have been a big help. *Saaida*. Good-bye."

Saleh slowly placed the receiver in its cradle and stared across at Thomson, his eyes growing hard and cold.

"Look, Captain, just because your friend doesn't know they've gone doesn't mean they're still there," the American insisted.

"He saw al-Baquri this morning," Saleh insisted.

"Call their headquarters. Ask!"

Saleh drummed his fingers on the desk, then picked up the receiver and asked for the headquarters of the Fourth Armored Regiment. They stared at each other without speaking as the connection was made. Saleh spoke first, but spent most of the time listening. "Then try the Third Armored! Tell them it is a police emergency, man."

Saleh listened impatiently, his forehead twisting into a worried frown as the minutes passed. Finally he said, "No, that is all. I shall try again later."

He seemed lost in his own thoughts. "They could not get through," he said quietly. "A problem with the phone lines. No one has been able to get through for two days. With our phone system, that is hardly remarkable," he joked, but even he wasn't laughing.

"Both regiments? At the same time?"

Saleh had no answer.

"I want two favors from you, Captain. First, find out what's really going on at Heliopolis. Find out, but be damned careful who you ask."

"Why?"

"Because people get killed whenever that place is mentioned in the wrong circles."

"And your other little . . . 'favor'?"

"Let me go."

"What?" Saleh sounded both surprised and amused. "Now I know you are insane, Mr. Thomson! Just because some phone lines in Alexandria are out of order, I am supposed to release the prime suspect in two murder cases? How big a fool do you take me for?"

"You asked me why I didn't get on that airplane, didn't you? Now you know why. Something stinks around here. You knew it when you found Yussuf's body. But you'll never find out by yourself."

"You do not know me very well."

"Oh, you'll try, I'll give you that much. But you're a company man. You'll let somebody con you into believing their story, but it won't be true. They'll say you've got nothing to worry about, but they're wrong. You've got plenty to worry about—like Yussuf did, and Landau, and me, and now you. You're part of the daisy chain now.

They'll be watching every move you make, and they'll kill
you if they suspect you know. That's why we need each
other. You're on the inside. If you're real careful, you might
get through to the right people while I chip away from the
outside. Working from opposite ends we might be able to
stop them before it's too late. Besides, what have you got
to lose? The worst thing that can happen is I get myself
killed, right?''

"No, the worst thing is you won't. But I shall deny myself that little pleasure and keep you right here, where you
can't bother anyone.''

Saleh pressed the buzzer on his desk and Sayyid stepped
quickly into the room. Obviously he'd been waiting, hoping he'd be needed even sooner. "Lock him up, Sayyid.
Quietly and with no fanfare. Put him in the isolation cell
and I want no records kept. Mr. Thomson doesn't exist, not
until I decide he does.''

Thomson shook his head, wanting to argue but knowing
it was useless. Slowly, he rose to his feet. "You're making
a big mistake. I just hope you learn how big before it's too
late.''

"You have an incredible imagination, Mr. Thomson.
Incredible! Take him away.''

Sayyid gripped the American's arm and pushed him into
the hallway. Thomson turned toward the main staircase,
but Sayyid steered him the other way, toward the back stairs
they had come up. Sayyid opened the fire door and motioned for the American to go first.

Thomson paused and looked down the dim stairwell.
Any thoughts he might be harboring about outrunning the
hulking sergeant evaporated as Sayyid laid a huge paw on
his shoulder. He gave Thomson a gentle push, not enough
to make him tumble head first down the stairs, but enough
to let him know he could, anytime he wanted to.

Sayyid was careful. He stayed off to one side, one stair back, his hand never leaving the American's shoulder. Thomson knew he had to do something. If he let them lock him up, it would all be over. And after all he'd been through, he couldn't let them do that.

They walked down in silence. Thomson stopped on the first narrow landing and let loose a loud, uncontrollable sneeze. "Dust," he mumbled as he wiped his coat sleeve across his nose.

Sayyid didn't smile. Thomson felt the grip on his shoulder tighten as the sergeant looked down the steep flight of stairs. Thomson didn't like the new expression on the big man's face. Sayyid shoved him again, and this time it wasn't for show. It was for real.

Thomson would have lost his balance and fallen down the stairs if it hadn't been for another monstrous sneeze that bent him over at the waist, just as Sayyid pushed forward and his fingers slipped off Thomson's shoulder. Suddenly, it was Sayyid who lost his balance. For a split second, he tottered on the edge of the stair, and that was all the opening Thomson needed. He grabbed Sayyid's shirt sleeve and pulled.

Like a runaway dump truck on a steep grade, nothing was going to stop the big man's momentum now. He tried to grab Thomson's arm, but the American knocked his hand away. Sayyid's expression turned from shock to terror as he found himself airborne, tumbling down a flight of stairs, arms and legs flailing wildly.

Fortunately, the police headquarters was made of huge quarry stones and thick timbers. Thomson cringed as he watched the mountain of angry muscle smack head-first onto the landing fifteen feet below. Sayyid bounced once and came to rest in a crumpled heap against the wall at the foot of the stairs. He was out cold.

Thomson took the rest of the stairs two at a time, and bent over to check Sayyid's pulse when he got to the bottom. He was alive, but he wouldn't forget his trip for a long time. Serves him right, Thomson thought. But why had Sayyid tried to push Thomson down the stairs? It didn't make any sense. Was it Saleh's idea? Had he planned this little 'accident' all along? Or had Sayyid thought it up on his own?

Thomson didn't know. And for the moment at least, he didn't care. He searched through the sergeant's pockets, taking the man's revolver, his money, and his keys. To make the job complete, he pulled out Sayyid's handcuffs and snapped one ring around Sayyid's wrist and the other around his ankle. That should hold him for a while. Then he ran for the back door, hoping he'd never meet the sergeant in another dark stairwell again—or anywhere else for that matter.

17

SALEH REMEMBERED it as if it were yesterday.

Could twenty-five years have passed since they were boys playing on that muddy riverbank near their village? They were like brothers: Hassan Saleh, Ali Rashid, and Gamal Nasser. They went everywhere and did everything together. Perhaps it was their youth, or the simpler era they grew up in, or the narrow world of experiences they shared, but it seemed that the three of them had but one dream and one destiny. It was all so clear back then, before the hot forge of time had bent and twisted even the hardest steel.

There had always been something different about Gamal. He wasn't the oldest, or the smartest or most serious, either. Ali Rashid bested him on those counts. That didn't matter. Gamal was their leader. No votes were ever taken and they never argued the point. They knew it instinctively, as Egypt itself would one day know. That was the effect Gamal Abdel Nasser had on people.

Their small village could never hold their ambitions. Each of them joined the army when he came of age, because it was the surest and quickest path out of the cane fields. To Ali Rashid, the army was the means to a far more important end. He was always the serious one—humorless, as only a man who talked back to God could be. He was consumed by the burning, blinding passion only reli-

gion could inflict on a man, and only a holy war could
quench.

Gamal Nasser had a burning cause as well, but his was
more secular and infinitely more rational. He was the politician. He would put on the uniform, until the time came
for even greater responsibilities.

Only Hassan Saleh joined the army for itself. He took to
the ritual and discipline with the pleasure and grace of a
man born to it. To him there was no higher calling. So much
greater the tragedy. The career he loved ended on the sands
of the Sinai in 1956 when an Israeli artillery shell nearly cost
him a leg, and his sanity.

Months later, an old friend visited him in the hospital.
He ordered Hassan to accept a position with the civilian
police, arguing that Egypt could not be denied his talents.
Hassan preferred to die, but he obeyed. How could one refuse an order from one's president and closest friend?

Hassan thought he'd lost everything, but he found much
more. He found a faith, every bit as real and burning as the
one that drove Ali Rashid. Hassan Saleh's faith was Egypt
and Gamal Abdel Nasser. To Hassán, the two had become
one, and Detective Captain Hassan Saleh was their high
priest and their protector.

Nasser was in the eye of the hurricane, the heart and soul
of the revolution he had unleashed. As the furies swirled,
tugging and pulling at him, he stood up to them like a block
of granite. Forty-two years old, he was at the height of his
power and abilities. With a hawklike face, rich olive skin,
and crinkly black hair, he looked every inch an Arab, but
he was unusually tall, thick-chested, and broad-shouldered.
Nasser didn't need his physical size to dominate other men.
He did it with his inner strength and the sheer force of his
will.

Those impressions hung on Hassan Saleh like heavy anchor chains as the insignificant police captain from Cairo went to visit the president of Egypt at his suburban home in Mansheet el-Bakr, outside the city.

The furnishings of Gamal's office were as meager as Saleh expected them to be. Nasser could perform on the world's grand stage with more pomp and ceremony than anyone, but the boy from the small village of Beni Murr who lived inside was far different. He was a quiet, introspective man. All he ever needed was a small desk, an old stiff-backed couch, a few chairs, a bowl of oranges, and a pitcher of lemonade. And his books. The man was an insatiable reader, and he was never beyond reach of his books.

He greeted Saleh with the genuine warmth of a brother, throwing his arm around Saleh's shoulder and bidding his old friend to sit beside him on the couch.

"The leg?" Gamal asked, focusing those large, pale-brown eyes on his friend's face. "It is better, I pray?"

"It is still there." Saleh shrugged. "Who can complain?"

"I wish I could accept my setbacks that gracefully. But it has been too long, Hassan. We can curse our responsibilities, but it has been far too long, my old friend."

"They are what we sought, are they not? And I'm not ready to lay them down and go back to one of those brown mud houses. Are you?"

"You are right, of course." Nasser laughed. "Still, those were good days, and we have lost much since then. But enough of that depressing talk. What brings you out here, Hassan? It must be a matter of grave importance, or you would not have come."

"An inquiry, my President..."

"Ah! So the matter is official." Nasser leaned forward and listened intently.

"Yes. A murder, I am afraid. And a most confusing one. Every homicide case begins with an alien landscape. Everyone has a map, except the police. So my task is to blunder about in the fog, tripping over the loose ends and groping at little facts, until I find a path or two. Most lead me nowhere, but I must walk each one to its end, regardless."

"How fascinating."

"Or frustrating. But such is my task: to follow those paths." It pleased Saleh to see Gamal listening with that old intensity, his head thrust forward and his jaw jutting out. He looked as if he'd topple forward, but he didn't, and he missed nothing. To Saleh, the expression on Gamal's face melted the years.

"From the first day, this case has taken me in strange directions, my President. I kept rejecting them, confident they were false leads. But each new path would only take me right back to where the others left off."

"They keep bringing you here, to me?" Nasser grinned.

"No, but you may be able to help." Saleh paused to gauge the president's reactions. "You see, they keep pointing into the desert, to an old British army base near Heliopolis." For a moment, Saleh saw an amused flicker in Nasser's eyes. Then it was gone.

"That is why this investigation is so confusing. It is a murder case. Several murders, in fact. I would waste your valuable time for nothing less. My path keeps pointing out there toward Heliopolis, so I must ask. Do we have a secret base there? A base that has something to do with rockets?"

Nasser's face opened in a broad smile. "I shouldn't be surprised or angry. Even state secrets cannot stay hidden when my best detective picks away at them, one thread at a time. So I might as well tell you, Hassan, before you unravel the whole cloth and drop it at my feet. Rockets, you ask?" He smiled proudly. "Yes."

"That is all I need to know." He began to rise.

"No! Sit a moment longer. I want you to understand. Yes, we are developing a rocket. Not a very big one, but it will suffice. The final test is the day after tomorrow, on Thursday. I want you to join me, at Heliopolis, to watch the test as my guest."

"It would be a great honor, my President."

"Nothing you do not deserve, Hassan, and more."

"But tell me," Saleh asked. "Are we using Germans to build these rockets?"

"Yes." Nasser nodded. "We do not have the skills to undertake a project like that. So who could we use? The Americans? All they offered me was Hollywood movies, refrigerators, and their insufferable arrogance. The Russians? They are even worse. They give us nothing but inferior weapons and a monstrous debt. What a lovely choice. The Communists are atheists and the Christians are hypocrites. So I turned to the Germans. Whomever! I would ask the devil himself, if he could make a rocket for me."

"I do not question . . ." Hassan feared an offense.

"We are desperate, Hassan. Farouk bankrupted us. He destroyed everything that held this nation together: our values, the ruling class, even the army. So what is left? The religious fanatics are pawing on the right, and the Communists are lurking on the left. This office is all that holds Egypt together today." Nasser paused, the strain showing on his face. "We are all prisoners of the Great Saladin. His legend haunts this place: the great warrior general who will ride in and save his people from the heretics and the sinners. Well, those days are gone. Warrior generals and lowly colonels can't save anything. Only the people can. So I need those rockets. They will restore our pride. And that will buy me the precious time I need to build this nation. When a people lift their eyes to the skies, they will never drop them back to the dirt. Then, there is nothing they cannot accomplish.''

Hassan Saleh couldn't agree more.

"Our future lies with the poor nations like ourselves. Together, we can cut the chains that bind us to the West and the East. Think of the age we live in, Hassan." His voice grew excited. "All the world's great leaders come from the developing nations—Nehru, Mao, Sukarno, Nkrumah, Castro, Ho—all from poor nations like ours. And the one thing each of us needs more than anything else is time. War has been our folly. We cannot afford another one. It will tear Egypt apart. But these rockets will be a symbol. That is why I am building them. They will be the salvation of our people.''

The power of Nasser's presence radiated across the couch. Those brown eyes expressed six thousand years of glory and pain.

"And I need you, Hassan. You and Ali Rashid are the only men in Egypt I trust to guard my back. Believe me, there are thousands who would plunge a knife in it. Six years ago, I had to move against the Ikhwan, the Moslem Brotherhood. Those fanatics have been after my blood ever since. And last year, it was the Communists. My patience has worn thin from these constant conspiracies, and so has my luck. So plod on with your investigation, old friend.'' He laughed as he looked into Hassan's eyes. "Follow those paths of yours. I need time, and you must see that I have it.''

Saleh swallowed hard as the weight of the man's words fell on him. "I will try, my President," he whispered.

"I know you will," Nasser said as he rose to his feet. Saleh rose too, knowing the meeting was over as Nasser slowly walked him to the door.

"One more question," Saleh asked. "I assume you stationed some troops at Heliopolis? Are there any armored units out there? Perhaps on maneuvers?"

"Armor?" Nasser frowned. "At Heliopolis? No. Just security guards. Tanks would only attract attention. We wouldn't want that. But do not worry." He dismissed the question with a knowing smile. "It is in the best of hands. You will see on Thursday. Join me out there, at noon. I promise a few surprises even my best detective will not expect!"

AFTER THE DOOR CLOSED, Nasser stared at it, then chuckled. He walked back to his desk and picked up a folder from the tall stack demanding his immediate attention. He began to read, but couldn't concentrate. Finally, he laid the folder down and reached for the telephone.

"Ring Heliopolis for me," he ordered. "The commandant. Personally." He replayed Saleh's words in his head, remembering those days. The feelings were old and dim, but warm. Until the ringing of the telephone brought him back.

"Yes, yes," he began. "No, nothing important. But I had a special visitor this afternoon. He asked me a number of sharp questions about Heliopolis . . . and about the rockets. . . ." Nasser paused, smiling to himself, letting the panic build at the other end. "So it appears your crack security might be a bit frayed.

". . . Who? I thought you might ask. Well, I'll give you a small hint. He is a homicide detective from Cairo, and I believe you are acquainted.

"... Yes! He didn't know all that much, but he knew enough. He asked me about the rockets, and he asked me about the German scientists, too. Something to do with a murder case he is working on.

"... Well, what do you think I told him? I invited him out on Thursday. What would you have done?"

Then Nasser laughed, even louder. "Oh, by the way, we don't have any armored units out there, do we? ... I didn't think so. But it is good to know he got something wrong.... Yes! Of course I will be there on Thursday. Noon. You couldn't keep me away!"

COLONEL ALI RASHID placed the receiver back in its cradle. He sat ramrod straight, staring down at the telephone, as his forced smile cracked and dropped away, piece by piece. Slowly, Rashid raised his eyes and focused them on the man sitting on the other side of the desk.

"Nasser knows about the tanks?" Grüber dared to ask, trying to deflect the rage he knew was coming. "How?"

"A mutual friend. A lowly homicide detective named Saleh!" Rashid said in an angry whisper. "And the only man in Egypt I truly fear."

"Did Nasser believe your story?"

"He has no reason not to believe me, does he? And we must see it stays that way."

"Then the problem is contained."

"Do not underestimate him." The colonel's eyes grew worried. "Nasser is a past master of conspiracies. How do you think he got where he is? The devil himself hasn't led such a charmed life. Many have tried to get at him, but no one has succeeded. If he gets the slightest hint of it, hears the faintest whisper, we are doomed."

"Then we must deal with Thomson ... and this policeman."

The colonel's eyes flared at the German's open challenge. "The American is yours. But you will stay away from Hassan Saleh. Do you hear me!" Rashid demanded, his powerful eyes glaring at Grüber. "Saleh is my concern, not yours. Is that clear?"

Grüber wanted to argue, but making the point was enough. For now.

"Attend to your duties," the colonel hissed. "And remember, Grüber. Thursday at noon. We may live or die, but it will all be over on Thursday at noon."

Grüber's expression was openly arrogant. He'd finally found the man's weak spot and he would use it against him, at the right time.

"Nothing is to be left to chance." The colonel's voice cut through the thick, hot air inside the small room. "Nothing! And none of your people are to leave this compound. Especially Fengler and his daughter. The American talked to her, and that cursed man can be all too persuasive."

18

THOMSON KNEW HE WOULDN'T last long, not in daylight on the streets of a foreign city, where his white face stood out like a neon sign. So he ran, as fast as his legs could carry him, heading for the main business district, where he might stand a chance of blending in. Then what? Where could he run? Where could he hide, at least a few hours until dark, where they wouldn't look?

Twenty hot sweating minutes later, Thomson entered the deserted alley behind Jeremy's bar. He tried the back door, but it was locked tight, barred from the inside. "That damned Brit," he mumbled, banging on the old wooden boards until his knuckles hurt. Jeremy rarely left the place, except to eat and sleep, but there was no response from inside. Nothing. The iron-ribbed door blocked his way, mocking him, as everything in this city had done for the past three days. He was exhausted and drained, feeling more alone and hopeless than ever.

He turned his head and glanced anxiously up the alley, expecting to see a police cruiser any second. "Jeremy, you Limey bastard, open up," he pleaded, but it was no use. The bar was empty. It was three P.M. and he couldn't wait any longer.

Tired and frustrated, he threw himself against the door, using his shoulder as a battering ram, trying again and again to force it open. All he got for his efforts was more pain. The door wouldn't budge and it wasn't about to. The damned thing was solid: braced, banded, barred, and bolted tight. He could blow the building to kindling wood, but the door would still be standing upright in the rubble.

Thomson was desperate. If he hung around much longer, some good citizen would call the cops for sure. If he took to the streets and kept running from one hiding hole to another, he'd only be putting off the inevitable. There was no escape and he was too tired to try.

He stepped back from the door, his eyes searching the rear wall of the building. High above the door he saw a narrow transom. The glass was filthy, covered by a generation of dust and grime. It didn't appear to have been opened in years. At the rear of the next store he saw an old, rusting trash bin and a stack of wooden packing crates. Thomson tossed the crates aside and wedged himself behind the trash bin, shoving and pushing until he had manhandled it across the rough concrete and into position beneath the transom. Still, it wasn't tall enough. He ran back and grabbed two of the crates, piling them on top of the trash bin, then climbing to the top of his rickety tower.

The transom was loose. He could rattle the frame, but the window, which was bolted shut and covered with heavy wire mesh, wouldn't open. "That damned Limey," Thomson swore. Too tired and angry to care, he pulled Sayyid's revolver from his jacket pocket, punched a hole in the rusted wire and ripped it out, then smashed the windowpane, knocking the loose pieces of glass into the storeroom. He pulled up on the rusted latch, only to have the entire window frame come out in his hands. In a rage, Thomson raised it over his head and tossed it across the alley, watching in delight as it smashed against the far wall. He turned back and wedged his head and shoulders through the transom, pulled himself inside, then carefully lowered himself into the dark.

When he reached the floor, his legs sagged and he let himself slump against the cool wall of the storeroom, exhausted. He was sweating hard and his heart was pounding, but he did feel a bit safer here in the dark. Safe? God. He shook his head and laughed out loud. How incredibly stupid could he be? He was too old for this crap, and he wasn't nearly good enough to pull it off, even in his prime, if he had ever had a prime. What was the old saying? A half step. A half step separated the quick and the dead.

He opened his eyes and squinted into the dark storeroom. Thomson groaned when he saw that the rear door he'd been beating on was braced with two wooden two-by-fours. Lord! No wonder he couldn't get the door to budge, he thought, rubbing his shoulder. He slowly rose to his feet, his aching body screaming in protest. With a soft sigh and a few threats, he made the old bones move. He shuffled over to the door and pushed up on the steel bars, one at at time. He opened the door and stuck his head outside, glancing quickly toward the street. No one was there. He tossed the crates across the alley so it wouldn't look as obvious. He tried to shove the trash bin back, but his strength was gone. The bin would have to stay where it was. Finally, feeling like an old, flat tire, he went inside and dropped the two-by-fours into place.

The events of the last two days were beginning to feel like sledgehammer blows to the gut. Funny, he thought sadly, fifteen years ago, when his body could hack almost anything, he was too damned stupid to know it shouldn't. Now, when it couldn't hack much at all, he was too damned stubborn not to try anyway.

He staggered out of the storeroom into more familiar haunts, plopping himself down on a stool. Reaching across the bar, he grabbed a fifth of gin, not bothering with a glass. He pulled out the cork with his teeth and took a long drink. Then he closed his eyes as his throat exploded, white hot. His eyes filled with tears and he was lucky to lower the bottle back onto the bar without dropping it.

"God! That's awful," he rasped, staring at the fifth. It had been two days. He couldn't remember when he'd gone that long between transfusions. Must be a modern record! Strange, though. He hadn't given it much thought, but he should have been crawling the walls by now. He wasn't. And instead of satisfying his need, the warm gin had turned his stomach. It had made him gag. He leaned forward on the polished oak bar for support, and felt sick.

He looked at the bottle and saw his own reflection in the greasy glass. Who was that guy? Not even a funhouse mirror could make him look that bad. Had to be some mistake, he thought, pushing the bottle away. He knew he'd wake up any second and find it was only a bad dream.

He looked toward the far end of the bar and saw the phone. He stared at it for a long minute, thinking, then slid off the barstool and made his feet walk the ten paces. Mechanically, Thomson lifted the receiver and dialed the number.

"Is Perper there?" he mumbled, wondering if Kilbride had bugged the whole embassy yet. When Perper finally came on the line, Thomson said quietly, "Hi, Reggie, remember me?"

"Oh, Jesus," Perper answered, his normal sarcasm completely gone. "Yeah"—Perper tried to sound casual—"how you doing, Uncle Tom?"

"I've been better. Can we talk?"

"Wouldn't be wise. You know how it is."

"Yeah, I remember."

"Thought you were leaving?"

"I decided to stay a couple more days."

"So I heard. Cairo can do that to a guy. In fact, some people never leave," Reggie said, regaining a touch of his old form. "Too bad you didn't."

"Well, I ran into some of your old pals. We had a nice chat and I couldn't drag myself away."

"The word's out, you know," Perper warned, his voice sounding deeply concerned.

"I can imagine."

"No. You can't. They say you crossed over, sold out. Know what that means?"

"Headhunters?"

"And a real big price. So give it up before it's too late. You're going to end up very dead, very quick."

"It isn't true, you know."

"Of course it isn't. And that doesn't mean shit, because it's as true as they want to take the trouble to make it. So come in. Maybe I can find a good Republican lawyer. You can plead insanity. Who could doubt you?"

"I need your help, Reggie," Thomson said quietly.

There was a long pause before Perper replied. "I was afraid you'd say that."

"A little research, that's all. Check the pedigrees on a Kraut named Fengler."

"Part of the comedy team out in the desert?"

"The one and only. During the war he worked at a place called Hechingen. In the Black Forest. It was some kind of research lab. Cable Bonn and find out what the hell he did there."

"You're amazing! You're floating in a toilet bowl and you want me to jump in with you."

"We can do laps, practice our backstroke. Besides, you're in it whether you want to be or not."

"Bullshit! You're the one they're after. Not me."

"This is big, Reggie. I know it is. I've got to find out about Fengler. What the hell? You only live once."

"That's what bothers me."

"Meet me?" Thomson pleaded. "Tonight. Eight o'clock. Where we met the last time, but out in back, in the alley. Okay?"

"Thomson!... I'll try. That's all I can promise. I'll try."

19

THOMSON HID IN THE STOREROOM until dark, napping until he heard Jeremy open the bar and putter around out front. Thomson stayed where he was. There was no sense in involving the Englishman. A half hour before Perper was due to arrive, Thomson slipped out the back into the alley. Two doors down, he spotted a row of garbage cans and chased two cats from their nesting place. Squatting behind the cans, he waited. Not that he was expecting any surprises from Perper, but Thomson was in no condition to handle any, either.

At the stroke of eight, he saw Perper's lumpy figure come into view at the far end of the dark alley. Reggie stopped and peered into the shadows, unsure of the situation. Thomson smiled. If Perper was scared, they'd get along just fine.

Reggie walked slowly up the alley, counting doors, until he came to the rear entrance to the bar. Then he pulled a white handkerchief from his pants pocket and mopped his brow, waiting for something to happen.

"For chrissakes, Thomson," he called out in a loud whisper. "Come on out. Can't you see I'm alone?"

"Okay, Reggie. Relax," Thomson answered as he stepped from the shadows and met Perper in the center of the alley, where he was sweating like a pig.

"Did they follow you?" Thomson asked.

"I don't think so. . . ."

"You don't think so?"

"How the hell should I know?" Perper shot back. "You phone me on a goddamn open line, then have the balls to ask if I was followed down a dark alley?"

"Okay, okay." Thomson surrendered. "Look, I'm not in much better shape than you are tonight."

"Tonight? Tonight ain't the problem. We're both a little dated for stunts like this."

"Relax. Did you find out anything?"

"Plenty! And I scared the hell out of myself doing it, too." Perper mopped his brow again, his eyes darting back and forth to the ends of the alley. "You were right. There were research labs at Hechingen, but they didn't have a damned thing to do with rockets. Let me give you a hint. Hechingen is a small town south of Stuttgart, near Haigerloch. That ring any bells?"

"Haigerloch? Oh, shit! The Krauts built a nuclear reactor there, didn't they?"

"Tried. They couldn't get the bugs out, but that didn't stop them from trying. All they needed was more time. Time they never got. Not back then, anyway."

"And Fengler?"

"He was small-time, more like a lab assistant, but he was in on everything, from '35 right to the bitter end," Perper said as the sweat rolled down his cheeks.

"The brains of the outfit was a guy named Werner Kaltenberg. He was at Haigerloch, with the reactor. His sidekick at Hechingen was Fritz Schlaerman. He was in charge of 'applied research.' These clowns weren't just scribbling on the blackboard, Thomson. They were making a bomb, a goddamn A-bomb!"

Thomson nodded slowly. "Fengler's a nuclear physicist."

"After I bust my ass, why do I get the sick feeling you already knew?"

"It was the only thing that made sense, but I didn't have proof. Anything else?"

"I'm saving the worst for last. Schlaerman could never make it work because he couldn't get his hands on enough high-grade uranium ore," Perper said. "Never did. That's where Fengler came in. He cooked up a substitute, using strontium ninety and cobalt sixty instead of uranium. They call it a 'poor man's bomb.' It goes up with a big bang, just like the real ones, but it's dirty as hell. It throws fallout all over the place. Schlaerman and Kaltenberg were scientists. They refused to make it, so Fengler took the idea to Himmler and Göring. He claimed his one bomb could level London. All they had to do was slip it up the Thames in a U-boat. They ran out of time, but Fengler was right. It would have worked. That's what I don't understand, Thomson. Nasser isn't nuts. He knows the world won't stand for it, not even the Russians. He'll be stopped, as soon as the word gets out."

"Not if they use it first," Thomson commented quietly.

Perper stared at him. "But why would Nasser do that?"

"I don't think he knows anything about it. Unless I miss my guess, they're going to dump him, and we haven't got much time."

"We? Perpers don't come in heroic flavors anymore, Thomson. Just plain vanilla."

"What the hell can I do by myself? Are you going to wait until they nuke Tel Aviv?"

"Then take it to Kilbride! I know, he's stupid and arrogant, but he couldn't know about the bomb. He'd have to listen, if I backed you up."

"I can't take that chance. What about your Israeli friends? Wouldn't they help?"

"Help?" Perper snorted. "They'd start a war. And don't kid yourself. They already have a bomb. Is that what you want?"

"What about Langley? Or the Pentagon? Can't you get a message out? If they started asking questions, Kilbride would have to do something."

"Me again? Thomson, when shit hits the fan, the distribution is never proportional." Reggie continued to argue, but Thomson saw the guilty look on his face. "Damn you!" he finally said. "Maybe I can try, later tonight on the graveyard—"

Perper never got to finish his sentence.

He and Thomson were blinded by the beam of a powerful searchlight coming from the far end of the alley. Thomson swore as he grabbed Perper by the arm and pulled him behind the garbage cans. He peered around the edge to see who was out there, but it was useless. The light was too bright. "Thomson," he heard a disgustingly familiar voice call out. "You too, Perper. Come out before you get hurt."

It was Collins.

Perper moved closer. "Thomson," he whispered. "Let me go out. Collins doesn't have a damned thing on me. I'll say you phoned and wanted to give yourself up. Okay?"

"Reggie. He didn't come to talk. He came here to kill me. And he'll kill you just as fast."

"He wouldn't dare. He hasn't got any authorization. Not on me. So let me draw their attention while you make a run for it.... Unless you've got a better idea?"

Thomson didn't, but he didn't think much of Reggie's idea, either. Finally he nodded. "Be careful. Collins isn't the type to fool around with."

"Neither am I. I'll be flat on my stomach if he even looks cross-eyed."

Then Perper stood up, holding his hands over his head. "Okay, Collins," he shouted. "No pyrotechnics. Thomson asked me to come so he could give up, nice and quiet. Don't blow it."

Perper stepped gingerly into the center of the alley, into the light, and began walking toward Collins. As he did, his body cast a broad shadow across the garbage cans where Thomson was still hiding.

It was the best chance Thomson was likely to get. He had to run fifty yards in the open before he reached the end of the alley, but there was no choice, not if he wanted to get out alive.

Perper kept babbling, halfway to them now. Thomson pulled Sayyid's revolver from his pocket and made his break, running like hell. He put ten quick strides behind him before he heard the first shots. They echoed in the narrow alley like cannon shells, and showered Thomson with pieces of brick and mortar as they ricocheted off the walls. That made him run even faster, bobbing and weaving like Jim Brown in the open field.

Collins wouldn't have been stupid enough to leave the other end unguarded. And he wasn't. With twenty feet to go, a large shape stepped into the alley and blocked Thomson's way. It was one of the meatballs from the airport. Backlit by the search light, Thomson was sandwiched between gunfire and a beefy roadblock dead ahead.

But the searchlight was shining straight into the meatball's eyes. He was holding a chrome-plated automatic in his right hand and dropped into a very professional-looking crouch, squinting, as he steadied the butt of the automatic in the palm of his other hand and set his sights on Thomson's chest. At this range, there was no way he could miss. Thomson raised the police revolver, even as he realized he was going to be too late, an eternity too late. Time seemed to hang suspended as Thomson saw the sadistic smile on the man's face. Thomson was too old, too stupid, and too slow. Now, he'd pay the price for it.

As the meatball looked down the barrel and started to take up the slack on the trigger, one of Collins's bullets skipped off the brick wall, flashed past Thomson's shoulder, and caught the meatball at the base of the throat.

The man's head popped back, his eyes bulged, and Thomson heard a shocked, gurgling grunt escape his mouth. In that moment, the man forgot all about Thomson. He dropped the gun, and his hands clawed at his throat, as if he could stop the blood now gushing from the jagged hole.

Thomson ran past him to the corner, turning his head for one last look at Collins. The other guards were after him now, trying to catch up. And as he looked back, Thomson saw something lying in the dust at the center of the alley. It was another crumpled body—Perper.

"You bastard," Thomson screamed. "You stupid bastard!"

He stopped and raised the revolver, pointing it back down the alley as he pulled the trigger. He kept pulling it, until the chamber clicked empty. Collins and his men dove for cover. The second shot doused the searchlight with a loud pop, and he heard several loud screams. That wasn't enough. It didn't begin to even the score. He'd do anything to make that bastard Collins pay for what he'd done.

Because it had gotten very personal.

20

THE HOUR WAS LATE. Captain Saleh leaned back in his desk chair and stared out the window into the darkness, content that he'd been right all along. Of course it was a CIA plot. Now there could be no doubt. Not that the plot wasn't a clever one. And the American, Thomson, was a superb liar, perfect for the role of the broken-down field agent.

He lit another long Turkish cigarette, and drew the acrid smoke deep into his lungs. The red glow of the cigarette ash was the only light in the office. It was a vile habit, but he'd acquired it years before, in the hospital. It would make him gag and cough, sending a racking pain through his chest, but for that brief moment he would forget about his leg.

It was clear now that Yussuf had been one of Thomson's agents. The first answers were always right, he thought. Experience taught that if nothing else. Believe your nose, not your brain. The American had hired the fat Arab to spy for him. They had had a falling-out, undoubtedly over money, so Thomson had him killed. But he underestimated the police. Criminals always do. He hadn't expected the police to unravel his story so fast. He hadn't expected Saleh to be in charge. He had staged the rest to cover his tracks: the phony kidnapping, the chase from the airport, even the manhunt and his escape from Sayyid. Yes, Thomson was clever.

And Saleh would see that he hung for it.

Then why was he still sitting in his office, he asked himself, instead of going home to his wife and children, confident the case was closed at last?

No case had ever gotten inside his skull as this one had. Saleh had met every type of criminal the sewers could spew up, but this American was different. The man's act was so complete, so pat. It was either a complete illusion, or the real thing. That was Saleh's choice. Was Thomson's story all lies, or all truth?

A soft knock at the door interrupted his thoughts.

Saleh looked up to see Sergeant Sayyid peering cautiously around the corner of the door frame. Saleh motioned for him to enter, frowning when he saw that Sayyid's face was bruised and his head wrapped with a thick white bandage.

"They permitted you to leave the hospital so soon, Sayyid?" he asked in surprise.

"I chose not to stay," the sergeant replied sternly. "It is a place of illness."

"Still, you should do what the doctors order. You took a vicious fall." From the look in Sayyid's eyes, the sergeant knew his injuries far better than the captain ever could. "Well, it is good to have you back. And have no fear, we shall find your American. And when we do, I'll give him to you as a present? Would that make you feel better?"

His hate-filled glare was answer enough. Thomson would be a dead man.

"Go home, Sayyid. Rest," Saleh added. "There is nothing for us to do. The net is out. He cannot use the airport or the border crossings. He shall not escape."

Sayyid nodded and quietly left the room. Good, Saleh thought. He was too bone-tired for argument. Well. He smiled. At least it gave him a chance to speak with Gamal.

It seemed ages ago, when they had sat on the riverbank, wondering what the future would bring them. They were three adolescent revolutionaries, fighting the boredom of those days with endless debates. When was that? 1936? 1937? They couldn't have been more than nineteen. Looking back, those days seemed such easy ones. Each of them, in his own way, had had all the answers.

IT WAS SUNSET. The three young men kept arguing as the big orange ball of a sun dropped behind the palm trees on the opposite shore of the river. Beyond the trees and the thin fringe of green farmland lay the great western desert. It dominated everything, filling the air with a thin veil of dust that refracted the waning rays of the sun and turned the evening sky into a rich kaleidoscope of purples, reds, and yellows. But sunsets were for poets. Hassan Saleh, Ali Rashid, and Gamal Nasser had far more serious matters on their minds.

"Gamal, have you gone mad!" Hassan's mouth hung open. "Why would you join the army?"

A faintly amused smile crossed Gamal's face. He shook his head, as a schoolteacher would to a backward pupil. "No, I haven't gone mad, Hassan. The past few months in Cairo have simply opened my eyes, that's all."

"But the army? They sleep with the British. Is that what you want to do, Gamal? Be one of their whores? What of the law? I thought you wanted to study the law?"

With anyone else, there would have been a violent argument. Not with Gamal. He never showed his emotions with words. Instead, he used those powerful brown eyes and a broad smile. The effect was disarming. It wasn't something you could argue with.

"I know it is hard for you to see, Hassan, sitting here in this wretched village—"

Ali had been listening intently, but he finally broke in. "How could Cairo improve anyone's vision, Gamal? It is an abomination, neither Arab nor Moslem. People strut about in Savile Row suits, passing themselves off as European. But they aren't. They can never be. The British laugh at this silly masquerade. And in the end, they are nothing. We are Moslems," he stated flatly. To Ali, life was filled with absolutes and sharp edges. "Our destiny lies in the Koran. There is nothing in Cairo, the army, or your cursed civil law that is any greater than that."

"As usual, Ali, you are right," Gamal apologized. "Cairo is not Egypt. This is," he said, as he patted the rich black soil of the riverbank. "Our roots are nourished by the Nile. Egypt is our village and thousands of others like it, ageless and unshackled. It is barefoot children, dirt streets, sugar beets, water buffalo. It is a place where mere survival depends on the next good crop, and that hasn't changed since the days of the pharaohs . . . or the time of Mohammed."

Ali's eyes narrowed as he studied Gamal. "Then you agree? Cairo is an abomination?"

"Certainly. But it is much more, Ali. Cairo is control. He who controls Cairo, controls Egypt. And he who controls Egypt, controls the Middle East."

Ali nodded, still suspicious. "To what end? I judge a man by his dreams, Gamal, not just his actions. What are your dreams? What do you do the morning after your revolution?" he demanded to know.

"Still breathing fire, Ali? Good!" Gamal laughed as he turned toward him. "We need men like you. And, yes. I want to change it all. Eventually I shall, if I have men like you beside me. Because no wall is too high for you. You would rip the bricks apart with your bare hands if you had to, wouldn't you?"

"If that was Allah's will. No wall ever built by man would ever stop me, Gamal. Nor would any man, not if it was Allah's will."

"Gamal doesn't claim to receive His daily messages, Ali," Hassan joked. "He doesn't sit on his prayer rug and scowl, waiting for the lightning bolt."

"Don't blaspheme." Ali's eyes warned. "I have less use for heretics than I do for politicians. Tell me what you would do with the wall, Hassan. Negotiate with it? Compromise? Read it the law? Or maybe you would convince it to tear itself down?"

Gamal placed himself between them. "You are right, of course, Ali. The wall is too high and too old for those things. Besides, our timing is all wrong. That is why I have decided to join the army. Why waste the time and sweat trying to tear the wall down when we can simply go around it. As I said, I learned a few things in Cairo."

Gamal raised his hand and pushed his hair back from his forehead. "See that scar?" he asked. "It is fresh, I assure you. And it came from a policeman's bullet."

"A bullet?" Hassan asked excitedly. "So it has begun! The police actually fired on their own people?"

"Yes, but they did not shoot very well. They didn't kill me, as you can see."

"Allah be praised for that, if nothing else," Ali answered.

"Allah had nothing to do with it," Hassan jeered. "Just bad marksmanship."

"Do not blaspheme!" Ali said angrily.

"The day has come to take up arms!" Hassan said. "You can pray all day long, Ali. But when you look up, Farouk will still be on the throne, the army and the police will still be guarding his fat backside, and a British regiment will be guarding them. But imagine it!'' He grinned. ''They dared to fire on the people! And if it is civil war they want—''

''Hush, both of you,'' Gamal said, silencing their bickering. ''You sound like you're the ones who got shot. Someday it may come to guns, but not for many, many years. That cannot work. You forget, I was there. I was part of the protests and the riots. We showed we could fill the streets with people, and the police showed they could fill them with blood just as quickly. In the end, what did we gain except more martyrs?''

''What will?'' Hassan demanded. ''We must drive the British out. Without them, the army and the police are nothing. Farouk's government would collapse, and we can begin the real revolution.''

''The British will leave on their own,'' Gamal replied patiently. ''We have a new and powerful weapon on our side: time. Time! The signs are everywhere. Europe is racing toward war. The Italians are in Ethiopia, bleeding like stuck pigs. The Germans are testing their new war machines in Spain, while the British and French bury their heads in the sand, telling themselves Hitler isn't serious. But he is. War will come and Hitler will do our job for us. Win or lose, the British will have no strength for the 'burdens of empire.' That is why it is merely a matter of time, Hassan. Time is our new weapon.''

''How much Gamal? How long must we wait?''

''Not long. But when the time does come, we must be ready. The bullet taught me that much.'' Gamal turned to each of them, asking, ''Was it the will of Allah that the bullet missed, Ali? Or just bad aim, Hassan? I accept them both. But the next time, the gun will be in my hand.''

They nodded and smiled, the tension broken.

''We cannot fight the police and the army,'' Gamal continued. ''We must take them over, absorb them into the revolution, and use them to lead the way. That is why I joined the army. And I am not alone. There are many others who see things as we do. We want change, but we cannot leave it to the mob in the streets. If we do, the victory will be hollow."

"What happens after this victory, Gamal?" Ali asked again, always returning to the point. "After we drive the British out, what then? Will we simply have a pharaoh in a khaki uniform? Is that all we get? Or will we have a Saladin, a Moslem leader who will rally the true believers from Baghdad to Morocco? Our enemy is not the British, it is Western secularism. That is what saps our strength. If we do not burn it out, we will always be a silly little people. So which will it be? A pharaoh? Or a Saladin?"

Gamal considered the question. This was how the equation always reduced itself. Even in the streets—among the Socialists, the Fascists, the New Youth Movement, the Communists, and the Moslem Brotherhood—they agreed on the means, but never on the end. He'd never understand them. Why couldn't it just be freedom? Why wasn't that enough? A breath of freedom, a better life for the people, and more social justice than they have now. Why wasn't that enough? But to the fanatics, the revolution was merely a prelude.

Gamal looked at Ali, trying to understand the man, but it was getting harder. "All I know, Ali"—he looked into those deep, fiery black eyes, answering honestly—"is that our people deserve better. And nothing can happen if we don't begin."

"Isn't that enough?" Hassan added "After twenty-five centuries, why isn't it enough to simply have an Egypt ruled by Egyptians? Let your precious Syrians, and Iraqis, and Moroccans take care of themselves."

"You've never seen my point, have you?" Ali asked, his eyes flashing. "We are Moslems, first and last. Egypt is merely a place: a narrow green valley squeezed between two deserts. What do I care about pharaohs? That was four thousand years ago. Now, we draw our strength from our faith. Yes, the revolution must start here, but it must not end here. Never! That is our sacred duty."

"But if it doesn't succeed here," Gamal said, throwing his arms around the two of them, "thirty years from now, we will still be sitting on this riverbank, cursing the same old problems. Won't we? We must band together and fight them, not each other."

NOW, IT WAS GAMAL who needed time, Hassan thought. His revolution had barely begun, yet his enemies were trying to pull him down. Gamal needed time and Hassan Saleh would make sure he got it.

He was exhausted. It was nearly midnight, long past the hour he should have taken his own advice and gone home to bed. He walked slowly to the door, stretching his cramped leg as he closed the office door behind him and headed for the stairs, lost in thought. He found his car, his mind still buried in old memories of far better days. He slipped his key into the lock and heard a soft voice calling from the shadows.

"Captain . . ."

Saleh turned and frowned. "Yes?" He squinted, trying to see who it was, then something struck him across the back of the head and knocked him to his knees. He fought the pain and numbness, struggling to clear his head and get to his feet, but was hit again. He toppled forward onto his face, stunned, only dimly aware of the voices and footsteps around him.

"No!" he heard a familiar voice shout. "Alive, you fool! Load him into the car. And hurry, before we are seen."

Hands lifted him off the pavement and he felt a sharp pinprick on his right bicep.

Shouts. Someone was shouting. There were bright lights and loud curses. The arms that held him up suddenly let go. He felt himself standing, hanging in midair, as feet ran away across the parking lot. He smiled, floating pleasantly on the air. Then he felt himself falling, as if down a long, bottomless, black chute.

21

THOMSON RAN THROUGH the dark sidestreets, chased more by his own rage than by Collins and his goons. He ran until his body wouldn't let him punish it any further and then collapsed in a doorway, soaked with sweat and gasping for air. Slowly, he felt the anger begin to fade. The flames flickered and died, leaving behind a bed of white-hot coals. He closed his eyes and remembered the old adage "Don't get mad, get even."

Maybe that was his problem. From the beginning, he'd acted too calmly and professionally. He'd been a bad boy, but not nearly bad enough. Even after he revolted, he kept playing by their rules, trying to keep the clinical detachment of a good field agent, just like he had been trained, just like they'd expected.

"Nothing personal, old man." Wasn't that what they had said? Just business, you understand. What was that? The blood? Perper and the others? Well, you can't make an omelette without breaking a few eggs, can you?

Not this time! The whole deal was sick. Whoever was behind it was nuts: an irrational fanatic. Thomson knew he deserved whatever he got, and in spades. That was the risk he had taken when he ran from the airport. He had accepted it. But he didn't accept their killing Perper. Perper was a noncombatant and the bastards had had no right to do it to him. When they did, they became the ones who had broken the rules.

Who the hell did they think they were? Collins? Kilbride? Even that damned Kraut Fengler? Thomson hated them, but it had to go higher. There weren't enough brains between the three of them to dream up a plan like this. No, someone else was behind it. Someone was lurking in the shadows, calling the shots, and he was the one Thomson was going to stick with the tab.

He opened his eyes and looked at his watch. It was almost nine P.M. That gave him eight hours of darkness. Eight hours. Not much, but they would be enough. And he knew exactly how to put them to good use.

STEALING A CAR should have been a snap for a polished pro like Thomson. But he hadn't used a hot-wire in more years than he could remember. He found a new Renault on a quiet sidestreet and plied all his skills under the dashboard. All he got for his trouble was a couple of painful shocks from the bare ignition wire. He gave up, cursing, determined to find a car that was a bit closer to his own age.

Two blocks away, he saw the rusting carcass of an old MG. Its owner probably left it out each night, hoping some thief would put it out of its misery. Thomson squeezed himself upside-down beneath the steering wheel and set to work. He had almost figured the wiring out when he saw the ignition key lying on the floor mat next to his head.

Minutes later he was driving northeast on the main highway, heading toward the desert—and Heliopolis.

THE SAND WAS COLDER than he remembered, or maybe it was just him. For the first time in years, he felt that old, grim determination welling up inside. It was how he had felt before those big drops into Germany: eager, with a fine edge of intensity.

Thomson looked through the fence and stared at the big aircraft hangar in the middle of the compound. If he was right, that was where they had hidden their new toys. He would have loved to blow the hangar to bits, but he had brought no explosives. All he had was a rusty tire iron from the MG and Sayyid's empty service revolver. It wasn't going to be much use, but it beat bluffing with the tire iron. Besides, he wasn't planning to shoot it out with Grüber's SS guards.

They weren't his biggest problem, anyway. No, his biggest problem would be time. He only had five or six hours of darkness, and like Dracula, he had to be safely hidden by the first light of dawn. So he set to work on the fence, putting the tire iron and some of that white-hot anger to use, digging and prying at a seam as if it were Collins's rib cage. The fence never stood a chance. In less than a minute, Thomson had ripped a hole big enough to squeeze through.

Ten minutes later, he was lying in the scrub ten yards from the rear of the hangar. Carefully, he worked his way through the shadows until he found a shallow hole where he could snuggle down and watch. The windows were painted black, but through the thin walls he could hear sounds of heavy equipment and metal clanging on metal, high-speed electric drills, and harsh voices shouting orders.

There were two guards on patrol outside. Like good Krauts, they circled the building, a hundred and eighty degrees apart. Thomson watched one guard walk away from him, up the near side of the building. When he reached the front corner, the other guard came into view at the opposite corner. They went round and round like that, with the regularity of mechanical figures on a Bavarian cuckoo clock. Thomson kept watching and waiting for the right opportunity. And sure enough, his patience paid off.

There was a small door set in the rear wall of the hangar. Thomson heard the rattle of a lock and saw the door swing open. A middle-aged man in a long white technician's smock stepped outside into the bright pool of light. He stretched and yawned, and pulled a pack of cigarettes from his coat pocket. With a furtive glance to each side, he slipped a cigarette into his mouth and lit a match, cupping his hands to shield the flame. The technician took a deep drag and leaned against the building, looking up at the stars and exhaling, as the smoke drifted across the face of a big sign hanging on the wall behind him. In bold red letters it said, NO SMOKING.

So much for crack discipline, Thomson told himself.

And right on schedule, one of the guards came marching around the far corner of the building. The technician smiled and mumbled a greeting, but the guard wasn't impressed. He frowned and walked closer, pointing at the man's cupped hand and the cloud of smoke hanging in the air. The technician began to argue, but he finally threw the cigarette on the ground and stepped on it, glaring at the stern-faced guard. That didn't help. The guard glared back and the technician got even madder. He stomped away, yanked the door open, and slammed it shut behind him.

The guard watched the door for a moment, then resumed his rounds, giving Thomson his chance. He sprinted toward the door and grabbed the knob, twisting it quickly and praying that the technician had been too angry to lock it behind him. The knob turned and Thomson pulled the door open far enough to see through the crack.

He blinked as he looked inside the brightly lit hangar. His view was partially blocked by a tall row of wooden crates, but he could see enough. There were dozens of men working near the center of the hangar, each dressed in a white smock. Some were leaning across their workbenches, working feverishly with wrenches and soldering irons. Others were looking up at the ceiling, directing the movement of a slow-moving overhead crane. The remainder were huddled around two long-bed trailers sitting in the middle of the floor. It was easy to pick out the supervisors. They were the ones with the crisp white smocks and clipboards, scowling and shouting orders.

Whatever the guys in the white smocks were doing, they seemed frantic to get it done. And with the other guard coming any second, the open doorway wasn't the place to be. Thomson opened the door wider and slipped inside. Bending low at the waist, he darted behind the crates, and worked his way to a dark corner where he had a better view.

His eyes were drawn to the trailers. It didn't take too many smarts to realize that the long, fat tubes lying on them were rockets. They were painted dark green, appeared to be about fifty feet long, and were short and fat, with four stabilizer fins at their rear ends. The nose cones tapered gracefully to sharp points. Thomson knew exactly where he'd seen these tired old war horses before. He'd been there, in London, in 1944, and he still carried the composite image of a thousand weary, terrified faces looking up at the sky as the next V-2 came into view. When he closed his eyes, he still saw the anger and frustration on those faces. And he remembered what a V-2 could do. Once launched, it was unstoppable. And it was deadly. With sixteen hundred pounds of TNT stuffed inside its nose, it could destroy a whole block of steel-and-glass high-rises. With one of Fengler's dirty little A-bombs, Egypt could change the political face of the Middle East forever.

Then he saw him.

It was Fengler. Funny, Thomson thought, some people never changed, even after twenty years. God wouldn't let them; when he made a good joke, he wanted to enjoy it. Fengler strutted across the floor, his head held high and his chin jutting out, older to be sure, and nearly bald, yet with the same prissy wire-rimmed glasses, sour expression, and cold, pitiless eyes he'd been born with. Yes, it was Papa Fengler.

He had just stepped out of his glassed-in office at the rear corner of the hangar. His body was bent forward at the waist and he had his hands stuffed deep into his pockets, looking like Groucho Marx lost in a rare serious thought. When he reached the others, he made a few frantic arm motions and began shouting orders, out-scowling even the nastiest of his supervisors. Then he turned on his heel and left as quickly as he had come, stomping back to his office and slamming the door behind him. From the expressions on the other men's faces, it was clear Papa Fengler was an easy man to dislike.

Farther along the rear wall was a large brick storeroom. Its walls ran from floor to ceiling, broken only by a single steel door. On the door was a large red sign. In its center, three yellow interlocking rings were painted. That was the international symbol for radioactive material, and Thomson knew that was where the warheads would be kept.

He pulled Sayyid's revolver from his rear pocket and slowly worked his way around the row of crates until he could see through the bank of windows into Fengler's office. Fengler was alone, his back to the door, and he was bent over a drafting table. With one quick move, Thomson walked to the door and pushed it open, far enough to slip inside and drop below the height of the windows.

Fengler heard the noise but was too busy to be bothered looking up. "Klaus?" he snapped. "Where is the other set of drawings on the fuel lines? I know you had them this morning... Klaus? Are you deaf, man!" he shouted, finally turning his head and seeing Thomson crouching behind the door.

"What is the meaning of this! Who let you—" When he saw the gun in Thomson's hand, he froze.

Thomson found it fascinating. In that one short second, Fengler's arrogance evaporated. His eyes filled with fear as he looked down the barrel. "Who are you?" he asked, trying to intimidate, but it wasn't working. He was a better coward than actor.

"Shut up!" Thomson gestured with the revolver. "Turn back to the table and look busy."

Not surprisingly, Fengler did exactly what he was told. "You are insane," he said, sweat popping out on his forehead. "You cannot—"

"I said shut up, or I'll kill you right now!" Thomson hissed, glancing quickly around the cluttered office, knowing he'd have little to fear from Papa, not with the gun pointed at him.

"I know who you are," Fengler said as his eyes narrowed and his face turned red. "You are that American, the one who kidnapped my Ilsa last night. Aren't you?"

"And if you don't want me to make your precious daughter an orphan, you'll do what I told you."

"You'll never get out of here—"

"No?" Thomson chuckled. "I got in, didn't I? Besides, I'm not leaving alone. You're coming, too—either with me, or in a casket—you can take your pick."

"We'll see," Fengler stated ominously. "This will gain you nothing. Kill me if you wish. You cannot stop us. Not now. It is too late. It took me twenty years to reach this moment, and you cannot stop me! Not now!"

"Give me the key to the bunker, Fengler."

The German's eyes bulged and he stepped back against the drafting table. "The warheads? No! You are insane. You cannot touch them. You'll have to kill me first."

"Nothing would give me greater pleasure." Thomson raised the revolver and aimed it at Fengler's forehead, trying to look angry and a bit demented. Fengler looked into the small black hole. He blinked, and Thomson saw his eyes turn away. He looked beyond Thomson, for just a split-second, at something just outside the room.

Thomson caught the look, but he was too late. Again, he had been a half-step too late. He heard a scraping sound behind him as someone slammed the door into his shoulder, knocking him off balance. That was all it took. He tried to swing his pistol around, but it was too late. Two of Fengler's technicians stood in the doorway, looking more surprised to see Thomson and his gun than he was to see them.

Fengler didn't let the opportunity pass. His arm swept out and he grabbed a roll of blueprints from the top of the drafting table. He flung them across the narrow gap that separated him from Thomson. The heavy tube crashed into Thomson's chest and knocked him against the wall. Their initial shock gone, Fengler's two men jumped on top and Papa followed right behind like a madman. The two technicians pinned Thomson's arms to the floor while Fengler grabbed a fistful of Thomson's hair and bashed the American's head on the concrete again and again.

Thomson struggled to break free, but after the fifth crack of his skull on the hard floor, he stopped counting.

22

ILSA FENGLER LAY on her bed, staring through the window into the empty silence of the desert night. The stars seemed so bright, yet so distant, like her dreams.

She was alone in the house, as usual. During the day, that didn't matter as much. She kept her hands busy and could tolerate the loneliness. But not at night. The night mocked her. She rolled over, pressed her face against the wall, and began to cry, praying that sleep would come. From years of practice, Ilsa knew it would, but some nights, it did not come for a long time.

How much more could she take? Papa dragged her from one godforsaken outpost after another, keeping her locked away, refusing to let her mix with the others, always protecting her from something or someone. "They aren't good enough," he always said. Why couldn't she make him understand how the loneliness ate at her?

"Soon, Ilsa. Very soon," he would always say, putting her off. "When our work is complete here, we'll leave. You'll see. We'll have respect then. You'll see. Soon."

Leave? And go where? To Germany? After fifteen years, that dream was as distant as ever. No, she was doomed to wandering, like the *Flying Dutchman*, never touching the Earth.

Her soft crying was broken by the sound of a car coming rapidly up the road. It slowed and turned into the driveway, its headlight beams flashing across the wall of her bedroom.

It must be Papa, she thought. He had worked later and later these past few weeks. But when she heard the loud, angry slam of his car door, she sat up and looked out the window. Strange, she thought, and so unlike him. He was never noisy, especially at this hour. Then she saw the headlights of a second car coming up the road, driving even faster. It swung into their driveway behind Papa's car. A man got out, and the argument began.

It was Major Grüber. Papa turned and walked toward him, wagging his finger in Grüber's face and talking in harsh, angry whispers. With Grüber's first word, Ilsa listened closely. She had always considered herself a kind and charitable person; she hated no one—except Grüber. He was always leering at her and making dirty comments, when he was certain no one else could hear him, of course. Couldn't Papa see what he was like? How could he work for someone like that? Couldn't he see the evil behind that mask?

"Calm down? Calm down, you say!" Papa's voice grew loud and even angrier. "He broke into the laboratory tonight. Into my laboratory, Grüber! It was me he was after, not you. He ... he would have killed me, no thanks to you or your cursed guards. The American was your responsibility. The colonel ordered you to take care of him, didn't he? It was your job, and you bungled it!"

Ilsa had never heard Papa raise his voice to Grüber before, certainly not like this.

"Well, I've had enough of your incompetence. I'm going to report this whole affair to Colonel Rashid in the morning."

Grüber did not respond. Instead, he smiled and shook his head, as if he pitied Papa. "I wouldn't be hasty if I were you, Herr Doktor.'' The threat implicit in Grüber's voice was open and menacing. "Remember who you are. Unless you're going to squat down on a prayer rug with those vermin—and stay there—you'd better not say a word to that camel driver Rashid. Not if you know what's good for you.''

"Good for me? Good for me, you ask? I've been giving that some thought, Grüber. And I've decided Colonel Rashid might be what's good for me after all. I am working for him, now. You can tell that to Hoess, and to Stuttgart, too. You are finished. All of you are finished.''

"Don't be naïve, Herr Doktor. No one is bigger than the movement. If you cross us, you're the one who'll be finished. You are German, don't ever forget that.''

"Don't threaten me, Grüber. This isn't 1943, it's 1962. You need me more than I'll ever need you. So does Rashid." His voice grew more confident. "I'm tired of doing your dirty work. What has it gotten me? Nothing. First you let that Jew inside the compound, now it is an American spy. It was me they were after, Grüber. And if my assistants hadn't walked in, he would have killed me.''

"I want the American,'' Grüber demanded.

"No! I have him locked up—bound and gagged—and that's where he'll stay, until I give him to Rashid tomorrow.''

"I want him. Do you hear me, Fengler?''

"You can't have him!''

"Don't cross swords with me. I'll carve you into little pieces before I'm finished.''

"I said no! I'll show the colonel who can handle security around here, and who cannot. This entire project should have been mine, all of it, not just the warheads. But you decided to put Schlaerman in charge, didn't you? Well, my work is finished, correctly and on time. Then I had to straighten out his mess too, didn't I? What did I get for it?

Nothing! I haven't failed. You have: you, and Schlaerman, and Hoess, and all the rest. You are the one who should be reporting to me! We all know whose idea this was. And we all know my part of the operation is flawless. You'll see. You'll all see what they can do. You'll all see! Now get out of my sight, Grüber."

"Give me the American!" Grüber shouted.

But Papa abruptly turned away and left Grüber standing alone in the front yard, fuming. Ilsa heard Papa's footsteps echo across the front porch and the screen door slam shut behind him.

Grüber was in a rage, his fists clenched at his sides. He stared at the door, then raised his eyes and looked up at her bedroom window. It was dark inside. She knew he couldn't see her, but the look on his face made her recoil. His eyes were burning with hatred. He stared at her window for several long minutes, then turned away and stomped back to his car. She heard an angry squeal of tires as Grüber drove away, and the desert night became quiet once again.

Ilsa looked up at the stars, Papa's words still ringing in her ears, unaware that the tears had stopped running down her cheeks. She knew what they were making in the hangar. She had always known, but had refused to admit it, even to herself. To her, Papa was just a simple scientist, puttering around his lab, doing research. But none of that was real: the research, the broken promises, or her forgotten dreams. As the harsh truth of Grüber's words sank in, Ilsa felt the terror grow inside her.

The American? Thomson? Could Papa really have caught him in the lab? Could Thomson really have come to kill Papa? No. She refused to believe that. But why would Thomson have come back? He had to be insane, but he wasn't dangerous. No, Grüber and Hoess were the dangerous ones. They had infected Papa with their megalomania, and Ilsa couldn't take it any longer. She must leave. She must leave, and she must persuade Papa to come with her, while there was still time.

In the next room, she heard him undressing. She wanted to run in and confront him, but that would accomplish nothing. He was too close to it, blinded by his own ambitions. No, he'd never understand. He'd never listen. Later? Perhaps. But that would take time.

She heard the bedsprings creak. Many long minutes later, after his heavy breathing had turned to soft snores, she rose and went to the dresser. She changed out of her nightgown and into a pair of dark slacks and a heavy sweater. Slipping downstairs to the kitchen, she remembered the old flashlight in the center drawer. The beam was weak, but it would do.

She walked to the back door and pulled it open, then stopped. She looked back into the kitchen, hesitating. Finally, she walked back to the cabinet and reached up to the top shelf, where her fingers found the butt of the old Luger. She gripped it firmly in the palm of her hand, then jammed the barrel into the waistband of her slacks, like she'd seen in the movies. She tried not to be afraid of the gun anymore. She had far worse things to fear. But this wasn't the movies, either. It was real. The feel of the oily metal on her skin made her break into a cold sweat.

It was clear to her now. Thomson held the key. If he escaped, with everything he knew, their plan would collapse. They'd be forced to stop, before someone got hurt. Nasser would throw them out of the country. That would even be better. It would be the end. They could go home. And if she was clever, no one would suspect who did it. Home! Maybe they could finally live a normal life. That was what Ilsa wanted, and she wanted it desperately.

Outside the house, she hurried to the old Fiat. She slipped it out of gear and leaned her shoulder against the doorpost, pushing the small sedan backward into the street. Then she got inside and turned the ignition key, nursing the gas to keep the engine quiet, not wanting to wake Papa up. But her nerves were frayed. To her, the little car sounded like a tank.

Well down the dark row of cottages, she dared to flick on the headlights, fearing the car would attract more attention without the lights than with them.

She approached the hangar slowly and looked at her watch. It was two A.M. Even the stragglers would be in bed by now. They would be up early to prepare for the test. That would leave only a few maintenance men and Grüber's guards to worry about. Ilsa tried to remain calm, trying not to attract attention. There was only one place they would have put Thomson: the paint locker. It was the only room with solid walls, a heavy door, and a lock. That was where he'd be.

She walked down the side of the building and counted the windows... five, six, seven. There were lights on inside those rooms, shining through the cracks, but the eighth room was dark. That was it, the paint locker. She inched closer and used her flashlight, shielding the beam as she peered through the rusty bars and painted glass. Still, she swore she saw a dim shape lying on the concrete floor. It must be Thomson, and he wasn't moving.

She hurried to the far end of the hanger, turned the corner, and ran right into one of the security guards.

"Oh," she stammered, backing away as the guard raised his gun. "Uh, you startled me." She tried to sound calm. "You see, Papa forgot some papers, and I..."

The guard glared at her for a few seconds, then lowered the gun barrel. "*Ja*, Fräulein Fengler." He nodded impatiently, motioning her toward the door.

Ilsa rushed past him and jammed her key into the lock, shoving the door open and letting it close behind her. Then she collapsed against the hangar wall, her legs trembling, her heart pounding with fear. She was so afraid she almost threw up. But she knew what she had to do. She knew if she didn't begin this instant, she'd lose her nerve.

The paint locker stood along the left wall of the hangar, halfway back, behind a tall stack of crates. She moved quietly along the rear wall of the hangar until she reached the corner and could look down on the far side of the crates. She suddenly stopped, terrified. Guards! Wouldn't Papa have posted guards inside too? She should have thought of that before. This whole idea was insane.

But no one was there. The corridor was empty. Maybe the guard had stepped away? Maybe he had gone outside? Or maybe there weren't any guards. Papa said they had Thomson locked up, bound and gagged. Whatever, she couldn't wait for an answer. Pulling the Luger from the waistband of her slacks, she walked slowly toward the door of the paint locker. It was shut tight and bolted from the outside. There was no lock, just a big sliding bolt. She grabbed it and tugged until it slid free and she could open the door.

As she did, she heard a smug voice call to her from a few feet away, from behind the crates. "Perhaps you could use some help, Fräulein?" the voice mocked her. And she didn't have to look to know whose voice it was. Grüber's.

He was standing between two wooden crates, leering at her with the same expression she had seen less than half an hour before. He came closer. "So, you want to help your

American friend again, eh? I suspected as much, but now we have the proof, don't we?"

"No! I . . . uh . . ." She tried to think.

"Oh, yes." He laughed as he stepped closer. "It seems you have gotten yourself—and your father—in a great deal of trouble this time, Ilsa," he said as he put his hand on her shoulder. "With other women, I can normally make some arrangements to help them out of jams like this. But you've never liked soldiers. Have you? No, you are one of those little virgins who are always looking down on us, like you've been looking down on us ever since you arrived, aren't you?"

"Not on all soldiers, Grüber. Just ones like you!"

Grüber's eyes flashed and he shoved her against the wall.

She raised the Luger from behind her back and held it out with both hands, pointing it at his chest. She was terrified, and they both knew it. "Stop right where you are," she ordered.

Grüber laughed. With one swift motion he slapped her across the face with one hand while grabbing the gun barrel with the other, twisting it out of her grasp as if he were taking a toy from a bad child.

Her cheek burned and she could feel the tears welling up inside.

"No, Ilsa, you know nothing of soldiers like me. But you will," he taunted her, as he casually tossed the Luger aside. With another quick move, he grabbed her shoulders and threw her onto the floor, hard, as if she were a stuffed doll. He jumped on top, digging a knee into her stomach and knocking the wind out of her. Then he straddled her. "In Russia, when we found a surly bitch like you, this usually did the trick. We always found them a bit more polite afterward!"

She tried to shove him away, but he grabbed her sweater and ripped it open, laughing as he looked down at her small, bare breasts. She reached up and scratched at his cheeks with her fingernails, gouging them like an angry cat, and drawing blood. He growled and slapped her across the face. She screamed in pain, but he kept slapping her, again and again, punishing her with each blow, until she had to cover her head with her arms. His assault came so fast, everything spun around inside her head. She heard him laughing at her, but she could do nothing.

His hands dropped to her breasts. He grabbed them, rubbing hard and pinching both nipples. She screamed again and shook her head. "If you aren't very nice," he warned sarcastically, "I'll hurt you a lot worse than that before I'm finished. And believe me, I know how to hurt a woman."

His powerful hand grabbed the waistband of her slacks and she felt them rip. Desperate, she turned her head and saw the Luger lying on the bare concrete floor near the wall. She stretched her hand as far as it would reach, and was able to wrap her fingers around the barrel and pull it toward her. Tightening her grip, she swung it at him and clubbed him across the forehead with all her strength.

He toppled off to one side, then righted himself. "You little..." he swore, grabbing her arm to halt the blows. He twisted her wrist backward until the sharp pain made her drop the gun. It was hopeless. She watched his eyes as he ran his free hand across his forehead, pausing to look at the blood, then holding his fingers in front of her eyes so she could see. "You'll pay dearly for this," he whispered angrily, as he ripped her slacks open and began to unfasten his belt.

She screamed again as she heard him say, "Yes, you'll pay, my dear..." but before he could finish the sentence or carry out his threat, his head suddenly snapped forward with a violent jerk. His eyes bulged out and he floated there above her, his body suddenly going limp. Then his eyes closed and Grüber toppled to one side, collapsing onto the floor next to her, unconscious.

Ilsa couldn't understand what had happened. She stared at Grüber's face, lying only inches away, but she was too terrified to move. She forced her eyes away, forced them to look up, and saw a dim figure towering above both of them, wobbling back and forth, holding a long wooden two-by-four in his hands.

"Thomson!" She began to cry hysterically.

23

SHE GRABBED THE TORN EDGES of the sweater and pulled them together, trying to hide her embarrassment and anger. Not that it mattered. His face was bloody and bruised. He was obviously in pain and barely conscious.

He stood over her, wobbling back and forth on legs that could no longer support him. Finally, the heavy board slipped from his grasp and clattered onto the concrete floor. His hand reached out and found the wall, stopping his fall. He collapsed against it, holding his ribs as he slid slowly down and joined her on the floor.

"That was nice." He tried to smile as he looked over at Grüber's unconscious form. He pointed at the two-by-four and nodded. "And that was the best swing I've taken since Little League. Never hit for the average, but I was a terror in the clutch. Sorry," he mumbled through clenched teeth. "I uh . . . I hope he didn't hurt you."

"No." She looked away, not knowing what to say to him. "Thank you. He didn't. But he would have. I'll be all right." Then she quickly turned back. "What about you? My God. What did they do to you?" she asked, deeply concerned. She sat up and leaned over him, carefully examining his cuts and bruises. As she did, her torn sweater fell open again, exposing her breasts, but this time she ignored it.

Thomson closed his eyes and felt her fingers gently touching his face. They were firm but delicate, and strangely comforting to him. "Don't worry." He smiled. "I'll live."

"Is anything broken?"

"Just my pride, and maybe a rib or two." He opened his eyes and looked up at her. "What brings you around? Visiting hours?"

"I...I wanted to help you escape, but Grüber caught me. Is... Is he the one who beat you up?"

"No. Sorry to say, it was your old man and two of his pals. But we can chat about that later. We have to get out of here—or did you think that far ahead?"

"Let me help you." She took his arm and helped pull him to his feet. "I have a car. It's parked outside. Can you make it that far?"

"That depends on who's chasing me. Wait a minute, though." He grimaced in pain as he bent down and retrieved her Luger from the floor. "This might come in handy," he said, as he leaned on her shoulder, letting her take his weight.

"What about him?" she asked angrily, as she looked down at Grüber, holding the sweater closed with her hand.

"Don't worry. Grüber's down for the count.... Unless you want me to kill him?" From the look on her face, he could see it wasn't much of a joke. "That's not such a bad idea after all. But we're running out of time." He motioned toward the rear door.

When they got there, she propped him against the wall and opened the door far enough to take a peek outside. "Quick," she said as she turned back, opening the door wide and taking a firm grip on his arm. "The guard must be around the other side. We must hurry before he comes back."

They stumbled across the tarmac until they reached the deep shadows and could slow down. They made it to the parking lot without being challenged. She crammed him into the passenger seat, quickly got behind the wheel and started the engine, then sat there, staring through the windshield with a worried frown on her face.

"This is as far as the plan went?" he asked calmly.

"No!... Uh, yes." She looked over helplessly. "I thought I could set you free and go back home. I didn't expect..."

"Okay. Look, Ilsa. Just head for the front gate. I can't stay here, that's for sure. Neither can you. Not anymore."

"I...I didn't expect to become this involved....I..."

"I'm sorry. I really am," he said. "I didn't want you in this either, but it's too late. We're in it together, whether we want to be or not."

She nodded and looked over at him with a sad smile. Then she gunned the engine, and the car kicked up a cloud of dust and gravel as she steered toward the road. Thomson laid a friendly hand on her shoulder and warned, "Take it easy, until we get to the gate."

"I can't talk us through like the last time, you know." She looked at him, then at her torn clothes.

"We're not going to try."

As they drove across the dark post in silence, Thomson looked across at her and began to wonder. It wasn't the way he wanted it. This was no place for an amateur, especially a woman. No, he knew he was kidding himself. He was beginning to like her, and that wasn't fair. She was too vulnerable, and too fragile. But what choice did he have?

As they got within sight of the gate, he saw the headlights of another car approaching from the opposite direction. "Slow down." He put his hand on her arm, trying to reassure her. "Relax. Time it so we reach the gate when they do. And for chrissakes, don't start thinking! Just do what I tell you to do, got that?''

She nodded and swallowed hard, trying to reassure him.

Thomson watched the guard step up to the heavy, counterbalanced wooden gate. He was looking the other way, toward the car coming in, and hadn't seen the Fiat. As the other car got closer, Thomson saw that it was a dark Mercedes sedan. The guard began to raise the gate to let it pass through.

Ilsa started to say something, but Thomson cut her off as he watched the guard. Finally, he heard the Fiat and turned his head to see who was coming up from behind.

"Steady," Thomson warned. "Slow down, just like you always do." But as they got within fifty feet of the barrier he snapped, "Now! Floor it!"

The small engine roared and the car leaped forward, accelerating as it headed for the opening. The gate was halfway up. All the bewildered guard could do was leap aside as the Fiat passed under the barrier, clipping the support pole and sending chunks of wood flying through the air.

As they raced past the Mercedes, Thomson turned his head and looked inside. He caught a brief glimpse of two Arab officers sitting in the rear seat, looking over in shock as the smaller car roared by unchecked, disappearing down the dirt road in a cloud of dust.

"WE HAVE LESS than twelve hours. Are all your units at their jump-off points, ready to move on the capital?" He continued his methodical questioning, staring vacantly out the car window as the dark desert landscape rolled past.

"Yes," General al-Baquri answered nervously. "I told you that before."

"And I shall ask you again." Rashid's head snapped around. "There is no margin for error here, al-Baquri. None."

"Do you think I don't know that? The rest of us have as much at risk here as you, Rashid," he argued, indulging his anger by using the colonel's surname. After all, al-Baquri did outrank him by three full grades. Not that rank mattered. In the larger scheme of things, the general didn't come up to the colonel's knees, and they both knew it.

"Good." Rashid's voice hinted at his amusement. "I'm glad you realize how much is at risk here, General. Because it is everything!" It was dark in the backseat, so al-Baquri couldn't see Rashid's piercing eyes. But he felt them, even in the dark. "You, and I, and the others are nothing. Our lives are nothing. What is at risk is the future of the entire Moslem world. Never forget that."

Al-Baquri kept quiet. His concerns were far less sweeping. Would he live to see one more sunset? Would he see his wife and children again? Or would tomorrow afternoon find him standing in front of a presidential firing squad?

"My tanks and men have been arriving in small groups for the past four days." Al-Baquri squirmed in his seat. "Two battalions are dug in here at Heliopolis and four more are waiting in the desert, ready to move on Cairo at noon. But you promised us that won't be necessary. You promised that the garrison in Cairo won't resist."

"And they won't. Once he is dead and the general staff arrested, there will be no resistance, will there?"

"You assured us there will be no shooting. I . . . I do not know how my troops would react if I ordered them to fire on other Egyptian soldiers."

"A good commander can get his men to do whatever he tells them. Isn't that so, al-Baquri?" Rashid leaned closer, his eyes boring in. "Isn't that so, General?"

Al-Baquri began to sweat. Rashid terrified him. At best, the man was a zealot. At worst, he was totally insane. But it was too late to stop any of it. General Faisal al-Baquri, Commander of the Egyptian Third Armored Regiment, was caught in a trap of his own making. All he could do was thank Allah he could hide in the darkness, so Rashid couldn't read the desperation written on his face.

"He phoned me today," Rashid said quietly, sounding faintly amused. "He asked me if we had any armored units out here."

"He? You mean Nasser!" Al-Baquri sat up, his back suddenly becoming ramrod straight.

"I do not speak the name unless I am forced to. It is an abomination to me!"

"He knows?" al-Baquri demanded. "My God! But how?"

"The police . . . the American got to Saleh."

"We are finished," the general groaned.

"The damage has been contained. Grüber finally caught the American. He has him locked up. And this will be the last time he meddles in my affairs."

"And Saleh? If he knows . . ."

"He knows nothing. Nasser assured him everything is fine. Why shouldn't he? But you have nothing to fear. The good police captain will not be around to upset our plans tomorrow. He is temporarily indisposed. And if I am prepared to deal with my oldest friend, then you may be assured I will deal even more harshly with anyone else who gets in my way."

Al-Baquri swallowed hard, knowing exactly what he meant.

"You know, the British used to have a saying about their accursed breakfasts." Rashid leaned back and mused.

"The chicken who contributes the eggs is 'involved.' But the pig who contributed the bacon, he is 'committed'!"

"Rashid! I assure you—"

"Don't assure me. Show me! Tomorrow!"

Al-Baquri chafed under the rebuke, but before he could reply the lights of the post came into view through the front windshield, saving him. He breathed a muffled sigh of relief. At last this inquisition would end.

"I want your best officers on duty tomorrow, particularly at the reviewing stand, officers we can trust."

"It has already been arranged," al-Baquri replied, as the sedan began to slow down.

"And I want this gate closed, immediately. No one is to enter or leave. No one."

"I know! You've said that before." Al-Baquri smiled nervously as he watched the sentry step behind the gate and block their way, seemingly alert, as if he knew what he was doing. Allah be praised for that, at least. The guard tried to see through the bright headlight beams, waiting for the car to stop. Good, al-Baquri thought. Rashid will find no fault with his troops tonight. The guard recognized the car and saluted. He had slung his rifle over his shoulder and was beginning to raise the wooden barricade when al-Baquri saw the headlights of a second car approaching from the opposite direction. He leaned forward, a sick, nervous feeling growing in the pit of his stomach.

The car slowed down, only to suddenly accelerate and race forward. The guard turned his head and signaled for it to stop, but it didn't. The guard jumped aside as the small car raced through the open gate. Al-Baquri turned his head and swore as the smaller car went past. For a brief second, he looked into the front seat of the Fiat, and gasped.

"The American!" he shouted. "And that is Fengler's daughter with him! Quick, after them!"

The driver slammed on the brakes and tried to throw the car in reverse, as Rashid shouted angrily, "No! Let them go! We'll never catch them in the dark. Besides, Thomson won't get far. There is only one place left for him to run. This is the last time that man will interfere with me."

24

"WHY AREN'T THEY following us?" Ilsa asked after they'd turned onto the main highway and she could see no headlights behind them.

"I don't know. But I don't like any of the answers that come to mind," he answered, leaning back and closing his eyes. He ran his fingers lightly across his ribs, wincing from the pain. If a couple of them weren't broken, they were the next best thing. "Pull over to the side for a minute," he said.

When the car stopped, Thomson sat up and unbuttoned his shirt and struggled to slip it off. "You can't go around like that," he said, pointing to the torn sweater she was trying to cover herself with. She said nothing, obviously still embarrassed, as she turned her back to him and let the sweater drop onto the seat.

He draped the shirt over her bare shoulders. She quickly put her arms through the sleeves and clutched it to her, then she paused and he heard her sob. She hid her face in her hands and he saw her begin to tremble.

Thomson laid his hand on her back, tenderly, wanting so much to console her. She stiffened at his touch, as if she'd received an electric shock. Finally, she relaxed. She slowly turned to face him. Tears were running down her cheeks and she tried to speak, but couldn't.

He raised his arms out toward her and she came to him. She threw her arms around his neck and buried her head against his shoulder, as it all fell in on her. He leaned back, holding her tight and stroking her hair for several long minutes until her crying stopped.

She lifted her head and started to speak. "Thomson..."

"Richard. And don't say anything. You'll break the spell," he said, knowing nothing seemed more natural than to be holding her like this. And it wasn't misplaced sympathy or a big-brother complex. He just wanted to hold her. She was different from any woman he'd ever known.

She raised her hands and tenderly touched his face, drawing it closer until their lips met and she closed her eyes.

When they parted, he looked at her and said, "Good thing for you I've got sore ribs."

She dropped her head on his shoulder again, as if it belonged to her. "What are we going to do, Richard?" she asked.

"I don't know. They'll be looking for the car at the borders. But there are ways. We might be able to get out—"

"Out?" She sat up and looked puzzled. "We can't leave. We have to stay here. You know what will happen if we don't."

"Ilsa, look at us. How much chance do you think we stand? And why should we? If we run, we might make it. If we try to stop them, we're going to lose everything, including each other. That isn't worth it."

"Richard, we *have* nothing. If we leave, I couldn't live with myself, or with you. I just couldn't. We've got to stay here and try to stop them."

"Including your father?"

"He doesn't know what he's doing."

Thomson tried to laugh, but it hurt too much. "He doesn't know how to break ribs, either. But for an amateur, he gave it a pretty good try."

"I knew you wouldn't understand."

"Look, Sweet Pea, you keep thinking Papa's pure as the driven snow, if that makes you feel better, but he's into this up to his eyeballs."

"Of course he knows what he is doing—in a theoretical sense. He's consumed by it. But he's only doing it to make a point, to prove something to them. That's all. He doesn't understand where it's all heading."

"And you're going to teach him? To save him from himself? You think you can wreck his plans, then convince him you did it for his own good?"

"No! I didn't…that's why I needed you. Can't you stop them? Can't your government?"

"*My* government?" He laughed. "I don't know. But it doesn't matter. He'll still hate you for it. He'll never see it your way. Never. Did you think about that? About what that will do to you? And to us?"

"I don't know!" she shouted. "It all happened too fast."

He felt sorry for her, and for himself. He would have rather run away, but only if she came with him. So he was stuck. He didn't owe them anything, certainly not this much, not after what they had done to him. But he couldn't refuse her, even though her harebrained idealism was going to get them both killed.

She stared through the windshield, driving in silence for several miles before she said, "Papa wasn't always like this. You must believe me. He was a kind man, before my mother was killed in a bombing raid. I was only twelve, but I saw what it did to him. After that, all he had left was his work. He turned bitter. He lost himself in it. A man can be excused for that, can't he?"

If he was a carpenter or a plumber? Sure, Thomson thought. But Papa Fengler wasn't one of those. He was a physicist. "How far has he gotten?"

"I think he's finished," she said quietly. "I can tell by the way he's been acting, by that strange look in his eyes. I've never seen him like this. He scares me."

"Me, too. Because the rockets are ready, too. One glance inside the hangar told me that much. What about the tanks? When did they show up?"

"Three days ago. We assumed it was part of the big demonstration they have planned for tomorrow. Everyone is going to be there, even Nasser himself. Wouldn't they want a lot of tanks and troops to protect him?"

"Said the spider to the fly," he mumbled.

FINDING A PAY PHONE wasn't difficult. Persuading Kilbride's butler to wake the ambassador in the middle of the night wasn't difficult either, not after Thomson said he was the secretary of state and demanded he get the dumb Mick on the line.

"Ambassador Kilbride here, Mr. Secretary." Thomson smiled as he heard the panic in the man's voice. "If you'll give me a few minutes, I'm sure I can explain this whole situation."

"I bet you can," Thomson said sarcastically. "And it'll make one hell of a fairy tale, won't it?"

"What? Who?... Thomson? When I get my hands on you, I'm going to personally wring your—"

"Shut up and listen for a minute, or you'll be wringing laundry in Leavenworth."

"Leavenworth? Me? This is all your fault. You did it good this time, boy. I had you nailed on espionage and treason. That wasn't good enough for you. You had to go shoot Perper, too. Well, that's murder. You know what these Arabs do with a murderer? They cut off his god-damned head with one of those big swords of theirs, that's what they do!''

"I didn't kill Perper," Thomson snapped, his voice turning angry. "Your pet, Collins, did that. You know it as well as I do."

"Tell that to the guy with the axe, Thomson. You're his problem now."

"Kilbride, listen to me, for chrissakes! Your Arab pals are setting you up. Can't you see that? Those rockets are ready to fire. I've seen them. And they've built a couple of A-bombs to go with them. Remember those old Nazis you didn't care about? Well, that's how they've been spending their summer vacations. There's a lot more going on out there, too, but I haven't got all the pieces."

"You never do, Thomson. And I don't want to hear any more about it—"

"Kilbride! Can't you see what they're going to do with those bombs?" he asked, until the answer to his own question finally hit home. "That's it, isn't it? You do see!"

"They aren't going to do a damned thing with them!" Kilbride screamed at him. "It's like I told you before, Thomson, but you wouldn't listen."

"Kilbride, call Washington. This thing's gotten out of control."

"No! I ain't calling anyone. You almost screwed it up for me good, Thomson. You just wouldn't leave it alone. You were too goddamned smart to listen, weren't you? Just like Washington. You're all too goddamned smart to listen to me. Well, we'll see who's right."

"Kilbride, don't do it. You're wrong!"

"Wrong? Me wrong, Thomson? Why don't you save us the trouble and go put a bullet in your head. That's all I want from you. Go kill yourself. Do anything. Just have the good sense not to let the Egyptians catch you!''

Then the ambassador slammed the phone down.

Thomson stared at the receiver and shook his head. "So much for that idea," he said as he looked at Ilsa, trying to think of something else. What about Saleh? he wondered. That would be like sticking his head down the lion's throat, but where else could he turn?

He dropped the coins into the phone and waited through the rings for someone to answer.

A bored receptionist finally came on the line. "Headquarters."

"May I speak with Captain Saleh, please?" Thomson asked.

"Captain Saleh is not available."

"Where can I reach him? It's urgent."

"The captain has had a serious accident. He's in the military hospital and will not be back to duty for some time. Who may I—"

Thomson hung up before she could finish asking.

"The police? But I thought they were chasing you too?" Ilsa asked.

"They are. Saleh was a good cop, though. He's tough and nasty, but I can't believe he knows a damned thing about the bombs. Not that it matters, because he's in the hospital." He closed his eyes and tried to think, but he was too tired. Where now? Where could he turn? Perper was dead, Kilbride wouldn't listen, and Saleh couldn't. That was strike three.

But maybe it wasn't. He frowned and picked up the phone again, trying to remember the number. On the fifth ring, someone answered.

"This is Thomson. Tell the old man that Perper's dead."

"We know," came the heavily accented reply.

"Tell Jani I'll be at that address in thirty minutes. I need your help."

HASSAN SALEH FOUGHT to regain consciousness. He was swimming in a thick white cloud, flailing at it with his arms and legs, but the harder he struggled, the denser the cloud became. He couldn't see his hands in front of his face. He couldn't even feel his hands, but he heard voices, arguing, nearby.

"I am not a visitor," the man said threateningly. "Can't you read my pass?"

"All right." The woman relented. "If they let you stay, I won't be held responsible for what happens. But Captain Saleh is in serious condition. He wasn't to have any visitors."

"I made that rule, you fool! I am his guard, not some . . . visitor," Sayyid nearly screamed at her.

Sayyid! And a nurse? Then he must be safe.

"He has a skull fracture. We must be very careful with him for at least forty-eight hours. How did it happen, anyway?"

"Hit and run . . . you know how those go."

"Hit by a car? And no other injuries? How strange."

"How fortunate," Sayyid corrected her.

"I suppose . . . I must leave now. You won't forget what I said? He is to have complete rest, for at least forty-eight hours."

"Oh, you may be sure of that." Sayyid's pleasant voice reassured her, and reassured Saleh.

Sayyid, here! He opened his eyes and saw Sayyid's dim shape leaning over him. He tried to smile. He wanted to say something to him, but he couldn't. His lips wouldn't move. His tongue seemed frozen.

"Is he waking up?" Sayyid sounded concerned.

"Soon," the nurse answered. "He was given a sedative. It will begin to wear off. Then he'll need lots of rest, and time."

Time, Saleh cursed, closing his eyes. The lids were too heavy. Time! He wanted so much to talk. There was something he wanted to say, but he couldn't remember. A car? Was he hit by a car? He couldn't remember.

The door swung shut and the room was quiet again. Then he heard footsteps and the sound of a telephone being dialed.

"Yes, sir," Sayyid said softly. "There was nothing I could do, I swear! A police cruiser came into the lot before we could lift him into the van. We had to pretend we found him lying there, or someone would have asked questions."

Saleh strained, trying to listen and understand, but it was hard.

"The Mahdi Military Hospital... Yes, sir," he went on. "I assure you. He is alive and in no danger.... A skull fracture, so there's no way he can interfere with our plans. I will stay here myself until the time has passed. And I will make sure he talks to no one. By noon, it won't matter, will it?"

Saleh didn't understand. None of it made sense. He opened his eyes and saw Sayyid put the phone back in its cradle. The sergeant turned to face him, and his hand reached inside his jacket. He pulled out a small leather case. He stepped toward the bed, then opened it and filled a hypodermic needle.

No! Saleh wanted to speak. He wanted to stop Sayyid, but he couldn't. All he could do was watch helplessly as Sayyid filled the needle and bent over. Saleh looked into Sayyid's eyes. They seemed so cold and so hard. They were the eyes of a stranger. Saleh wanted to say something, but the words drifted away. His eyelids closed, and he couldn't remember. He was lost again in that thick white cloud.

25

As THEY APPROACHED the house, Thomson got a sick feeling in his gut. Maybe he was tired, maybe it was just nerves, but he told her to drive through the neighborhood one more time anyway. She gave him a perplexed look and did what he said.

"I don't see a thing," she finally commented.

"That's the whole point. Humor me and keep driving," he said, as he scanned the dark alleyways of the working-class neighborhood. If it was just nerves, Thomson didn't appreciate them one bit. Everything looked too calm and too quiet.

They found the address easily enough. The house sat by itself near the side of an old brickyard. He had to hand it to the Israelis. It was the perfect place for a meet—quiet and secluded. Too secluded, he thought. There wasn't a single car on the street and there were no lights on inside the house. No matter how hard he looked, he could find no signs of surveillance or the hint of any guards. None. They were good, but nobody was that good. There wasn't a thread out of place. It looked perfect. Just like Damascus.

Maybe that was what set off the little alarm bells in the back of his head. Whatever it was, he heard them clanging like a four-alarm fire, telling him to get away as fast as his feet could carry him. Carry him where? He knew the alarm bells were probably right. It reeked of a setup. But even if it was, there wasn't a damned thing he could do about it. Thomson had to go in, because there wasn't anywhere else to go.

He told Ilsa to park the car two streets over from the house. "You got a flashlight in this thing?" he asked as he struggled with the latch on the glove compartment.

"Don't bother. It's been broken since we got the car. Here." She dug into the clutter beneath the front seat and handed him a flashlight.

He tried to take it from her, but she wouldn't let go. She shook her head. "I'll carry the flashlight. You carry the gun."

"That would be nice," he replied with a smile, "if you were coming along . . . but you're not."

Ilsa got out of the car anyway and stood in the road with her arms folded, staring down at him through the front windshield, watching as he struggled to get out the other side by himself. Finally, she walked around and took his arm, pulling him up onto his feet.

She looked up at him, glaring. "First, I'm not staying here alone." She was absolutely certain about that. "Not after what I've been through tonight. And second, you cannot make it very far on your own. If you try, and go stumbling around out there in the dark, you'll wake up half of Cairo. But don't worry about me, Richard. You're the one they're after. Besides, if anything does happen, I can take care of myself."

"Like you did in the hangar!"

"I can take care of myself! I'm not your responsibility. There are other things that are more important. So you worry about you, and I'll worry about me. If we don't, we're never going to get anywhere."

He turned his eyes away and said sheepishly, "I just don't want to see you hurt."

Her expression softened and she smiled. She ran her hand down his cheek. "I know. And I appreciate the sentiment. Really. But we seem to be trapped by the . . . practicalities of the moment."

"Damned thick-skulled Germans," he muttered. He reluctantly turned away and led her on a slow, limping course between two houses, down a narrow alley, and up to a thick hedge, where they had a clear view of the rear of the house. He peered through the bushes and studied each door and window, probing the dark shadows but not learning a damned thing he didn't know before. There were no lights inside the house, no guards he could see, and no signs of life.

Thomson pulled the old Luger from his belt and ran his fingers down the barrel, examining it closely, making sure the safety was off, the clip of bullets seated firmly in the butt, and a round in the chamber. Then he grabbed Ilsa firmly by the hand and set off for the rear door of the house.

The yard was in complete darkness, but he sensed something was wrong. The back door was hanging open, sagging, as if it had been kicked off its hinges. Nearby, a window frame had been knocked out onto the ground. It looked as if someone had tried to get inside quickly and didn't care how he did it.

Thomson eased up on to the porch and listened intently at the rear door. All he heard were the soft sounds of the Egyptian night, but not a single sound from inside the house. Nothing. He peeked around the door frame, trying to see inside, but it was too dark. He tightened his grip on the old Luger and held it out waist-high as he leaned forward, looking into the house. He flicked on the flashlight. In the bright circle of light at the end of its narrow beam he saw snatches of a kitchen, as if through a keyhole. The room had been turned inside out and upside down, and shot to pieces. A cheap wooden table and a matched set of chairs were lying on their sides, and the floor was littered with pots and broken crockery. The far wall was stitched with a line of bullet holes. Huge chunks of plaster were gouged from the archway that led to the front rooms of the house.

Ilsa began to whisper something, but Thomson put his finger to her lips and hushed her.

"Stay close," he whispered. He turned off the flashlight and limped into the kitchen, carefully stepping over the debris and working his way toward the front of the house. That would be the living room, he told himself, and that was where he found the first body.

Thomson almost tripped over it as he groped his way through the dark. He bent down and used the flashlight again, taking the risk because he had to know more. He held the beam low, studying the body. It was a young man, dressed in a cheap brown suit. There were three bullet holes in his chest. From the look of total shock on his face and the angle of the body, it looked as if they had shot him from the rear door, probably before he even knew they were there. Could he be one of the men with Jani last night? Thomson wondered. It was hard to tell.

There was an Uzi submachine gun lying next to the man, with a long silencer screwed onto its barrel. Thomson picked it up and sniffed the barrel. It hadn't been fired. Whatever had hit him had come quick, Thomson thought grimly. At least he hadn't suffered.

"Richard," he heard Ilsa softly moan. She was kneeling behind him in the corner. When he turned the flashlight in her direction, he saw more bodies.

He quickly lifted her aside and propped her against the wall, facing the other way. The last thing he needed right now was a sick woman on his hands. He turned the light back on the bodies, looking for the two he prayed wouldn't be there.

There were five men, lying where they'd fallen, like sides of beef on a slaughterhouse floor. The guy in the brown suit might not have known what hit him, but these guys had. Someone had lined them up and gunned them down—shot them to pieces. The wall was full of holes, splattered with blood as if it were a set in a cheap Hollywood gangster movie. Thomson had seen his share of killing, but this massacre threw his stomach right up into his throat.

On the left side of the stack, Thomson saw Jani's body. He was lying on top of someone else, as if he had tried to shield him from the bullets. How sadly futile. Thomson reached out and touched the hand of the man on the bottom. It looked old and wrinkled. The fingers were lifeless now, but Thomson remembered how eloquent and expressive they had once been. He turned the flashlight beam on the old man's face. Thomson frowned. The old man looked very ordinary now. Twenty-four hours ago, he had been something special. He'd been alive.

"Rest in peace," Thomson mumbled. "You should have stayed back on the farm, because you deserved better than you got here." He stood up, ignoring the sharp-edged pain in his chest and side. He wanted it. He wanted the pain and the hurt. Maybe it would make him feel better. If he punished himself enough, maybe he could forgive himself for not doing something sooner, and for being the one still standing here, alive, while better men had died.

The list was getting long and heavy, too long and too heavy for Thomson to keep carrying. There was the old man and Jani, and the rest of the guys lying there. And before them Perper. And before him that fat slob Yussuf, the one without the head. He counted too, but not for much. And then there was Landau. He'd been the first, but was

a long way from the last. Thomson shook his head. Somebody had left an awful trail of bodies behind him, and
somebody was going to pay.

He was mad, and could feel his adrenaline pumping. The
old engine was running fine now, racing flat-out without a
twitch, as he felt his reflexes on full alert. Maybe the bodies and the blood had done it, but each of his senses seemed
heightened. He turned off the flashlight and stood silently
in the dark room, listening hard.

He swore he heard a faint rustling in the front yard. He
picked up the Uzi and several spare magazines from the
floor, jamming them into his pants pocket. Then he stepped
closer to Ilsa and took her trembling hand. "Let's get out
of here," he whispered, as he pressed the Luger into her
fingers and led her toward the rear door. But the rustling
sound was followed by footsteps and a soft voice in German
telling someone to go around the back.

Thomson pulled Ilsa quietly through the kitchen until
his foot bumped against a chair in the dark. The footsteps
near the front door became louder and he heard someone
enter the house. If they didn't move fast, he knew they'd
be surrounded, trapped inside.

He pushed her against the wall and stepped outside onto
the small porch. Dropping into a low crouch, he saw a soldier dressed in dark combat fatigues with a rifle in his hands
walking toward him not five feet away. It was hard to tell
who was the more surprised, but Thomson was the one who
was ready. Taking a quick step forward, he swung the barrel of the Uzi in a compact arc and raked it across the man's
throat before he could even break stride. The soldier let out
a soft gurgle and crumpled backward onto the ground.
Dropping even lower, Thomson brought the Uzi down to
waist level and scanned the backyard.

He saw nothing. Quickly, he reached inside the kitchen door and grabbed Ilsa's hand, then took off in a painful loping run across the yard. Looking back, he saw a dark shadow step through the rear door of the house. Thomson didn't think twice. Holding the Uzi out at arm's length, he pointed it at the door and pulled the trigger, firing a muffled burst across the narrow doorway. The barrel jumped and the shadow fell backward into the kitchen. Two down, he thought. That would do for a down payment on the debt. And maybe it would slow them up for a few moments.

Holding her with one hand and the Uzi with the other, Thomson headed for the hedge as he heard angry shouts in German and running feet converging on the house from several directions. The Germans had laid their little trap with skill.

In the dark, even running as slowly as they were, he and Ilsa might have made it, if it hadn't been for the man who came plunging through the hedge, heading directly toward them. They saw each other at the same time, and Thomson's Uzi was still pointed at the house. He tried to bring it around as the other man raised his automatic rifle, and Thomson saw he'd be too late. The German had his gun at waist level and was about to shoot when a loud *crack* split the night. It was the Luger. Ilsa had pulled the trigger. The heavy nine-millimeter slug hit the German and lifted him off his feet. It was a clean hit, dead center in the chest. Still, the German managed to squeeze the trigger on his automatic rifle as he fell.

The short burst missed Thomson, digging up the ground behind him. But he felt a sudden, heavy pull on his arm that almost made him lose his balance as Ilsa tumbled forward. As she fell, her hand slipped from his grasp. His head whipped around, and he stopped and looked back at where she lay on the ground.

"Richard!" she gasped as she rolled onto her side, holding her thigh with both hands.

Thomson looked at her in desperation, then back at the house. He raised the Uzi and fired off the rest of the magazine at the rear door. That might buy them a few seconds, but not much more. Then he tried to get his hands under her and lift her to her feet. "Quick! Let me carry you."

"No!" She pushed his hands away. "Get out of here. Go! Before they catch you, too. We are on our own, remember?"

"I can't leave you here," he insisted.

Her hand lashed out and slapped him across the face. "If you love me, then you'll keep going, and you'll stop them. Go. I'll never forgive you if you don't. Please!"

He heard more voices and the sound of running feet. He looked down at her and hated her for forcing him to make the choice. "I'll get you out of this," he said. Then he stood up and began running, the ache in his heart greater than the one in his side as he limped through the backyards and sidestreets, trying to fight off the anger, the frustration, and the tears.

ILSA LAY ON THE GROUND, her eyes filled with hate. She ignored the pain. Holding her thigh, she looked up at the men with the dark faces and guns.

Then she heard the voice, the one voice that made her blood run cold.

"My, my!" Grüber looked down at her, gloating. "Look what has fallen into my hands again. And won't Papa Fengler be pleased to learn what his darling daughter has been up to this evening."

26

EVEN PAINTED in the fresh glow of a midsummer sunrise, the Mahdi Military Hospital looked somber and imposing. Four stories tall, its dull reddish-brown brick covering an entire city block, it resembled nothing so much as a medieval fortress or a prison. Thomson sat in the Fiat studying the façade of the building, nervously gripping the steering wheel, knowing that Saleh was somewhere inside. Saleh was the last chance he had.

His eyes scanned the street and caught his reflection in the rearview mirror. His? He barely recognized the gaunt face staring back at him. It looked too exhausted and battered to continue. The eyes were a dull streaked red and set above dark bluish-black pouches. His hair was greasy and matted, in bad need of a combing. And his clothes were torn and spotted with grease. Was that what he'd worn to the airport that morning? That morning? Hell, he groaned. That was yesterday morning!

It wasn't an illusion. It was him. That was the toll the past four days had levied. Clearly, he couldn't simply walk up to the information desk of the hospital with a bouquet of flowers in his hand and ask for Saleh's room.

He turned the key in the ignition and started the car's engine, pulling out slowly into the thin morning traffic and circling the old hospital again and again, studying it, looking for a crack in their armor, and finding none.

On the fourth pass, he heard the high-pitched wail of an emergency siren. Coming down the street in the opposite lane was a khaki-colored army ambulance with a bright red flasher on its roof. It roared past and made a sharp turn into the hospital driveway, nearly tipping onto its side before it skidded to a halt at the emergency room entrance. Two white-clad attendants jumped out and ran to the rear door of the ambulance. Together, they hauled the stretcher out and made a bone-jarring dash to the emergency room door.

Thomson smiled. He made a U-turn and followed the same route, parking behind the ambulance. It was still early. The street was deserted. No one noticed the seedy-looking man climb into the back of the ambulance, or the somewhat scruffy attendant emerge a few minutes later, complete with a white smock, hospital cap, and clipboard.

The trick is to keep your eyes straight ahead. Walk fast and scowl. Act like you know exactly what you're doing, and like you're too important to be bothered with stupid questions. Then again, two out of four wasn't all bad.

Fortunately, the directory signs inside the hospital dated from colonial days. The hospital departments were listed in Arabic and English. Still, Thomson didn't have the slightest idea where they had put Saleh. Emergency? Orthopedics? Surgery? Who knew? He began to prowl the halls, starting with the first and second floors, where the major departments were housed. Taking them one at a time, he walked through Post-Op and Intensive Care, and ended up in the Internal Medicine wing. But he found nothing.

So he went back to the main corridor and the central bank of elevators. He stepped into the first one that came down and pushed the buttons for the top two floors. When the door opened for the fourth floor, he stuck his head out for a quick look up and down the hall. From the signs on the wall, he realized they were convalescent wards. He doubted they'd park a police captain in such plebeian surroundings, so he let the door close and rode up to five.

As the door opened, he noticed that plush carpeting and wallpaper had replaced the faded paint and bare tile of the four lower floors. If they had a VIP area, this was most likely it, Thomson thought.

He stepped out of the elevator and walked briskly down the long hallway, holding the clipboard high to shield his face, pretending he was a near-sighted maintenance man checking the ceiling fixtures. Several orderlies walked past and gave him curious stares, but continued on. You never ask for trouble from a man with a clipboard.

Thomson was beginning to think he might actually pull it off when the door at the far end of the hall opened and he saw Sayyid step out. The big sergeant yawned and stretched, then began walking toward Thomson.

Thomson raised the clipboard higher and did a quick about-face. The hairs on the back of his neck stood up as he remembered their last meeting. He held his breath, listening for a shout or even a threatening growl, but none came. Sayyid must not have seen him after all. Thomson kept retreating toward the opposite end of the hall, with Sayyid's heavy footsteps keeping pace behind him. One thing was sure, he wasn't going to let them catch up.

The footsteps stopped. Thomson kept walking, but risked a quick glance back. Sayyid was standing at the bank of elevators. When the elevator door opened, Sayyid stepped forward and disappeared from view.

This was the break Thomson had been praying for. He dashed back to the other end of the hall, to the door Sayyid had come out of. He pressed his ear to the wood and listened, but heard nothing. Reaching under the smock, he pulled out the Luger and held it behind the clipboard, then opened the door and slipped inside.

The room was dark except for a dim floor lamp standing in the corner. The shades were drawn, but Thomson could see that the furnishings were plush—one hell of a lot bigger and nicer than your average *fella* would get. The bed and nightstand stood along the near wall. There was a soft couch along the far wall and a wheelchair and tall lounger in the corner by the window. He saw that he was alone, except for the man lying beneath a sheet on the bed.

Thomson lowered the clipboard and kept the Luger aimed at the bed, determined not to walk into another trap. "Don't move," he rasped, trying to sound calm as he edged closer. Then with a quick motion he switched on the reading lamp that hung on the headboard above the bed.

In the harsh light, he recognized Saleh. The cop's face was pale. His head was heavily bandaged and his eyes shut tight. His facial muscles were slack and it was obvious he hadn't heard a word Thomson said.

"Come on, Saleh," Thomson said in frustration, as he shook the policeman's shoulder and poked him gently in the ribs with the Luger. "It's springtime. You're Queen of the May, you bastard, so rise and shine! I'm in no better shape than you are."

Saleh frowned and grunted from the prodding, trying to clear his head. One eye opened, then a second, but they were glassy, the pupils dilated.

"Oh hell," Thomson mumbled, turning toward the nightstand next to the bed. "What did they pump into you, anyway?" he asked, noticing the hypodermic needle and a vial. He picked it up, but the inscription was in Arabic. Not that he would have understood it in English.

There was a water jug on the table. He carried it over and splashed some of it on Saleh's face. The Egyptian's eyes blinked again, and it was obvious he was trying to focus them. "What? Who?... Thomson?" Saleh shook his head and frowned. "Where am I? Something... You were right... You were right all along. It's tomorrow... I've got to stop them..."

"Great! That's really great," the American commented dryly. "You've got to stop them. So let's get you on your feet and the hell out of here, before your playmate comes back."

Thomson grabbed the wheelchair and rolled it to the side of the bed, bent over, and tried to lift Saleh up and into it. The captain was still babbling, pleading with him. "We've got to go... go to Gamal."

"Sure, we'll do just that, Sport."

"He'll know what to do. We must leave..." But Saleh's words drifted away as his eyes focused on something behind Thomson.

That was when the American knew he'd made a mistake.

"You should have taken the captain's advice," Sayyid's angry voice whispered from the doorway. Thomson turned his head and saw a large-caliber revolver pointing at him. "You should have gone a long time ago, Thomson. Now it is too late. Stand up, very slowly, and move away from the bed."

Thomson did what Sayyid said, dropping Saleh's head back onto the pillow. "No, Sayyid! No!" Saleh kept muttering. "You must help us..."

The big sergeant kicked the door shut behind him and came across the room with all the subtlety of a tornado. The wheelchair was in his path, so one of his big paws lashed out and swatted it against the far wall. "I should have given the captain another injection before I left, Thomson. But it wasn't necessary. He would have kept sleeping, if someone hadn't come in and tried to wake him up. Yes, Captain Saleh would have slept through the whole thing. He wouldn't have known a thing about it until it was too late. It would have been over, if you hadn't interfered again."

Sayyid's eyes turned vicious as the paw lashed out and slammed Thomson against the wall this time. "I'll take that present you left on the bed," he added as he leaned over and grabbed the Luger. "If there is going to be any shooting done around here, I will be the one doing it."

"Why, Sayyid?" Saleh asked in disbelief, his eyes straining to understand. "Not you, too... not you. The voice I heard... I thought I was dreaming, but it was you, wasn't it? Why? Why would you involve yourself in this? It is treason!"

"Treason? Treason!" Sayyid bristled at the word. "I respect you deeply, Captain. But you have no right to accuse me of such things. There is only one treason in this country. It comes from that abomination you call president. But his hours are numbered, Allah be praised."

Saleh moaned and shook his head. "Sayyid, this is wrong. I beg of you. Why?"

"Why? He is a traitor to his faith, and there is no greater treason a man can commit! He has set himself up as a false prophet, gaining the confidence of his people, then compromising it away until we have nothing. No more! We shall strike a blow that will purify our land with fire. We will rid ourselves of him and the Jews. That is just the beginning. Today begins the rebirth of the Moslem people. Nothing else matters. So how can you dare call it treason?"

"Those are not your words, Sayyid. I know you too well," Saleh groaned. "It is the Ikhwan again, isn't it? The Moslem Brotherhood? Has their secret society infected you with this venom, Sayyid?"

"Infected? We are the people, not him. Nasser has tried to blot us out, twice. But he can't. No one can. And this time, we shall be the ones who survive, not him. This time, we have a true leader with the vision to govern this land. When those rockets soar in the sky at noon and begin their downward arc toward Tel Aviv and Haifa, a million Arab voices will rise as one, shouting the name of Colonel Ali Rashid. As his oldest friend, you should be honored. He is the one who spared your life, Captain. Not I."

But Saleh had stopped listening. He had pressed his palms against his ears, trying to block out the truth. When they couldn't, his eyes flared and he screamed an oath in Arabic, suddenly bolting upright on the bed and lunging for Sayyid.

The sergeant's pistol was pointed at Thomson, and he never expected a threat from this new quarter. But before Sayyid could react, Saleh had his arms locked around Sayyid's chest, pinning his gun arm to his side, and hanging on. Sayyid stepped backward, dragging Saleh off the bed, but lost his balance and stumbled. As they crashed to the floor, Sayyid's elbow hit the hard floor and his revolver bounced away.

Even in top shape, the frail captain would have been no match for the burly sergeant, but the little man was possessed. Sayyid pushed himself up to his knees and tried yanking his arm free. He roared and slammed Saleh up and down, finally bouncing him against the metal railings of the bed before the captain's grip was broken and he rolled aside, stunned.

The American dove for him as soon as Saleh grabbed Sayyid's arm, but he had too far to go. He leaped on Sayyid's back as the big sergeant broke Saleh's grip, and became the object of the sergeant's fury. Sayyid swung his arm around and caught Thomson in the ribs with an elbow that seemed to be the size of a small ham. The blow lifted Thomson off his feet and slammed him against the bed. The sergeant was a powerful man and he knew how to use every muscle. Thomson had only caught a glancing blow, but it took his breath away. His ribs screamed and for a moment he saw a bright flashing light inside his head. He stumbled forward, bent over at the waist.

Sayyid could have finished him right then. There was nothing Thomson could have done to stop him. But Sayyid didn't. He took a step toward Thomson, then stopped. He straightened up and threw his chest out, content to rub his sore elbow as he looked down on his two trophies. There was no question he would kill Thomson, but he would do it his own way, slowly, with his bare hands, and when he had the time to savor it. He laughed, taking a confident step backward as he looked for his revolver on the floor. He smiled when he saw it under the bed and bent down to pick it up.

As Sayyid's fingers touched the gun, Thomson blocked out the pain and took a long, desperate stride forward, lunging out with his foot and giving Sayyid a monstrous kick in the face. He got all his leg into it, and felt bone meet bone. Sayyid staggered backward. The kick sat him down on the floor, hard, but very much conscious. He looked up at Thomson and growled like a wounded animal, shaking his head to clear the cobwebs, and started to get back up. From the look in his eyes, that was one thing Thomson didn't want to let happen. The American grabbed the front legs of the steel nightstand, picked it up, and swung it around in a short arc. Bottles and metal trays flew across the room, but Thomson didn't care. All his attention was focused on Sayyid. The corner of the table caught him on the side of the head and staggered him. His eyes turned glassy and he dropped to all fours. Thomson wound up again. The second shot caught the sergeant flush on the jaw and laid him out flat on the floor. Sayyid heaved a final groan, then went out cold.

Thomson stood there, holding the nightstand in his shaking hands as he looked down at Sayyid, ready to hit him again if he moved. He didn't, but Thomson was still suspicious. "Ah, shit," he said, then gave the sergeant a kick to the side of the head for good measure.

"Help me up," he heard Saleh call from beneath the bed. "For God's sake, Thomson. Help me up. We've got to get out of here. Quick."

"Yeah," he muttered sarcastically as he lowered the nightstand to the floor. He grabbed his side and tried to catch his breath. "You want to get out of here? Good thing you reminded me, Captain. I'd have never thought of it on my own."

Saleh couldn't be more right, though. Thomson staggered back to the side of the bed and slumped down, reaching under it to give Saleh a helping hand to his knees. Saleh had to make it the rest of the way on his own. But he did. Thomson joined him on the mattress and they sat next to each other surveying the damage.

"I am sorry," Saleh gasped. "I've been so stupid. You came to get me out, didn't you?"

"Yeah. It was all going so nice and quiet, too." Thomson smiled as he saw the wheelchair sitting against the far wall and got back to his feet. He was bone-tired, but he managed to limp over and roll it back to the side of the bed.

"Come on, Captain," he said as he helped Saleh off the bed and pushed him to the small closet near the lavatory. Saleh's suit was there and so were his shoes. Thomson scooped them up and dropped them in the captain's lap, then wrapped a blanket around him. Saleh looked deathly pale. "You aren't going to pass out on me, now are you?" he asked.

"I . . . I don't think so."

"Don't!" Thomson ordered as he picked up the Luger and Sayyid's revolver from the floor and slipped them beneath the blanket. "Sit up straight and smile. It's going to take both of us to talk our way out of here, Sport."

Thomson wheeled Saleh out of the room and pulled the door closed behind them. He steered a path down the center of the hall, keeping his eyes straight ahead until he reached the elevator. He pushed the down button and waited, sweating out each second as the elevator rose in its shaft.

The bell chimed. As the door opened, a thin, dark orderly stepped out and greeted them. "Here." He smiled politely and stepped back, holding the door open. Thomson tried to return the smile but saw the orderly's gaze drop to the floor, to his battered brown leather shoes. The orderly frowned, then looked up at Thomson's face and frowned again.

"Where do you work?" the orderly demanded.

But before Thomson could answer, the barrel of the heavy revolver poked out from beneath the blanket and jabbed the orderly in the groin. "Get in that elevator!" Saleh said, poking him again for emphasis. "And be sure your flapping mouth does not make you a eunuch."

The man's eyes grew round. He swallowed hard and began to sweat, but backed into the elevator, his eyes never leaving the barrel of the gun.

Thomson followed with the wheelchair and pushed the button for the first floor.

"Well?" Saleh asked in an exasperated voice.

"Oh, yeah." Thomson remembered and landed a roundhouse right on the man's chin. His ribs flashed with pain, but the orderly crumpled in a heap at his feet. When the elevator reached the first floor, Thomson wheeled Saleh out. He reached back and pushed the fifth-floor button. Then he headed for the first street-level door he could find.

27

COLONEL ALI RASHID stared vacantly at the maps lying before him on his desk, pretending to listen as al-Baquri droned on about the positions of his troops. Rashid knew he should be more attentive, but he could no longer concentrate on such trivialities. His body might be trapped here in the office, sitting behind the desk as straight and rigid as a steel girder, but his mind was elsewhere. He simply had no patience for little men, for cretins like al-Baquri and the rest of them. Besides, it was all in Allah's hands now. Allah would strike His enemies down at the same moment He raised Rashid up, all in His Name.

Al-Baquri was incapable of comprehending it. That wasn't his fault. It was Allah's will. He only blessed a few with His gift, and Colonel Ali Rashid was one of them. There was no question of that. He was one of the Chosen, one of those very few given the vision. Even more importantly, He had chosen Rashid as the one to act.

Rashid rested his chin on his fingertips and stared up at the general. Why couldn't they understand? Rashid could have done it all by himself; he had the power. It burned inside him with a force stronger than all the tanks and rockets and atomic bombs put together. Nothing could stop him now. *He* was the chosen one.

Fengler sat in a nearby armchair, cleaning his fingernails, fidgeting and bored, and paying even less attention than Rashid. As usual, Fengler wanted only to return to his precious blockhouse. That could wait, Rashid thought. Then he frowned. Where was Grüber? He was essential to the plan, yet he was late. That was not like him. Grüber was a compulsive paranoid, and he rarely showed the impertinence or the courage to be late when he was summoned.

Rashid looked at his watch. Ten A.M. In less than two hours, his dream, the dream of centuries, the dream he had been born to fulfill, would be complete. He ran his fingers across his forehead and felt the heat. He was on fire, but those two couldn't see it. They never would. They never could. Not that it mattered. All that mattered was that they carry out the orders he gave them.

The telephone on his desk rang. He stared at it, irritated by the interruption. Finally, he moved his hand the few inches it took to reach the receiver and raise it to his ear. "Yes," he said quietly. Al-Baquri stopped his briefing and waited. Even Fengler looked up, curious. "No, no," Rashid added, as a faint smile crossed his lips. "If he insists on seeing me, then let him come in."

The door swung open and Ambassador Kilbride stepped into the Spartan office, accompanied by Collins. "Colonel!" The big white-haired Irishman feigned his usual bravado as he smiled and thrust a meaty hand toward Rashid.

The Egyptian didn't respond or rise to greet him. Instead, he sat steely-eyed, with his hands beneath his chin. The time for such games had passed, he thought. It was time Kilbride understood that.

"Well," the ambassador mumbled as his smile faded and his hand dropped to his side. "Colonel, I know it's damned rude of me to barge in like this, but I wonder if I could take a few minutes of your time . . . alone?" He winked as he cocked his head toward Fengler and al-Baquri.

"Alone?" Rashid asked, his tone of voice rejecting the idea out of hand. "There is no need for us to speak alone, Mr. Ambassador. No need at all." He glanced briefly at the other two and chuckled, observing that they were even more nervous than Kilbride. "These are my closest associates. Permit me to introduce them, Mr. Ambassador. This is General Faisal al-Baquri, the distinguished Commander of our elite Third Armored Regiment. Seated in the chair is Professor Ernst Fengler, the noted German physicist. I'm certain you have heard of them."

"Uh, yes." Kilbride frowned and turned a noticeable shade of gray. "The physicist?" he muttered then took a deep breath. "That's what I wanted to talk to you about, Colonel. Look," he began again, more seriously this time. That always worked. "You're a busy man, and I know you're the kind of guy a fellow can talk straight with. Right? We've had a real good understanding over the past few months. Real good."

"Quite true," Rashid conceded pleasantly.

"Damned right! The way I see it, we've got a lot going for us right now. And we're going to have a lot more going for us real soon, if you know what I mean." Kilbride edged even closer to the desk, dropping his voice to a conspiratorial whisper. "But I gotta tell you something, Colonel. Man to man, that is. And I know I don't have to beat around the bush with you, do I? You see, there's some wild stories floating around."

"Wild stories?" Rashid smiled. "Well, you know what these backwater capitals are like, Mr. Ambassador. In the Souk, one can always find stories: new conspiracies, a new war someone is about to start, or rumors of a coup by a band of Moslem fanatics out to overthrow the government. Is that the kind of wild stories you've been hearing?"

"You see"—Kilbride slapped his hands together in relief—"that's exactly what I told them! I knew there wasn't—"

"Then again," Rashid interrupted, "you can't always dismiss a rumor that lightly. Sometimes they carry a kernel of truth. For instance, have you heard the story about the secret base someone is building out in the desert? That's where this group of fanatics is supposed to be making rockets and atomic bombs. Imagine that! Isn't it ridiculous, Mr. Ambassador?"

"Yes ... yes," Kilbride answered uncertainly, turning his eyes toward Collins for help. The young agent was still standing there smiling as the whole conversation went right over his head. "Yes, ridiculous," Kilbride finally answered. "Naturally, I didn't believe a word of it. But we have this troublemaker over at the embassy ... or had!"

"Ah! That must be Thomson." Rashid nodded fondly. "Clearly the best man you had, Kilbride ... very resourceful, and persistent. But you asked about the atomic bombs. What would we do with such weapons? We are nothing more than poor, ignorant Arabs. What would we do with such bombs? Annihilate the Zionist cancer you visited upon us? Why would we want to do that? Or push all the foreign devils out of the Middle East? All of them, even you? Perhaps you have a reason to be concerned after all, Kilbride!" He paused to focus the full power of his eyes on the ambassador.

Kilbride shrank back in confusion. "Yes. I ... I can see what you boys are getting at. You want a little clout, that's all. Sure! Stir things up a little. Get some attention. Make a few threats so folks will sit up and take notice. We all gotta keep up with the Joneses, so to speak." He chuckled, convincing himself he was right as usual. "Isn't that about the size of it?"

"If you say so, Mr. Ambassador." Rashid leaned forward, toying with him like a large cat with a very small mouse. "But perhaps I misunderstood. Weren't you the one who told me that no one 'at your end' would shed a tear if our 'dear president' was no longer 'in the picture'? Weren't those the words you used?"

"Well. Yes, but—"

"And didn't you say 'those Jews should be taught a lesson,' one that will put them 'in their place'?" Rashid's voice bore in.

Kilbride became flustered. "But I never figured—"

"Figured? You never figured what? That anyone would take you seriously?" Rashid mocked him. "Well, you needn't worry. I don't! As for the stories you heard, you'll find out how true they are at noon. But don't fret about us making new military pacts with the Russians...or with you, either. Those days are gone! After noon today, the Zionist menace will trouble us no more. Professor Fengler's warheads will see to that. Won't they, Professor?" He gave the German a sharp warning glance.

Fengler quickly sat up and nodded, swallowing hard.

"Then"—Rashid turned his full attention back on Kilbride, watching the ambassador twist and turn under his powerful gaze—"once that task is complete, General al-Baquri's troops and tanks will move on Cairo. They will seize the barracks, the bridges, the key government offices, and the radio tower. When my message is broadcast to the army and the people—once they understand what we have accomplished—there will be dancing in the streets."

"No—no resistance?" Kilbride stammered. "Do—do you think Nasser will just sit there and let you take over?"

"Ah." Rashid smiled. "Our beloved president! You need not worry about him, Mr. Ambassador. He will already be dead. Weren't you the one who said the only thing standing in my way was Gamal Abdel Nasser? Wasn't this whole thing your idea? Like the British king who asked, 'Will no one rid me of this cursed priest?'"

Kilbride's face turned beet red. The man was near panic. "I—I never meant rockets or nuclear bombs, Rashid! You can't be serious about—"

"Serious? Serious! Do you think this is some game we are playing?" He sat forward and slammed his fist on the desk. "Today is the day I redraw the map of the Middle East, Kilbride. When those rockets lift into the desert sky, they'll signal an uprising that will sweep the Moslem lands clean. All the foreign devils in our midst shall die, including you!"

The ambassador's eyes bulged out. Rashid watched his reaction and smiled. "Of course, you shall remain here as my guest, until this business is completed, won't you, Mr. Ambassador? I wouldn't want you spreading any more of these ridiculous rumors of yours."

That was when the door to Rashid's office flew open and slammed against the wall, and Grüber stomped into the room. His head was bandaged, his uniform was filthy, and he was dragging Ilsa Fengler behind him, her leg wrapped in a bloody bandage.

"What is the meaning of this!" Fengler jumped to his feet as Grüber dropped her on the floor.

"Don't worry, Herr Professor," Grüber taunted him. "Your darling daughter will live. She helped the American escape, and got in the way of a bullet. Afterward, she had the misfortune of getting caught. By me!"

"What of the American?" Rashid's voice silenced them.

Grüber's arrogant tone vanished. "He . . . he escaped."

"Thank God!" Kilbride moaned.

"And he will stop you," Ilsa Fengler shouted defiantly as she rose to her knees. "This plan of yours is madness.

Don't you understand that, Papa? Can't you see it for what it is?'' she pleaded. But all her father could do was turn his eyes away, too embarrassed to look at her.

"Take them away!" Rashid shouted to Grüber in a fit of rage. "Lock them in the blockhouse, all of them: Kilbride, his lackey, Fengler, and the girl. As your reward for letting Thomson escape, you will stay inside with them, Grüber, and I shall post men outside the door. If there is the slightest mistake, none of you shall leave that bunker alive. None of you! Do you hear me, Professor? If those rockets do not fly at precisely noon, you will all die!"

THOMSON DROVE the old Fiat back into the city, keeping to the sidestreets so he wouldn't attract any attention. Attention? One quick look inside was all it would take: two men dressed in hospital clothes, bandaged, beat-up, and bloody—that would be the end of it.

He turned into a narrow alleyway and drove the car halfway to the end before he stopped and turned the engine off.

"Where are we?" Saleh's groggy voice asked as Thomson helped him out.

"The only friendly place in town." Thomson took him by the arm and carried him to a doorway. "Jeremy! For God's sake, open up!" He banged on the wood until his knuckles were raw.

"The Englishman's bar?" Saleh mumbled as he heard footsteps and a heavy steel bar being raised. The door swung open a few inches and Saleh smiled. "I knew I should have had him deported."

"That's gratitude," Thomson snorted as he pushed the door open the rest of the way and carried Saleh past the surprised bartender and into the storeroom.

"Are you wacko, mate!" Jeremy fumed, but he didn't stop them. "You're the hottest ticket in town, and that's one trouble I don't need." He glanced at their strange outfits and took a closer look at Saleh. "What the hell have you gotten yourself into? And who's this wog? He in as much trouble with the coppers as you are?"

"Jeremy, he is the coppers! Or at least he was. Meet Captain Saleh of the Metropolitan Police. So you better be nice."

Jeremy groaned and closed the door behind them.

"The time . . . what is the time?" Saleh asked, ignoring their chatter.

"Time? Uh, about eleven o'clock I guess," Jeremy answered.

"A telephone. I must have a telephone."

"Whatever you say, mate. Whatever you say!" Jeremy grabbed Saleh's other arm, still not certain, but quickly led them into the bar anyway. "Right here in the corner."

Saleh leaned heavily against the wall and lifted the receiver. He tried to focus his eyes as he stabbed a shaky finger at the dial, and waited impatiently for someone to answer. When he spoke, Saleh's voice was hoarse and angry. The words were Arabic, spoken quickly.

Thomson saw the disappointment written across his face as he got his answer. Saleh slowly lowered the receiver into its cradle and hung up. "I have failed." His voice cracked. "Gamal has already left for Heliopolis." He turned toward Thomson and pleaded with him. "You must take me there. I must reach him before it is too late."

"Saleh"—Thomson tried to sound kind—"look at yourself. You can't even stand up."

But the small policeman would hear none of it. "Get me there, Thomson. Get me there! I know you intend to go, but you will fail if you try it alone. You need me, because I'm the only one who can get you through the gate. You must take me with you."

Thomson looked at him and rolled his eyes, regretting what he was about to agree to.

28

THE GUARDS SNAPPED to rigid attention as the motorcade drove through the gate. In the lead was a long, black Cadillac, the one that had formerly transported King Farouk on his infrequent excursions into the countryside. The car's well-stocked bar had been replaced by a small writing desk and a basket of fresh fruit. That was more befitting of the life-style of its new owner. Still, the limousine had its uses. Its heavy-duty tires and reinforced suspension could carry the weight of the extra steel plates hidden inside its door panels and beneath its floorboards.

Today, two small pennants flew from the Cadillac's front fenders. One was the red, green, and black flag of Egypt. The other bore the gold seal of its president. As the car swept past, the guards could be excused for turning their heads and stealing a glimpse of the unmistakable square chin, jutting hawk nose, and round, dark profile of Gamal Abdel Nasser.

Following behind the limousine were two staff cars, filled with his aides and personal bodyguards. The short convoy didn't stop. Instead, it raced through the gate and kept going down the sand-swept concrete road that led to the open field at the far end of the big airplane hangar and the reviewing stand.

Nasser glanced at his watch and smiled. It was eleven-fifty. By design, he was always early or late, but never on time. Too many close calls over the past seven years had taught that lesson dearly. A modest degree of unpredictability was preferable to being polite—and dead.

As the Cadillac approached the reviewing stand, he surveyed the large, select crowd that had gathered, waiting impatiently beneath the scorching noonday sun, just as he expected them to do. Most were old comrades in arms, that network of friends and allies that any leader must rely on, particularly in the fragile arena of rifle-barrel politics. He needed them as much as they needed him. Still, it never hurt to remind them who ran Egypt—Nasser, the desert, and the sun. The order did not matter.

"Park behind the stands," he said quietly to his driver. The big car rolled to a stop only a few feet away from the horde of assembled generals and politicians. Before they could lunge forward to open the door and greet him, his personal bodyguards had arrived and pushed them back, clearing a wide circle around the car, and a path for him through the crowd. Nasser waited a long, well-timed moment before he stepped out.

They all recognized the curly black hair and broad shoulders of their president. The crowd broke into eager applause as Nasser looked around at their faces and smiled. It was a proud moment. They all knew why he had invited them here. They all knew what this day would mean, for them, and for Egypt. So he paused, smiling triumphantly, and returned their greeting with a wave of his hand.

It had not been easy. Twenty-five centuries of foreign domination and domestic dry rot had brought Egypt to its knees. Her people yearned for independence and social justice. He had already given them the first, and he was working day and night on the second. The people knew that. They believed he would keep his word. But for how long? For how long? Less than five percent of the land was even habitable, much less arable. One fourth of Egypt's population lived in the teeming slums of Cairo, suffering under a terrible burden. They would not wait forever.

"My President, welcome to Heliopolis," a loud, commanding voice called to him from the rear of the crowd. Heads turned. When they saw the tall, dark officer in the colonel's uniform, a path seemed to open for him. Slowly, the colonel strode toward the sedan, confident, untouched by the guards.

"Colonel Rashid. How good to see you again!" Nasser's face beamed and the formality disappeared. "It has been too long, hasn't it, Ali?" Nasser lifted his eyes to the sky. "You certainly picked a perfect day for your tests. Not a cloud. Perfect, eh?"

"Yes. It was Allah's will that this day should be perfect." Rashid's eyes flashed. "And I guarantee it shall be a memorable one. Come walk with me." He made a grand, sweeping gesture toward the reviewing stand with his arm.

Nasser's entourage of aides and guards fell in step behind them, but Rashid turned his head and looked slightly embarrassed. "Your staff may care to sit on the far side of the stands," he said in a quiet voice. "I reserved a whole section for them. With all the special guests you invited, I hate to offend anyone else. I was certain you would agree."

Nasser paused and looked around at the crowd, ignoring the anxious frowns of his aides.

"As a special surprise, I invited some of our oldest friends to attend the test," Rashid added. "I assumed you would prefer to have them sit near you.... But if you find the security a problem..."

"No! Of course not, Ali." Nasser waved their protests aside, while noticing that a ring of heavily armed soldiers had quietly taken up positions around the reviewing stand. "It seems you have those matters well in hand." Nasser took a few steps, then stopped again and looked back at the soldiers, squinting, as he tried to make out the insignias on their uniforms. "Is that the Third Armored Regiment?" he asked, his voice faintly puzzled. "I thought they were still in the Delta?"

"They are," Rashid replied quickly. "But under these circumstances, I asked for a special detachment."

"Does that also explain the tanks I saw as I drove in—the ones hidden in the trees?"

"Obviously not hidden well enough, at least not from such an experienced eye!" Rashid flattered him. "You can tell that to General al-Baquri. He wouldn't be pleased to hear it from me."

"Al-Baquri? He is here, too?" Nasser asked, feeling the first tremor of uneasiness pass through him as he remembered Hassan's strange questions. The Third Armored? Here? He looked into Ali's eyes, searching for the answer, but found none.

Rashid confessed, "I realize al-Baquri isn't one of your favorites, but I hesitated to offend anyone important. Perhaps the day might help him see the light, my President?"

"Stranger things have happened." Nasser smiled. He looked deeper into Ali's eyes, as he had when they were boys in the village. He had always found friendship there— warm, bright colors, and a residue of the many happy hours they had once shared. This time, he found nothing. It was as if someone had erected a high concrete wall across an old, familiar path. The wall was a featureless, cold gray. He saw nothing beyond it—none of the old warmth or fondness, no love or hate either. Nothing. The man was a stranger. Nasser shook his head, convinced that he must be wrong.

"You are right, Ali. And you are a better politician than I'll ever be. You were right to invite old al-Baquri. He is an insufferable bore, but a necessary one. I only wish the man could find an ounce of humor. That would make him a bit more bearable."

A large crowd of officers stood waiting at the foot of the reviewing stand, resplendent in their gaudiest dress uniforms. Behind them, the remaining rows were filled with high government officials—those faceless bureaucrats who kept the wheels of his government moving along, perhaps creaking ineptly, but moving.

Nasser began dutifully shaking hands, giving each man a smile and a friendly word, until he reached the safe haven of his own seat at the far end. Pausing to look up and wave, he found himself staring into the dour, nervous face of General al-Baquri himself. Nasser broke the awkwardness of the moment by reaching out and grasping al-Baquri's hand. "Good to see you again, General." He feigned a smile, and noticed that the man's hand was drenched with sweat. "You must be more careful in this blistering heat. It can sneak up on you if you're not careful."

"Yes." Al-Baquri pulled his hand back and wiped it on his pants leg, glancing over at Rashid, pleading for help.

"The president is right!" Rashid quickly agreed. "General al-Baquri has been here since dawn, supervising every detail of our security plan. And I assure you, that is hot work indeed, is it not, General?"

Al-Baquri shrank back with a thin, pathetic smile, seemingly relieved when Nasser turned away to scan the rest of the faces standing behind the presidential box. The president said a few words to some other familiar faces, then turned back toward Rashid and asked, "Where is Hassan Saleh? Hasn't he arrived yet?"

"Ah! You did not get the message then?" Rashid's voice sounded deeply pained. "There was some kind of accident last night. Hassan was struck by a car—not seriously, Allah be praised—but the doctors made him stay in the hospital overnight, for observation. He telephoned me this morning. You can imagine how disappointed he was that he could not be with us today. It meant a great deal to him."

"So he told me. How unfortunate. I hoped the three of us could stand here together and watch. How fitting that would have been, eh? From that dusty old village, to—this!" He swept his hand across the horizon, ending at the two trailers parked on the desert. They were hundreds of feet away, but their dark green color stood out against the hot, coppery-red sand. And standing on top of each trailer, tall and straight as arrows, were the rockets, their noses pointed up at the clear blue sky.

Nasser said nothing. All he could do was stand and stare for several long minutes. "Look at our children, Ali." He smiled. "They are our magnificent new children. And when I think what you have done to make this day happen, you make me proud!"

Nasser turned to face Rashid, his eyes wet with tears. He clapped both hands on the colonel's shoulders and said in a loud, booming voice: "You make all Egypt proud, Colonel Ali Rashid. That is why I placed these new children of mine in your hands. You are one of the few men in Egypt who has my complete trust."

29

"THE TIME, MAN! What time is it?" Saleh asked for at least the tenth time in as many minutes.

"It's noon—maybe a few minutes after. And asking won't get us there any faster." Thomson was driving the old Fiat as fast as he could, but it wasn't fast enough. While they were on the main highway, he had pushed himself into doing all the things he never did with a car: speeding, cutting other cars off, and racing down the ragged shoulder when he had no other choice. Now that they were on an old dirt road he had to slow down. It took all his concentration just to keep the small car's wheels in the ruts and keep it from bouncing off the road into the rocks.

"Did you see the line of army trucks on the highway? Did you see them?" Saleh asked as he lay slumped against the car door, obviously in pain, his eyes closed. "They were troop transports, and they were heading for Cairo. Pray we are not too late."

"Pray you can figure out what we're going to do when we get there!" Thomson said in an exasperated voice.

"I was invited."

"But I wasn't! And this isn't exactly an official police car, you know. How far do you think we're going to get? Look at yourself. Look at me!"

He and Jeremy had managed to get Saleh into his white linen suit. It was an improvement over the hospital gown, but not by much. The shoulder seam of the jacket was ripped open and the pants showed large black grease stains. His shirt was missing several buttons and the collar was smeared with dried blood. If that wasn't bad enough, Saleh's head was wrapped with a thick white bandage and his face was pale enough to match.

"Why did you come to get me out of the hospital?" Saleh asked.

"You were my last chance."

"Last chance for what? This is my country, not yours. And don't give me any altruistic nonsense, Thomson. It won't work, not coming from you."

"I made a promise to somebody...and to myself. That's all there is to it."

Saleh frowned.

"Fengler's daughter. I think Grüber has her," Thomson finally confessed. "And you're supposed to be the big detective?"

"Then get me there, Thomson. It looks like we both have our reasons."

"I see you've finally stopped calling me 'Mister,'" Thomson said.

"Under the circumstances, it seemed a a bit dated."

"Now that we have that solved, I hope you've thought up a good story." Thomson pointed ahead. "Because we've arrived." Around the next bend in the road lay the entrance to the base, and the heavy wooden gate was down.

Thomson powered through the curve and hit the brakes, skidding to a halt a few feet short of the barrier and the three sentries standing behind it. They were Egyptians, but these were first-line shock troops, not rent-a-cops like the last bunch. They were dressed in full combat gear and held their assault rifles at the ready, pointing straight at the little Fiat. They looked as if they knew what they were doing, and they didn't look pleased at the unexpected interruption.

Saleh looked out the passenger window and flashed his badge at the closest soldier. "Police! Open this gate immediately and let me pass. I am here on official business."

"Police?" The man shrugged indifferently. "That means nothing here. Our orders are to keep this gate closed until after—"

"Who gave that order? Quickly, man!"

"I did!" Thomson heard a loud, arrogant voice call to them. He turned his head and saw a muscular Egyptian army lieutenant standing with his foot propped on the front fender of the Fiat. From the size of the man, it was lucky the tires hadn't blown. Slowly, the officer sauntered around to Saleh's side of the car so he could get a better look inside. "I gave those orders," he bellowed as he glared down at them. "Who the hell are you to question my men?"

Saleh looked up, his fists clenched into two white balls, his face turning crimson. "Who?" Saleh's voice cracked like a whip through the hot air. "I am Saleh, Captain Saleh of the Metropolitan Police! And I was invited here by my closest personal friend, Colonel Ali Rashid."

The officer blinked. Thomson could have sworn he saw the man actually flinch. Not that Saleh's words, or the tone of his voice, could have had that much effect, but something had.

"Now, you tell me one thing, Lieutenant," Saleh went on, leaning even farther out the window and sounding even angrier. "Are you going to let me pass, or do I have to give the colonel the name of the dumbest officer in his command?"

"Captain . . . Saleh?" The lieutenant's arrogant tone began to vanish. He looked down at Saleh's badge, all the while running through the consequences of letting or not letting the little man through.

Saleh kept the pressure on. "Now open that gate, you fool! Or would you prefer to be patrolling the Sudanese border tomorrow morning, on a camel?"

Thomson watched in silent amazement, afraid to speak or to move, afraid the magic spell would be shattered. In a matter of seconds, the big officer was shouting orders, and his men couldn't open the gate fast enough.

Saleh turned his head toward Thomson and pointed a trembling hand down the open road. "Go, go!" That was all Thomson needed. He popped the clutch and slammed the accelerator to the floor.

"Well, I'll be damned!" He laughed. "Just like 'open sesame.'" He looked in the rearview mirror and saw the guards disappear in a billowing cloud of brown dust. Saleh dropped his arm and slumped against the door again, his eyes closed and his breathing labored. "You all right?" Thomson asked.

"I will be fine. Drive, man!"

"I've got to hand it to you, Captain." He chuckled over the high-pitched whine of the engine. "Your name's got more clout around here than I thought."

"It wasn't my name." Saleh's voice dropped to a thin whisper. "It was Rashid's. He's the one behind this. I should have seen it from the beginning. Rashid! How could he do this?" His whisper turned harsh and sarcastic. "Rashid, and I, and Nasser grew up together. He has the best tactical mind in the army. And you're supposed to be the big American spy?"

Thomson looked across the seat, and they shared a pathetic smile. It was the first one he had ever seen from Saleh. The man was human after all.

"Where is the revolver? The one you took from Sayyid?" Saleh held his hand out. "Give it to me."

Thomson looked over at him again. The smile was gone, determination in its place. Finally, Thomson reached inside his jacket and pulled out the heavy revolver. Reluctantly, he set it in the palm of Saleh's hand. "That's supposed to be my part. Remember? You were just supposed to get us in."

"We both knew I was lying," Saleh answered grimly as he checked the cylinder, counting the rounds. "Even you can see the necessity of my going. Can't you?"

"No. All I see is the condition you're in." Thomson shook his head. "You're nuts. Look at yourself. You can't even hold the gun steady, much less use it. Hell, you're in no shape to even get out of the car!"

"Thomson, you'd be surprised to learn what a man can do, when he must—when he has no choice." Saleh tapped the barrel of the revolver against his bad leg. "Besides, I saw the Uzi you hid beneath the car seat. That is all you will need."

It was hopeless. In the distance, Thomson could see dozens of cars and trucks parked in the open field behind the reviewing stand. It was a full house. Beyond the reviewing stand he could see a small concrete building—the blockhouse. And farther still, he could see the two trailers, sitting at the edge of the desert. Thomson recognized them immediately. They were the same ones he had seen inside the hangar. But now they were standing erect instead of on their backs, their noses pointed toward the sky, ready to fire.

Saleh's eyes swept across the desert. "Do you know what we Bedouin call it, Thomson?" he asked sadly. "Do you know what we call the desert? We call it *la siwa hu*. It means 'where there is nothing but God.' Today, that seems like a very fitting name, doesn't it?''

"I didn't come here to die, Saleh. I came here to stop them. If you go waltzing in there and start blasting, you'll blow the only chance we've got. So don't get emotional on me."

"Emotional?" The police captain sat up, his angry eyes fixed on Thomson. "I am not getting emotional. They may have your woman, Thomson, but they have my country. Don't you understand what is at stake here? Or the kind of men we are dealing with? Look out there!" He pointed to the rockets. "If that is Ali Rashid's work, then the only way to stop *them* is to stop *him*. You would not get ten feet alone. Believe me! If Rashid planned this, he is too smart to leave you an opening. My way is the only way."

"There *is* no way!" Thomson finally laughed at the absurdity of it all. He smiled and pointed at the cordon of soldiers standing around the reviewing stand, staring at the small fast-moving car that was coming at them. They began to scatter and take up their positions. "We're going to get our butts shot off, and you know it!"

The policeman slowly nodded. "Perhaps. Perhaps not. But I'm going for Rashid anyway. If we fail, at least we can do enough damage to slow them down, to let them know we tried. We can do that much, can't we?"

Thomson looked over at Saleh and grinned. "Yeah," he said. "We can let them know we tried. That's the first sensible thing you've said in a week."

"Agreed." Saleh nodded. "And I'm sorry for all the things I said to you. Most of them were not terribly nice, especially since you were the one who was right, and I was the one who was so terribly wrong."

"Yeah, but most of what you said was true." Thomson made a wide, banking turn as he swung the car into the parking area behind the reviewing stand and hit the brakes. With the strong desert wind blowing from behind them, the Fiat was quickly engulfed in a cloud of choking, brown dust.

"There! Let me out there," Saleh's voice rasped as he pointed toward the reviewing stand and jammed the revolver into his belt. "That is where Rashid will be. You head for the blockhouse. If I cannot stop him, you must prevent the rockets from being fired. And do not worry"— his mouth twisted into a thin smile—"they will know I tried."

The car skidded to a halt on the hard sand. Saleh opened the door and jumped out, then he was gone.

THOMSON WANTED TO WATCH the little man, but found himself with more than enough problems of his own. First, he heard confused but angry shouts as the soldiers began closing in around him. He couldn't see them, but he heard the sound of running feet and the unmistakable jangle of loose military equipment heading his way. That was enough. Saleh was on his own now. All Thomson could do was put the accelerator to the floor and hope for the best.

He couldn't see a damned thing through the billowing cloud of dust that hung around the car. He coughed and felt his eyes watering, but he knew the troops that were trying to find him couldn't see much either. Maybe they wouldn't shoot after all. Why should they? They couldn't have the vaguest idea who was driving the car. Could they?

Getting into the parking lot had been easy. Getting out of the maze of cars and trucks was going to be a far different matter: nearly blind, in something more than a big hurry, and chased by God knows how many angry men with loaded assault rifles.

Thomson spun the wheel left and right, maneuvering around a dozen cars and trucks that materialized out of the thick haze in front of him. With a succession of bone-jarring crunches, he bounced the small car off a fender here and a bumper there as if he were the last survivor in a demolition derby. Each time he crashed, he'd gun the engine, back away, and send up another billowing cloud of dust. Occasionally, he caught a quick glimpse of soldiers running through the haze, but they couldn't see much of him, either. Maybe they really won't shoot, he kept trying to convince himself, as he kept the car hidden in the dust. Maybe they won't.

That pleasant delusion was shattered by the hazy outline of a man in army fatigues who suddenly appeared through the dust, not twenty feet in front of the car. Thomson wanted to spin the steering wheel or tromp his foot on the brake, but it was too late. He had no time to stop and no time to hide. The soldier dropped into a crouch and leveled his automatic rifle at the windshield of the car. It happened so fast, Thomson never even got a clear view of the man. The image that burned itself into the back of his skull was a blur of brown and green, a pair of large, jet-black eyes, and the ugly hole at the shooting end of a gun.

Instead of hitting the brakes, Thomson pushed the accelerator pedal to the floor and dove sideways across the seat, raising his forearm to protect his eyes and praying to the dashboard. The last thing he saw of the Egyptian was an open mouth, the jet-black eyes turning white, and an orange tongue of flame leaping from the rifle barrel. The spray of bullets shattered the windshield and blew chunks of broken glass into the passenger compartment. The soldier seemed to disappear as fast as he had appeared, and Thomson heard the unmistakable crunch of a steel bumper colliding with muscle and bone.

The bullets punched a neat line of holes through the windshield and across the back cushion where Thomson had sat only a second before, missing their target, but the chunks of razor-sharp glass that followed didn't. They hit Thomson's arm and chest like a swarm of angry bees. He screamed and cursed as he sat up and tried to regain control of the speeding car, blocking out the rush of pain and anger from dozens of cuts.

He fought with the steering wheel, but could only watch helplessly through the holes in the windshield as the Fiat rammed the side of a truck. The impact threw him forward and the bridge of his nose smacked against the steering wheel with a loud *snap*! The small car bounced off the side of the truck and then its engine died.

Thomson knew his nose was broken. He shook his head and blinked, wiped away the blood, and then busied himself picking pieces of glass out of his arm and trying to ignore the flashing red and white stars that filled his eyes. They hurt, but so did every other part of his body. As his vision cleared, he realized he wasn't seeing stars after all. It was the high desert sun, refracted into a thousand rays of light through the shattered glass of the windshield.

The sun! Somehow he'd bashed his way through the maze of cars and trucks and was looking up at the sun, a blue sky, an open desert, and the blockhouse! It sat on a low ridge, no more than two hundred yards away. The blockhouse! And all he had to do now was travel the rest of the way there. He laughed to himself. That, and get inside. What the hell? After what he'd gone through to get this far, nothing seemed impossible.

Thomson wiped his shirt sleeve across his face and felt the sticky wetness. He looked down. The sleeve and the front of his shirt were drenched with fresh blood from the hailstorm of broken glass. He heard more gunshots and felt the Fiat shudder from the impact of more bullets. He turned the ignition key and swore as the starter made a sickening groan. It groaned again, and a third time, before the engine finally kicked over. He threw the little car into gear and pointed its broken hood ornament at the door of the blockhouse.

Thomson had nothing left to prove to himself, but he'd made a promise. And they'd have to kill him before he failed to keep it.

30

SALEH STOOD WITH HIS BACK to the hot desert wind, shielding his eyes as the last of the choking dust cloud blew on by. He tottered back and forth, dizzy and light-headed, fighting with all his strength to remain erect. Finally, the hissing died away and he opened his eyes. He was standing alone in the bright sunlight less than twenty paces from the front corner of the reviewing stand. He blinked and wiped the coarse sand from his eyes. Straining to see, he searched the faces of the men sitting there. But everything was still blurred from the blow to the head. If he'd told Thomson about the double vision, he wouldn't have brought him along, so Saleh had said nothing. For a brief moment, the eyes would clear and he could recognize a face or two, then the scene would shimmer and the rows of heads become featureless circles again.

They hadn't noticed him yet. They had been looking the other way, watching some maniac crash his way through the hazy rows of cars and trucks behind them. One by one, they turned around, still waving angry fists in the air as they coughed and swore at the rapidly disappearing Fiat. Not that the guards were any more attentive. They hadn't noticed Saleh either. He simply appeared before them, standing motionless, like some long forgotten marble statue that had been uncovered by the windstorm.

It was the movement that caught their attention. Saleh took a few short, halting steps to his right, placing himself closer to the center of the reviewing stand. Without his cane, he had to drag his bad leg behind him through the coarse sand. It was that awkward, halting motion that finally made them notice the small dark man with the torn clothes, the large white bandage wrapped around his head, and the black, angry eyes.

At last, he saw their faces, and they saw his. Saleh watched their expressions change from surprise to shock. Every man in the stands recognized him. Most had been old comrades. And they knew his record of fierce courage and devotion to one man. Fingers pointed and elbows nudged as the crowd fell into an uneasy silence. Saleh paused and lifted his head high in defiance as he forced his battered body to stand upright. He searched the tightly packed rows, his head moving back and forth, looking for that one face in the crowd.

The troops saw him too. He heard a panicked cry and saw the line of soldiers spin about, their officers suddenly shouting contradictory orders at them. Some of the troops placed themselves between him and the reviewing stand, knowing they should do something, but unsure of what. An officer finally pointed at him, and three men dashed forward.

Saleh did not move as the first soldier rushed at him and lashed out with his rifle barrel, striking him in the shoulder. He fell to the ground in a daze and saw the dark blur of a steel-toed army boot coming for his head, but there was little he could do to block the vicious kick. Feebly, he lifted his forearm. The boot glanced off his wrist and struck him in the ribs, its force unabated. The air rushed from his chest and his head dropped to the sand. Too weak and too dazed to offer any further resistance, he lay sprawled on the ground, his eyes vacant, seeing nothing but a circle of heavy boots and rifle barrels, all pointed down at him, ready to fire.

Saleh had no doubt they would have shot him that very moment, if not for the loud, commanding voice that called down to them from the reviewing stand: "*Laa, laa!* No, no! Release that man!"

The soldiers stopped. The voice had that unmistakable ring of authority. Dimly, through the pain, Saleh realized the voice had saved his life. He looked up and watched the guards' eyes as they exchanged quick, confused glances. Their heads turned toward their officers, then up at the voice in the stands, still not sure what to do. But when they saw the face of the man who had given the order, they began to back away from Saleh, only inches at first, then more rapidly, as their confused looks turned to worry. The voice belonged to Gamal Abdel Nasser.

The crowd fell silent. This wasn't the show they had bargained for when they came to this dusty outpost, but every eye was now riveted on Saleh and the guards. They had suddenly become the dangerous new act in the center ring of the circus. But the crowd was confused. Some of the dignitaries continued to stare at Saleh and the guards. Others turned toward the man who had called them back. They were all confused—and scared.

Without the uniforms and the ribbons, these were simple men—bureaucrats and career soldiers who had risen through the ranks by quietly following orders and worshiping regularity. It wasn't a system that rewarded originality or deep thought. These were men who hated the dangerous little surprises that crept into their safe, dull routines. They had come to this little demonstration to see and to be seen, but the sound of gunfire now loomed as a terrifying threat to the fragile world of their existence. They had no use for bullets or speeding cars, or for strange apparitions that appeared out of sandstorms.

Saleh saw the fearful apprehension in their eyes as they cocked their heads and frowned at the bandaged, battered figure lying in the middle of a ring of soldiers. They grew restless, and pointed him out to others, whispering, their faces growing more animated. Worried eyes darted back and forth as they tried to unravel the bizarre turn of events.

Slowly and painfully, Saleh rolled onto his side and propped himself up on an elbow. He felt like a drowning man: exhausted, numb, and unable to breathe. He was treading water with frozen legs, feeling himself sinking lower and lower. With each desperate second, he almost longed to be done with it. Just give in, he thought. Just give in and let go. But a tiny voice deep inside his brain screamed, No! No! You can't let them do that to you! Fight back!

The sweat rolled down his face and neck, turning the caked sand into dark brown rivulets. He blinked and lifted his eyes, searching the crowd of worried faces once more, determined to find Gamal. A smile crossed his lips and grew wider as he recognized him. It was Gamal! He was standing in the front row, looking down at him. And in that instant, as their eyes met, Saleh felt all the years and all the pain melt away.

Get up! his brain screamed at him. He forced himself to his knees and managed to prop his good leg beneath him for support. He placed his fingers on the burning sand and tried to push himself up, but he didn't have the strength. His left arm failed him and he tipped forward onto his elbow. He watched it collapse, too limp and numb from the vicious kick it had absorbed to support his weight. He tried again, but his body wouldn't respond. He cursed as he slumped onto his side, the faces and the reviewing stand itself blurring into an indistinct haze. He shook his head, but couldn't even remember why he had come.

"Help that man up!" the loud, commanding voice in the stands called out once more. That voice: it drifted in and out of his head like a distant radio station on a stormy night. But slowly, he began to remember. He felt hands reach out to him. They weren't rough this time. They were unusually gentle, even terrified, as if he were a rare porcelain they feared they might break. They raised him to his feet, then backed away, leaving him standing there, alone, wobbling back and forth on rubbery legs as he looked up at the stands and smiled.

Of course, he thought. Of course the guards were worried. That should come as no surprise. Even as groggy as Saleh was, he recognized the voice of the president. Nasser was standing in the front row of the reviewing stand. Saleh stared up at him and forced his weak, mutinous body forward. One painful step at a time, he moved toward the reviewing stand, toward Gamal, as his head cleared, and he remembered. He remembered the rockets. He remembered the tanks. He remembered the troops, and the American, and he remembered the treachery of Ali Rashid.

Nasser took a step forward and leaned over the railing that ran along the front of the reviewing stand. His face was grim and his eyes hard and angry. Then he turned and looked back over his shoulder at the crowd. He stared at their faces, one at a time. His penetrating eyes scanned the confused faces of the guards, the shocked face of General al-Baquri, and finally the face of Colonel Ali Rashid, standing at his side. He studied Rashid's expression as he had never studied it before. The gray wall had vanished and he could see beyond, but all he saw there was hate. Their eyes met as strangers, as enemies, as if he had never even known the man, much less understood him. Never.

The crowd fell silent. Every ear strained to listen.

"Isn't this wonderful?" Nasser finally asked Rashid in a quiet, almost melancholy voice. "It appears you were wrong, Ali. Our dear brother Hassan Saleh has joined us after all, hasn't he?" Nasser paused. A sad, puzzled expression came across his face. "Perhaps you have some explanation for his sudden recovery?"

With his fists clenched tightly at his sides, Ali Rashid's face twisted with rage as he stared down at the battered figure standing on the sand in front of them. Then his head whipped around. He looked directly into Nasser's eyes and met the challenge. "Surely, it is the will of Allah." His voice cracked. Rashid raised his arm and looked at his wristwatch. "It seems the hour has arrived. It is noon. The test will proceed immediately—"

"No!" Saleh shouted with all his strength as he fought to stay on his feet. The reviewing stand was dancing before his eyes and his head spinning in circles. He dropped back to his knees, barely able to focus his eyes on them. "No," he repeated, but his voice had shrunk to little more than a hollow whisper. "You are a traitor!"

Nasser cocked his head to one side, still watching Rashid's eyes intently. With the word "traitor," Nasser saw the man's thin, false façade crumble away, releasing years of pent-up anger and frustration. Nasser shuddered. He shook his head and said, "No, Ali." His voice was sad but firm. "These tests will be delayed for the time being. First, we shall attend to our dear friend Hassan Saleh. You do agree with that, don't you? . . . Colonel?"

But Rashid wasn't listening. He stared down at Saleh as the anger inside him reached the flash point and exploded. He shook his fist at him. "Traitor? Traitor! You dare call me traitor?" he shouted at Saleh, then at Nasser himself. "We'll see who the traitor is."

In one lightning-quick motion, Rashid stepped behind Nasser, threw an arm around his neck, and pulled the president's revolver from its holster. He jammed the gun barrel against the side of Nasser's neck and spun him around until they both faced the stands. Pressing back against the railing, Rashid used Nasser's thick torso as a shield. But he need not have worried. No one else was armed; no one, except the troops loyal to him, and Nasser's bodyguards. But all they could do was watch helplessly from the far end of the reviewing stand, where Rashid had carefully placed them.

"Quickly," he shouted triumphantly to al-Baquri. "Have your men clear this rabble away. Do it now!"

But al-Baquri could only stare, dumb and speechless. He was already in over his head. Their careful plan lay in shreds at his feet. And things were moving too fast. His eyes darted back and forth between Rashid and Nasser, his mouth open, gaping. He was clearly terrified.

"Now, I said! And get a gun, you fool, before I have you shot with the rest of them!" Rashid shouted at him. But al-Baquri was in a trance, unable to move.

Rashid jabbed the revolver deeper into Nasser's neck. "Delay my tests?" He laughed sarcastically. "Never! These 'tests' will proceed as planned, and you shall have the pleasure of standing here and watching them, oh 'my President'! Yes, you shall watch them, because this is the one thing you should have done a long time ago. Signal the blockhouse!" he shouted at one of the junior officers. "You see, dear Gamal. This is no test. And those are not dummy warheads, either."

Rashid twisted his head around so he could stare down at Saleh, his eyes radiating the power and madness of the twisted mind inside. "Traitor? Traitor, you say? Is that what you dare call me? You never could understand, could you? You never understood what this revolution was all about. Did you think I fought and bled simply to throw the British out, to replace them with toads like these?" He glared up at the stunned faces around them.

"Perhaps that was enough for you, but it could never be enough for me. It could never be enough for the Brotherhood, for the true believers. And it could never be enough for the people! No, in the end, all we did was to trade one arrogant, godless tyrant for another: for a tyrant of our own. And that makes his sin a mortal one."

Saleh could say nothing. He knelt on the burning sand, slumped forward, his head bowed as the rush of Rashid's words crashed down on him like an avalanche.

"For six years, we waited in vain, praying he would act, praying he would rid us of this corruption and lead his people back to the word of Allah. He did nothing. We waited for him to declare a Holy War, but he did none of those things. Now, we will wait no longer!"

The faces around him were stunned as he shouted to them, "Here is your traitor!" He jabbed Nasser with his gun barrel again. "Not I. Soon, you will all understand, those of you who rise up with us. You will understand when you see Tel Aviv and Haifa lying at your feet in ashes. That is when the real revolution begins. It will sweep the filth of this nation into the gutter where it belongs. Today is that day. By sunset, the entire Moslem world will stand behind me."

"You are mad." Nasser's hoarse voice finally spoke. "The world will never let you—"

"The world?" Rashid crowed. "The world? The world will do...nothing! By tonight, our hands will be tightly wrapped around the oil valves of Saudi Arabia, Iran, Syria, Abu Dhabi, and Iraq. We will control the natural gas pipeline in Libya and Jordan, and we will close the Suez Canal.

The world? Indeed!'' He goaded him. ''Who? Your Russians? Maybe the Americans? Or the British? The French? They are nothing if not realists. When we control the oil, we control them, and they know it. What do you think they will do? Invade? If they do, it will all go up in flames. All of it! And compared to that, what value do you think they place on the lives of a few Zionists? No, the world will do precisely... nothing!''

31

THE WIND AND SAND blew through the gaping hole in the windshield, lashing at Thomson's eyes. He drove half-blind, bouncing up and down on the front seat as the Fiat raced across the hard-packed desert sand. He could barely keep his grip on the steering wheel as it tried to twist itself out of his hands. The car would bottom out on the rocks with the gut-wrenching scream of tortured metal, only to scrape free, charge at the next hill, and soar over its ridge line. Through it all, Thomson managed to keep the hood ornament of the Fiat pointed at the steel door of the block-house. As he cut the distance in half and got a clearer image of his destination, he saw he wasn't going to be alone when he arrived. There were two soldiers guarding the blockhouse door.

Thomson reached beneath the front seat and grabbed the barrel of the Uzi submachine gun. His mind flashed back to the Israelis, to Grüber's slaughterhouse in the suburbs, and to Ilsa lying on the bare ground as he had run away. He shouldn't have listened to her, regardless of what she had said. He should have stayed there. And with that grim thought, he laid the Uzi across his lap and flicked the safety off. It was time they paid some bills. They owed him, and the loan company was about to come knocking on their door.

The two soldiers had had a clear view of his approaching car ever since he'd left the parking lot, which gave them more than enough time to make their plans. With the nonchalance of battle-hardened veterans, he saw them talking casually to each other. They pointed at the Fiat and slipped their own weapons from their shoulders, checked the magazines, and stood in front of the door, seemingly unconcerned, as if they were waiting for a bus.

Finally, when the Fiat got within two hundred feet of them, the guard on the left moved, sprinting away from the door of the blockhouse and running about thirty feet before he dropped to his stomach on the top of a sandy rise. He had chosen his ground well, placing himself in a perfect position to rake the driver's side of the Fiat as soon as Thomson was stupid enough to bring it into range.

The other guard chose to stand his ground in front of the door with a Schmeisser machine pistol dangling from his hands, daring Thomson to keep coming. It was Klaus, the thick-necked SS sergeant who had been at the gate two nights before when Ilsa talked her way out. And judging from the arrogant smirk on his face, Thomson knew he could see who was driving the Fiat and couldn't wait to pay him back. Klaus looked like a matador with his sword drawn and ready, waiting for the last futile charge of the bull. He let Thomson drive within a hundred feet, then seventy-five, without moving a muscle. But when the Fiat crossed the imaginary line at fifty feet, Klaus jerked the barrel of the Schmeisser up and began firing on full automatic.

Thomson was waiting too, and he almost waited too long. The German was fast and he was damned good at his deadly little business. Thomson dove sideways across the car seat, flattening himself out as a fusillade of bullets blew away the rest of the windshield. But he was able to keep a tight grip

on the steering wheel with his left hand while his foot
pressed down on the gas pedal. The only other thing he
could do was pray the speeding car was still headed for the
front door of the blockhouse, and for Klaus.

Not that the second guard had any intentions of letting
him get that far. Thomson looked across helplessly as a half-
dozen black holes appeared in the beige fabric on the inside of the door. The bullets whizzed above his shoulder
and gouged big chunks of foam rubber from the seat cushion where he had just been sitting. But the car raced on. The
guard fired a second burst, riddling the car door from top
to bottom, probing its interior for the flesh and bones that
were hiding there. The man was too good a shot to keep
missing, and Thomson's leg suddenly burned with pain.
He raised his head and saw that one of the large-caliber
bullets had dug a bloody furrow across his thigh.

Klaus continued firing, all too aware that his first shots
had also missed and that the car was now getting danger-
ously close. But he wasn't worried. They had the small car
trapped in a vicious cross fire, so he set his aim lower, going
for the engine, hoping to cripple the car this time. Why not?
He'd prefer to finish with the driver at his leisure, anyway.

Thomson heard the heavy slugs bounce off the engine
block with a loud *clang*! The Fiat shuddered from the impact of lead exploding on its working parts. Then the engine quit and the car began to slow down, mortally
wounded. Still, it had too much momentum to be stopped
completely. Thomson heard a panicked scream as Klaus
realized it too. The car crashed into the wall and crushed
Klaus between its bumper and the heavy steel of the door
frame.

The Fiat hit hard. The initial impact lifted its rear end
off the ground and sent pieces of brick and metal flying.
Then the car bounced back, as fast as it had come in,

springing both doors wide open. The hood flew up and a basketful of spare parts popped straight up into the air. The car careened back ten feet before it rolled to a stop. Like a gun-shot animal, the little car lay down and died.

The impact threw Thomson against the dashboard and deposited him in a dazed heap on the floor. His sore ribs were somewhere beyond pain, but at least he wouldn't have any more trouble with Klaus. That evened the odds, but it didn't stop the shooting. He was still too stunned from the violent collision to do much more than watch as the instrument panel above his head exploded from the impact of more bullets. He scooped the Uzi off the floor and cradled it in the crook of his arm as he rolled out the passenger-side door and fell to the ground.

He landed on his face. The white-hot sand burned his eyes and mouth, and that helped. The pain snapped him wide awake. He scrambled to all fours and crawled beneath the car, where he could look out and search the sandy hills for the other German. He was coming fast from the far side, having every intention of finishing Thomson off. Thomson knew he couldn't wait. The man's shiny black boots were barely ten feet away. He didn't aim. He extended his arm, pointing the barrel of the Uzi in the general direction of the boots, and pulled the trigger. Close enough works with horse shoes, government contracts, and the quick burst of a submachine gun.

The first shots missed, and the recoil pushed the back of Thomson's hand against the Fiat's red-hot tailpipe. He ignored the pain and the smell of singed flesh long enough to loose off a longer burst, keeping his finger on the trigger until he saw a bullet clip the man's shinbone. The German crashed to the ground like a big oak. Thomson watched as the man's knees, his waist, his chest, his head, and then his gun dropped into view through the narrow slit between the car and the sand.

Now we're both equal, Thomson thought.

They were both lying flat on the ground with a bad case of the hurts. Well, they were almost equal. The German appeared to be in top shape and probably had the aging American by at least ten years. Then again, Thomson was the only one with a gun in hand.

The German screamed in pain, trying to grab his leg with one hand and the Schmeisser with the other. Thomson gave a loud whistle. "Yoo-hoo!" He shook his head. "I wouldn't if I were you." That got the German's attention. His head twisted around and his mouth dropped open as he looked beneath the car and saw Thomson's smiling face above the open sights of the Uzi.

The soldier tried desperately to raise the Schmeisser anyway, but he was too late, a lifetime too late. Besides, Thomson thought, the German had that look in his eyes. It was the look he had learned to hate years before. It was the look of a killer who had spent his entire life at the "right" end of a gun, taking his pleasure in using it to terrorize others. That look was probably the last thing Jani and the old man had seen, but they weren't the first. Funny, though. No one had ever told Superman he might find himself in the same position someday. The look in his eyes wasn't pretty. It was filled with equal measures of arrogance, shock, and cowardice. Thomson put an end to it when he squeezed the trigger and shot him in the chest.

Thomson closed his eyes. He had never enjoyed killing. It made his stomach turn. But he had learned long ago that there were some men who deserved nothing less.

Slowly, he rolled out from under the car. He lay motionless on the sand, taking deep breaths one after another, and letting them out slowly. He felt numb, incapable of moving, and very, very old. Perper had been right, he thought. He was out of his league. He should have known better. He ached all over, but the worst of it was coming from his throbbing left leg. He looked down and saw the deep gouge from the German's bullet and his own blood running onto the sand. Well, he thought, maybe they'd finally give him that purple heart.

He reached up and found the door handle. Using all his strength, he pulled himself to his knees and leaned against the side of the car. The blockhouse was still standing there, barely ten feet away, and looking every bit as solid and impregnable as it had before. Thomson knew he'd need more than an old Italian sedan to crack through the reinforced concrete. The Uzi dangled from his hand, but the light submachine gun wouldn't do much good against that thick steel door.

Putting his weight on his good leg, Thomson rose to his feet and leaned against the car's fender. Back by the reviewing stand and parking lot, the opposition was already forming. Men were running toward him on foot, and three jeeps mounted with large-caliber machine guns were following his tracks across the sand. Thomson had about given up all hope when he heard the sharp *click* of a lock. He turned his head and looked up. There was movement in the doorway of the blockhouse. The door had opened a few inches. Through the crack between the door and the frame, he saw Grüber's face.

Grüber's expression turned to shock when he saw the American standing barely five feet away. "Thomson!" he shouted angrily. He had a Luger in his fist and already had his arm extended, with plenty of time to take careful aim. Thomson tried to bring the Uzi up, but his reflexes were too far gone. Grüber sensed it too. He smiled, knowing he could get off a careful shot. And from the look in his eyes, Thomson knew the German wouldn't miss.

Grüber wouldn't have, either, if something or someone hadn't shoved him from behind and knocked him off balance. He squeezed the trigger anyway, but the shot sailed high over Thomson's head. Grüber had lost his edge. He tried to bring the barrel back down for a second shot, but it was his turn to be late. By the time he found his target again, Thomson had the Uzi pointed at the doorway. The short barrel kicked in his hand and he managed to fire off a half-dozen rounds before it clicked empty. Those were the last rounds in the magazine, but they were enough. The small-caliber bullets found the seam between the door and the wall, ripping into Grüber's arm and shoulder and punching him backwards into the blockhouse.

Thomson rushed after him, hobbling in pain. What he wanted was inside, and he was determined not to let Grüber lock him out again. He rammed his shoulder into the door and jumped inside, waving the Uzi around the room. He need not have worried. No one inside was about to argue with him, not the way he looked—battered and bloody, his clothes shredded, with a crazed look in his eyes and an Uzi in his hands. The magazine might be empty, but they didn't know that. And it wasn't something a sane man wanted to take odds on.

Thomson slammed the door shut behind him and leaned back against the dented steel. It was all he could do to stand upright, with his ribs aching and the blood oozing down his leg onto the floor. His eyes darted quickly around the room and saw total chaos. Fengler and two of his German technicians were standing at their makeshift command console along the side wall, frozen with fear as they looked at him and the gun. Grüber had made it to the center of the room, where he had dropped to his knees, head bowed, his shattered arm hanging limp at his side. And next to him, lay Ilsa, stunned, where she must have fallen. That explained Grüber's bad aim. To make the picture complete, Thomson saw Kilbride's tousled white mane cowering in the far corner behind Collins.

"Thomson," Kilbride began to babble. "Holy Mother of God, you were right, my boy! They were about to—"

"Shut up!" Thomson cut him off, his eyes hard and angry as he watched Kilbride flinch. He turned quickly back toward Fengler and raised the Uzi. "Get away from those controls. Now! Back up against the far wall, or you'll die right where you are. Move!"

Once they were safely away from the console, he looked down at Ilsa. She tried to sit up, but was still stunned. He wanted to go to her right then. He wanted to forget about Grüber and Fengler and the rockets and just take her in his arms, but he couldn't. He knew he'd pass out if he took the first step. Her eyes met his and they opened wide. He could imagine what he must look like, even to her.

"Well? What the hell did you expect?" He smiled. "John Wayne and the cavalry?"

"No. You will do," she answered quietly, her eyes filled with tears and her face lined with pain.

He leaned as far as he could and held out his hand to her. But as their fingers touched and he took her hand in his, Grüber came alive. His good arm lashed out and shoved Ilsa forward. As she fell against Thomson's legs, Grüber lunged for the control panel. With a triumphant shout, he slammed his hand down again and again on the row of brightly colored buttons.

Thomson lost his balance and he and Ilsa toppled over onto the floor together. Out of bullets, the best he could do was throw the empty Uzi at Grüber in frustration, and even that was too late.

Through the thickness of the concrete walls, Thomson heard the beginning of a dull rumble. The ground began to tremble. In seconds, the noise had increased to a roar. It grew louder and louder until the walls of the blockhouse shook. And in those agonizing seconds of understanding, Thomson knew one of the rocket engines had just fired.

32

THE ELECTRICAL IGNITION inside the rocket's engine exploded with a loud *pop* and a momentary flash of light, drawing every eye toward the two dark-green trailers sitting on the desert sand in front of the reviewing stand. In that instant, the crowd forgot the grim struggle taking place between their president and Colonel Ali Rashid. Somehow, it paled in comparison to the miracle of modern technology unfolding before their eyes.

For a second, there was nothing but a painful silence. Both rockets stood motionless on their narrow trailers, their tapered cones silhouetted against the blue sky. Suddenly, a shower of orange sparks cascaded from the base of one of the rockets. The sparks splashed off the deflector plate and bounced onto the desert sand, flaring up and quickly burning away to gray ash. No explanation was necessary. Everyone in the crowd had seen the pictures. They should have known what to expect. But these were simple men, the sons of farmers and shopkeepers. Pictures were one thing. Actually being there and seeing it happen was something else. They were awestruck. They pointed their fingers. Their mouths hung open, gaping at the power being unleashed just for them.

The sparks ceased to fly, but the rocket still hadn't moved. Inside, ethyl alcohol and liquid oxygen quickly filled the firing chamber, until the swirl of vapors flashed.

A withering blast of smoke and orange flame erupted from the rocket's engine. The devastating fireball exploded hundreds of feet in all directions. Even in the reviewing stand, the crowd could feel the distant rocket's hot breath, hotter and louder than the cruelest sandstorm. The noise was deafening. They could barely hear themselves think. Smoke and flames filled the air, driving a gritty cloud of dust across the low, empty hills. Still, no one in the crowd could tear his eyes away.

That was merely the preface. When the rocket's powerful main engine sprang to life, the steel frame of the reviewing stand shook and vibrated beneath their feet. It felt as if they were trapped in an earthquake. The flames danced across the sand in a mad, frightening rush of power, burning brighter and whiter than the harshest noonday sun. The rocket trembled, straining, determined to lift its own bulk off the ground or explode in angry frustration. And slowly, an inch at a time, then a foot at a time, it broke free from the trailer and was airborne. The smoke and flames billowed out in triumph, and the rocket rose higher and higher.

For the first few seconds, it followed a perfectly vertical flight path. Faster and faster it went, soaring higher into the sky, its power defying gravity until it began the faintest dip to the right. Its path began to bend and the dip became a gentle arc. Like a falcon, the fast-moving rocket had homed in on its target.

With one voice, the crowd broke into a wild, tumultuous cheering. Men hugged other men. They pounded each other on the back and began to dance, so caught up in the triumph of the moment they couldn't care about anything else. This was the achievement of their generation, their pyramid, their Sphinx, their canal. And to a man they cheered.

All except Rashid. He stood silently in the front row, watching the rocket soar upward, and watching his ever larger dreams rise into the sky on its back. The crowd disgusted him. They were like children watching fireworks. He was the only one who truly understood, and he could not bring himself to cheer. There would be time enough for that, but not now. Too many things still hung in the balance.

Nasser stood silently, too. He had invested heavily in dreams of his own, but he was watching them be perverted into someone else's nightmare. He knew he should do something, but Rashid's arm was still locked around his throat and the gun barrel still pressed into his neck. Yet that wasn't what stopped him. It was the rocket. He was hypnotized by it as everyone else was, and as incapable of offering the slightest resistance. Like the rest of them, the awesome power and majesty of the rocket made him feel petty, impotent, and mortal. It sapped him of his strength, for the first time in his life.

They were all watching its flight; everyone, except Saleh. He knelt on the sand in front of the reviewing stand with his back to the rocket, fighting with all his strength just to remain conscious. He swayed back and forth, oblivious to the crescendo of sound and flame rising behind him. He didn't hear the rocket's roar, because Ali Rashid's words had filled his ears as if they were molten lead. The words burned into his brain with hate and revulsion, and filled him with more agony than he had ever felt in his life.

Slowly, Saleh looked up at the front row of the reviewing stand. Through the haze he saw his two oldest friends locked in a deadly embrace. One of them held a pistol to the other man's throat, to the throat of his president. Saleh's world had crashed down around him. Something inside him snapped. He no longer knew why this was happening,

and he no longer cared. All he knew was that he must stop
Ali Rashid, and he was the only one who could.

He reached a trembling hand inside his jacket and closed
his fingers around the butt of the revolver he had jammed
inside the waistband of his slacks. The hand felt weak and
limp, but he forced it to obey. He tugged at the revolver and
pulled it free. But it felt heavy, so very heavy that he
couldn't hold it up. It dropped into his lap. He gripped it
tight with both hands, putting his thumbs on the hammer
and straining with all his might to pull it back. He broke
into a sweat. Finally, the hammer came back and the cylinder rotated with a sharp *click*. Straining, he raised his
arms in front of his chest and tried to point the revolver at
the reviewing stand.

"No!" his hoarse voice screamed in anguish, barely able
to carry across the fifteen feet that separated them. "No!"
he screamed a second time, praying he could make Ali stop
before it was too late.

Rashid heard a noise above the fading roar of the rocket.
He frowned, almost irritated by the distraction. He turned
his head to identify the source, and looked down, his eyes
slowly focusing on the slumped figure of Hassan Saleh. For
a moment Rashid didn't believe what he saw. He even
seemed faintly amused, until he saw the heavy revolver in
Saleh's hands. Then Rashid's eyes flared and the expression on his face filled with anger.

"No," Saleh moaned, still refusing to believe the trans-
formation he was watching. Rashid's eyes were aglow,
burning with a power and madness Saleh had never seen
before. The face was that of his oldest friend. Forty years
of friendship didn't lie. It was Rashid's face, but there was
little else about the man up on the reviewing stand that he
recognized. Ali had changed. It was as if he were now possessed by some sick and alien force.

"Do not be a fool, Hassan," Rashid warned, as he saw the revolver wavering back and forth in Saleh's hand. "Look!" He motioned toward the rocket. "You are too late. Can't you see that? It is done. And look at them." He snorted arrogantly at the crowd. "You wouldn't dare shoot their new hero. Would you?" He broke into a loud, confident laugh. "No. They would tear you to pieces! You see, I understand them. I understand what they want. And I am giving it to them."

Rashid jammed the gun barrel deeper into Nasser's neck. "Do you seriously think they care about this scum now? Don't be ridiculous. He is the man who failed them. He failed his people every bit as much as he failed his God. Neither will ever forgive him. Do you know why, Hassan? Because our dear Gamal forgot that a revolution never stops halfway. It may be betrayed, but the revolution never stops."

Saleh squinted down the barrel of the revolver, watching Rashid's face dance above the front sight. He tried to hold his arms steady, but he couldn't. The pistol seemed to have a will of its own. Sweat rolled down his forehead and burned his eyes. The knuckles on his hands turned white from the strain, but the gun barrel wouldn't stop moving.

"This does not involve you!" Rashid shouted his final warning. "Look! Look at the rocket. Think what it will mean to our people. It is power, power we can use to liberate all Islam, once and for all. That is why I spared your life. Don't betray me too, Hassan. I need you at my side. So join with me! Join me now." But Saleh's pistol still pointed at him and Rashid's eyes flared angrily at the rejection. He tightened his grip on Gamal's neck and swung the president's body around, putting it in the line of fire from Saleh's gun.

"There, 'old friend.'" He smiled bitterly. "You have no one to blame but yourself. You have chosen your side, and you'll die for it, just as he will. So go ahead and shoot. Shoot! Unless you think you might hit the wrong man?"

Saleh blinked as he tried to distinguish between the two dancing shapes, but he couldn't. Rashid was right. Even if he did shoot, he might hit Nasser by mistake. But in his heart, he knew that wasn't the only reason. Despite everything Rashid had done, he had been like a brother. How could he shoot him? And Rashid knew that. From the supremely confident expression on his face, he knew Saleh wouldn't shoot. Colonel Ali Rashid had made it his business to know men, to know their weaknesses, and to use those weaknesses against them. In the end, Rashid knew Saleh would never shoot him. He was depending on it.

But this time he was wrong. Maybe it was the way his eyes tormented Saleh, or the look of complete superiority on his face, or that cynical laugh. Saleh never knew which and he never even realized he had pulled the trigger, until he felt the revolver recoil in his hand.

The sharp crack of the pistol shot cut through the dying roar of the rocket. The men standing behind Rashid ducked, but they were in no danger. The shot wasn't even close. Saleh was an expert marksman with a handgun, yet he missed Rashid by at least ten feet. Something deep within him had made him squeeze the trigger, but something else even more powerful made him jerk his wrist up as he fired. The bullet soared harmlessly into the sky.

Still, the pistol shot left Rashid in shock. He flinched as he realized Saleh had actually fired at him. He had been wrong. He had misjudged the one man he knew best. The expression of supreme confidence on his face suddenly vanished. His eyes filled with cold, raw anger and he was consumed in a fit of rage. He forgot all about his hostage.

He pulled the revolver away from Nasser's neck and twisted his body around to face Saleh. Then he lowered the barrel of the gun and pointed it at the crippled figure kneeling on the sand in front of him. Rashid's gun hand did not waver. He did not hesitate either. He aimed purposefully at Saleh and pulled the trigger.

Saleh never felt the bullet hit him. All he knew was that something slammed into his shoulder and punched him backwards onto the hard sand, taking the breath from his lungs. His eyes remained locked on Rashid's, looking up in disbelief at the hatred and cruelty he saw there. The pain from those eyes was far worse than the pain from the bullet. The bullet might kill him, but the eyes had already done far worse. He lay on his back, feeling his own hatred rise and explode inside him. His eyes never left Rashid's as he raised the barrel of his pistol again and squeezed the trigger.

It was those eyes, he kept telling himself. They were the enemy, not the shell of the man who had once passed for a friend. But to stop one, he had to stop the other. And this time, Saleh did not miss.

The thirty-eight-caliber slug struck Rashid in the forehead and snapped his head back. He staggered, his arms flailing the air as he tried to remain upright. His body refused to fall. His eyes refused to accept any of it, refused to accept their own mortality. Rashid's twisted mind still controlled those eyes, but it couldn't control his body. It was dying. His legs buckled at the knees. His lips curled into a hideous groan as his own body defied him. How dare it! He would not permit that.

Rashid's hand went limp. The gun slipped from his fingers and clattered on the wooden platform of the reviewing stand. Slowly, his body followed, stiff and rigid, pitching forward and crashing onto the hard planks. In those last, brief seconds, those hateful, uncomprehending eyes remained locked on Saleh's, until his body went limp, the eyes turning to smoked glass. The fires inside had consumed all of him. Colonel Ali Rashid was dead.

33

THOMSON KNEW he had failed. He closed his eyes and slammed his fist on the hard concrete floor, but the pain couldn't block out the sound of the rocket engine. He had failed again, as he had failed at every really important thing he tried in his life—two wives, a long career of unbroken mediocrity, Damascus, now this—and he hated himself for each one of them.

The deafening rumble slowly faded away and Thomson knew in the pit of his stomach that Fengler's warhead was on its way toward some unsuspecting Israeli city. Landau, Jani, the old man, and all the rest had died for nothing. There would be no warning, not that a warning would do much good with a nuclear bomb. He didn't know how large Fengler's warhead was, but its size wouldn't make a hell of a lot of difference. If any atomic bomb detonated above the crowded streets and tall buildings of a modern steel-and-glass city like Tel Aviv, the death and destruction would be total.

Thomson tried to sit up. He had fallen against the wall with Ilsa sprawled on top of him. She lay there holding her head in her hands. He wanted to roll her aside and get to his feet. What was the use? His legs were too weak to stand on. He leaned back against the wall and pulled her to him, cradling her in his arms. He felt like a punched-out boxer, glassy-eyed and unable to force his aching body to go another round. Each of the bumps, bruises, and countless blows it had absorbed over the past four days and the past forty years had taken its inevitable toll. Besides, he thought, as he glanced at the control panel, there wasn't a damned thing he could do even if he wanted to.

Grüber leaned awkwardly against the console, sneering triumphantly at Thomson. His shattered left arm hung limp at his side, and blood ran down the back of his hand and dropped on the floor. Grüber was finished but he didn't seem to care. He looked down at the American and laughed. "*Zu Befehl*, Thomson," his raspy voice called out defiantly. "Do you know what that means? To obey! Those are the words every SS officer swears on the day he is commissioned. It is our oath of honor—my oath of honor. What would you know of any of that, of a soldier's honor?"

"You're right, Grüber," Thomson answered quietly, stroking Ilsa's hair, too tired to argue.

He turned his head toward Kilbride. The ambassador was still hiding in the far corner, his mouth hanging open, gaping alternately at Grüber and at Thomson. "You dumb Irish bastard," Thomson called over to him. "You wanted it all, didn't you? Well, you won't be able to run for dog catcher after they get through with you." Kilbride hadn't moved a muscle to help. He'd reduced himself to the role of a mere spectator, unable to even comprehend the result of the ugly little game he'd been playing. All he could do was watch it unfold, like some damned tennis match in Quincy.

The German technicians were watching too, standing against the far wall, still scared. Slowly, they lowered their hands. Like vultures, they were all too aware they had nothing to fear from Thomson any longer.

Fengler moved first. He took a few cautious steps toward Grüber and joined him at the command console. He put his arm around Grüber's shoulder, smiling anxiously, eyeing the dials and switches on the panel. "Let me help you, Herr Sturmbannführer," he said, as he tried to gently ease Grüber aside.

But Grüber would hear none of it. He turned and shoved Fengler away with a look of complete contempt. "No! I need none of your help! I will finish what I started."

Fengler quickly backed off, a half step at least, but he continued to hover as he watched Grüber slump forward against the console. The pool of blood at their feet was growing in size. Grüber looked weak and pale. His strength was fading, and Thomson couldn't understand what was keeping the man up.

"Yes, I still have some unfinished business. Don't I, Thomson?" Grüber tried to laugh through the pain, but he couldn't. He was convulsed by a wracking cough as he looked back to the controls. And in that instant, Thomson remembered. There was a second rocket, and Grüber was looking for its firing button!

Grüber studied the row of buttons, shaking his head as he tried to focus his eyes. Finally, he smiled. He stretched his fingers, groping for the button that would send the second rocket racing into the sky after its twin. "Yes," he mumbled. "Unfinished business. Do you know what that means? I, Sturmbannführer Ernst Grüber, will finish what Himmler and Heydrich and all the rest of them could never do."

Thomson shoved Ilsa aside. He had failed to stop the first rocket, but he'd be damned if he'd let Grüber fire the second one. That might not mean much anymore, but it meant everything to Thomson. It had come down to him or Grüber and one of them was going to die.

Thomson pressed his hands against the wall, trying to find a handhold so he could get to his feet. Frantic, he rolled onto his knees and tried to stand, but his shoe slipped on the slick, damp floor. He reached out to break his fall and found nothing to grab onto. He tumbled sideways, his hand striking something hard lying on the bare concrete. It skittered away and bounced off the wall. His hand chased after it. He didn't think, just grabbed, desperate to find something he could throw at Grüber. But as his fingers wrapped around the hard, irregular shape, he realized he was gripping the barrel of Grüber's Luger, still lying on the floor where the German had dropped it.

Thomson rolled onto his side. He grabbed the butt in his other hand and raised the gun, not bothering to aim. He simply pointed its barrel toward Grüber, ready to shoot, but found Ilsa sitting directly in his line of fire. Grüber's face seemed to float above her shoulder, glowing triumphantly, as his eyes finally found the button he was looking for. He reached out for it, stretching his arm until his fingers touched it. Thomson pushed Ilsa's head aside with his free hand and squeezed the trigger. He fired once, then a second time, and prayed.

The nine-millimeter slugs roared like howitzer shells inside the bare masonry walls of the blockhouse. And the bullets were every bit as deadly as they were deafening. The first shot hit Grüber in the face, stood him upright and obliterated that cruel smirk forever. The heavy bullet spun the German around like a top and ripped his fingers off the firing button. The second shot followed close behind, striking him in the upper chest and knocking him backward onto the floor. The German lay there for a moment and raised his head. His eyes were glassy, but he reached his hand toward the control panel once more.

The American looked down the barrel at him, ready to pull the trigger one last time, but there was no need. Grüber's head stayed upright for a long moment, then his features went limp and his head fell onto the concrete at Fengler's feet, stone dead.

Fengler stood in a trance. The only sound inside the blockhouse was the faint hum of a generator. Fengler's terrified eyes looked down at Grüber's body, at the gun in Thomson's hand, and at the firing button on the control panel. He moaned but stayed where he was.

"Go ahead, Fengler. Give me an excuse," Thomson offered.

The German's face turned pale as he stared down the barrel of the Luger. Thomson had it pointed at the bridge of his nose, and from the look in the American's eyes, he didn't need much of an excuse to shoot. But Fengler wasn't about to give him one. He jerked his hands away from the control panel and held them high over his head, then quickly backed up against the wall.

The long empty silence ended when Ilsa pushed herself off the floor and saw Grüber's body. She screamed, and twisted her head around, toward Thomson, seeking help, but only saw the gun and the look of anger in his eyes. She screamed again, and Thomson saw Fengler's nerves shatter.

"Ilsa . . . Ilsa . . . What have they—"

But she would hear none of it. Her head whipped around and she glared at her father. She raised her hand and silenced him. "They? They?" she asked. "They did nothing, except stop you and Grüber from going through with this madness. And I can only thank God they did."

"The rockets?" Thomson asked in a tired voice. "You're too late. Grüber fired the first one before I could stop him."

"Oh, no!" She cupped her hands over her ears, digging her fingers into her hair. Her face filled with anguish. Then she slid halfway across the floor on her knees, getting even closer to her father. "You must stop it, Papa! Stop it. Destroy the rocket now!'' she begged, but he refused to even look at her.

"Stop it?" Thomson quickly demanded. "Can he do that? Can he still stop the rocket?"

But she didn't answer. Her eyes were riveted on her father. She pleaded with him, as if it were a private conversation between the two of them. "Papa! Grüber is dead. They can't force you to do these things anymore." Her voice became more desperate as he continued to refuse to look at her. "Papa, please! Use the destruct button. Destroy it before the rocket gets out of range."

Thomson listened, watching as Fengler's terrified eyes finally looked down at her. He wanted to do or say something, but he was afraid to move. It had to come from Ilsa. The old bastard would never do it for him, but maybe he would do it for her. Fengler swallowed hard. He took the first halting step toward the console. Then another. And he probably would have taken the rest, if a fierce pounding of rifle butts on the blockhouse door hadn't interrupted him. Fengler turned and looked at the door. He looked down at Ilsa, then Thomson, and stopped walking.

"Damn!" Thomson cursed his luck. They had been living on borrowed time ever since he'd forced his way inside. Thomson had known the soldiers would arrive sooner or later, but why had they picked now? Still, they were swarming outside, but they hadn't gotten inside, not yet anyway.

He had slammed the heavy metal door shut behind him and thrown the bolt across. That might slow them down, but it wouldn't keep them out for long. They had stopped pounding on the door, proving they weren't complete morons, but he knew they were regrouping. The door's steel frame and heavy hinges had taken a beating from the Fiat, and were bent and twisted. It wouldn't take much more before they gave way completely, not if the soldiers really made a concerted effort to get inside.

Fengler knew that, too. His eyes suddenly cleared and he thrust his chin in the air, supremely confident once more. He refused to even look at Ilsa now. "Destroy it, my dear? Destroy the rocket, and my warhead?" He shook his head, his voice sounding incredulous. "You don't know what you are asking of me. This is *the* test, Ilsa! This is the moment I have worked for...dedicated my life to...for more than twenty years. Destroy it? You . . . you cannot be serious. You cannot ask me to do such a thing."

"Papa," she screamed. "This is not a test. You know it isn't! That warhead is live and it will kill many people, if you don't destroy it. Now. Please, Papa. Do it. Destroy the rocket before it is too late."

"Do what she says, Fengler," Thomson warned as the pounding on the door resumed with a new ferocity. He saw the door shake. The soldiers were throwing their shoulders into it, again and again, and the hinges were beginning to bend. The door wouldn't hold them out much longer, only seconds at best. Thomson raised the barrel of the Luger and lined it up on the bridge of Fengler's nose. "Do it, or you'll never live to see the results."

Fengler never wavered. He looked down at Grüber's body and shook his head. "Do you think he made me do this? Don't be foolish. Grüber could never make me do anything I did not want to do. This is my work. Mine! And I will die before I see it ruined." He folded his arms across his chest and backed away from the console, resigned to let events sweep him along, whether that meant being shot or being rescued.

Thomson leaned forward and grabbed Ilsa by the hair. He pointed the Luger at her head.

"Okay, Papa!" Thomson's sarcastic voice challenged him. "What's it going to be? I won't shoot you after all. That would be a waste of time. I'm going to shoot her instead. So take your pick. Your precious daughter, or your new toy? Which is it going to be?"

Fengler's eyes narrowed, cold and hateful. "You wouldn't do that." He was trying to convince himself.

"Look." Thomson leaned forward and pushed the barrel into her ear, cocking his head toward the door. "I'm a dead man anyway. So which of your babies dies with me? Huh?"

Fengler cursed and his lips quivered with hate, but he took that first, fateful step toward the console. His hands shook as he pulled a brass key from his pocket and jammed it into the top of a small red plate at one end. The plate popped up, and from the agonized look on the German's face, Thomson knew the destruct button lay beneath it. Fengler reached his hand out, then stopped, his fingers suspended in midair, as if something had grabbed his arm and was holding it back. He looked at Thomson and at Ilsa, but couldn't make his hand move.

Whether Fengler couldn't or wouldn't do it, Thomson neither knew nor cared. All that mattered was that the button hadn't been pushed.

Ilsa knew that too. "Papa!" she screamed in anguish as she broke free from Thomson's grasp. She threw herself forward and lunged at her father like a desperate animal. He raised his arms in defense, startled by the onslaught, as she struck him and pushed him away from the console. He staggered backward, his eyes filled with shock and horror when she fell across the console and reached for the destruct button.

"No, Ilsa," he cried, grabbing for her and hitting her on the back with his fists. "Stop. Don't do it!" He tried to pull her away.

Thomson didn't wait. He aimed the Luger at Fengler's legs and pulled the trigger. The bullet struck the German in the thigh and knocked his legs out from under him. He fell to the floor but kept reaching out, his desperate hands pulling at her leg, still screaming, "Ilsa, no! No!" as she pushed the button.

GAMAL ABDEL NASSER collapsed against the metal railing of the reviewing stand. Like everyone else, he was staring in shock at the body of Ali Rashid lying at his feet. Still stunned, he took several deep breaths and tried to clear his head. As he slowly pushed himself upright, he heard the sharp explosion followed by a low rumble high in the sky above the horizon. Nasser raised his hand to shield his eyes, looking up, trying to locate the source of the noise.

The rocket's thin white vapor trail stretched across the bright blue sky, then suddenly ended in a dense cloud of orange flame and black smoke. The sharp explosion died away in a muffled rumble. That too faded as quickly as it had come, leaving the crowd standing in silence. Nasser nodded and ran his tongue across his parched lips, quickly collecting his wits. He said nothing. Not yet.

Once more, he looked down at Rashid's body, then at Saleh's, sprawled on the sand in front of the reviewing stand. "Send for a doctor. Quickly," he said harshly, then lifted his head and straightened himself to his full height. He knew if he didn't seize the moment, everything could still be lost. Only then did he turn and scan the crowd of faces standing behind him, focusing his powerful brown eyes on General al-Baquri.

"General," he stated calmly but authoritatively, "it appears this business of ours has now been concluded. Do you not agree?"

Al-Baquri shrank back, trying to think, but events had moved too fast for him. He had left the thinking to Rashid; it was not his job. He needed time, but the power of Nasser's will closed in around him, overwhelming and suffocating him. He could not think, not like this. He swallowed hard, his eyes darting through the stands looking for help from the other conspirators, and finding none. In every face, all al-Baquri found was hostility.

His troops still surrounded the reviewing stand. They were the ones who were armed, but he saw them backing away from him, exchanging worried glances. His men looked shocked and confused as they deserted him, one by one. And why not? They could see the fear in their general's eyes. And they saw the power in Nasser's.

Al-Baquri had the troops, the tanks racing toward Cairo, and the guns; but he no longer had Colonel Ali Rashid. Against an unarmed Gamal Nasser, it was no contest. It had been Rashid's job to kill Nasser, not his. Al-Baquri suddenly found himself alone, and that was the one thing he wasn't prepared for. The day belonged to Nasser.

"Good," the president said quietly as he nudged al-Baquri back in his seat with the tip of his finger. "And, General, I want to thank you and your men for the excellent job they did today. You may dismiss them now. Send them back to their barracks."

Al-Baquri nodded. His head ached. He slumped down on the seat and lowered his eyes to the ground as he heard the running feet of Nasser's bodyguards coming up behind him. Rough hands gripped his arms and he felt himself being led away, dazed, pale, and shattered.

"Quickly!" Nasser snapped his fingers and began to shout angry orders at the gaggle of staff officers standing near him in the front row. "Round up those troops! Send some of them to the blockhouse. Now! And arrest everyone inside. Go!"

Nasser watched the colonels push and shove each other aside, scrambling over fallen chairs as they tried to get as far away from him as they could. Then he turned back to the desert. He bent down at the waist and squeezed his large frame between the metal railings at the front of the reviewing stand. He jumped down onto the ground and with three loping strides reached Hassan Saleh's unconscious body. He knelt on the sand and raised the policeman's head into his lap.

Three medics ran over and joined him. He supervised their every move. Two of them wrapped bandages around the bullet wound in Saleh's shoulder while the third man struggled to open a stretcher. Nasser glared at each of them in turn. "Do your work well, my friends. Because I hold the three of you personally responsible for the life of this man. Is that clear?"

34

"WELL, MATE? You going to tell me about it?" Jeremy asked as he set the drink down in front of Thomson. "Or are you going to sit there and play dumb?" The Englishman had noticed the bruises on the American's face when he limped into the bar. He grimaced at the two fading black eyes and the white Band-Aid that stretched across the bridge of Thomson's nose. Obviously it had been broken. Jeremy flipped his towel over his shoulder, still irritated. "You owe me that much, you know."

Thomson looked up over the rim of his glass and shrugged. "What's to tell? I got hit by a truck. Don't I look like it?"

"The same truck that ran over Reggie Perper?"

Thomson took a small sip of gin and winced. He looked away and set the glass down in disgust. "You make this batch yourself? Or did you dip it out of the sewer?"

"You never complained before."

"That was then. Now's now," Thomson answered quietly as he glanced around the nearly empty bar. Funny. He had never noticed how seedy the place really was. It never paid to get too sober.

"Look, Thomson. You run out the door with that wog and disappear for nearly two weeks without so much as a peep. What's a man supposed to think? You ain't been around to hear all the crazy stories, either!"

"Stories?" Thomson asked innocently.

"Yeah. Like a lot of people getting arrested and others getting deported. There were troops all over town for a week, and Nasser canned half of his government. Me? I've been sitting here hugging my goddamned passport, waiting for the meat wagon to arrive. I figured the two of you were dead, and I was going to find my ass in jail any minute. But nothing happened. Nothing! Then you come waltzing in here tonight and have the nerve to just sit there, looking like a four-car smashup."

Jeremy was just getting started. "And after all I done to help? A Christian man would at least tell a body what happened. I know, I know!" he fumed. "Blame it all on the CIA. National security. Your bleeding mouth's been sewn shut, right? Don't worry, old Jeremy's learned not to expect a damned thing from an ingrate like you!"

The Englishman pulled the towel off his shoulder and snapped it at a pair of flies sitting on Thomson's table. "No, old Jeremy expects no better," he chided. "But if he got a simple word of thanks, or even one of your smart-mouthed jokes, at least he'd know the wogs didn't chop off your private parts with one of those big curved swords of theirs. If that's too much to ask, then go bugger yourself!"

"Thank you! Thank you!" Thomson tried not to smile. "I quit. Okay? And don't worry. I think I still got all my private parts. You want some jokes?" He was the one who sounded irritated this time. "Well, go watch Uncle Milty. I'm fresh out. You caught me at a bad time. Two weeks in one of their stinking jail cells can do it to the best of us."

Jeremy looked impressed. "I guess so." He nodded, as if he understood. "But I know you, Thomson. When you start being nice, something's wrong."

"Yeah? Well, it happens. So leave me alone, huh? And stop asking so goddamned many questions. I just ain't got the answers anymore."

"Your game. Your rules. But questions go with the territory." Jeremy shrugged and walked away.

Two weeks, he thought. Not that they were all that bad, at least after the first few days. In the beginning, they were rough as hell, after half the Egyptian army broke into the blockhouse and hauled him away. A couple of days later, they suddenly eased up. They got him clean clothes and even sent in a doctor. They sewed up his leg, set his broken nose, and ordered his food from a restaurant. Impressive, to a guy who expected a firing squad. Even the guards got strangely polite and friendly, as if they were afraid of him and wouldn't say why. Not that they had much to be afraid of. Thomson hurt everywhere there was a place to hurt.

That kind of pain he could take.

What was worse was the way he had left things with Ilsa. It was strange that she mattered that much to him now, but she did. The last time he had seen her, she was sitting on the floor of the blockhouse, staring up at him, her face pale and drawn.

"Would you? Would you have?" she asked.

"Ilsa! What do you think?" was all he'd had time to say as the Egyptians poured into the blockhouse. Three of them had jumped on him and that was all he remembered.

Thomson had kicked himself in the head a hundred times a day ever since, thinking of all the clever things he should have said to her and didn't. No, he shouldn't have said something clever. That was a reflex, a defense against getting hurt again. He should have said something serious, but he had forgotten how. Now it was too late. Ilsa had gotten to him. He had found something fragile yet very strong about her, and he wanted to know more.

When the bastards had finally let him out of jail this morning, he'd rented a car and raced out to Heliopolis, but the camp had been deserted, the gate hanging open, unattended. Even the old aircraft hangar was empty. The reviewing stand was gone, and the swirling desert sand had begun to cover all traces of what had happened there. He drove to the bungalow she and her father had shared, but the house was empty. Even the furniture and the geraniums on the window ledge were gone. She was nowhere to be found.

Thomson had tried the German Embassy, but all he got was loud official silence. So he had come back to Jeremy's bar, like a homing pigeon with nowhere else to go, and had done the two things he swore he would never do again. He ordered a gin, and he began to feel sorry for himself.

He sat staring at the glass, watching the ice melt. The front door opened and he looked up as sunlight briefly filled the empty room. A dark, thin man stood in the doorway, leaning on an ebony cane for support, waiting for his eyes to adjust to the darkness. The man's face was hidden in the shadows, but Thomson knew who it was.

"Oh, Lord," he heard Jeremy mutter under his breath. "You got company, Thomson. You! And leave me the hell out of it this time!"

Saleh was wearing his usual immaculate white linen suit, but the jacket was draped awkwardly over his shoulder and his left arm hung limply in a sling. His head wasn't wrapped in bandages anymore. Still, he looked pale and weak as he stood in the doorway, his eyes slowly focusing on Thomson. Saleh took his first halting steps toward him, leaning heavily on his cane, his face drawn with pain and determination. When he finally reached the table, Saleh pulled out a chair and sat down wearily. Then he looked across at Thomson with an unusual expression of warmth and friendship. "*Mister* Thomson, it has been a while, has it not?"

"*Captain* Saleh," Thomson mimicked, "can I buy you a drink? Or don't you use the stuff?"

Saleh turned toward Jeremy and called out, "Scotch, please. Neat." Then he looked back at Thomson. "Not all of us take our religion that seriously. I thought you would have known that by now."

Thomson looked across the table and waited, but Saleh said nothing more. Finally, the American shook his head, getting mad. "I don't understand you. I really don't. Why the hell did you come in here, anyway?"

Saleh nodded, his face devoid of emotion. "To thank you for your assistance," he stated simply and eloquently. "Without it, this would be a far different nation to-day... and a far different world, I am afraid. Rashid's plan came close to succeeding."

"Well"—Thomson leaned forward, barely keeping his anger and mouth under control—"if I'm such a god-damned 'national hero,' why'd you keep me locked up in that stinking jail of yours for two weeks?"

"One week!" Saleh was insistent on correcting him. "One week. Things were most confused for the first few days, as you can well understand. State Security kept you and all the other foreigners in jail, until they 'sorted out the pieces,' as you would say. Unfortunately, I knew nothing of that. I was... incapacitated. As for the rest of your time in jail..." He smiled. "Well, I must admit that was my idea. But I gave strict orders that you were to be treated well."

"Why? What the hell did I do?"

"Oh, nothing wrong. But I could not permit you to leave before I had a chance to speak with you."

"So speak!"

"I am! For one thing, I had an obligation to thank you. And that is what I am trying to do, if you will let me."

Jeremy edged up to the table and carefully set the drinks down. "I, uh . . . I don't suppose you remember me, Captain?"

"Mr. Throckmorton? Of course I do. And I want to thank you for your help as well. It was nearly as invaluable as the help I received from Thomson here. The Egyptian people owe you a debt of gratitude."

Jeremy stared down at Saleh with his mouth hanging open, waiting for the punch line. There were many things he expected to hear from an Egyptian cop, but a "debt of gratitude" wasn't one of them. "Well, uh. Pleased, I'm sure," he managed to reply as he backed away, not knowing what to make of it all.

Saleh sat back and looked across the table at Thomson. "Questions?" he asked.

"No," Thomson demanded, "answers!"

"Well, I would prefer to think of these past few weeks as . . . a minor exercise in nation building. It has forced us to undertake certain . . . realignments . . . within our civilian government and our military command structure."

"What happened, Saleh? What about the bombs?"

"Bombs? What bombs? If you are referring to what I think you are referring to, it never happened. Stop and think about it, about everything and everyone involved. You will agree, it never happened."

"Cut the crap. Just tell me what happened."

Saleh looked at him and shrugged. "Well, you forget I was not in the best condition myself. I am told the rocket you managed to destroy scattered itself, along with a thousand little chunks of radioactive warhead, across a desolate area of the southern Sinai. Your government was kind enough to offer its assistance in the rather nasty job of cleaning it all up. Not that they did not have a large share of guilt to atone for.''

"Kilbride?"

"You know," Saleh said as he leaned on the table, "somehow, year in and year out, the world manages to survive your government's predilection toward rewarding minor political hacks with major diplomatic posts. I guess every nation can be guilty of that from time to time. But Kilbride was too stupid to be posted to Dublin! After we declared him persona non grata, I was surprised your State Department did not send him to the Sinai with a dust-broom.'' The corners of Saleh's mouth curled into a faint smile as he considered the thought. That was the second time Thomson had seen him smile. "We had the other warhead dismantled. We shall keep the rocket, but conventional weapons are quite sufficient for our needs at the present.''

"What about Fengler . . . and his daughter?" Thomson tried not to sound anxious.

"Ah! Nasser's first inclination was to have all the foreigners shot—including you—but that tends to depress the market for foreign labor. Next, he decided to deport you all. That would have attracted too much unwanted attention. Besides, the West Germans refused to accept them. It seems some of them are wanted for war crimes, and the German government wants that type of public scrutiny even less than we or your people do.''

"You should have given them to the Israelis," Thomson replied, without a trace of humor.

"Not a bad idea! But we did not. We put them on a charter flight for Paraguay. I believe they have friends there.''

"What happened to the girl?"

"Ilsa Fengler? A most delightful person. She asked to see me in the hospital, before she left."

"You bastard!"

"Can't you sit and listen for a moment, Thomson? You are the most exasperating man I have ever met. She happens to be the other reason I came."

Thomson glared at him and held his tongue.

"I am sorry. I remembered what you said about your 'promise,' and I told her that. But it was her desire that you cool your heels for a while. I felt an obligation to respect that wish. Besides, I had other reasons to keep you out of trouble."

"Where did she go?"

"West Germany. She would not say precisely where. Their government had no reason to deny her a visa, and she seemed anxious to get as far away from her father and the rest of his ilk as she could. She left a week ago, I believe. But she gave me a message for you. She said if you really wanted to find her, you would. If not, she said she would understand."

Thomson nodded, thanking him with his eyes.

"I do not want to get personal," the Egyptian said. "But surely 'the big American spy' has sufficient resources to find anyone he wants to find, especially in a nation filled with such fanatical bookkeepers as Germany. If you cannot find her, you aren't half as good as I think you are. If you do not want to find her, then you are a damned fool. Unless you would prefer to sit here and drink yourself into a stupor."

Thomson said nothing. He looked across at Saleh and smiled. "Actually, I lost my taste for the stuff a couple of weeks ago," he said as he pushed the glass away. "What about you, Captain? What are you going to do?" he asked, looking at the sling.

"I will survive." Saleh smiled. "The last time it was a leg. This time it was the shoulder. I will survive. As I told you that night we met, I am Bedouin. We are a tough people."

"So are Nebraskans," Thomson retorted.

"Nebraskans? I am not familiar with them, but if that is what you are, then I agree. Yes, you are tough, too, Thomson. I dismissed you too lightly at first. I took you for a burned-out alcoholic, a hard case, and an incredibly stupid one at that. That was a serious misjudgment on my part, one of all too many I made in that last week. In retrospect, I believe my misjudgment of you was for the best. And since you are so tough, and so resilient, you will understand why I must now order you out of my country. You have twenty-four hours to be gone or be thrown back in jail, for a much longer stay this time."

"What?" Thomson nearly exploded. "What the hell happened to all the thanks?"

"Those were most sincere, I assure you." Saleh smiled. "But think, for a moment at least, of all the laws you have trampled on—breaking and entering, grand theft, espionage, destruction of government property, conspiracy, and numerous homicides, even if I do not count the Germans, which I do not. You are simply too hot a commodity around here. To be frank, many of our people think I am letting you off far too lightly. But for the moment, rank still has its privileges."

"You? Since when do the damned police order foreign nationals out of the country?"

"Ah, I forgot to tell you." Saleh seemed almost embarrassed. "The president has appointed me chief of State Security. So the expulsion order will stick, I am afraid. Besides, you know too much for your own good, far too much—too much for anyone to harm you, but too much to permit you to stay in our midst, either."

Thomson looked across the table and started to argue, but Saleh cut him off with a wave of his hand.

"There is a bright side to this affair, if you'll permit me to explain." Saleh's eyes sparkled. "I kept you in jail because I had some arrangements to make. That took time. When you go back to your embassy, you shall find your government most accommodating. In truth, they are terrified of you. As well they should be. I told them you wrote some interesting memoirs while you were in jail, and that I have a copy. I assured them, if you do not live out a long and prosperous life, those memoirs will find their way to the *London Times*."

"Another Bedouin prophecy?" Thomson tipped his head back and roared with laughter. "I bet you did. And I can imagine the looks on their faces."

"Consider it a going-away present. But you no longer fit here in Cairo. You are a bad memory that cannot keep strolling about among us. Our wounds are too fresh. You understand."

Thomson looked at Saleh and nodded, then reached over and picked up his glass. "A final toast then, Captain. Let's never darken each other's doorways. Okay?"

"Okay!" Saleh's face opened in a broad grin. He clinked his glass against Thomson's and threw the raw whiskey down his throat. "Take care of yourself, Thomson," he said affectionately, as he reached into his coat pocket. He pulled out a small folder and laid it on the table. "One last gift. An airplane ticket. For the morning flight...to Frankfurt."

Then Saleh rose to his feet and limped away. Thomson watched him go. The little man never even turned back. He reached the door, pushed it open, and left the bar without another word.

"Well, don't that beat all!" Jeremy stomped over to the table, his hands on his hips. "He's really sending you packing? And here I thought he was different!"

"Oh, he is, Jeremy. Believe me, he is. But he isn't like us, either. Thank God for that much."

"I think I'm going to miss you, Thomson."

"But not much?"

"Why split hairs?" Jeremy laughed. "And I have a goodbye present for you, too. Been working on it for ten days now, hoping you'd come back." He giggled as he sat down in the chair across from Thomson.

Jeremy shoved the glasses and ashtray aside, giving himself room to draw nine dots on the greasy tabletop. They were aligned in three rows of three dots each, all evenly spaced.

"Now, Thomson. All you have to do is connect all nine of the little buggers by drawing four straight lines. No more! And you can't lift your damned finger off the tabletop, either. Four straight lines," he warned. "So let's see how bloody bright you are for a change!"

"You? Challenging me?" Thomson rolled his eyes toward the ceiling, giving Jeremy the type of condescending look Thomson usually reserved for stupid eight-year-olds. He glanced down at the tabletop, deigning to give the puzzle a few seconds of his time. He looked at it again and frowned, shifting uncomfortably in his chair as he heard Jeremy walking away, chuckling to himself.